About the Au

Elizabeth Bevarly is the award-winning, nationally number one bestselling author of more than seventy novels and novellas. Her books have been translated into two dozen languages and published in three dozen countries. An honours graduate of the University of Louisville, she has called home places as diverse as San Juan, Puerto Rico and Haddonfield, New Jersey, but now resides back in her native Kentucky with her husband, her son, and two neurotic cats (as if there were any other kind).

In a testosterone filled home (one husband, five boys between ages fourteen and eighteen, and one squeaky boy guinea pig), it's hard to imagine not going insane. The trick is to escape. So in her charming Southern world filled with politics, football, and after school snacks, **Carolyn Hector** utilises her knack for spinning every plausible situation into a romance story. Find out what she is up to on Twitter @WriteOnCarolyn or find her on Facebook.

USA Today bestselling author **Lynne Marshall** used to worry she had a serious problem with daydreaming, then she discovered she was supposed to write those stories! A late bloomer, she came to fiction writing after her children were nearly grown. Now she battles the empty nest by writing romantic stories about life, love, and happy endings. She's a proud mother and grandmother who loves babies, dogs, books, music, and travelling.

Once Upon a Time

Once Upon a Time:
Beauty

ELIZABETH BEVARLY

CAROLYN HECTOR

LYNNE MARSHALL

MILLS & BOON

First Published in Great Britain 2023
by Mills & Boon, an imprint of HarperCollins*Publishers* Ltd,
1 London Bridge Street, London, SE1 9GF

www.harpercollins.co.uk

HarperCollins*Publishers*
Macken House, 39/40 Mayor Street Upper,
Dublin 1, D01 C9W8, Ireland

Special thanks and acknowledgement are given to Lynne Marshall for her contribution to *The Hollywood Hills Clinic* series

ISBN: 978-0-263-31933-0

MIX
Paper | Supporting responsible forestry
FSC™ C007454

This book is produced from independently certified FSC™ paper to ensure responsible forest management.

For more information visit: www.harpercollins.co.uk/green

Printed and Bound in the UK using 100% Renewable Electricity at CPI Group (UK) Ltd, Croydon, CR0 4YY

A BEAUTY FOR THE BILLIONAIRE

ELIZABETH BEVARLY

Prologue

There was nothing Hogan Dempsey loved more than the metallic smell and clink-clank sounds of his father's garage. Well, okay, *his* garage, as of the old man's death three years ago, but he still thought of it as his father's garage and probably would even after he passed it on to someone else. Not that he was planning on that happening anytime soon, since he was only thirty-three and had no one to leave the place to—his mother had been gone even longer than his father, and there hadn't been a woman in his life he'd consider starting a family with since…ever. Dempsey's Parts & Service was just a great garage, that was all. The best one in Queens, for sure, and probably the whole state of New York. People brought their cars here to be worked on from as far away as Buffalo.

It was under one of those Buffalo cars he was working at the moment, a sleek, black '76 Trans Am—a gorgeous piece of American workmanship if ever there was one. If Hogan spent the rest of his life in his grease-stained coveralls, his hands and arms streaked with engine guts, lying under cars like this, he would die a happy man.

"Mr. Dempsey?" he heard from somewhere above the car.

It was a man's voice, but not one he recognized. He looked to his right and saw a pair of legs to go with it, the kind that were covered in pinstripes and ended in a pair of dress shoes that probably cost more than Hogan made in a month.

"That's me," he said as he continued to work.

"My name is Gus Fiver," the pinstripes said. "I'm an attorney with Tarrant, Fiver and Twigg. Is there someplace we could speak in private?"

Attorney? Hogan wondered. What did an attorney need with him? All of his affairs were in order, and he ran an honest shop. "We can talk here," he said. "Pull up a creeper."

To his surprise, Gus Fiver of Tarrant, Fiver and Twigg did just that. Most people wouldn't even know what a creeper was, but the guy toed the one nearest him—a skateboard-type bit of genius that mechanics used to get under a car chassis—and lay down on it, pinstripes and all. Then he wheeled himself under the car beside Hogan. From the neck up, he didn't look like the pinstripe type. He looked like a guy you'd grab a beer with on Astoria Boulevard after work. Blonder and better-looking than most, but he still had that working-class vibe about him that was impossible to hide completely.

And Hogan should know. He'd spent the better part of a year when he was a teenager trying to keep his blue collar under wraps, only to be reminded more than once that there was no way to escape his roots.

"Sweet ride," Fiver said. "Four hundred and fifty-five CUs. V-8 engine. The seventy-six Trans Am was the best pony car Pontiac ever made."

"Except for the sixty-four GTO," Hogan said.

"Yeah, okay, I'll give you that."

The two men observed a moment of silence for the holy land of Detroit, then Fiver said, "Mr. Dempsey, are you familiar with the name Philip Amherst?"

Hogan went back to work on the car. "It's Hogan. And nope. Should I be?"

"It's the name of your grandfather," Fiver said matter-of-factly.

Okay, obviously, Gus Fiver had the wrong Hogan Dempsey. He could barely remember any of his grandparents since cancer had been rampant on both sides of his family, but neither of his grandfathers had been named Philip Amherst. Fortunately for Hogan, he didn't share his family's medical histories because he'd been adopted as a newborn, and—

His brain halted there. Like any adopted kid, he'd been curious about the two people whose combined DNA had created him. But Bobby and Carol Dempsey had been the best parents he could have asked for, and the thought of someone else in that role had always felt wrong. He'd just never had a desire to locate any blood relations, even after losing what family he had. There wasn't anyone else in the world who could ever be family to him like that.

He gazed at the attorney in silence. Philip Amherst

must be one of his biological grandfathers. And if Gus Fiver was here looking for Hogan, it could only be because that grandfather wanted to find him. Hogan wasn't sure how he felt about that. He needed a minute to—

"I'm afraid he passed away recently," Fiver continued. "His wife, Irene, and his daughter, Susan, who was his only child and your biological mother, both preceded him in death. Susan never married or had any additional children, so he had no other direct heirs. After his daughter's death in a boating accident last year, he changed his will so that his entire estate would pass to you."

Not even a minute. Not even a minute for Hogan to consider a second family he might have come to know, because they were all gone, too. How else was Gus Fiver going to blindside him today?

He had his answer immediately. "Mr. Amherst's estate is quite large," Fiver said. "Normally, this is where I tell an inheritor to sit down, but under the circumstances, you might want to stand up?"

Fiver didn't have to ask him twice. Hogan's blood was surging like a geyser. With a single heave, he pushed himself out from under the car and began to pace. *Quite large.* That was what Fiver had called his grandfather's estate. But *quite large* was one of those phrases that could mean a lot of different things. *Quite large* could be a hundred thousand dollars. Or, holy crap, even a million dollars.

Fiver had risen, too, and was opening a briefcase to withdraw a handful of documents. "Your grandfather was a banker and financier who invested very wisely. He left the world with no debt and scores of assets. His main residence was here in New York on the Upper East Side, but he also owned homes in Santa Fe, Palm Beach and Paris."

Hogan was reeling. Although Fiver's words were making it into his brain, it was like they immediately got lost and went wandering off in different directions.

"Please tell me you mean Paris, Texas," he said.

Fiver grinned. "No. Paris, France. The *Trocadéro*, to be precise, in the sixteenth *arrondissement*."

"I don't know what that means." Hell, Hogan didn't know what any of this meant.

"It means your grandfather was a very rich man, Mr. Dempsey. And now, by both bequest and bloodline, so are you."

Then he quoted an amount of money so big, it actually made Hogan take a step backward, as if doing that might somehow ward it off. No one could have that much money. Especially not someone like Hogan Dempsey.

Except that Hogan did have that much money. Over the course of the next thirty minutes, Gus Fiver made that clear. And as they were winding down what the attorney told him was only the first of a number of meetings they would have over the next few weeks, he said, "Mr. Dempsey, I'm sure you've heard stories about people who won the lottery, only to have their lives fall apart because they didn't know how to handle the responsibility that comes with having a lot of money. I'd advise you to take some time to think about all this before you make any major decisions and that you proceed slowly."

"I will," Hogan assured him. "Weird thing is I've already given a lot of thought to what I'd do if I ever won the lottery. Because I've been playing it religiously since I was in high school."

Fiver looked surprised. "You don't seem like the lottery type to me."

"I have my reasons."

"So what did you always say you'd buy if you won the lottery?"

"Three things, ever since I was eighteen." Hogan held up his left hand, index finger extended. "Number one, a 1965 Shelby Daytona Cobra." His middle finger joined the first. "Number two, a house in Ocean City, New Jersey." He added his ring finger—damned significant, now that he thought about it—to the others. "And number three..." He smiled. "Number three, Anabel Carlisle. Of the Park Avenue Carlisles."

One

"You're my new chef?"

Hogan eyed the young woman in his kitchen—his massive, white-enamel-and-blue-Italian-tile kitchen that would have taken up two full bays in his garage—with much suspicion. Chloe Merlin didn't look like she was big enough to use blunt-tip scissors, let alone wield a butcher knife. She couldn't be more than five-four in her plastic red clogs—Hogan knew this, because she stood nearly a foot shorter than him—and she was swallowed by her oversize white chef's jacket and the baggy pants splattered with red chili peppers.

It was her gigantic glasses, he decided. Black-rimmed and obviously a men's style, they overwhelmed her features, making her green eyes appear huge. Or maybe it was the way her white-blond hair was piled haphazardly on top of her head as if she'd just grabbed it in two fists and tied it there without even looking to see what she was doing. Or it could be the red lipstick. It was the only makeup she wore, as if she'd filched it from her mother's purse to experiment with. She just looked so...so damned...

Ah, hell. Adorable. She looked adorable. And Hogan hated even thinking that word in his head.

Chloe Merlin was supposed to be his secret weapon in the winning of Anabel Carlisle of the Park Avenue Carlisles. But seeing her now, he wondered if she could even help him win bingo night at the Queensboro Elks Lodge. She had one hand wrapped around the handle of a duffel bag and the other steadying what looked like a battered leather bedroll under her arm—except it was too skinny to be a bedroll. Sitting beside her on the kitchen island was a gigantic wooden box filled with plants of varying shapes and sizes that he was going to go out on a limb and guess were herbs or something. All of the items in question were completely out of proportion to the rest of her. She just seemed...off. As if she'd been dragged here from another dimension and was still trying to adjust to some new laws of physics.

"How old are you?" he asked before he could stop himself.

"Why do you want to know?" she shot back. "It's against the law for you to consider my age as a prerequisite of employment. I could report you to the EEOC. Not the best way to start my first day of work."

He was about to tell her it could be her last day of work, too, if she was going to be like that, but she must have realized what he was thinking and intercepted.

"If you fire me now, after asking me a question

like that, I could sue you. You wouldn't have a legal leg to stand on."

Wow. Big chip for such a little shoulder.

"I'm curious," he said. Which he realized was true. There was just something about her that made a person feel curious.

Her enormous glasses had slipped down on her nose, so she pushed them up again with the back of her hand. "I'm twenty-eight," she said. "Not that it's any of your business."

Chloe Merlin must be a hell of a cook. 'Cause there was no way she'd become the most sought-after personal chef on Park Avenue as a result of her charming personality. But to Hogan's new social circle, she was its latest, and most exclusive, status symbol.

After he'd told Gus Fiver his reasons for wanting to "buy" Anabel that first day in his garage—man, had that been three weeks ago?—the attorney had given him some helpful information. Gus was acquainted with the Carlisles and knew Anabel was the current employer of one Chloe Merlin, personal chef to the rich and famous. In fact, she was such a great chef that, ever since her arrival on the New York scene five years ago, she'd been constantly hired away from one wealthy employer to another, always getting a substantial pay increase in the bargain. Poaching Chloe from whoever employed her was a favorite pastime of the Park Avenue crowd, Gus had said, and Anabel Carlisle was, as of five months prior, the most recent victor in the game. If Hogan was in the market for someone to cook for him—and hey, who wasn't?— then hiring Chloe away from Anabel would get the latter's attention and give him a legitimate reason to reenter her life.

Looking at the chef now, however, Hogan was beginning to wonder if maybe Park Avenue's real favorite pastime was yanking the chain of the new guy, and Gus Fiver was the current victor in that game. It had cost him a fortune to hire Chloe, and some of her conditions of employment were ridiculous. Not to mention she looked a little...quirky. Hogan hated quirky.

"If you want to eat tonight, you should show me my room," she told him in that same cool, shoulder-chip voice. "Your kitchen will be adequate for my needs, but I need to get to work. *Croque monsieur* won't make itself, you know."

Croque monsieur, Hogan repeated to himself. Though not with the flawless French accent she'd used. What the hell was *croque monsieur*? Was he going to be paying her a boatload of money to cook him things he didn't even like? Because he'd be fine with a ham and cheese sandwich.

Then the other part of her statement registered. The kitchen was *adequate*? Was she serious? She could feed Liechtenstein in this kitchen. Hell, Liechtenstein could eat off the floor of this kitchen. She could bake Liechtenstein a soufflé the size of Switzerland in one oven while she broiled them an entire swordfish in the other. Hogan had barely been able to find her in here after Mrs. Hennessey, his inherited housekeeper, told him his new chef was waiting for him.

Adequate. Right.

"Your room is, uh... It's, um..."

He halted. His grandfather's Lenox Hill town house was big enough to qualify for statehood, and he'd just moved himself into it yesterday. He barely knew where his own room was. Mrs. Hennessey went home at the end of the workday, but she'd assured him there were "suitable quarters" for an employee here. She'd even shown him the room, and he'd thought it was pretty damned suitable. But he couldn't remember now if it was on the fourth floor or the fifth. Depended on whether his room was on the third floor or the fourth.

"Your room is upstairs," he finally said, sidestepping the problem for a few minutes. He'd recognize the floor when he got there. Probably. "Follow me."

Surprisingly, she did without hesitation, leaving behind her leather bedroll-looking thing and her gigantic box of plants—that last probably to arrange later under the trio of huge windows on the far side of the room. They strode out of the second-floor kitchen and into a gallery overflowing with photos and paintings of people Hogan figured must be blood relations. Beyond the gallery was the formal dining room, which he had yet to enter.

He led Chloe up a wide, semicircular staircase that landed on each floor—there was an elevator in the house, too, but the stairs were less trouble—until they reached the third level, then the fourth, where he was pretty sure his room was. Yep. Fourth floor was his. He recognized the massive, mahogany-paneled den. Then up another flight to the fifth, and top, floor, which housed a wide sitting area flanked by two more bedrooms that each had connecting bathrooms bigger than the living room of his old apartment over the garage.

Like he said, pretty damned suitable.

"This is your room," he told Chloe. He gestured

toward the one on the right after remembering that was the one Mrs. Hennessey had shown him, telling him it was the bigger of the two and had a fireplace.

He made his way in that direction, opened the door and entered far enough to give Chloe access. The room was decorated in dark blue and gold, with cherry furniture, some innocuous oil landscapes and few personal touches. Hogan supposed it was meant to be a gender-neutral guest room, but it weighed solidly on the masculine side in his opinion. Even so, it somehow suited Chloe Merlin. Small, adorable and quirky she might be, with clothes and glasses that consumed her, but there was still something about her that was sturdy, efficient and impersonal.

"There's a bath en suite?" she asked from outside the door.

"If that means an adjoining bathroom, then yes," Hogan said. He pointed at a door on the wall nearest him. "It's through there." *I think*, he added to himself. That might have actually been a closet.

"And the door locks with a dead bolt?" she added.

He guessed women had to be careful about these things, but it would have been nice if she hadn't asked the question in the same tone of voice she might have used to accuse someone of a felony.

"Yes," he said. "The locksmith just left, and the only key is in the top dresser drawer. You can bolt it from the inside. Just like you said you would need in your contract."

Once that was settled, she walked into the room, barely noticing it, lifted her duffel onto the bed and began to unzip it. Without looking at Hogan, she said, "The room is acceptable. I'll unpack and report to the kitchen to inventory, then I'll shop this afternoon. Dinner tonight will be at seven thirty. Dinner every night will be at seven thirty. Breakfast will be at seven. If you'll be home for lunch, I can prepare a light midday meal, as well, and leave it in the refrigerator for you, but I generally spend late morning and early afternoon planning menus and buying groceries. I shop every day to ensure I have the freshest ingredients I can find, all organic farm-to-table. I have Sundays and Mondays off unless you need me for a special occasion, in which case I'll be paid double-time for those days and—"

"And have an additional day off the following week," he finished for her. "I know. I read and signed your contract, remember? You have Christmas Eve, Christmas Day and Thanksgiving off, with full pay, no exceptions," he quoted from it. "Along with three weeks in August, also with full pay."

"If I'm still here then," she said. "That's ten months away, after all." She said it without a trace of smugness, too, to her credit. Obviously Chloe Merlin knew about the Park Avenue chef-poaching game.

"Oh, you'll still be here," he told her. Because, by August, if Hogan played his cards right—and he was great at cards—Anabel would be living here with him, and his wedding present to her would be a lifetime contract for her favorite chef, Chloe Merlin.

Chloe, however, didn't look convinced.

Didn't matter. Hogan was convinced. He didn't care how many demands Chloe made—from the separate kitchen account into which he would deposit a specific amount of money each week and for which she alone would have a card, to her having complete dominion over the menus, thanks to his having no dietary restrictions. He was paying her a lot of money to cook whatever she wanted five days a week and letting her live rent-free in one of New York's toniest neighborhoods. In exchange, he'd created a situation where Anabel Carlisle had no choice but to pay attention to him. Actually not a bad trade, since, if history repeated—and there was no reason to think it wouldn't—once he had Anabel's attention, they'd be an item in no time. Besides, he didn't know what else he would do with all the money his grandfather had left him. It was enough to, well, feed Liechtenstein.

Hogan just hoped he liked...what had she called it? *Croque monsieur.* Whatever the hell that was.

Chloe Merlin studied her new employer in silence, wishing that, for once, she hadn't been driven by her desire to make money. Hogan Dempsey was nothing like the people who normally employed her. They were all pleasant enough, but they were generally frivolous and shallow and easy to dismiss, something that made it possible for her to focus solely on the only thing that mattered—cooking. Even having just met him, she found Hogan Dempsey earthy and astute, and something told her he would never stand for being dismissed.

As if she could dismiss him. She'd never met anyone with a more commanding presence. Although he had to be standing at least five feet away from her, she felt as if he were right on top of her, breathing down her chef's whites, leaving her skin hot to the touch. He was easily a foot taller than she was in her Super Birkis, and his shoulders had fairly filled the doorway when he entered the room. His hair was the color of good semolina, and his eyes were as dark as coffee beans. Chloe had always had a major thing for brown-eyed blonds, and this man could have been their king. Add that he was dressed in well-worn jeans, battered work boots and an oatmeal-colored sweater that had definitely seen better days—a far cry from the fresh-from-the-couturier cookie-cutter togs of other society denizens—and he was just way too gorgeous for his own good. Or hers.

She lifted her hand to the top button of her jacket and twisted it, a gesture that served to remind her of things she normally didn't need reminding of. But it did no good. Hogan was still commanding. Still earthy. Still gorgeous. Her glasses had begun to droop again, so she pushed them up with the back of her hand. It was a nervous gesture she'd had since child-hood, but it was worse these days. And not just be-cause her big black frames were a size larger than they should be.

"So…how's Anabel doing?" he asked.

Of all the questions she might have expected, that one wasn't even in the top ten. Although he didn't strike her as a foodie, and although he'd already filled out a questionnaire she prepared for her employers about his culinary expectations and customs, she would have thought he would want to talk more about her position here. She'd already gathered from Ana-bel that her former employer and her new employer shared some kind of history—Anabel had tried to talk Chloe out of taking this position, citing Hogan's past behavior as evidence of his unsophisticated palate. But Chloe neither cared nor was curious about what that history might be. She only wanted to cook. Cooking was what she did. Cooking was what she was. Cooking was all that mattered on any given day. On every given day. Chloe didn't do well if she couldn't keep every last scrap of her attention on cooking.

"Anabel is fine," she said.

"I mean since her divorce," Hogan clarified. "I understand you came to work for her about the same time her husband left her for one of her best friends."

"That was none of my business," Chloe told him. "It's none of yours, either. I don't engage in gossip, Mr. Dempsey."

"Hogan," he immediately corrected her. "And I'm not asking you to gossip. I just..."

He lifted one shoulder and let it drop in a way that was kind of endearing, then expelled his breath in a way that was almost poignant. Damn him. Chloe didn't have time for endearing and poignant. Especially when it was coming from the king of the brown-eyed blonds.

"I just want to know she's doing okay," he said. "She and I used to be...friends. A long time ago. I haven't seen her in a while. Divorce can be tough on a person. I just want to know she's doing okay," he repeated.

Oh, God. He was pining for her. It was the way he'd said the word *friends*. Pining for Anabel Carlisle, a woman who was a nice enough human being, and a decent enough employer, but who was about as deep as an onion skin.

"I suppose she's doing well enough in light of her... change of circumstances," Chloe said.

More to put Hogan out of his misery than anything else. Chloe actually didn't know Anabel that well, in spite of having been in her employ for nearly six months, which was longer than she'd worked for anyone else. Now that she thought about it, though, Anabel was doing better than *well enough*. Chloe had never seen anyone happier to be divorced.

"Really?" Hogan asked with all the hopeful earnestness of a seventh-grader. *Gah. Stop being so charming!*

"Really," she said.

"Is she seeing anyone?"

Next he would be asking her to pass Anabel a note during study hall. "I don't know," she said. But because she was certain he would ask anyway, she added, "I never cooked for anyone but her at her home."

That seemed to hearten him. Yay.

"Now if you'll excuse me…" She started to call him *Mr. Dempsey* again, remembered he'd told her to call him *Hogan*, so decided to call him nothing at all. Strange, since she'd never had trouble before addressing her employers by their first names, even if she didn't prefer to. "I have a strict schedule I adhere to, and I need to get to work."

She needed to get to work. Not wanted. Needed. Big difference. As much as Chloe liked to cook, and as much as she wanted to cook, she needed it even more. She hoped she conveyed that to Hogan Dempsey without putting too fine a point on it.

"Okay," he said with clear reluctance. He probably wanted to pump her for more information about Anabel, but unless his questions were along the lines of how much Anabel liked Chloe's pistachio *financiers*, she'd given him all she planned to give.

And, wow, she really wished she'd thought of another way to put that than *He probably wanted to pump her*.

"If you need anything else," he said, "or have any questions or anything, I'll be in my, uh…"

For the first time, he appeared to be unsure of himself. For just the merest of moments, he actually seemed kind of lost. And damned if Chloe didn't have to stop herself from taking a step forward to physically reach out to him. She knew how it felt to be lost. She hated the thought of anyone feeling that way. But knowing it was Hogan Dempsey who did somehow seemed even worse.

Oh, this was not good.

"House," he finally finished. "I'll be in my house."

She nodded, not trusting herself to say anything. Or do anything, for that matter. Not until he was gone, and she could reboot herself back into the cooking machine she was. The cooking machine she had to be. The one driven only by her senses of taste and smell. Because the ones that dealt with hearing and seeing and, worst of all, feeling—were simply not allowed.

A ham and cheese sandwich.

Hogan had suspected the dinner Chloe set in front of him before disappearing back into the kitchen without a word was a sandwich, because he was pretty sure there were two slices of bread under the crusty stuff on top that was probably more cheese. But his first bite had cinched it. She'd made him a ham and cheese sandwich. No, maybe the ham wasn't the Oscar Mayer he'd always bought before he became filthy, stinking rich, and the cheese wasn't the kind that came in plastic-wrapped individual slices, but *croque monsieur* was obviously French for *ham and cheese sandwich*.

Still, it was a damned good ham and cheese sandwich.

For side dishes, there was something that was kind of like French fries—but not really—and something else that was kind of like coleslaw—but not really. Even so, both were also damned good. Actually, they were better than damned good. The dinner Chloe made him was easily the best not-really ham and cheese sandwich, not-really French fries and not-really coleslaw he'd ever eaten. Ah, hell. They were better than all those spot-on things, too. Maybe hiring her would pay off in more ways than just winning back the love of his life. Or, at least, the love of his teens.

Chloe had paired his dinner with a beer that was also surprisingly good, even though he was pretty sure it hadn't been brewed in Milwaukee. He would have thought her expertise in that area would be more in wine—and it probably was—but it was good to know she had a well-rounded concept of what constituted dinner. Then again, for what he was paying her, he wouldn't be surprised if she had a well-rounded concept of astrophysics and existentialism, too. She'd even chosen music to go with his meal, and although he'd never really thought jazz was his thing, the mellow strains of sax and piano had been the perfect go-with.

It was a big difference from the way he'd enjoyed dinner before—food that came out of a bag or the microwave, beer that came out of a longneck and some sport on TV. If someone had told Hogan a month ago that he'd be having dinner in a massive dining room at a table for twelve with a view of trees and town houses out his window instead of the neon sign for Taco Taberna across the street, he would have told that person to see a doctor about their hallucinations. He still couldn't believe this was his life now. He wasn't sure he ever would.

The moment he laid his fork on his plate, Chloe appeared to remove both from the table and set a cup of coffee in their place. Before she could escape again—somehow it always seemed to Hogan like she was trying to run from him—he stopped her.

"That was delicious," he said. "Thank you."

When she turned to face him, she looked surprised by his admission. "Of course it was delicious. It's my life's work to make it delicious." Seemingly as an afterthought, she added, "You're welcome."

When she started to turn away, Hogan stopped her again.

"So I realize now that *croque monsieur* is a ham and cheese sandwich, but what do you call those potatoes?"

When she turned around this time, her expression relayed nothing of what she might be thinking. She only gazed at him in silence for a minute—a minute where he was surprised to discover he was dying to know what she was thinking. Finally she said, "*Pommes frites*. The potatoes are called *pommes frites*."

"And the green stuff? What was that?"

"*Salade de chou.*"

"Fancy," he said. "But wasn't it really just a ham and cheese sandwich, French fries and coleslaw?"

Her lips, freshly stained with her red lipstick, thinned a little. "To you? Yes. Now if you'll excuse me, your dessert—"

"Can wait a minute," he finished. "Sit down. We need to talk."

She didn't turn to leave again. But she didn't sit down, either. Mostly, she just stared at him through slitted eyes over the top of her glasses before pushing them into place again with the back of her hand. He remembered her doing that a couple of times earlier in the day. Maybe with what he was paying her now, she could afford to buy a pair of glasses that fit. Or, you know, eight hundred pairs of glasses that fit. He was paying her an awful lot.

He tried to gentle his tone. "Come on. Sit down. Please," he added.

"Was there a problem with your dinner?" she asked.

He shook his head. "It was a damned tasty ham and cheese sandwich."

He thought she would be offended that he relegated her creation—three times now—to something normally bought in a corner deli and wrapped in wax paper. Instead, she replied, "I wanted to break you in slowly. Tomorrow I'm making you *pot au feu*."

"Which is?"

"To you? Beef stew."

"You don't think much of me or my palate, do you?"

"I have no opinion of either, Mr. Dempsey."

"Hogan," he corrected her. Again.

She continued as if he hadn't spoken. "I just happened to learn a few things about my new employer before starting work for him, and it's helped me plan menus that would appeal to him. Which was handy since the questionnaire I asked this particular employer to fill out was, shall we say, a bit lean on helpful information in that regard."

"Shouldn't I be the one doing that?" he asked. "Researching my potential employee before even offering the position?"

"Did you?" she asked.

He probably should have. But Gus Fiver's recommendation had been enough for him. Well, that and the fact that stealing her from Anabel would get the latter's attention.

"Uh…" he said eloquently.

She exhaled a resigned sigh then approached the table and pulled out a chair to fold herself into it, setting his empty plate before her for the time being. "I know you grew up in a working-class neighborhood in Astoria," she said, "and that you're so new money, with so much of it, the Secret Service should be crawling into your shorts to make sure you're not printing the bills yourself. I know you've never traveled farther north than New Bedford, Massachusetts, to visit your grandparents or farther south than Ocean City, New Jersey, where you and your parents spent a week every summer at the Coral Sands Motel. I know you excelled at both hockey and football in high school and that you missed out on scholarships for both by *this much*, so you never went to college. I also know your favorite food is—" at this, she bit back a grimace "—taco meatloaf and that the only alcohol you imbibe is domestic beer. News flash. I will *not* be making taco meatloaf for you at any time."

The hell she wouldn't. Taco meatloaf was awesome. All he said, though, was, "How do you know all that? I mean, yeah, some of that stuff is probably on the internet, but not the stuff about my grandparents and the Coral Sands Motel."

"I would never pry into anyone's personal information on the internet or anywhere else," Chloe said, sounding genuinely stung that he would think otherwise.

"Then how—"

"Anabel told me all that about you after I gave her my two weeks' notice. I didn't ask," she hastened to clarify. "But when she found out it was you who hired me, and when she realized she couldn't afford to pay me more than you offered me, she became a little... perturbed."

Hogan grinned. He remembered Anabel *perturbed*. She never liked it much when she didn't get her way. "And she thought she could talk you out of coming to work for me by telling you what a mook I am, right?" he asked.

Chloe looked confused. "Mook?"

He chuckled. "Never mind."

Instead of being offended by what Anabel had told Chloe, Hogan was actually heartened by it, because it meant she remembered him well. It didn't surprise him she had said what she did. Anabel had never made a secret of her opinion that social divisions existed for a reason and should never be crossed—even if she had crossed them dozens of times to be with him when they were young. It was what she had been raised to believe and was as ingrained a part of her as Hogan's love for muscle cars was ingrained in him. Her parents, especially her father, had been adamant she would marry a man who was her social and financial equal, to the point that they'd sworn to cut her off socially and financially if she didn't. The Carlisle money was just that old and sacred. It was the *only* thing that could come between Hogan and Anabel. She'd made that clear, too. And when she went off to college and started dating a senator's son, well... Hogan had known it was over between them without her even having to tell him.

Except that she never actually told him it was over between them, and they'd still enjoyed the occasional hookup when she was home from school, in spite of the senator's son. Over the next few years, though, they finally did drift apart.

But Anabel never told him it was over.

That was why, even after she'd married the senator's son, Hogan had never stopped hoping that someday things would be different for them. And now his hope had paid off. Literally. The senator's son was gone, and there was no social or financial divide between him and Anabel anymore. The blood he was born with was just as blue as hers, and the money he'd inherited was just as old and moldy. Maybe he was still feeling his way in a world that was new to him, but he wasn't on the outside looking in anymore. Hell, he'd just drunk beer from a glass instead of a longneck. That was a major development for him. It wouldn't be long before he—

"Hang on," he said. "How does Anabel know I only drink domestic beer? I wasn't old enough to drink when I was with her."

"That part I figured out myself," Chloe said.

"There are some damned fine domestic beers being brewed these days, you know."

"There are. But what you had tonight was Belgian. Nice, wasn't it?"

Yeah, okay, it was. He would still be bringing home

his Sam Adams on the weekends. *So there, Chloe Merlin.*

"Is everything you cook French?" he asked. He wasn't sure why he was prolonging a conversation neither of them seemed to want to have.

"Still angling for that taco meatloaf, are we?" she asked.

"I like pizza, too."

She flinched, but said nothing.

"And chicken pot pie," he threw in for good measure.

She expelled another one of those impatient sighs. "Fine. I can alter my menus. Some," she added meaningfully.

Hogan smiled. Upper hand. He had it. He wondered how long he could keep it.

"But yes, all of what I cook is French." She looked like she would add more to the comment, but she didn't.

So he tried a new tack. "Are you a native New Yorker?" Then he remembered she couldn't be a native New Yorker. She didn't know what a mook was.

"I was born and raised in New Albany, Indiana," she told him. Then, because she must have realized he was going to press her for more, she added, with clear reluctance, "I was raised by my grandmother because my parents…um…weren't able to raise me themselves. Mémée came here as a war bride after World War Two—her parents owned a bistro in Cherbourg—and she was the one who taught me to cook. I got my degree in Culinary Arts from Sullivan University in Louisville, which is a cool city, but the restaurant scene there is hugely competitive, and I wanted to open my own place."

"So you came to New York, where there's no competition for that kind of thing at all, huh?" He smiled, but Chloe didn't smile back.

He waited for her to explain how she had ended up in New York cooking for the One Percent instead of opening her own restaurant, but she must have thought she had come to the end of her story, because she didn't say anything else. For Hogan, though, her conclusion only jump-started a bunch of new questions in his brain. "So you wanted to open your own place, but you've been cooking for one person at a time for... how long?"

She met his gaze levelly. "For five years," she said.

He wondered if that was why she charged so much for her services and insisted on living on-site. Because she was saving up to open her own restaurant.

"Why no restaurant of your own by now?" he asked.

She hesitated for a short, but telling, moment. "I changed my mind." She stood and picked up his plate. "I need to see to your dessert."

He wanted to ask her more about herself, but her posture made clear she was finished sharing. So instead, he asked, "What am I having?"

"*Glissade.*"

"Which is? To me?" he added before she could.

"Chocolate pudding."

And then she was gone. He turned in his chair to watch her leave and saw her crossing the gallery to the kitchen, her red plastic shoes whispering over the marble floor. He waited to see if she would look back, or even to one side. But she kept her gaze trained on the kitchen door, her step never slowing or faltering.

She was a focused one, Chloe Merlin. He wondered why. And he found himself wondering, too, if there was anything else—or anyone else—in her life besides cooking.

Two

The day after she began working for Hogan Dempsey, Chloe returned from her early-afternoon grocery shopping to find him in the gallery between the kitchen and dining room. He was dressed in a different pair of battered jeans from the day before, and a different sweater, this one the color of a ripe avocado. He must not have heard her as she topped the last stair because he was gazing intently at one photograph in particular. It was possible that if she continued to not make a sound, he wouldn't see her as she slipped into the kitchen. Because she'd really appreciate it if Hogan didn't see her as she slipped into the kitchen.

In fact, she'd really appreciate it if Hogan never noticed her again.

She still didn't know what had possessed her to reveal so much about herself last night. She never told anyone about being raised by a grandmother instead of by parents, and she certainly never talked about the desire she'd once had to open a restaurant. That was a dream she abandoned a long time ago, and she would never revisit it again. Never. Yet within hours of meeting Hogan, she was telling him those things and more. It was completely unprofessional, and Chloe was, if nothing else, utterly devoted to her profession.

She gripped the tote bags in her hands more fiercely and stole a few more steps toward the kitchen. She was confident she didn't make a sound, but Hogan must have sensed her presence anyway and called out to her. Maybe she could pretend she didn't hear him. It couldn't be more than five or six more steps to the kitchen door. She might be able to make it.

"Chloe?" he said again.

Damn. Missed it by that much.

She turned to face him. "Yes, Mr. Dempsey?"

"Hogan," he told her again. "I don't like being called 'Mr. Dempsey.' It makes me uncomfortable. It's Hogan, okay?"

"All right," she agreed reluctantly. "What is it you need?"

When he'd called out to her, he'd sounded like he genuinely had something to ask her. Now, though, he only gazed at her in silence, looking much the way he had yesterday when he'd seemed so lost. And just as she had yesterday, Chloe had to battle the urge to go to him, to touch him, and to tell him not to worry, that everything would be all right. Not that she would ever tell him that. There were some things that could never be all right again. No one knew that better than Chloe did.

Thankfully, he quickly regrouped, pointing at the photo he'd been studying. "It's my mother," he said. "My biological mother," he quickly added. "I think I resemble her a little. What do you think?"

What Chloe thought was that she needed to start cooking. Immediately. Instead, she set her bags on the floor and made her way across the gallery toward him and the photo.

His mother didn't resemble him *a little*, she saw. His mother resembled him a lot. In fact, looking at her was like looking at a female Hogan Dempsey.

"Her name was Susan Amherst," he said. "She was barely sixteen when she had me."

Even though Chloe truly didn't engage in gossip, she hadn't been able to avoid hearing the story of Susan Amherst over the last several weeks. It was all the Park Avenue crowd had talked about since the particulars of Philip Amherst's estate were made public, from the tearooms where society matriarchs congregated to the kitchens where their staff toiled. How Susan Amherst, a prominent young society deb in the early '80s, suddenly decided not to attend Wellesley after her graduation from high school a year early, and instead took a year off to "volunteer overseas." There had been talk at the time that she was pregnant and that her ultra-conservative, extremely image-conscious parents wanted to hide her condition. Rumors swirled that they sent her to live with relatives upstate and had the baby adopted immediately after its birth. But the talk about young Susan died down as soon as another scandal came along, and life went on. Even for the Amhersts. Susan returned to her rightful place in her parents' home the following spring and started college the next year. For all anyone knew, she really had spent months "volunteering overseas."

Until Hogan showed up three decades later and stirred up the talk again.

"You and she resemble each other very much," Chloe said. And because Susan's parents were in the photograph, as well, she added, "You resemble your grandfather, too." She stopped herself before adding that Philip Amherst had been a very handsome man.

"My grandfather's attorney gave me a letter my grandfather wrote when he changed his will to leave his estate to me." Hogan's voice revealed nothing of what he might be feeling, even though there must be a tsunami of feeling in a statement like that. "The adoption was a private one at a time when sealed records stayed sealed, so he couldn't find me before he died.

"Not that I got the impression from his letter that he actually *wanted* to find me before he died," he hastened to add. Oh, yes. Definitely a tsunami of feeling. "It took a bunch of legal proceedings to get the records opened so the estate could pass to me. Anyway, in his letter, he said Susan didn't want to put me up for adoption. That she wanted to raise me herself. She even named me. Travis. Travis Amherst." He chuckled, but there wasn't an ounce of humor in the sound. "I mean, can you see me as a Travis Amherst?"

Actually, Chloe could. Hogan Dempsey struck her as a man who could take any form and name he wanted. Travis Amherst of the Upper East Side would have been every bit as dynamic and compelling as Hogan Dempsey of Queens. He just would have been doing it in a different arena.

"Not that it matters," he continued. "My grandparents talked Susan out of keeping me because she was so young—she was only fifteen when she got pregnant. They convinced her it was what was best for her and me both."

He looked at the photo again. In it, Susan Amherst looked to be in her thirties. She was wearing a black cocktail dress and was flanked by her parents on one side and a former, famously colorful, mayor of New York on the other. In the background were scores of people on a dance floor and, behind them, an orchestra. Whatever the event was, it seemed to be festive. Susan, however, wasn't smiling. She obviously didn't feel very festive.

"My mother never told anyone who my father was," Hogan continued. "But my grandfather said he thought he was one of the servants' kids that Susan used to sneak out with. From some of the other stuff he said, I think he was more worried about that than he was my mother's age." He paused. "Not that that matters now, either."

Chloe felt his gaze fall on her again. When she looked at him, his eyes were dark with a melancholy sort of longing.

"Of course it matters," she said softly. "Your entire life would have been different if you had grown up Travis Amherst instead of Hogan Dempsey." And because she couldn't quite stop herself, she added, "It's…difficult…when life throws something at you that you never could have seen coming. Especially when you realize it's going to change *every*thing. Whatever you're feeling, Hogan, they're legitimate feelings, and they deserve to be acknowledged. You don't have to pretend it doesn't matter. It matters," she repeated adamantly. "It matters a lot."

Too late, she realized she had called him Hogan. Too late, she realized she had spilled something out of herself onto him again and made an even bigger mess than she had last night. Too late, she realized she couldn't take any of it back.

But Hogan didn't seem to think she'd made a mess. He seemed to be grateful for what she'd said. "Thanks," he told her.

And because she couldn't think of anything else to say, she replied automatically, "You're welcome."

She was about to return to the kitchen—she really, really, really did need to get cooking—but he started talking again, his voice wistful, his expression sober.

"I can't imagine what my life would have been like growing up as Travis Amherst. I would have had to go to some private school where I probably would have played soccer and lacrosse instead of football and hockey. I would have gone to college. I probably would have majored in business or finance and done one of those study-abroads in Europe. By now Travis Amherst would be saddled with some office job, wearing pinstripes by a designer whose name Hogan Dempsey wouldn't even recognize." He shook his head, clearly baffled by what might have been. "The thought of having to work at a job like that instead of working at the garage is…" He inhaled deeply and released the breath slowly. "It's just… A job like that would suffocate me. But Travis Amherst probably would have loved it."

"Possibly," Chloe said. "But maybe not. Travis

might have liked working with his hands, too. It's impossible to know for sure."

"And pointless to play 'what if,' I know," Hogan agreed. "What's done is done. And the idea that I would have never known my mom and dad or have the friends I've had all my life... The thought of all the memories that live in my head being completely different..."

Chloe winced inwardly at the irony of their situation. They both grieved for the unknown. But with him, it was a past that hadn't happened, and for her, it was a future that would never be.

"I need to cook," she told him. She pushed her glasses into place with the back of her hand and took a step backward. "I'm sorry, but..." She took another step back. "I need to cook. If you'll excuse me..."

"Sure," he said. "No problem." He didn't sound like there wasn't a problem, though. He sounded really confused.

That made two of them.

When Chloe turned to head back to the kitchen, she saw Mrs. Hennessey topping the last stair. Hogan's housekeeper reminded her of her grandmother in a lot of ways. She wore the same boxy house dresses in the same muted colors and always kept her fine white hair twisted into a flawless chignon at her nape. She was no-nonsense and professional, the way Chloe was. At least, the way Chloe was before she came to work for Hogan. The way she knew she had to be again if she wanted to keep working here.

And she did want to keep working here. For some reason. A reason she wasn't ready to explore. It was sure to be good, whatever it was.

Mrs. Hennessey announced to the room at large, "There's an Anabel Carlisle downstairs to see you. I showed her to the salon."

That seemed to snap Hogan out of his preoccupation with what might have been and pull him firmly into the here and now. "Anabel is here? Tell her I'll be right down."

"No, Mr. Dempsey, she's here to see Ms. Merlin."

Hogan's jaw dropped a little at that. But all he said was, "Hogan, Mrs. Hennessey. Please call me Hogan." Then he looked at Chloe. "Guess she refigured her budget and wants to hire you back."

Chloe should have been delighted by the idea. Not only did it mean more money coming in, but it also meant she would be free of Hogan Dempsey and his damnable heartache-filled eyes. She should be flying down the stairs to tell Anabel that she'd love to come back to work for her and would pack her bags this instant. Instead, for some reason, she couldn't move. "Tell Anabel we'll be right down," Hogan told Mrs. Hennessey.

The housekeeper nodded and went back down the stairs. Chloe stood still. Hogan gazed at her curiously.

"Don't you want to hear what she has to say?"

Chloe nodded. She did. She did want to hear what Anabel had to say. But she really needed to cook. Cooking was something she could control. Cooking filled her head with flavors and fragrances, with methods and measurements. Cooking restored balance to the universe. And Chloe could really use some balance right now.

"Well then, let's go find out," Hogan said.

Chloe looked at him again. And was immediately

sorry. Because now he looked happy and eager and excited. And a happy Hogan was far more overwhelming, and far more troubling, than a conflicted one. A happy Hogan reminded her of times and places—and people—that had made her happy, too. And those thoughts, more than anything, were the very reason she needed to cook.

Hogan couldn't understand why Chloe looked so unhappy at the thought of seeing Anabel. Then again, Chloe hadn't really looked happy about anything since he met her. He'd never encountered anyone so serious. Even cooking, which she constantly said she wanted to do, didn't really seem to bring her any joy.

Then he remembered she'd never actually said she *wanted* to cook. She always said she *needed* to. For most people, that was probably a minor distinction. He was beginning to suspect that, for Chloe, there was nothing minor about it at all.

"C'mon," he told her. "Let's go see what Anabel wants." And then, because she was standing close enough for him to do it, he leaned over and nudged her shoulder gently with his.

He might as well have jabbed her with a red-hot poker, the way she lurched away from him at the contact. She even let out a soft cry of protest and lifted a hand to her shoulder, as if he'd struck her there.

"I'm sorry," he immediately apologized, even though he had no idea what he needed to apologize for. "I didn't mean to..."

What? Touch her? Of course he meant to touch her. The same way he would have touched any one of his friends, male or female, in an effort to coax them out of their funk. People always nudged each other's shoulders. Most people wouldn't have even noticed the gesture. Chloe looked as if she'd been shot.

"It's okay," she said, still rubbing her shoulder, not looking like it was okay at all.

Not knowing what else he could say, he extended his arm toward the stairs to indicate she should precede him down. With one last, distressed look at him, she did. He kept his distance as he followed her because she seemed to need it, but also because it gave him a few more seconds to prepare for Anabel. He'd known he would run into her at some point—hell, he'd planned on it—but he'd figured it would be at some social function where there would be a lot of people around, and he'd have plenty of time to plan. He hadn't thought she would come to his house, even if it was to see someone other than him.

What Mrs. Hennessey called a "salon," Hogan thought of as a big-ass living room. The walls were paneled in maple, and a massive Oriental rug covered most of the green marble floor. A fireplace on one wall had a mantel that was dotted with wooden model ships, and it was flanked by brown leather chairs—a matching sofa was pushed against the wall opposite.

Three floor-to-ceiling arched windows looked out onto a courtyard in back of the house, and it was through one of those that Anabel Carlisle stood looking, with her back to them. Either she hadn't heard them come in, or she, too, was giving herself a few extra seconds to prepare. All Hogan could tell was that the black hair that used to hang in straight shafts to the middle of her back was short now, cut nearly to her chin.

And her wardrobe choices were a lot different, too. He remembered her trying to look like a secondhand gypsy, even though she'd probably spent hundreds of dollars in Fifth Avenue boutiques on everything she wore. Today's outfit had likely set her back even more, despite merely consisting of sedate gray pants and sweater. But both showcased lush curves she hadn't had as a teenager, so maybe they were worth the extra expense.

As if he'd spoken his appraisal out loud, Anabel suddenly spun around. Although she looked first at Chloe, she didn't seem to be surprised by Hogan's presence. But whether the smile on her face was for him or his chef, he couldn't have said. "Hogan," she said in the same throaty voice he remembered. God, he'd always loved her voice. "Good to see you."

"You, too, Anabel. How have you been?"

She began to walk toward where he and Chloe stood in the doorway. She still moved the way she used to, all grace and elegance and style. He'd always loved watching her move. She was just as gorgeous now as she'd been when they were kids. Even more, really, because she'd ditched the heavy eye makeup and dark lipstick she used to wear, so her natural beauty shone through. Strangely, the lack of makeup only made her blue eyes seem even bluer than he remembered them and her mouth even fuller and lusher.

He waited for the splash of heat that had always rocked his midsection whenever he saw her, and for the hitch of breath that had always gotten caught in his chest. But neither materialized. He guessed he'd outgrown reactions like that.

"I imagine you've already heard most of the highlights about how I've been," she said as she drew nearer. "My divorce was the talk of the town until you showed up." She smiled again, but there was only good humor and maybe a little nostalgia in the gesture. "I should actually probably thank you for that."

"You're welcome," he said, smiling back.

It really was good to see her. She really did look great. So what if his heart wasn't pumping like the V-8 in a Challenger Hellcat, the way he would have thought it would be. People grew up. Hormones settled down.

With one last look at Hogan she turned her attention to Chloe.

"I want you to come back to work for me," she said, straight to the point. "I can pay you three percent more than Hogan offered you."

Hogan looked at Chloe. She still seemed shell-shocked from whatever the hell had happened between them in the gallery. She glanced at Hogan, then back at Anabel, but said nothing.

Cagey, he thought. She was probably thinking if Anabel was offering three percent, she could get more from Hogan. Fine. Whatever it took to keep Chloe on, Hogan would pay it. Especially if it meant Anabel might come around again.

"I'll raise your salary five percent," he told her.

Anabel looked at him, her lips parted in surprise. Or something. Then she looked back at Chloe. "I can go six percent," she said coolly. "And you can have the entire month of August off, with pay."

Again, Chloe looked at Hogan, then back at Anabel. Again, she remained silent.

"Eight percent," Hogan countered.

Now Anabel narrowed her eyes at him in a way he remembered well. It was her *I'll-get-what-I-want-or-else* look. She always wore it right before he agreed to spring for tickets for whatever band happened to be her favorite at the time, or whatever restaurant was her favorite, or whatever whatever was her favorite. Then again, she'd always thanked him with hours and hours of hot *I-love-you-so-much* sex. Well, okay, maybe not hours and hours. He hadn't been the most controlled lover back in the day. But it had for sure been hot.

Anabel didn't up her salary offer this time, but she told Chloe, "And I'll give you the suite of rooms that face the park."

Chloe opened her mouth to reply, but Hogan stopped her with another counteroffer. "I'll raise your pay ten percent," he said. He didn't add anything about a better room or more time off. Not just because she already had a damned suitable room and more time off than the average person could ever hope to have, but because something told him money was way more important to Chloe than anything else.

What she needed the money for, Hogan couldn't imagine. But it was her salary that had been the most important part of her contract, her salary that lured her from one employer to another. Chloe Merlin wanted money. Lots of it.

For a third time she looked at Hogan, then at Anabel. "I'm sorry, Anabel," she said. "Unless you can offer to pay me more than Mr...." She threw another glance Hogan's way, this one looking even more edgy than the others. Then she turned so that her entire body was facing Anabel. "Unless you can offer me more than...that... I'm afraid I'll have to remain here."

There was a brief expectant pause, and when Anabel only shook her head, Chloe made her way to the doorway. "I'll draw up a rider for my contract and have it for you this evening," she said to Hogan as she started back up the stairs.

And then she was gone, without saying goodbye to either of them.

"She is such an odd duck," Anabel said when Chloe was safely out of earshot.

There was nothing derogatory in her tone, just a matter-of-factness that had been there even when they were teenagers. She wasn't condemning Chloe, just stating the truth. His chef was pretty unique.

"But worth every penny," she added with a sigh. She smiled again. "More pennies than I can afford to pay her. Obviously, she's working for someone who's out of my league."

Hogan shook his head. "Other way around, Anabel. You were always out of my league. You said so yourself. More than once, if I remember."

She winced at the comment, even though he hadn't meant it maliciously. He'd learned to be matter-of-fact from her. "I was a dumb kid when we dated, Hogan," she told him. "I was so full of myself back then. I said a lot of things I shouldn't have."

"Nah," he told her. "You never said anything I wasn't thinking myself. You were right. We came from two different worlds."

"Even so, that didn't give me the right to be such an elitist. My parents just taught me their philosophy well. It took me years to figure out I was wrong."

Now there was a loaded statement. Wrong about what? Wrong about the prejudice her parents taught her? Wrong about some of the comments she'd made? Wrong about their social circles never mixing? Wrong about leaving him for the senator's son?

Probably better not to ask for clarification. Not yet anyway. He and Anabel had rushed headlong into their relationship when they were kids. The first time they'd had sex was within days of meeting, and they'd almost never met without having sex. He'd sometimes wondered if maybe they'd gone slower, things would have worked out differently. This time he wasn't going to hurry it. This time he wanted to do it right.

"So how have you been?" she asked him. "How are your folks? I still think about your mom's Toll House cookies from time to time."

"My folks are gone," he told her. "Mom passed five years ago. Dad went two years later. Cancer. Both of them."

She looked stricken by the news. She lifted a hand to his shoulder and gave it a gentle squeeze. "Oh, Hogan, I am so sorry. I had no idea."

He covered her hand with his. "You couldn't have known. And thanks."

For a moment neither of them said anything, then Anabel dropped her hand. She crossed her arms over her midsection and looked at the door. Hogan told himself to ask her something about herself, but he didn't want to bring up her divorce, even if she didn't seem to be any the worse for wear from it. Her folks, he figured, were probably the same as always. Maybe a little more likely to invite him into their home than they were fifteen years ago, but then again, maybe not.

But for the life of him, he couldn't think of a single thing to say.

"I should probably get going," she said. "I have a thing tonight. My aunt and uncle are in town. We're meeting at the Rainbow Room." She expelled a sound that was a mixture of affection and irritation. "They always want to meet at the Rainbow Room. Which is great, but really, I wish they'd expand their repertoire a bit. Try Per Se or Morimoto sometime. Or Le Turtle. I love that place."

Okay, she'd just given Hogan the perfect opening. Three different restaurants she obviously loved. All he had to do was say, *What a coincidence, Anabel, I've been wanting to expand my repertoire, too. Why don't you and I have dinner at one of those places? You pick.* And they'd be off. For some reason, though, he just couldn't get the words to move out of his brain and into his mouth.

Not that Anabel had seemed to be angling for an invitation, because she didn't miss a beat when she continued, "Ah, well. Old habits die hard, I guess."

Which was another statement that could have been interpreted in more ways than one. Was she talking about her aunt and uncle now, and their dining habits? Or was she talking about her and Hogan, and how she still maybe had a thing for him? It didn't used to be this hard to read her. And why the hell didn't he just ask her out to see how she responded?

"It was good to see you again, Hogan," she said as she took a step in retreat. "I'm glad Philip Amherst's attorneys found you," she continued as she took another. "Maybe our paths will cross again before long."

"Maybe so," he said, finding his voice.

She lifted a hand in farewell then turned and made her way toward the exit. Just as she was about to disappear into the hallway, Hogan thought of something to ask her.

"Hey, Anabel."

She halted and turned back around, but said nothing.

"If I'd grown up an Amherst..." Hogan began. "I mean, if you'd met me as, say, a guy named Travis Amherst from the Upper East Side who went to some private school and played lacrosse and was planning to go to Harvard after graduation, instead of meeting me as Hogan Dempsey, grease monkey..."

She smiled again, this one definitely nostalgic. "Travis Amherst wouldn't have been you, Hogan. He would have been like a million other guys I knew. If I'd met you as Travis Amherst, I never would have bothered with you."

"You bothered with the senator's son," he reminded her. "And he had to have been like those million other guys."

"Yeah, he was. And look how that turned out."

Good point.

"You take care, Hogan."

"You, too, Anabel."

She threw him one last smile, lifted a hand in goodbye then turned around again and made her way down the hall. He heard her footsteps gradually fade away, then heard Mrs. Hennessey open and close the front door for her. Then, as quickly as she'd shown up in his life again, Anabel was gone.

And as the front door clicked shut behind her, it occurred to Hogan that, just like last time, she never actually told him goodbye.

Three

Although Chloe had Sundays and Mondays off, she rarely used them to relax. She generally went out in the morning and often didn't return until nearly dark—or even after—but the hours in between were almost always devoted to things related to cooking. Sometimes she explored new shops or revisited old favorites to familiarize herself with what they had in stock or to pick up a few essentials. Sometimes she sat in on lectures or classes that addressed new methods or trends in cooking. Sometimes she checked out intriguing restaurants to see what was on their menus that she might adapt for her own. Sometimes she attended tastings of cheeses, charcuterie, beers or wines.

It was to one of the last that she was headed out late Monday afternoon when she ran into Hogan, who was coming in the back door. She'd been exceptionally good at avoiding him since last week when Anabel had tried to hire her back—the same afternoon she'd shared those odd few moments with Hogan in the gallery that had ended with her completely overreacting when he nudged her shoulder with his.

She still wanted to slap herself for recoiling from him the way she had. There had been nothing inappropriate in his gesture. On the contrary, he'd obviously been trying to be friendly. There was a time when Chloe loved having her shoulder nudged in exactly that same way by…friends. It had just been so unexpected, that was all. Especially coming from someone who wasn't…a friend.

And, okay, it had also been a long time since someone had touched her with anything resembling friendship. It had been a long time since anyone had touched her at all. She went out of her way to avoid physical contact these days. With everyone. It just wasn't professional. Among other things.

It was those *among other things* that especially came into play with Hogan. Because even an innocent touch like a nudge to the shoulder felt… Well. Not innocent. Not on her end anyway. Not since it had been so long since anyone had touched her with anything resembling friendship. Or something.

Which was why she had been super careful not to let it happen again. Since that afternoon, dinner every night had been nothing but serving, identifying and describing Hogan's food. No more sitting down at his table. No more spilling her guts. And certainly no more touching. She was his chef. He was her employer. Period. Thankfully, he finally got the message, because after three or four nights of her sidestepping every question he asked about her by replying with something about the food instead, he'd finally stopped asking.

At least, that was what she'd thought until she saw him today. Because the minute he stepped inside he smiled that damnably charming smile of his and said, with much friendliness, "Chloe, hi. Where you going?"

It was the kind of question, spoken with the kind of expression that was almost always followed by *Can I come, too*? He just looked so earnest and appealing and sweet, and something inside Chloe that had been cold and hard and discordant for a very long time began to grow warm and soft and agreeable.

Stop that, she told that part of herself. *Stop it right now.*

But that part wouldn't listen, because it just kept feeling better. So she did her best to ignore it.

"Must be someplace really nice," he added. "'Cause you look really nice."

Had she thought that part of her was only growing warm? Well, now it was spontaneously combusting. The man's smile just had that effect. As did the fact that he was wearing garage-issue coveralls streaked with machine oil, an outfit that should have been unappealing—and on anyone else in her social sphere, it probably would have been—but only served to make Hogan look even more handsome.

She'd always found the working-class hero too damnably attractive. Men who worked with their hands *and* their brains could, at the end of the day, point to something concrete that was actually useful to society and say *Hey, I did that with my bare hands*. Inevitably, that always made her think about what else a man like that could do with his bare hands—especially at the end of the day. And, inevitably, she always remembered. Men like that could make a woman feel wonderful.

She pushed her glasses up with the back of her hand—it was a nervous gesture, she knew, but dammit, she was nervous—and, without thinking, told him, "You look really nice, too."

Only when he chuckled did she realize what she had said and immediately wished she could take back the words.

But Hogan shrugged off the comment. "No, I look like I've spent the better part of the afternoon under a 1957 Mercedes-Benz Three Hundred SL Gullwing that belonged to my grandfather. Which I have been. *You* look really nice. So where you going?"

It was nice of him to say so, but Chloe was the epitome of plain in a black pencil skirt, white shirt, claret-colored cardigan and black flats—all of which she had owned since college—with her hair piled on top of her head, the way it always was.

"Thank you," she made herself say, even though she was uncomfortable with the compliment. "I'm going to a wine-tasting."

She thought the announcement would put an end to any idea he might have about joining her. She was still serving him beer with his dinner—though he had certainly expanded his horizons there—and was hoping to find a few wines at this tasting today that might break him in easily.

"Sounds like fun," he said. Even though he didn't sound like he thought it was fun. In spite of that, he added, "Want some company?"

Of course she didn't want company. Chloe hadn't wanted company for years. Six years, in fact. Six years and eight months, to be precise. Six years, eight months, two weeks and three days, to be even more precise.

"I mean, knowing about wine," Hogan continued, "that could help me in the Anabel department, right? I need to know this stuff if I'm going to be moving in her circles. Make a good impression and all that."

He wasn't wrong, Chloe thought. She knew for a fact that Anabel Carlisle knew and enjoyed her wines. She could invite Hogan to come along, if for no other reason than that. And what other reason could there be?

Even so, she hedged, "Actually, I—"

But Hogan cut her off. "Great. Gimme ten minutes to clean up and change clothes. Be right back."

She was so stunned by his response that it took her a minute to react. She spun around and said, "But—"

But she knew he wouldn't hear her, because he was already pounding up the stairs.

She told herself to leave before he got back and explain her disappearance later by saying she'd assumed he was joking so went her merry way. She really didn't want company today. Or any day. So why didn't she slip out the door and make her way up 67th Street to Madison Avenue, where she could lose herself in both the crowd and the sunny October afternoon? Why did her feet seem to be nailed to the floor? More to the point, why did a part of her actually kind of like the prospect of spending the rest of the afternoon with Hogan?

She was still contemplating those questions and a

host of others when he reappeared ten minutes later. The man was nothing if not punctual. And also incredibly handsome. So far she'd seen him in nothing but jeans and sweaters and greasy coveralls, but, having clearly taken a cue from her own outfit, he now wore a pair of khaki trousers, a pinstriped oxford and a chocolate-colored blazer. And in place of his usual battered work boots were a pair of plain leather mocs—not quite as well-worn as the boots, but still obviously, ah…of a certain age. Just like everything else he had on.

How could a man have inherited as much money as Hogan had and not have spent at least some of it on new shoes and clothes? Then again, who was she to judge? The last time Chloe bought a new article of clothing for herself, it had been for… Well, it wasn't important what she'd bought the dress for. It had been six years since she'd worn it. Six years, eight months, two weeks and six days, to be precise. And she'd gotten rid of it soon after.

As Hogan began to walk toward her, heat bloomed in her midsection again, only this time it was joined by a funny sort of shimmying that only made it more enjoyable.

No! she immediately told herself. *Not enjoyable.* What she was feeling was…something else. Something that had nothing to do with enjoyment.

As he drew nearer, she noticed he hadn't managed quite as well with his grooming as he had his clothing. There was a tiny streak of oil over his eyebrow that he'd missed.

"All set," he said when he stopped in front of her.

"Not quite," she told him.

His expression fell. "I've never been to a wine-tasting. Should I change my clothes?"

She shook her head. "No, your outfit is fine. It's a casual event. It's just that…"

He was within touching distance now, and she had to battle the urge to lift a hand to his face and wipe away the oil herself. The gesture would have been no more inappropriate than his nudging of her shoulder had been last week. For some reason, though, the thought of touching him in such a way felt no less innocent than that one had.

So instead, she pointed at his eyebrow and said, "You missed a spot of grease there. Over your left eyebrow."

He swiped the side of his hand over the place she indicated…and missed the streak by millimeters.

"It's still there," she said.

He tried again, this time with the heel of his palm. But again, he missed it by *that much*.

"Still there," she said again.

He uttered an impatient sound. "Do you mind getting it for me?"

He might as well have asked her if she minded picking him up and heaving him out the window. Did he really not understand that physical contact was a physical impossibility for her after the way she'd overreacted to being touched by him last week? Were they going to have to endure another awkward moment to make that clear?

Strangely, though, the thought of touching Hogan now was slightly less…difficult…than it should have been. Resigning herself, she reached toward his face. Hogan's gaze hitched with hers, making it impossible for her to untether herself. Those brown, brown eyes, richer than truffles and sweeter than muscovado, made her pulse leap wildly, and her mouth go dry. Finally, finally, her hand made contact with his face, the pad of her index finger skimming lightly over his brow.

Her first attempt to wipe away the smudge was as fruitless as his had been—not surprising, since she was barely touching him. She tried again, drawing her thumb over his skin this time—his warm, soft skin—and that was a bit more successful. But still, the stain lingered. So she dragged her thumb across it again, once, twice, three times, until at last, the spot disappeared.

She didn't realize until that moment how her breathing had escalated while she was touching him, or how hot her entire body had become. Her face, she knew, was flushed, because she could feel the heat in her cheeks, and her hand felt as if it had caught fire. Worse, her fingers were still stroking Hogan's forehead, lightly and idly, clearly not to clean up a speck of oil, but simply because she enjoyed the feel of a man's skin under her fingertips and didn't want to stop touching him yet. It had been so long since Chloe had touched a man this way. So long since she had felt the simple pleasure of warmth and strength and vitality against her skin. Even a fingertip.

Worst of all, Hogan seemed to realize exactly what she was feeling. His face was a little flushed, too, and his pupils had expanded to nearly eclipse the dark brown of his irises. Seemingly without thinking, he covered her hand with his and gently removed it. But instead of letting it go after maneuvering it between them, which she had thought he would do—which he really should do—he held on to it, stroking his thumb lightly over her palm.

The warmth in her midsection went supernova at that, rushing heat to her every extremity. So acute was the sensation that she actually cried out—softly enough that she hoped he might not have heard her... except she knew right off he did. She knew because he finally severed his gaze from hers...only to let it fall to her mouth instead.

For one insane moment she thought he was going to kiss her. She even turned her head in a way that would keep her glasses from being a hindrance, the way she used to when— The way a person did when they knew something like that was about to happen. That was just how far she had allowed her desire to go. No, not desire, she immediately corrected herself. Appetite. Instinct. Drive. It had been too long since she'd enjoyed the sexual release every human being craved. Hogan was a very attractive man. Of course her body would respond to him the way it did. It was a matter of hormones and chemistry. There was nothing more to it than that.

Not that that wasn't more than enough.

He still hadn't released her hand, so, with much reluctance, she disengaged it herself and took a giant step backward. Then she took a breath, releasing it slowly to ease her pulse back to its normal rhythm and return her brain to its normal thoughts.

"There," she said softly. "All better."

She hoped he would think she was only talking about the removal of the oil streak from his face. But *all better* referred to herself, too. Her physical self, anyway. The emotional parts of her, though...

Well. Chloe knew she would never be *all* better. Not with so much of herself missing. But she was better now than she had been a few minutes ago, when touching Hogan had made so much of her feel so alive. That feeling was just a cruel ruse. She knew she would never feel alive again.

"All better," she tried again, forcefully enough this time that she sounded as if she actually believed it. "We should get going," she added. "We don't want to be late."

Hogan watched Chloe escape through the back door, his hand still hanging in the air between them. And he wondered, *What the hell just happened?* One minute he was asking her to wipe away a smudge of grease—an action that should have taken less than a second and been about as consequential as opening a jar of peanut butter—and the next, they were staring at each other, breathing as hard as they would have been if they'd just had sex. Really good sex, too.

His hand was even trembling, he noted as he forced himself to move it back to his side. And his whole body was hot, as if she'd run her fingers over every inch of him, instead of just his forehead. What the hell was up with that? The only person who was supposed to be making his hands shake and his skin hot was Anabel. Certainly not a near-stranger with a chip on her shoulder the size of the Brooklyn Bridge.

He gave his head a good shake to clear it. Then he made his feet move forward to follow Chloe, who had already gone through the back door. Outside on 67th Street, she was standing near a tree with her back to him, her face in profile as she gazed toward Madison Avenue—though she didn't look as if she was in any hurry to get anywhere. In fact, her expression was kind of distant and dreamy, as if it wasn't tasting wine she was thinking about, but tasting...uh... something else instead.

Hogan shoved the thought away. He had to be imagining things. Chloe Merlin had made it clear that she wanted to keep her distance from him, physically, mentally, emotionally, spiritually and every other-*ly* there was. Ever since that day last week when she'd reeled away from him in the gallery, she'd been professional to a fault. Every effort he'd made to get to know her better—because he always wanted to know a person better who was working for him, the same way he knew the guys who worked for him at the garage— had fallen flat.

Then again, he'd never met anyone like Chloe, so maybe it was just because of that.

By the time he drew alongside her on the street, she was back to her regular cool composure. When she looked at him now, it was with the same sort of detachment she always did. Her red-lipsticked mouth was flat, and she straightened her glasses with her fingers this time, instead of the back of her hand, a much less anxious gesture than usual. But he still couldn't quite forget that erotic little sound of surrender that had escaped her when he dragged his thumb along the inside of her palm. It would be a long time before he forgot about that.

"We're going to a new restaurant on Madison Avenue, just around the corner from sixty-seventh," she told him. "*L'Artichaut.* They don't actually open until next week, so it will be nice to have a little sneak peek in addition to the wine-tasting."

It suddenly occurred to Hogan that there might be a charge for him to participate. "Is it okay if you show up with someone? I mean, I have my wallet, but I don't have a lot of cash on me."

It was something he might have said in the past, when not having cash on him was a fairly regular occurrence. Saying something like that now, in light of his new financial situation, made him think he sounded like he was expecting Chloe to pick up the tab for him.

"There's no charge," she said. "It's by invitation. And mine included a plus-one. I just didn't, um, have a plus-one to invite."

Wow. She really was a Park Avenue sensation if she got invited to stuff like this. Then the second part of her statement registered. And made him a lot happier than it should have.

"I hope you don't mind having one now," he said.

"It's fine," she told him. But she still didn't sound like it was.

"Now that all the legalities of inheriting my grandfather's estate have been settled, it's kind of hard for me to keep busy, you know? I mean, I don't really have to work anymore, and, as much as I liked working in the garage, I thought I'd like not working more. Isn't that what everyone wants? Even people who like their jobs? To not have to get up every day and go to work?"

"I don't know," she said. "Is that what everyone wants?"

Well, everyone except, apparently, Chloe Merlin. Then again, she'd never said she liked her work. She said she needed it. He still wanted to know what the difference was. "*I* always thought it was," he said. "I started working for a paycheck in my dad's garage when I was fourteen, cleaning up and manning the cash register and running errands until I was old enough to work on the cars. When I was in high school, I worked another job, too, at a market up the street from us, delivering groceries."

Because it had taken the income from two jobs to keep Anabel in the style to which she was accustomed. Not that Hogan regretted a bit of it. She'd been worth every extra minute on his time cards.

The point was that he'd been working hard for more than two-thirds of his life. When Gus Fiver told him how much money he had now, Hogan had realized he could sleep late every morning and stay up late every night and enjoy a million different pursuits. Problem was, he wasn't much of a night owl—he liked getting up early. And he didn't really have any pursuits. Not yet. He hadn't even been away from his job for two weeks, and already, he was restless.

"I don't understand how the idle rich handle being idle," he said. "It feels weird to have all this money I didn't work for. I don't want to be one of those people who gets everything handed to them, you know? I need to figure out a way to earn my place in the world."

"Some wealthy people who don't work keep themselves busy by finding causes to support and raising money to help them. You could become a philanthropist."

He shook his head. "I'd rather just have someone tell me who needs something and write them a check."

Which was something he'd actually started doing already. "There's nothing wrong with charity work," he hurried to add. "It's just not my thing. I'm not comfortable asking people for money, even if the money's not for me."

"But you are comfortable giving it away."

"Well, yeah. It's not like I need it. Just the income I get from my grandfather's investments has me set for life. Not only do I have that incredible house," he added, jabbing a thumb over his shoulder toward the place they'd just left, "but he left me three other houses to boot. The guy had four houses. Who needs that many?" Before she could answer—not that the question had really required an answer—he added, "And he collected cars. There are four parked under the town house and another eight in a storage facility in New Jersey. Not to mention another ten at his other houses. Twenty-two cars. Hell, even I think that's too many, and I've always wondered what it would be like to collect cars."

She almost smiled at that. Almost. It didn't quite make it into her eyes, though. Still, he guessed hearing some mook complain about having too many houses and cars was pretty funny. Her reaction made him feel better. Maybe they could get back on solid, if weird, ground again.

"So that was what you were doing this afternoon?" she asked. "Looking at the ones parked at the house?"

He nodded. "Yeah. They're in incredible condition. Maybe Philip Amherst wasn't a huge success in the father and grandfather departments, but the guy knew wheels. In addition to the Merc Gullwing, there's a 1961 Ferrari Spyder, a 1956 Maserati Berlinetta, and, just when I thought the guy was going to be one of those European snobs, I pull the cover off this incredible 1970 Chevy Chevelle SS 427 in absolute mint condition that's—"

He stopped midsentence, because Chloe was looking at him now with an actual, honest-to-God smile on her face, one that had reached her eyes this time, and the sight nearly knocked the breath out of his lungs. He'd been thinking all this time that she was cute. Quirky, but cute. But when she smiled the way she was smiling now, she was… She was a… She was an absolute… Wow. Really, really…wow.

But all he could manage to say was, "What's so funny?"

She looked ahead again. "I think you've found your purpose."

"What? Collecting cars?" he asked. "No, that's too much. I'm already having trouble justifying keeping them all."

"Then maybe you could do something else with cars," she suggested. "Start designing your own line."

He shook his head. "I don't have that kind of talent."

"Then invest in someone who does."

He started to shoot down that idea, too, but stopped. That actually wasn't a bad idea. He even already knew somebody he could put some money behind. The daughter of one of the guys who worked at the garage. She was still in high school, but the kid knew cars inside and out, and had some great ideas for what to do with them. No way could her parents afford to send her to college. But Hogan could. And there were probably dozens of kids like her in New York…

But he still needed to figure out what to do with

himself. Investing in the future generation was great and all that, but Hogan needed a purpose, too. He'd worked with his hands all his life. He just couldn't see himself never working with them again.

Chloe halted, and Hogan realized they were standing in front of their destination. Looked like, for now, at least, what he would be doing was spending a few hours in a French restaurant tasting wine he knew nothing about. A couple of months ago the idea of doing something like that would have made him want to stick needles in his eyes. Today, though, it felt like a good way to spend the time.

He looked at Chloe again, at how the afternoon sun brought out sparks of silver in her white-blond hair and how the breeze had tugged one strand loose to dance it around one cheek. He saw how the smile had left her lips, but hadn't quite fled from her eyes.

Yeah, tasting wine with Chloe Merlin didn't seem like a bad way to spend an afternoon at all.

Four

Since she began working as a personal chef five years earlier, Chloe had lived in some seriously beautiful homes, from her first job cooking for Lourdes and Alejandro Chavez in their charming Tribeca brownstone to Jack and Martin Ionesco's Fifth Avenue mansion a few years later to Anabel Carlisle's Park Avenue penthouse just weeks ago. All had been breathtaking in their own ways, and all of her employers had generously made clear she had the run of their homes in her off-time, be it their dens or their balconies or—in the case of the Ionescos—their home cinema. Hogan, too, had assured her she was welcome in any part of his house at any time.

But Chloe had never ventured out of her room in any of her previous postings unless it was to cook in her employers' kitchens or to explore the culinary aspects of their various neighborhoods. She'd always been perfectly content to stay in her room reading books, watching movies or searching the internet for articles—but always something about cooking. She'd just never had the desire to involve herself any further in the homes or lives of her employers beyond cooking for them.

So why did she feel so restless in her room at Hogan's house? she wondered a few nights after their excursion to the wine-tasting—which had ended up being surprisingly enjoyable. And not just because Hogan had been such an agreeable companion, either. He'd also proved to have a fairly sophisticated palate, something that had astonished him as much as it had Chloe, and he had discovered some wines he actually enjoyed, all of them labels she would have chosen for him. She would have put his until then unknown oenophilia down to his Amherst genes, but somehow she suspected that whatever made Hogan Hogan was the result of Hogan alone. In any event, Chloe had actually almost had fun that day. She couldn't remember the last time she'd almost had fun.

Which was maybe why she suddenly felt so restless in her room. A part of her was itching to get out and almost have fun again. And no matter how sternly she told that part of herself to stop feeling that way, that part of herself refused to listen.

She looked at the clock on the nightstand. It was nearly midnight. Hogan, she knew, always turned in before eleven. She knew this because she often went to the kitchen to make a cup of *Mariage Frères* tea about that time before turning in herself, and the house was always locked up tight—dark and silent save a small lamp in the kitchen she required be kept on so that she could make late-night forages for things like *Mariage Frères* tea. She was confident enough he was in his own room by now that she didn't worry about having already donned her pajamas. Or what passed for pajamas for her—a pair of plaid flannel pajama pants and a T-shirt for François and the Atlas Mountains, her latest favorite band.

Even so, she padded as silently as she could in her sock feet down the stairs to the third floor—slowing only long enough at the fourth to ensure that, yes, Hogan's bedroom door was closed, and all the lights were off—where there was a library teeming with books, even though she was fairly sure they would be about things besides cooking. There might be a novel or two in the mix somewhere, and that would be acceptable.

The only light in the library was what spilled through the trio of arched floor-to-ceiling windows from a streetlamp outside—enough to tell her where the largest pieces of furniture lay, but not enough to distinguish any titles on book spines. So she switched on the first lamp she found, bathing the room in a pale, buttery glow.

She went to the set of shelves nearest her, pushing her glasses up on her nose so she could read the books' spines. All the titles there seemed to have something to do with maritime history. The next grouping was mostly atlases. After that came biographies, predominantly featuring robber barons, autocrats and politicians. So much for fun.

She went to the other side of the room and began working her way backward. Toward the middle, she finally came across novels. Lots of them. To her surprise, she found a number of historicals by Anya Seton, whom her grandmother had adored. She plucked out a title from the mix she recognized as one of Mé-mée's favorites, opened it to the first page, read a few lines and was immediately hooked. So hooked that she didn't look where she was going when she turned around and stepped away from the shelf, so she inadvertently toppled a floor lamp.

It fell to the ground, hitting the marble with what seemed like a deafening crash in the otherwise silent room. Hastily, she stooped to right it. No harm done, she decided when it was upright again with its shade back in place. Just to make sure, she flicked it on to see if the bulb still worked—it did—then turned it off again. After that the room—and the house—were silent once more.

She opened the book and went back to her reading, making her way slowly across the library as she did, skirting the furniture until she arrived back at the lamp she had turned on when she first entered. She stood there and continued to read until she finished a few more paragraphs, then absently turned off the light, closed the book and began picking her way through the darkness toward the wide library entrance—which, since she wasn't yet accustomed to the darkness, she had to struggle to make out, so her steps slowed even more. The moment she made her way through it and into the adjoining study, however, someone surged up behind her, wrapping an iron-hard arm around her waist to pull her back against himself—hard.

Chloe screamed at the top of her lungs and, simultaneously, elbowed him viciously in the gut and stomped down as hard as she could on his foot. When his grip on her loosened in response, she lurched away from him so fiercely that her glasses fell from her face and onto the floor. She barely noticed, though, because all of her attention went to hurling the heavy hardback as viciously as she could in the direction of her assailant—and hitting him square in the face with it if the expletive he yelled in response was any indication.

She was opening her mouth to scream again and about to race for the stairs when her attacker cried out, "Whoa, Chloe! I'm sorry! I didn't know it was you!"

Immediately, she closed her mouth. Hogan. Of course it was Hogan. Who else would it be? The house, she'd learned her first day on the job, had more security than Fort Knox, something she and Hogan both appeared to have forgotten. Realizing that now, however, did little to halt the flow of adrenaline to every cell in her body. Her heart was hammering, her breathing was ragged, her thoughts were scrambled and her body was trembling all over.

"I thought you were an intruder," he said.

He, too, sounded more than a little rattled—she could hear him breathing as heavily as she was. But his eyes must have been better adjusted to the dark, because he made his way effortlessly across the study to switch on a desktop lamp that threw the room into the same kind of soft, golden light the library had enjoyed only moments ago. In fact, the study was pretty much a smaller version of the room she'd just left.

Hogan, too, was bathed in soft, golden light, something that made him seem softer and more golden himself. His nightwear wasn't much different from hers, except that he was wearing sweatpants, and his T-shirt read "Vinnie's House of Hubcaps." And where her shirt hung loosely on her frame, Hogan's was stretched taut across his, so that it hugged every bump and groove of muscle and sinew on his torso. And there was a lot of muscle and sinew on his torso. And on his arms, too. Holy cow. His shirtsleeves strained against salient biceps that tapered into a camber of muscles in his forearms in a way that made her mouth go dry.

The moment Chloe realized she was staring, she drove her gaze back up to his face. But that didn't help at all, because his hair was adorably disheveled, his cheeks were shadowed by a day's growth of beard and his bittersweet-chocolate eyes were darker and more compelling than ever. Something exploded in her belly and sent heat to every extremity, but not before much of it pooled deep in her chest and womb.

Why did he have to be so handsome? So magnetic? So damnably sexy? And why couldn't she ignore all of that? She encountered handsome, magnetic, sexy men all the time, and she never gave any of them a second thought. What was it about Hogan that made that impossible to do?

He was gripping a baseball bat about a third of the way up, but he loosened his hold and let it slip to the knob as he lowered it to his side. With his free hand, he rubbed a spot on his forehead that was already turning red—the place where the book had hit him.

"I am so sorry," she said. "I thought you were an intruder, too."

He looked at his fingers, probably to check for blood, and when he saw that they were clean, hooked that hand on his hip. "Don't apologize for defending yourself. It was a nice shot."

She tried to smile at that, but she was so rusty at smiling these days, she wasn't sure she succeeded. "Thanks."

"I heard a loud noise," he said. "I thought someone had broken in."

"That was me. I knocked over a lamp in the library. I came down to look for a book, and then I got so caught up in my reading that I didn't look where I was going. I didn't realize it was that loud. I mean, it sounded loud when it went down, but I thought that was just because the room was so quiet. I mean this house must have walls like a mausoleum, and—"

And she made herself shut up before she started to sound like an idiot, even though it was probably too late for that.

"No worries," he told her. "It's fine."

Oh, sure. Easy for him to say. He wasn't staring at some luscious blond wondering what he looked like under that T-shirt. And those sweatpants. And socks. And anything else he might be wearing. Or not wearing.

Oh, she really wished she hadn't thought that.

They stood there for another moment in silence, their gazes locked, their breathing still a little broken. Though hers was doubtless more a result of her thoughts than any lingering fear for her safety. Her physical safety anyway. Her mental and emotional safety were another matter at the moment.

Finally, Hogan said, "I think I need a drink." One more look at her, and he added, "You look like you could use one, too."

She told herself to say no. Then said, "I wouldn't say no."

He nodded once, leaned the bat against a wide, heavy desk then crossed to a cabinet on the opposite side of the study, opening it to reveal a fairly substantial bar. Without even having to look through the options, he pulled down a bottle of very nice bourbon, along with a cut-crystal tumbler—obviously, he'd spent some time in this room—then turned around to look at Chloe.

"What's your poison?" he asked. "This is all bourbon. Something else my grandfather collected, I've discovered. If you'd rather have a glass of wine, I can go down to the cellar for some."

But she'd already recognized a familiar favorite on the shelf and shook her head. "I'll have a couple of fingers of the Angel's Envy," she told him.

His eyebrows shot up at that. "I never would have pegged you for a bourbon drinker."

"We're even, then," she said. "I wouldn't have guessed you'd be one, either." She'd been surprised enough at how quickly he'd taken to wine.

"I wasn't before," he admitted. "But after exploring my grandfather's study and discovering the bar, I realized cars weren't his only passion. I wanted to see if maybe we had this—" he gestured toward the spirits behind him "—in common, too." He grinned. "Turns out we do."

He withdrew her chosen label and a second tumbler for her and splashed a generous portion from each bottle into their respective glasses. Then he made his way back to her and handed her her drink, which she accepted gratefully.

He lifted his glass in a toast. "Here's to nonexistent intruders."

She lifted hers in response. "I'll drink to that."

They clinked their glasses and did so with enthusiasm, but after one taste, both seemed to lose track of where the conversation should go next. Chloe tried to focus on the heat of the bourbon as it warmed her stomach, but the heat in Hogan's eyes kept distracting her. He was looking at her differently from what she was used to, as if he were seeing something in her face that wasn't there before.

She realized what that was when he said, "You're not wearing your glasses. Or any lipstick. You're cute in them, but without them…"

It was only his mention of her glasses that made her remember she'd lost them in the scuffle. She really didn't need them that badly—only for up-close work—and mostly wore them because they were another way to keep distance between herself and others.

"I lost them when you, uh…when you, um…" *When you pulled me back against your rock-hard abs and made me want to crawl under your shirt to see them for myself* was the thought that tumbled through her mind, but she was pretty sure it wasn't a good idea to say that out loud. Especially since, at the time, what she'd really been thinking was that she needed to run for her life.

Then again, maybe the two thoughts had something in common after all.

He must have realized what she was trying to say—and thankfully not what she was actually thinking—because he glanced over toward the door where the two of them had been embraced a few minutes ago. Uh, she meant *embattled*, not *embraced*. Of course that was what she meant. Then he strode to the entryway, looked around on the floor and found them with little trouble. He picked up the book on his way back to Chloe and brought them both to her.

"Thanks," she said as she took her glasses from him. She started to put them back on then instead settled them on top of her head. She told herself it was only because she was sure they needed cleaning after what they'd just been through. It wasn't to get rid of any distance that might linger between Hogan and herself.

He looked at the spine of the book before handing it to her, eyeing her thoughtfully when he saw the unmistakably romantic title.

"It was Mémée's favorite," she said. Then, when she realized he would have no idea who Mémée was, clarified, "My grandmother. Anya Seton was her favorite author, and when I saw all the books in the library by her, it made me think of Mémée, and I just—"

She'd just felt kind of lonely, she remembered, when she saw all the books that reminded her of the grandmother who passed away when she was in college. She thought about Mémée often—nearly every time she cooked—but somehow, seeing all those novels had roused feelings Chloe hadn't felt for a very long time. Or maybe it was something else that had done that. Since coming to work for Hogan, nothing in her life had felt normal.

"I thought reading it might make me feel closer to her," she said halfheartedly. Then, because she couldn't quite stop herself, she added, "I just miss her."

Hogan nodded. "I lost my folks young, too," he said. "How old were you when your grandmother died?"

"Nineteen."

"Which means you were even younger when you lost your parents."

"I never actually knew my parents," Chloe said, again without thinking. Wondering why she offered the information to Hogan when it was something she never discussed with anyone. She really must be frazzled by the whole intruder thing. Because even though she told her brain to stop talking, her mouth just kept it up. "My father was never in the picture—I'm not even sure my mother knew who he was—and not long after my mother had me, she sort of…disappeared."

Which was something Chloe *really* never talked about. Only one other person besides her grandmother knew about her origins. And that person was gone, too. What was possessing her to say all this to Hogan?

Whatever it was, it had such a hold on her that she continued, "My mother was troubled. Mémée did her best, but you can only do so much for a person who refuses to get help."

Hogan said nothing for a moment, then, softly, he told her, "I'm sorry." Probably because he didn't know what else to say. Not that Chloe blamed him. She wasn't sure what to say about her origins, either. Other than that they had made her what she was, so she couldn't—wouldn't—regret them.

"It's okay," she said. "Mémée was a wonderful parent. I had a nice childhood, thanks to her. I loved her very much, and she loved me."

Hogan gazed down into his drink. "So I guess you and I have something in common with the biological mother, what-if-things-had-been-different, kind of stuff, huh?"

Chloe started to deny it, started to tell him that her own upbringing would have been virtually the same if her mother had been healthy, then realized there was no way she could know that was true. Maybe her upbringing would have been better, maybe not. Who knew? But her mother would have been the one to mold her, not Mémée, and there was no way of even speculating about what shape Chloe would have taken. Would she have ever discovered her love of cooking under her mother's care? Or would she be passionate about something else now? Had her childhood been different, she might never have come to New York. She might never have met Hogan. Or anyone else.

"Maybe," she finally said. "But things happen to people every day that change their lives, many of them events that are out of their hands. Or by the smallest choices they make. Even opting to cross the street in one place instead of another could have devastating results if you get hit by a bus."

He smiled at that. "Yeah, well, I was thinking more in terms of our quality of life."

"You don't think you had quality of life growing up in Queens?"

"I had great quality of life growing up in Queens. The best. I'm kind of getting the impression that growing up here with the Amhersts would have left me at a disadvantage."

His response puzzled her. "Growing up in a breathtaking, multimillion-dollar home with unlimited funds at your disposal would have left you at a disadvantage?"

This time he nodded. "Sure. If no one here loved me."

Her heart turned over at the matter-of-fact way he said it. As if it was a given that he wouldn't have been loved here in this world of excess.

"You don't think your mother would have loved you?" she asked.

He expelled an errant breath and moved to sit in one of the leather chairs. Chloe followed, seating herself in the one next to it. She wasn't sure why—she really should be going back to her room and making the effort to get into bed—but something in his demeanor prohibited her from abandoning him just yet.

"I don't know," he said. "She was awfully young when she had me. She might have started looking at me as a liability who kept her from living the kind of life her friends did. She might have started resenting me. But I know my grandfather wouldn't have cared for me. His letter to me was—" he inhaled deeply and released the breath slowly "—not the warmest thing in the world. I mean, he wasn't mean or anything, but it was pretty clear he was only leaving his estate to me because the Amhersts dating all the way back to the time of knights and castles considered bloodline to be more important than anything else. He obviously wasn't happy about doing it."

He looked at something above the door. Chloe followed his gaze and saw an ornate coat of arms hanging there.

"The Amherst crest," he said. "There's one of those hanging in nearly every room in this house. Have you noticed?"

In truth, she hadn't. But when it came to physical surroundings, Chloe deliberately wasn't the most observant person in the world.

"No," she told him. "I suppose if there are that many, then bloodlines did indeed mean a lot to him."

"In his letter, he even asked that I consider legally changing my last name to Amherst so the direct line to the family name wouldn't die out with him. I guess he always figured Susan would forget about me and go on with her life. Get married and have other kids whose names she could hyphenate or something. Kids he could proudly call his progeny. His legacy. Instead of some grease monkey whose blue collar was stained with sweat."

"I'm sure Susan never forgot you, Hogan," Chloe said with absolute conviction. "And I'm sure she loved you very much. In a way, you were probably her first love. No one ever forgets or stops loving their first love."

He gave her another one of those thoughtful looks, the kind where the workings of his brain fairly shone in his eyes. His dark, beautiful, expressive eyes. "You sound like you're talking from experience."

She said nothing in response to that. She'd said too much already.

But her response must have shown on her face, too, because Hogan grinned a melancholy grin. "So there's some guy back there in your past you're still pining for, huh? The same way I've been pining for Anabel all these years? Is that something else you and I have in common?"

Maybe it was the bourbon. Maybe it was the pale, otherworldly light. Maybe it was the last lingering traces of mind-scrambling adrenaline. Maybe it was just the way Hogan was looking at her. Whatever it was, Chloe couldn't resist it.

"I'm not pining for him," she said. "I'll never get him back. He's gone."

Hogan's grin fell. He met her gaze levelly, and whatever he saw in her eyes made his eyebrows arrow downward and his jaw clench tight. "Gone," he repeated. "Gone like…he moved to another country?"

Chloe shook her head. It wasn't the bourbon. It wasn't the light. It wasn't the adrenaline. It was definitely Hogan this time and the way he was looking at her that made her say the rest.

"Samuel was my husband. He was a chef, too. We were going to open our own restaurant. We were going to have kids and teach them to cook, too. We were going to have a long life together, full of family and food. We were going to retire fat and happy in Lyon, and we were going to have our ashes scattered together in the Pyrenees. Instead, his ashes were scattered in Brown County State Park, where he and I had our first date when we were in ninth grade."

Hogan was looking kind of horrified now, confirming what Chloe already suspected—she had made her biggest mess yet. So she gripped her glass and downed what was left of its contents. Then she rose and carried it back to the cabinet from which Hogan had taken it. She started to leave it there for him to take to the kitchen with his own glass when he was ready. Instead, she picked up the bottle of bourbon that was still sitting on the bar and left with both it and the glass. It was definitely time to go back to her room and make the effort to get into bed. Somehow, though, she knew it was going to be a while before she actually made it to sleep.

Five

Hogan didn't expect to see Chloe the morning after she bared the depths of her soul to him. Not just because a person as private as she was would obviously be embarrassed about having revealed what she had last night, but because he knew firsthand what too much bourbon—even good bourbon—could do to a person. She'd looked pretty serious about making a dent in the bottle she'd taken back to her room.

So it surprised him when he went into the kitchen Friday morning to make himself breakfast and found her in there cooking. She was wearing one of her gigantic chef's jackets and gaudy pants—these decorated with silhouettes of pigs and the word "oink"—and had her hair gathered at the top of her head the way she always did. Her glasses were back in place, her red lipstick was perfect and she looked none the worse for wear for having been up late drinking and grieving for a man she would have loved for the rest of her life if he hadn't died far too soon.

He still couldn't believe she was a widow at twenty-eight. Had been a widow since twenty-three or younger, considering she'd been in New York cooking for people for the past five years. Though her revelation last night went a long way toward explaining why she was the way she was, cool and aloof and serious to a fault. Had Hogan experienced what she had, had he, say, married Anabel and then lost her so young, he would have been putting his fist through something every chance he got. And there wouldn't have been enough bourbon in the world to keep him numb.

Then he remembered that Chloe wasn't cool or aloof or serious to a fault. There had been moments since he'd met her when her veneer had cracked enough for him to see through to the other side. That day in the gallery when she told him his feelings of confusion about his place in the world were valid. That afternoon of the wine-tasting when she uttered that erotic little sound at the touch of his thumb. Last night when she fought like a tiger for her safety. Chloe Merlin had a sensitive, passionate, fiery soul, one that clawed its way out of wherever she buried it whenever her guard was down. Though, now that he knew more about her, he understood her guardedness. He just wished she didn't feel like she had to be so wary around him.

"Good morning," he said as he headed for the cof-feemaker.

She jumped at the sound of his voice and spun

around, but her expression offered nothing of what she might be feeling.

"Your breakfast will be ready in ten minutes," she said in reply.

"Great," he told her. "But you know, after last night, you didn't have to—"

"Your breakfast will be ready in ten minutes," she repeated before he could finish, in exactly the same way.

"But—"

"Your breakfast will be ready in ten minutes," she said a third time, more adamantly. Then, to drive that point home, she added, "Have a seat in your dining room, and I'll bring it out to you."

Ah. Okay. So they were just going to ignore what happened last night and go back to the way things were. Pretend she never said all the things she said—and pretend he never saw her looking all soft and vulnerable and pretty.

Which should have been fine. They had separate lives that didn't need to intersect except for mealtimes or if he happened to run into her in the house at some point.

Like he had last night.

He guessed that was beside the point—Chloe's point anyway. And it was a good point. For some reason, though, Hogan didn't want to take it. He didn't want to forget last night happened. He didn't want to forget what she said. He didn't want to forget how she looked. And he didn't want to go back to their old routine and roles.

Chloe obviously did, though. So, without saying anything more, he poured himself a cup of coffee—

ignoring her frown, since, as far as she was concerned, that was her job—then went to the dining room to wait for his breakfast.

But when he sat down at the table—the same way he'd sat down at the table every morning for a few weeks now—he didn't feel any more comfortable than he had on any of the other mornings waiting for his breakfast. Maybe a legal document had made this place his house, but it still didn't feel like home. Maybe he never had to work another day in his life, but his life right now didn't have any purpose. Maybe he was eating better than he ever had before, but he didn't like eating by the clock and by himself. Hell, at least he'd had the Mets and the Knicks to keep him company before.

Hogan's point was that he didn't like having someone else fixing and bringing him his breakfast. Even if hiring Chloe to do just that had been—and still was—the best way to bring Anabel back into his life. Which was something he needed to be focusing his attention on. And he would. ASAP. Just as soon as he figured out a way to do it that would keep Anabel in his house for longer than the few minutes she'd been here last time.

For now, though, he'd just have to keep putting up with breakfast Chloe's way instead of making his own, the way he'd been doing from the time he was a pre-schooler splashing more milk out of the cereal bowl than into it all the way up to grabbing a cruller from Alpha Donuts on his way to work. That was breakfast for normal people. Breakfast wasn't—

Chloe arrived at his side and set a plate in front of him. Beside a couple of slices of melon settled into what he'd come to recognize as chard was a wedge of something layered with… Ah, hell. He was too tired to try to identify what all the layers were.

So he asked, "What's that?"

"*Tartiflette avec les lardons, le reblochon et les truffes noires.*"

"Which is?"

"Potato casserole with bacon, cheese and mushrooms."

Hogan sighed. Breakfast wasn't *tarti*-whatever. It wasn't even potato casserole with bacon, cheese and mushrooms. He started to tell Chloe he'd have breakfast out this morning. He could take the train to Queens and stop by Alpha Donuts to treat himself to a baker's dozen. He could visit the garage while he was in the neighborhood, maybe go back to his old apartment for a few things he hadn't thought he'd need here. And then he could grab lunch at Taco Taberna across the street before he came ho— Before he came back to Lenox Hill.

He glanced at Chloe. Up close, she didn't look as put together as he first thought. In fact, up close, he could see smudges of purple beneath red-rimmed eyes and a minuscule smudge of lipstick at the corner of her usually flawlessly painted mouth. Not to mention an expression on her face that was a clear mix of *I'm-the-fiercest-human-being-in-the-world* and *I'm-barely-holding-it-together*. She'd gotten up early on a morning when she probably felt like crap because she had to do her job. She'd dressed and hauled herself into work, even though she probably felt uncomfortable facing her boss. Hogan would be the biggest mook in New York if he left now.

"It looks delicious," he told her. "Thank you."

She looked surprised by his gratitude. This after he'd thanked her every time she brought him a meal. But she replied, as she always did, "You're welcome." Then she spun on her heel to return to the kitchen.

As he often did, Hogan turned around to watch her retreat. Usually, she headed straight for her sanctuary, head held high, her step never faltering. This morning, though, she moved sluggishly, her head dipping down. She even lifted her hand to her face at one point, and he was pretty sure she was wiping something out of her eyes.

He turned back around and looked at his breakfast. Even if it wasn't what he usually ate, it was, like everything else she'd cooked, very…artful. In fact, it was, like everything else she'd cooked, almost too artful to eat.

He suddenly wondered what chefs fed themselves. Did Chloe prepare her own breakfast as painstakingly as she made his? Or was she in the kitchen right now, jamming a Pop-Tart into her mouth without even bothering to toast it first? Would her lunch be a slice of reheated pizza? With maybe some Sara Lee pound cake for dessert? Hogan really liked Sara Lee pound cake. He missed Sara Lee pound cake. And, while he was at it, when did Chloe eat dinner anyway? Before or after she made his? Did she fix a double batch of everything? One for him and one for her? Or did she just throw together a ham and cheese sandwich to eat while she was waiting for him to finish? A real ham and cheese sandwich. Not a French one.

He was still wondering about all that as he picked up his fork and dug in to the potato whatever. And he wondered about something else, too: How did he convince his chef there was more to life than timetables and fancy potato casseroles?

By the time Chloe left for her grocery shopping Friday afternoon, she felt almost human again. A midmorning nap—which she took completely by accident in Hogan's wine cellar when she lay down to look at the bottles on the very bottom shelf—had helped. What helped more was Hogan's acceptance that they pretend last night never happened. But what helped most of all was losing herself in the sounds and sights and smells of Greenmarket, scouring the farmers' stalls for what seasonal finds this early November day had to offer. She needed shallots for the *confit de canard* she would be making for dinner, Brussels sprouts and mesclun to go with, and pears for the *clafoutis* she planned for dessert.

She took her time as she wandered through the market, stopping at a stall whenever she saw a particularly delectable-looking piece of produce to wonder what she could make with it. The apples always smelled so luscious this time of year. And there was a vendor with maple syrup. Had to have some of that. Oh, and fennel! She hadn't made anything with fennel for a long time. Fennel was delicious in vichyssoise. Had to have some of that, too. And this would be the last of the tomatoes until next year. She should probably pick up a few and use them for something, too. Maybe a nice *tartine*...

By the time Chloe returned from Greenmarket, she had two canvas totes teeming with vegetables and fruits and other goodies, more than enough to get her through Friday and Saturday both. Enough, really, so that Hogan could have leftovers on Sunday if he wanted to fix something for himself while she was out doing something. Something that wasn't staying in Hogan's house. Something that kept her mind busy with thoughts that had nothing to do with Hogan. Or the way Hogan looked last night after she told him about Samuel. Or thoughts about Samuel, for that matter. Or anything other than food and its preparation. Its wonderful, methodical, intricate preparation that could keep even the most prone-to-wandering-to-places-it-really-shouldn't-wander mind focused on the task at hand.

She couldn't wait to get started on dinner.

She had just finished putting everything away— save what she would be using tonight—and was about to head to her room to change from her khaki cargo pants and baggy pomegranate-colored sweater into her chef's duds, when Hogan entered the kitchen carrying two white plastic bags decorated with the red logo of a local grocery chain.

"I'm cooking tonight," he said without preamble when he saw her. Before she could object, he hurried on, "I was in my old neighborhood today to stop by my old place, and I dropped in at the market where I used to shop, and—"

"Why did you have to go to the market there?" Chloe interrupted.

She didn't mean to be rude. She was just so surprised and flustered by his appearance in the kitchen again—save this morning, he hadn't ventured into the room once since that first day when he greeted her here—that she didn't know what else to say. And that could also be the only explanation for why she sounded not just rude, but also a tad jealous, when she said what she did.

Hogan must have heard the accusatory tone in her voice, too, because he suddenly looked a little guilty. All he said, though, was, "I needed a few things."

"What kind of things?"

His guilty look compounded. "Uh…things. You know. Personal things. Things I needed to get. That are personal."

"And you had to go all the way to Queens? Does Manhattan not have these personal things you needed?"

And could she just stop talking? Chloe demanded of herself. She sounded like a suspicious wife. Where Hogan went, what he bought, why he went there and bought it was none of her business. *For God's sake, shut* up, *Chloe.*

"Sure, I could have gotten them here," he said. "But C-Town is right up the street from the garage, and it was on the way to the train, so I went in there. For some things. And while I was there, I picked up some stuff for dinner. I thought I could give you a break."

A break? she echoed incredulously to herself. She hadn't even been working for him for a month, and already he was tired of her cooking? No one got tired of Chloe's cooking. Not only was it the best in New York, they also paid her too much to get tired of her cooking.

"Dinner is my job," she reminded him. "It's what you pay me to do. I don't need a break."

"I know, but I thought—"

"Am I not performing to your standards?" she asked.

Now he looked surprised. "What? Of course you are. I just—"

"Have I not cooked you acceptable meals?"

"Yes, Chloe, everything you've cooked has been great, but—"

"Then why do you suddenly want to cook for yourself?"

And why did she still sound like a possessive spouse? Bad enough she was grilling him about things she had no business grilling him about. She was only making it worse sounding like she thought she was entitled to do it. Even if she did have some bizarre desire to actually be Hogan's spouse—which she of course did *not*—it was Anabel Carlisle he wanted to cast in that role. Chloe was his *chef.* So why wasn't she acting like one?

Hogan didn't seem to be offended by her outburst, though. In fact, he suddenly looked kind of relieved. He even smiled. "No, Chloe, you don't understand. I'm not cooking for myself. I'm cooking for us."

Okay, now she was really confused. As weird as it was for her to be behaving like a scorned lover, it was even weirder for Hogan to be acting like a cheerful suitor. Especially one who could cook.

Before she could say anything else, though, he was emptying the contents of the bags onto the kitchen island. A pound of ground chuck, a couple of white onions, a bag of shredded, store brand "Mexican blend" cheese, a bag of tortilla chips and a jar of salsa—both of those were store brand, too—a packet of mass-produced taco seasoning, a bottle of mass-produced taco sauce and a half dozen generic white eggs.

She hastily added up the ingredients in her chef's brain and blanched when she calculated the sum. "Oh, my God. You're going to make taco meatloaf, aren't you?"

He was fairly beaming as he withdrew a burned and battered loaf pan.

"Yep," he said proudly. "In the sacred Dempsey meatloaf pan, which is the mother of all meatloaf pans. On account of it was my mother's. And it gets even better."

He spoke as if that were a paean.

What he withdrew from the second sack was a bag of frozen "crinkle cut" carrots, which he said would be divine with a glaze of butter and Sucanat—except he really said they would taste great stirred up in a pan with some margarine and brown sugar, both of which he was sure Chloe had on hand—then came a tube of prefab biscuits whose label proudly proclaimed, "With flaky layers!" And then—*then*—to her absolute horror, he withdrew the single most offensive affront to gastronomy any chef could possibly conceive: a box of—Chloe could scarcely believe her eyes—macaroni and cheese.

"But wait, that's still not the best part," he told her.

Well, of course it wasn't the best part. There was no *best part* of anything sitting on the counter. He could pull a rabid badger out of the bag, and it would still be better than anything he'd removed so far. But it wasn't a rabid badger he pulled out of the bag. It was far, far worse. A ready-made pound cake wrapped in tinfoil that looked dense enough to, if there were a few thousand more of them, build a garage, followed by a gigantic plastic tub of something called Fros-Tee

Whip, which self-identified as a "non-dairy whipped topping." Chloe couldn't help but recoil.

"I know, right?" Hogan said, evidently mistaking her flinch of repugnance for a tremor of excitement. "It's the greatest dessert ever invented by humankind."

This was going to be news to the creators of *crème brûlée, crêpes Suzette* and *soufflé au chocolat*.

"Look, I know you're not big on the processed foods," he said when he saw her looking at the assortment of, um, groceries. "But you're going to love all this. And I got the good kind of mac and cheese. The kind with the liquid cheese in the pouch, not the powdered stuff in the envelope."

Oh, well, in *that* case...

When she looked at him again, he was grinning in a way that let her know he was perfectly aware that the meal he was proposing was the complete antithesis of epicurean. But he clearly intended to prepare it anyway.

"Hogan, do you realize how much sodium there is in that pile of...of...?" she asked.

"I think 'food products' is the phrase you're looking for," he supplied helpfully.

Actually, she had been thinking of another word entirely. Even so, the *products* part of his suggestion, she would concede. It was the *food* part she found debatable. So she only reiterated, "Hogan, do you realize how much sodium there is in that pile?"

He grinned. "Chloe, I don't care how much sodium there is in that pile. No one cares how much sodium comes out of their grocery bags."

"People who want to live to see their first gray hair do."

"This—" he pointed at his purchases on the island "—is a lot closer to the typical American diet than that is." Now he pointed at the items from her shopping trip she'd left on the counter. "Not to mention the typical American diet is a lot easier to prepare."

"Ease does not equate to edible. Or enjoyable."

"It does when it's taco meatloaf."

"If this—" now Chloe was the one to point to the… groceries…he'd bought "—is the sort of thing you want to eat, then why did you hire me to cook for you in the first place?"

She knew the answer to that question, of course. He was using her to get Anabel Carlisle's attention. Chloe knew that because Hogan himself had said so and, hey, it hadn't made any difference to her. It was irrelevant. She worked for whoever paid her the most. That was rule number one when it came to choosing her employers. For some reason, though, it suddenly kind of bothered her to be used as a means to an end. Especially that end in particular.

Hogan's reply, however, had nothing to do with Anabel. In fact, it wasn't a reply at all. At least not to the question she'd asked.

"Come on. Let me cook dinner tonight," he cajoled. "Have you ever even eaten taco meatloaf?"

She gave him one of those *What do you think?* looks and said nothing.

"Then how do you know you won't like it?" he asked.

"Two words. Butylated hydroxyanisole."

"Gesundheit." He grinned again.

And damn that grin anyway, because every time she saw it, something in Chloe's chest grew warmer.

At this point, it was also spreading into body parts that really shouldn't be feeling warm in mixed company.

"I guarantee you'll love it," he told her. "If you don't, I promise I'll never invade your kitchen again."

She started to remind him that the room they were standing in was actually *his* kitchen, but hesitated. For some reason she did feel a little proprietary when it came to Hogan's kitchen. Certainly more than she had any other kitchen where she'd worked. She told herself it was because it was less sterile than most with its tile the color of the French Riviera and its creamy enamel appliances and its gleaming copper pots that dangled like amaranth from the ceiling and its gigantic windows that spilled more sunshine in one morning than she'd seen working for months in most places. From the moment she'd set foot in here, she'd coveted this kitchen. In the weeks that followed, she'd come to feel as if she never wanted to leave.

Though, if she were honest with herself, there were days, she supposed, when she wasn't sure that was entirely because of the kitchen.

"Fine," she conceded reluctantly. "You can cook dinner tonight."

"For us," he clarified.

Although she wasn't sure why he needed or wanted that concession—and although she wasn't sure it was a good idea for her to make it—Chloe echoed, "For us."

When Hogan had gotten the bright idea to cook taco meatloaf for Chloe, he'd been wanting something for dinner that was a taste of home—his real home, not his adopted one. He'd been lying under the chassis of a Dodge Charger at the time—one Eddie Deflorio was thinking of buying, to give it a once-over and make sure Eddie wasn't about to get shafted—when Eddie said something about Hogan's mom's taco meatloaf. And just like that, Hogan had been jonesing for it more than he had in years. And not just the taco meatloaf, but also the carrots and biscuits and mac and cheese his mom always made to go with it. And—it went without saying—some Sara Lee pound cake for dessert.

It had just felt so good to be back in the garage, surrounded by familiar sounds and smells and people, talking about familiar stuff—not to mention *doing* something—that Hogan had just wanted the day to go on for as long as it could. And he'd wanted to keep *doing* something. Even if it was making taco meatloaf. If he was going to do that, then he had to go up to his old apartment to get his mom's meatloaf pan. Then, once he was back in his apartment…

He'd just felt better than he had in weeks. He'd felt like he was home. Then he'd realized he wanted to share that feeling with someone. And the person that popped into his head was Chloe Merlin. She had shared something of herself with him last night and obviously wished she hadn't. Now he wanted to share something with her so she wouldn't feel like she had to hide her emotions. From him or anyone else.

What better way to share a piece of his neighborhood home with her than to bring a taste of Queens into a kitchen of Lenox Hill?

Thankfully, Chloe had hung around while he was putting together the meatloaf to tell him where everything was, even if he sometimes had to walk clear across the room to find what he needed. Mostly, she had sat on a stool sipping a glass of red wine, throwing out words like *monosodium glutamate* and *propyl gallate* and *potassium bromate*. But she'd at least poured him a glass of wine, too, and turned on some halfway decent music to cook by, even if he didn't understand a word of what was being sung.

He had managed to combine all the ingredients of the dish and make a fairly serviceable loaf out of it— even if it was a little bigger on one end than the other, something that, now that he thought about it, actually made it more authentic—and was ready to put in the oven, when he realized he forgot to turn on the oven to preheat it. Which, now that he thought about that, too, also made the experience more authentic. What didn't make it authentic was that he had no idea how to work the damned stove, because it was three times the size of a normal stove and had roughly a billion knobs on it.

"How do you turn this thing on?" he asked Chloe.

She had finally ended her indictment of the processed food industry and was now reading a book about somebody named Auguste Escoffier—in French. She looked up at the question, studying Hogan over the tops of her glasses for a moment. Then she pushed them into place with the back of her hand, set her book down on the counter and rose to cross to the stove.

"What temperature do you need?" she asked.

"Three-fifty," he told her.

She flipped one of the knobs, and the oven emitted a soft, satisfying hiss. "Give it a minute."

She looked at the meatloaf, still sitting on the kitchen island in its pan, surrounded by stray bits of onion and cheese, splatters of salsa and a fine dusting of taco seasoning. Okay, and also a little puddle of wine, the result of Hogan having an accident during a momentary wild idea to add some red wine to the meatloaf, thinking maybe that would make Chloe like it better. Fortunately, he came to his senses before doing it, mostly to keep his mother from spinning in her grave, but also because he wasn't sure he was ready to wing it in the kitchen just yet. Chloe looked back at him, took off her glasses and met his gaze levelly. *"Ce travail, c'est pas de la tarte, n'est-ce pas?"*

He had no idea what she said, but he was pretty sure by her expression that she was commiserating with him. He was also pretty sure that the reason he was suddenly getting kind of aroused was because she just spoke French. And call him crazy, but arousal probably wasn't a good idea in the middle of a kitchen when the meatloaf wasn't even in the oven yet. Which was *not* a euphemism for *any*thing sexual.

"Uh…" he began eloquently.

She emitted a soft sigh, folded her glasses and set them on the counter, then gave him another one of those almost-smiles he'd seen from her once or twice. And liked. A lot.

"Cooking isn't for the fainthearted," she told him. "It's harder than people think."

Yeah, and he was only using like five ingredients, most of which came out of boxes and bags. He couldn't imagine how much trouble Chloe went to whenever she prepared a meal.

"Thanks for your help," he said.

"I didn't do anything."

"You told me where to find the scissors. That was major."

She almost smiled again.

"And you poured me a glass of wine. That was really major."

"It was the least I could do."

"Thanks again."

They stood staring at each other for another minute, Hogan trying not to notice how beautiful her green eyes were, or how great she looked wearing something besides her giant chef clothes, or how her hair was longer than he first thought, falling past her shoulders in a rush of near-white silk. Those weren't things he should be noticing about his chef. They were things he should be noticing about Anabel. Things he doubtless *would* notice about Anabel, once the two of them got together again. Just as soon as he called her up and invited her to, um, do something. Which he would totally figure out. Soon.

"The stove is ready," Chloe said.

Stove? he wondered. What stove? Oh, right. The one they were standing right next to. That must be the reason he was suddenly feeling so hot.

"Isn't there a beeper or something that's supposed to go off to tell us that?" he asked.

She shook her head. And kept looking at him as intently as he was looking at her. "Not on a stove like this."

"Then how do you know it's ready?"

"I just know."

Of course she did.

"So I guess I should put the meatloaf in the oven,

then," he said. Not thinking about any kind of sexual euphemisms *at all*.

"I guess you should."

Hogan nodded. Chloe nodded. But neither of them did anything. Finally, she took the initiative and picked up the pan. Then she opened the oven and pushed in the meatloaf. Really deep. Pretty much as far as it would go. Hogan tried not to notice. He did. Honest.

"There," she said, straightening as she closed the oven door. "How long does it need to go?"

Oh, it needed to go for a very long time, he wanted to say. Hours and hours and hours. Maybe all night. What he said, though, was, "Sixty minutes ought to do it."

Chloe nodded. Hogan nodded. And he wondered how the hell he ever could have thought it would be a good idea to cook dinner for Chloe in a hot kitchen with an even hotter oven.

"I should probably clean up my mess," he said.

But there weren't enough cleaners in the world to take care of the mess he'd made today. He was supposed to be focused on winning back Anabel. But lately, he was hardly ever even thinking about Anabel. Because, lately, his head was too full of Chloe.

Yeah, Chloe. A woman who had pledged her life to a man she'd lost much too young. And who was still grieving for him five years later. And who would probably never want anyone else again.

Six

"So? Come on. What did you think?"

Chloe looked at Hogan from her seat on his right at his gigantic dinner table. He was beaming like a kid who'd just presented for show-and-tell a salamander he fished out of the creek all by himself.

"You liked it, didn't you?" he asked. "I can tell, because you cleaned your plate. Welcome to the clean plate club, Chloe Merlin."

"It was...acceptable," she conceded reluctantly.

He chuckled. "Acceptable. Right. You had second helpings of everything, and you still cleaned your plate."

"I just wanted to be sure I ate enough for an accurate barometer of the taste combinations, that's all."

"And the taste combinations were really good, weren't they?"

All right, fine. Taco meatloaf had a certain *je ne sais quoi* that was surprisingly appealing. So did the carrots. And even the biscuits. Chloe had never eaten anything like them in her life. Mémée had never allowed anything frozen or processed in the house when Chloe was growing up. Her grandmother had kept a small greenhouse and vegetable garden in the backyard, and what she hadn't grown herself, she'd bought at the weekly visits she and Chloe made to the farmers' markets or, in the coldest months, at the supermarket—but organic only.

Chloe had just never felt the urge to succumb to the temptation of processed food, even if it was more convenient. She *enjoyed* prepping and cooking meals. She *enjoyed* buying the ingredients fresh. The thought of scooping food out of bags and jars and boxes was as alien to her as having six limbs. It wasn't that she was a snob about food or cooking, it was just that…

Okay, she was kind of a snob about food and cooking. Clearly, her beliefs could use some tweaking.

"You know," she told Hogan, "I could make some taco seasoning myself for you to use next time, from my own spice collection. It would have a lot less sodium in it."

He grinned. "That would be great. Thanks."

"And salsa is easy to make. I could make some of that fresh, the next time you want to cook this."

"I'd love that."

"Even the biscuits could be made—"

"I have to stop you there," he interjected. "I'm sorry, but the biscuits have to be that specific kind. They're what my mom always made. It's tradition."

And it was a taste of his childhood. Chloe got that. She felt the same way about *gratin Dauphinois*.

"Okay," she conceded. "But maybe fresh carrots next time, instead of frozen?"

He thought about that for a minute. "Okay. I mean, we already changed those anyway, since that stuff you call brown sugar is actually beige sugar, and you didn't have any margarine. By the way, what kind of person doesn't have margarine in their kitchen?"

Before, Chloe would have answered a question like that with some retort about hexane and free radicals. Instead, she said, "Butter is better for you."

She managed to stop herself before adding, *And you need to stay healthy, Hogan*. Because what she would have added after that was *I need you to be healthy, Hogan*.

She refused to think any further than that. Such as *why* she needed Hogan to be healthy. She told herself it was for the same reason she wanted anyone to be healthy. Everyone deserved to live a long, happy life. No one knew that better than Chloe, who had seen one of the kindest, most decent human beings she'd ever known have his life jerked out from under him. She didn't want the same thing to happen to Hogan. Not that it would. The man looked as hearty as a long-shoreman. But Samuel had looked perfectly healthy, too, the day he left for work in the morning and never came home again.

She pushed the thought away and stood. "Since you cooked, I'll clean up. It's only fair."

Hogan looked a little startled by her abrupt announcement, but stood, too. "You helped cook. I'll help clean up."

She started to object but he was already picking up his plate and loading it with his flatware. So she did likewise and followed him to the kitchen. Together they loaded the dishwasher. Together they packed the leftovers in containers. Together they put them in the fridge.

And together they decided to open another bottle of wine.

But it was Hogan's suggestion that they take it up to the roof garden. Although he'd told her on her first day at work the house had one, and that she should feel free to use it whenever she wanted, especially since he probably never would, Chloe hadn't yet made her way up there. She really did prefer to stay in her room when she wasn't working or out and about. Save that single excursion to the library—and look how that had turned out. When they made it up onto the roof, however, she began to think maybe she should reconsider. New York City was lovely at night.

So was Hogan's rooftop garden. The living section—which was nearly all of it—was a patchwork of wooden flooring and was lit by crisscrossing strings of tiny white lights woven through an overhead trellis. Terra-cotta pots lined the balustrade, filled with asters and camellias and chrysanthemums, all flaming with autumn colors from saffron to cinnamon to cayenne. Beyond it, Manhattan twinkled like tidy stacks of gemstones against the night sky.

Knowing the evening would be cool, Chloe had grabbed a wrap on her way up, a black wool shawl that had belonged to her grandmother, embroidered with tiny red flowers. She hugged it tightly to herself as she sat on a cushioned sofa pushed against a brick access bulkhead and set her wine on a table next to it. Hogan sat beside her, setting his wine on a table at his end. For a long moment neither spoke. They only gazed out at the glittering cityscape in silence.

Finally, Chloe said, "I still have trouble sometimes believing I live in New York. I kind of fell in love with the city when I was a kid, reading about it and seeing so many movies filmed here. I never actually thought I'd be living here. Especially in a neighborhood like this."

"Yeah, well, I grew up in New York," Hogan said, "but this part of the city is as foreign to me as the top of the Himalayas would be. I still can't believe I live here, either. I never came into Manhattan when I was a kid. Especially someplace like Park Avenue. I never felt the need to."

"Then how did you meet Anabel?" Chloe asked. "She doesn't seem like the type to ever leave Park Avenue."

He grinned that damnably sexy grin again. He'd done that a lot tonight. And every time he did, Chloe felt a crack open in the armor she'd worn so well for so long, and a little chink of it tumbled away. At this point, there were bits of it strewn all over his house, every piece marking a place where Hogan had made her feel something after years of promising herself she would never feel anything again. What she ought to be feeling was invaded, overrun and offended. Instead, she felt…

Well. Things she had promised herself she would never feel again—had sworn she was incapable of ever feeling again. Things that might very well get her into trouble.

"How I met Anabel is actually kind of a funny story," Hogan said. "She and a couple of her friends were going to a concert at Shea Stadium, but they pissed off their cab driver so bad on the way, he stopped the car in the middle of the street in front of my dad's garage and made them get out. She and the guy got into a shouting match in the middle of Jamaica Avenue, and a bunch of us working in the garage went out to watch." He chuckled. "I remember her standing there looking like a bohemian princess and cursing like a sailor, telling the cabbie she knew the mayor personally and would see to it that he never drove a cab in the tristate area again."

Chloe smiled at the picture. She couldn't imagine Anabel Carlisle, even a teenaged one, behaving that way. Her former employer had always been the perfect society wife when Chloe worked for her.

"Anyway, after the cabbie drove off without them, all us guys started applauding and whistling. Anabel spun around, and I thought she was going to give us a second helping of what she'd just dished out, but she looked at me and..." He shook his head. "I don't know. It was like how you see someone, and there's just something there. The next thing I knew, me and a couple of the guys are walking up the street with her and her friends, and we're all going for pancakes. After that she came into Queens pretty often. She even had dinner at my house with me and my folks a few times. But she never invited me home to meet hers."

There was no bitterness in his voice when he said that last sentence. There was simply a matter-of-factness that indicated he understood why she hadn't wanted to include him in her uptown life. That was gentlemanly of him, even if Chloe couldn't understand Anabel's behavior. She imagined Hogan had been just as nice back then as he was now. Anabel must have realized that if she'd become involved with him. Who cared what neighborhood he called home?

"It was her parents," he said, as if he'd read her mind. "Her dad especially didn't want her dating outside her social circle. She would have gotten into a lot of trouble if they found out about me. I understood why she couldn't let anyone know she was involved with me."

"If you understood," Chloe said, "then how come you're still unattached after all this time? Why have you waited for her?"

She thought maybe she'd overstepped the bounds—again—by asking him something so personal. But Hogan didn't seem to take offense.

"I didn't sit around for fifteen years waiting for her," he said. "I dated other girls. Other women. I just never met anyone who made me feel the way Anabel did, you know? There was never that spark of lightning with anyone else like there was that night on Jamaica Avenue."

Chloe didn't understand that, either. Love wasn't lightning. She did, however, understand seeing a person and just knowing there was something there. That had happened to her, too. With Samuel. The day he walked into English class in the middle of freshman year, she'd looked up from *The Catcher in the Rye* and into the sweetest blue eyes she'd ever seen, and she'd known at once that there was something between them. Something. Not love. Love came later. Because love was something so momentous, so stupendous, so enormous, that it had to happen over time. At least it did for Chloe. For Hogan, evidently, it took only a sudden jolt of electricity.

"And now Anabel is free," she said, nudging aside thoughts of the past in an effort to get back to the present. "You must feel as if you're being tasered within an inch of your life these days."

Even if he hadn't done much in the way of trying to regain the affections of his former love, she couldn't help thinking. She wondered why he hadn't.

He looked thoughtful for a moment. "I think maybe I've outgrown the fireworks part," he said cryptically. "But yeah. I really need to call her and set something up."

"Why don't you have a dinner party and invite her?" Chloe suggested. Wondering why her voice sounded so flat. She loved preparing meals for dinner parties. It was great fun putting together the menus. "You could ask her and a few other couples. Maybe she's still friends with some of the girls who were with her the night you met her," she added, trying to get into the spirit. And not getting into the spirit at all. "Other people would offer a nice buffer for the two of you to get reacquainted."

By the time she finished speaking, there was the oddest bitterness in Chloe's mouth. Maybe the wine had turned. Just to make sure, she took another sip. No, actually, the pinot noir tasted quite good.

"Maybe," Hogan said.

"No, definitely," she insisted. Because…

Well, just because. That was why. And it was an excellent reason. Hogan clearly needed a nudge in Anabel's direction, since he wasn't heading that way himself. He'd made clear since Chloe's first day of employment that he was still pining for the woman he'd loved since he was a teenager. He needed a dinner party. And Chloe needed a dinner party, too. Something to focus on that would keep her mind off things it shouldn't be on.

"Look, Chloe," he said, "I appreciate your wanting to help, but—"

"It will be perfect," she interrupted him. "Just a small party of, say, six or eight people."

"But—"

"I can get it all organized by next weekend, provided everyone is available."

"But—"

"Don't worry about a thing. I'll take care of all the details. It will be your perfect entrée into society, which, for some reason, you haven't made yet."

"Yeah, because—"

"A week from tomorrow. If you'll supply the names, I'll make the calls to invite everyone."

"Chloe—"

"Just leave it to me."

He opened his mouth to protest again, but seemed to have run out of objections. In fact, he kind of looked like the proverbial deer in the headlights. Okay, proverbial stag in the headlights.

Then he surprised her by totally changing the subject. "So what was it like growing up in… Where did you say you're from? Someplace in Indiana."

"New Albany," she replied automatically. "It's in the southern part of the state, on the Ohio River."

"I'm going to go out on a limb and say it probably

wasn't much like Manhattan," he guessed. "Or even Queens."

"No, not at all. It's quiet. Kind of quirky. Nice. It was a good place to grow up." She couldn't quite stop herself from drifting back into memories again. "Not a whole lot to do when you're a kid, but still nice. And Louisville was right across the river, so if we wanted the urban experience, we could go over there. Not that it was as urban as here, of course. But there were nights when we were teenagers when Samuel and I would ride our bikes down to the river and stare at Louisville on the other side. Back then it seemed like such a big place, all bright lights and bridges. Compared to New York, though…"

When she didn't finish, Hogan said, "You and your husband met young, huh?"

And only then did Chloe realize just how much she had revealed. She hadn't meant to bring up Samuel again. Truly, she hadn't. But it was impossible to think about home without thinking of him, too. Strangely, though, somehow, thinking about him now wasn't quite as painful as it had been before.

"In high school," she heard herself say. "Freshman year. We married our sophomore year in college. I know that sounds like we were too young," she said, reading his mind this time—because everyone had thought marrying at twenty was too young. Everyone still thought that. For Chloe and Samuel, it had felt like the most natural thing in the world.

"How did he…?" Hogan began. "I mean…if you don't mind my asking… What happened?"

She expelled a soft sigh. Of course, she should have realized it would come to this sooner or later with

Hogan. It was her own fault. She was the one who'd brought up her late husband. She couldn't imagine why. She never talked about Samuel with anyone. Ever. So why was she not minding talking about him to Hogan?

"Asymptomatic coronary heart disease," she said. "That's what happened. He had a bad heart. That no one knew about. Until, at twenty-two years of age, he had a massive heart attack that killed him while he was performing the physically stressful act of slicing peppers for *tastira*. It's a Tunisian dish. His specialty was Mediterranean cooking," she added for some reason. "We would have been an unstoppable team culinarily speaking, once we opened our restaurant."

Hogan was silent for a moment, then, very softly, he said, "Those are his chef's jackets you wear, aren't they?"

Chloe nodded. "After he was… After we sprinkled his ashes in Brown County, I realized I didn't have anything of him to keep with me physically. We didn't exchange rings when we married, and we weren't big on gift-giving." She smiled sadly. "Symbols of affection just never seemed necessary to either of us. So, after he was gone, I started wearing his jackets when I was cooking."

She had thought wearing Samuel's jackets would make her feel closer to him. But it hadn't. It wasn't his clothing that helped her remember him. If she'd needed physical reminders for that, she never would have left Indiana. But she'd been wearing them for so long now, it almost felt wrong to stop.

She reached for her wine and enjoyed a healthy taste of it. It warmed her mouth and throat as she swallowed, but it did nothing to combat the chill that suddenly enveloped her. So she put the glass down and wrapped her shawl more tightly around herself.

"I'm sorry, Chloe," Hogan said, his voice a soft caress in the darkness. "I shouldn't have asked for details."

"It's okay," she told him, even though it really wasn't okay. "It was a long time ago. I've learned to...cope with it. The money I make as a chef goes into a fund I started in Samuel's name that makes testing for the condition in kids less expensive, more common and more easily accessible. Knowing that someone else—maybe even a lot of someone elses—might live longer lives with their loved ones by catching their condition early and treating it helps me deal."

Hogan was being quiet again, so Chloe looked over to see how he was handling everything she'd said. He didn't look uncomfortable, though. Mostly, he looked sympathetic. He'd lost people he loved at a young age, too, so maybe he really did understand.

"I lied when I said the reason I came to New York was to open my own restaurant," she told him. "There's no way I could do that now, without Samuel. It was our dream together. I really came to New York because I thought it would be a good place to lose myself after he died. It's so big here, and there are so many people. I thought it would be easier than staying in a place where I was constantly reminded of him. And it's worked pretty well. As long as I'm able to focus on cooking, I don't have to think about what happened. At least I didn't until—"

She halted abruptly. Because she had been *this close* to telling Hogan it had worked pretty well until she met him. Meeting him had stirred up all sorts of feelings she hadn't experienced in years. Feelings she'd only ever had for one other human being. Feelings she'd promised herself she would never, ever, feel again. She'd barely survived losing Samuel. There was no way she could risk—no way she *would* risk—going through that again. No way she would ever allow someone to mean that much to her again. Not even—

"At least you did until I asked about it." Hogan finished her sentence for her. Erroneously, at that. "Wow. I really am a mook."

"No, Hogan, that's not what I was going to say." Before he could ask for clarification, however, she quickly concluded, "Anyway, that's what happened."

The temperature on the roof seemed to have plummeted since they first came outside, and a brisk wind riffled the potted flowers and rippled the lights overhead. Again, Chloe wrapped herself more snugly in her shawl. But the garment helped little. So she brought her knees up on the sofa and wrapped her arms around her legs, curling herself into as tight a ball as she could.

"You know how people say it's better to have loved and lost than to never have loved at all?" she asked.

"Yeah," Hogan replied softly.

"And you know how people say it's better to feel bad than to feel nothing at all?"

"Yeah."

"People are full of crap."

He paused before asking even more softly than before, "Do you really think that?"

She answered immediately. "Yes."

Hogan waited a moment before moving closer,

dropping an arm across her shoulders and pulling her to him, tucking the crown of her head beneath his chin. Automatically, Chloe leaned into him, pressing her cheek to his shoulder, opening one hand over his chest. There was nothing inappropriate in his gesture or in her reaction to it. Nothing suggestive, nothing flirtatious, nothing carnal. Only one human being offering comfort to another. It had been a long time since anyone had held Chloe, even innocently. A long time since anyone had comforted her. And now here was Hogan, his heat enveloping her, his scent surrounding her, his heart thrumming softly beneath her palm. And for the first time in years—six years, nine months, one week and one day, to be precise—Chloe felt herself responding.

But there, too, lay problems. After Samuel's death, she'd lost herself for a while, seeking comfort from the sort of men who offered nothing but a physical release for the body and no comfort for the soul. The behavior had been reminiscent of her mother's— erratic and self-destructive—and when Chloe finally realized that, she'd reined herself in and shut herself up tight. Until tonight.

Suddenly, with Hogan, she did want holding. And she wanted comforting. And anything else he might have to offer. She reminded herself that his heart and his future were with someone else. He was planning a life with Anabel. But Chloe didn't want a future or a life with him. She'd planned a life once, and the person she'd planned it with was taken from her. She would never make plans like that again. But a night with Hogan? At the moment a night with him held a lot of appeal.

She tilted her head back to look at his face. His brown eyes were as dark as the night beyond, and the breeze ruffled his sandy hair, nudging a strand down over his forehead. Without thinking, Chloe lifted a hand to brush it back, skimming her fingers lightly along his temple after she did. Then she dragged them lower, tracing the line of his jaw. Then lower still, to graze the column of his throat. His pupils expanded as she touched him, and his lips parted.

Still not sure what was driving her—and, honestly, not really caring—she moved her head closer to his. Hogan met her halfway, brushing her lips lightly with his once, twice, three times, four, before covering her mouth completely. For a long time he only kissed her, and she kissed him back, neither of them shifting their position, as if each wanted to give the other the option of putting a stop to things before they went any further.

But neither did.

So Chloe threaded her fingers through his hair, cupped the back of his head in her palm and gave herself more fully to the kiss. At the same time, Hogan dropped his other hand to her hip, curving his fingers over her to pull her closer still. She grew ravenous then, opening her mouth against his, tasting him more deeply. When he pulled her into his lap, wrapping both arms around her waist, she looped hers around his neck and held on for dear life.

She had no idea how long they were entwined that way—it could have been moments, it could have been millennia. Chloe drove her hands over every inch of him she could reach, finally pushing her hand under the hem of his sweater. The skin of his torso was hot and hard and smooth beneath her fingertips, like silk-covered steel. She had almost forgotten how a man's body felt, so different from her own, and she took her time rediscovering. Hogan, too, went exploring, moving his hand from her hip to her waist to her breast. She cried out when he cupped his hand over her, even with the barrier of her sweater between them. It had just been so long since a man touched her that way.

He stilled his hand at her exclamation, but he didn't move it. He only looked at her with an unmistakable question in his eyes, as if waiting for her to make the next move. She told herself they should put a stop to things now. She even went so far as to say, "Hogan, we probably shouldn't..." But she was unable—or maybe unwilling—to say the rest. Instead, she told him, "We probably shouldn't be doing this out here in the open."

He hesitated. "So then...you think we should do this inside?"

Chloe hesitated a moment, too. But only a moment. "Yes."

He lowered his head to hers one last time, pressing his palm flat against her breast for a moment before dragging it back down to her waist. Then he was taking her hand in his, standing to pull her up alongside him. He kissed her again, long and hard and deep, then, his fingers still woven with hers, led her to the roof access door. Once inside the stairwell, they embraced again, Hogan pressing her back against the wall to crowd his body against hers, their kisses deepening until their mouths were both open wide. She drove her hands under his sweater again to splay them open against the hot skin of his back, and he dropped a hand between her legs, petting her over the fabric of her pants until she was pushing her hips harder into his touch.

Somehow they made it down the stairs to Hogan's bedroom. Somehow they made it through the door. Somehow they managed to get each other's clothes off. Then Chloe was naked on her back in his bed, and Hogan was naked atop her. As he kissed her, he dropped his hand between her legs again, growling his approval when he realized how damp and ready for him she already was. He took a moment to make her damper, threading his fingers through her wet flesh until she was gasping for breath, then he drew his hand back up her torso to her breast. He thumbed the ripe peak of one as he filled his mouth with the other, laving her with the flat of his tongue and teasing her with its tip. In response, Chloe wove her fingers together at his nape and hooked her legs around his waist as if she intended to hold him there forever.

Hogan had other plans, though. With one final, gentle tug of her nipple with his teeth, he began dragging openmouthed kisses back down along her torso. He paused long enough to taste the indentation of her navel then scooted lower still, until his mouth hovered over the heated heart of her. Then he pressed a palm against each of her thighs and pushed them open, wide enough that he could duck his head between them and taste the part of her he'd fingered long moments ago.

The press of his tongue against her there was almost more than Chloe could bear. She tangled her fingers in his hair in a blind effort to move him away, but he drove his hands beneath her fanny and pushed her closer to his mouth. Again and again, he darted his tongue against her, then he treated her to longer, more leisurely strokes. Something wild and wanton coiled tighter inside her with every movement, finally bursting in a white-hot rush of sensation that shook her entire body. Before the tremors could ebb, he was back at her breast, wreaking havoc there again.

After that Chloe could only feel and react. There were no thoughts. No cares. No worries. There was only Hogan and all the things he made her feel. Hogan and all the things she wanted to do to him, too. When he finally lifted his head from her breast, she pulled him up to cover his mouth with hers, reaching down to cover the head of his shaft with her hand when she did. He was slick and hard, as ready for her as she was for him. But she took her time, too, to arouse him even more, palming him, wrapping her fingers around him, driving her hand slowly up and down the hard, hot length of him.

When he rolled onto his back to facilitate her movements, Chloe bent over him, taking as much of him into her mouth as she could. Over and over she savored him, marveling at how he swelled to even greater life. When she knew he was close to coming, she levered her body over his to straddle him, easing herself down over his long shaft then rising slowly up again. Hogan cupped his hands over her hips, guiding her leisurely up and down atop himself. But just as they were both on the verge of shattering, he reversed their bodies so that Chloe was on her back again. He grinned as he circled each of her ankles in strong fists, then he knelt before her and opened her legs wide. And then—oh, *then*—he was plunging himself into her as deep as he could go, thrusting his hips against hers again and again and again.

Never had she felt fuller or more complete than she did during those moments that he was buried inside her. Every time he withdrew, she jerked her hips upward to stop him, only to have him come crashing into her again. They came as one, both crying out in the euphoria that accompanied climax. Then Hogan collapsed, turning their bodies again until he was on his back and she was lying atop him. Her skin was slick and hot. Her brain was dazed and shaken. And her heart...

Chloe closed her eyes, refusing to complete the thought. There would be no completion of thought tonight. There would be completion only for the body. And although her body felt more complete than it had in a very long time, she already found herself wanting more.

Her body wanted more, she corrected herself. Only her body. Not her. But as she closed her eyes against the fatigue that rocked her, she felt Hogan press a kiss against the crown of her head. And all she could think was that, of everything he'd done to her tonight, that small kiss brought her the most satisfaction.

Seven

Chloe awoke slowly to darkness. She hated waking up before the alarm went off at five, because she could never get back to sleep for that last little bit of much needed slumber. Invariably her brain began racing over the list of things she had to do that day, not stopping until she rose to get those things done. Strangely, though, this morning, her brain seemed to be sleepier than she was, because it wasn't racing at all. There were no thoughts bouncing around about the intricacies of the asparagus-brie soufflé she planned for this morning's breakfast. No reminders ricocheting here and there that her savory and marjoram plants were looking a little peaked, so she needed to feed them. No, there were only idle thoughts about—

Hogan. Oh, my God, she'd had sex with Hogan last night. Worse, she had woken up in his bed instead of her own. Now she would have to sneak out under cover of darkness before he woke up so she could get ready for work and make his breakfast, then figure out how to pretend like there was nothing different about this morning than any of the mornings that had preceded it and *Just have a seat in the dining room, Hogan, and I'll bring you your breakfast the way I always do, as if the two of us weren't just a few hours ago joined in the most intimate way two people can be joined.*

Oh, sure. *Now* her brain started working at light speed.

Thankfully, Mrs. Hennessey had weekends off, so Chloe didn't have to worry about explaining herself to the housekeeper. Even if Mrs. Hennessey did remind her of her grandmother, who Chloe could just imagine looking at her right now and saying with much disappointment, *"Mon petit doigt me dit..."* which was the French equivalent of "A little bird told me," a phrase Mémée never had to finish because as soon as she started to say it, Chloe would always break down in tears and confess whatever it was she'd done.

And now she'd *really* done it.

Panicked by all the new worries rioting in her head, Chloe turned over, hoping to not wake Hogan. But the other side of the bed was empty. She breathed a sigh of relief...for all of a nanosecond, because her gaze then fell on the illuminated numbers of the clock on the nightstand beyond.

It was almost nine thirty! She never slept until nine thirty! Even on her days off! Which today wasn't!

By now she should have already finished cleaning up breakfast and should be sipping a cup of rose and lavender tea while she made a list for her afternoon shopping. She had completely missed Hogan's breakfast this morning. Never in her life had she missed making a meal she was supposed to make for an employer. How could she have slept so late?

The answer to that question came immediately, of course. She had slept so late because she was up so late. And she was up so late because she and Hogan had been... Well. Suffice it to say Hogan was a very thorough lover. He'd been even more insatiable than she.

Heat swept over her at some of the images that wandered into her brain. Hogan hadn't left an inch of her body untouched or untasted. And that last time they'd come together, when he'd turned her onto her knees and pressed her shoulders to the mattress, when he'd entered her more deeply than she'd ever felt entered before, when he threaded his fingers through her damp folds of flesh and curried them in time with the thrust of his shaft, then spilled himself hotly inside her...

Oh, God. She got hot all over again just thinking about it.

How could she have let this happen? She wished she could blame the wine. Or Hogan's unrelenting magnetism. Or the romance of New York at night. Anything besides her own weakness. But she knew she had only herself to blame. She had let her guard down. She had opened herself up to Hogan. She had allowed herself to feel. And she had lost another part of herself as a result.

No, not lost, she realized. She had surrendered herself this time. She had given herself over to Hogan willingly. And she would never be able to get that part of herself back.

She'd barely been able to hold it together after Samuel died. She'd had to tie herself up tight, hide herself so well that nothing outside would ever get to her again. Because losing something—someone—again might very well be the end of her.

She tried looking at it a different way. Okay, so she and Hogan had sex. So what? She'd had sex before. It was just sex. She'd been physically attracted to Hogan since the minute she met him. He was a very attractive man. Last night she'd simply acted on that attraction. As had he. But it was just an attraction. Hogan was in love with Anabel. He'd been in love with Anabel for nearly half his life. And Chloe still loved her late husband. Just because she and Hogan had enjoyed a little—okay, a lot of—sex one night didn't mean either of them felt any differently about each other today. It was sex. Not love.

So why did everything seem different?

She had to get out of Hogan's room and back to her own so she could regroup and figure out what to do. She was fumbling for a lamp on the nightstand when the bedroom door opened, throwing a rectangle of light onto the floor and revealing Hogan standing before it. He was wearing jeans and nothing else, and his hair was still mussed from the previous night's activities. He was carrying a tray topped with a coffeepot and a plate whose contents she couldn't determine.

"You're awake," he said by way of a greeting, his voice soft and sweet and full of affection.

Chloe's stomach pitched to hear it. Affection wasn't allowed. Affection had no place in a physical reaction. No place in sex. No place in Chloe's life anywhere.

"Um, yeah," she said, pulling the covers up over

her still-naked body. "I'm sorry I overslept. I can have your breakfast ready in—"

"I made breakfast," he interrupted.

Well, that certainly wasn't going to look good on her résumé, Chloe thought. Mostly because she was afraid to think anything else. Like how nice it was of Hogan to make breakfast. Or how sweet and earnest he sounded when he told her he had. Or the warm, fuzzy sensation that swept through her midsection when he said it.

"I mean, it's not as good as what you would have made," he continued when she didn't respond. "But I didn't want to wake you. You were sleeping pretty soundly."

And still, she had no idea what to say.

Hogan made his way silently into the dim room. He strode first to the window and, balancing the tray in one hand, tugged open the curtains until a wide slice of sunlight spilled through. Then he smiled, scrambling Chloe's thoughts even more than they already were. When she didn't smile back—she couldn't, because she was still so confused by the turn of events—his smile fell. He rallied it again, but it wasn't quite the same.

When he set the tray at the foot of the bed, she saw that, in addition to the coffee, it held sugar and cream, along with a modest assortment of not-particularly-expertly-cut fruit, an array of not-quite-done to far-too-done slices of toast, some cheese left over from last night and a crockery pot of butter.

"I wasn't sure how you like your coffee," he said. "But I found cream in the fridge, so I brought that. And some sugar, just in case."

When Chloe still didn't reply, he climbed back into bed with her. But since it was a king-size, he was nearly as far away from her as he would have been in Queens. Even so, she tugged the covers up even higher, despite the fact that she had already pulled them as high as they would go without completely cocooning herself. Hogan noticed the gesture and looked away, focusing on the breakfast he'd made for them.

"It's weird," he said. Which could have referred to a lot of things. Thankfully, he quickly clarified, "You know what I like for every meal, but I don't even know what you like to have for breakfast. I don't even know how you take your coffee."

"I don't drink coffee, actually," she finally said.

He looked back at her. "You don't?"

She shook her head.

"Then why is there cream in the fridge?"

"There's always cream in the fridge when you cook French."

"Oh. Well. Then what do you drink instead of coffee?"

"Tea."

"If you tell me where it is, I could fix you—"

"No, that's okay."

"If you're sure."

"I am."

"So…what kind of tea?"

"Dragon tea. From Paris."

"Ah."

"But you can get it at Dean and DeLuca."

"Gotcha."

"I don't put cream in it, either."

"Okay."

"Or sugar."

"Noted."

The conversation—such as it was—halted there. Chloe looked at Hogan. Hogan looked at Chloe. She fought the urge to tug up the sheet again. He mostly just sat there looking gorgeous and recently tumbled. She told herself to eat something, reminded herself that it was the height of rudeness to decline food someone had prepared for you. But her stomach was so tied in knots, she feared anything she tried to put in it would just come right back up again.

Before she knew what she was doing, she said, "Hogan, about last night…" Unfortunately, the cliché was as far as she got before she realized she didn't know what else to say. She tried again. "What happened last night was…" At that, at least, she couldn't prevent the smile that curled her lips. "Well, it was wonderful," she admitted.

"I thought so, too."

Oh, she really should have talked faster. She really didn't need to hear that he had enjoyed it, too. Not that she didn't already know he'd enjoyed it. Especially considering how eagerly he'd—

Um, never mind.

She made herself say the rest of what she had hoped to get in before he told her he'd enjoyed last night, too, in case he said more, especially something about how eagerly he'd—

"But it never should have happened," she made herself say.

This time Hogan was the one to not say anything in response. So Chloe made an effort to explain. "I was feeling a little raw last night, talking about Samuel and things I haven't talked about to anyone for a long time. Add to that the wine and the night and New York and..." She stopped herself before adding *and you* and hurried on, "Things just happened that shouldn't have happened. That wouldn't have happened under normal circumstances. That won't happen again. You're my employer, and I'm your employee. I think we can both agree that we should keep it at that."

When he continued to remain silent, she added, "I just want you to know that I'm not assuming anything will come of it. I don't want you to think I'm under the impression that this—" here, she gestured quickly between the two of them "—changes that. I know it doesn't."

And still, Hogan said nothing. He only studied her thoughtfully, as if he was trying to figure it all out the same way she was.

Good luck with that, Chloe thought. Then again, maybe he wasn't as confused as she was. Maybe he'd awoken this morning feeling perfectly philosophical about last night. Guys were able to do that better than girls were, right? To compartmentalize things into brain boxes that kept them neatly separate from other things? Sex in one box and love in another. The present moment in one box and future years in another. He probably wasn't expecting anything more to come of last night, either, and he'd just been sitting here waiting for her to reassure him that that was how she felt, too.

So she told him in no uncertain terms—guys liked it when girls talked to them in no uncertain terms, right?—to make it perfectly clear, "I just want you to know that I don't have any expectations from this. Or from you. I know what happened between us won't go any further and that it will never happen again. I know you still love Anabel."

"And you still love Samuel," he finally said.

"Yes. I do."

He nodded. But his expression revealed nothing of what he might actually be feeling. Not that she wanted him to feel anything. The same way she wasn't feeling anything. She wasn't.

"You're right," he agreed. "About all of it. What happened last night happened. But it was no big deal."

Well, she didn't say *that*. Jeez. Oh, wait. Yes, she did. At least, she'd been thinking it before Hogan came in with breakfast. Looking and sounding all sweet and earnest and being so gorgeous and recently tumbled. Okay, then. It was no big deal. They were both on the same page.

She looked at the breakfast he'd prepared. She had thought getting everything about last night out in the open the way they had would make her feel better. But her stomach was still a tumble of nerves.

Even so, she forced a smile and asked, "Could you pass the toast, please?"

Hogan smiled back, but his, too, looked forced. "Sure."

He pulled up the tray from the foot of the bed until it was between them, and Chloe leaned over to reach for the plate of toast. But the sheet began to slip the moment she did, so she quickly sat up again, jerking it back into place.

"I should let you get dressed," Hogan said, rising from bed.

"But aren't you going to have any breakfast?"

"I had some coffee while I was making it. That'll hold me for a while. You go ahead." He started to back toward the door. "I have some things I need to do today anyway."

"Okay."

"And, listen, I'm pretty sure I won't be here for dinner tonight, so don't go to any trouble for me."

"But I was going to make *blanquette de veau*. From my grandmother's recipe."

"Maybe another time."

Before she could say anything else—not that she had any idea what to say—he mumbled a quick "See ya," and was out the door, leaving Chloe alone.

Which was how she liked to be. She'd kept herself alone for six years now. Six years, nine months, one week and… And how many days? She had to think for a minute. Two. Six years, nine months, one week and two days, to be precise. Alone was the only way she could be if she hoped to maintain her sanity. Especially after losing her mind the way she had last night.

She was right. It shouldn't have happened.

As Hogan bent over the hood of Benny Choi's '72 Mustang convertible, he repeated Chloe's assertion in his head again. Maybe if he repeated it enough times, he'd start believing himself. Chloe had been spot-on when she said last night was a mistake. It had been a mistake. An incredibly erotic, unbelievably satisfying mistake, but a mistake all the same.

She was still in love with her husband. First love was a potent cocktail. Nothing could cure a hangover from that. Hell, Hogan knew that firsthand, since he was still punch-drunk in love with Anabel fifteen years after the fact. Right? Of course right. What happened between him and Chloe last night was just a byproduct of the feelings they had for other people, feelings they'd both had bottled up for too long. Chloe had been missing her husband last night. Hogan had been missing Anabel. So they'd turned to each other for comfort.

Stuff like that happened all the time. It really was no big deal. Now that they had it out of their systems, they could go back to being in love with the people they'd loved half their lives.

Except that Chloe couldn't go back to her husband. Not the way Hogan could go back to Anabel.

"Thanks for coming in to work, Hogan," Benny said when Hogan dropped the hood of his car into place. "Now that your dad's gone, you're the only guy I trust with my baby."

Benny and Hogan's father had been friends since grade school. With what was left of Hogan's mother's family living solidly in the Midwest, Benny was the closest thing to an uncle Hogan had here in town. He was thinning on top, thickening around the middle and wore the standard issue blue uniform of the New York transit worker, having just ended his shift.

"No problem, Benny," Hogan assured him. "Feels good to come in. I've been missing the work."

"Hah," the other man said. "If I came into the kind of money you did, I wouldn't even be in New York. I'd be cruising around the Caribbean. Then I'd be cruising around Mexico. Then Alaska. Then… I don't even know after that. But I sure as hell wouldn't have my head stuck under Benny Choi's Mach One, I can tell you that."

Hogan grinned. "To each his own."

They moved into Hogan's office so he could prepare Benny's bill. Which seemed kind of ridiculous
since Hogan wasn't doing this for a living anymore,
so there was no need to charge anyone for parts or
labor. With the money he had, he could buy a whole
fleet of Dempsey's Garages and still have money left
over. He knew better than to tell Benny the work was
on the house, though. Benny, like everyone else in
Hogan's old neighborhood, always paid his way. Even
so, he knocked off twenty percent and, when Benny
noticed the discrepancy, called it his new "friends and
family" rate.

Hogan sat in his office for a long time after Benny
left, listening to the clamor of metal against metal
as the other mechanics worked, inhaling the savory
aroma of lubricant, remembering the heft of every tool.
He couldn't give this up. A lot of people would think
he was crazy for wanting to keep working in light of
his financial windfall, but he didn't care. Hogan had
been working in this garage for nearly two decades,
most of it by his father's side. It was the only place
he'd ever felt like himself. At least it had been until
last night, when he and Chloe had—

A fleet of Dempsey's Garages, he thought again,
pushing away thoughts of things that would never happen again. He actually kind of liked the sound of that.
There were a lot of independent garages struggling in
this economy. He could buy them up, put the money
into them that they needed to be competitive, keep everyone employed who wanted to stay employed and
give everything and everyone a new purpose. He could
start here in the city and move outward into the state.

Then maybe into another state. Then another. And another. This place would be his flagship, the shop where he came in to work every day.

And it would be a lot of work, an enterprise that ambitious. But Hogan always thrived on work. Being away from it was why he'd been at such loose ends since moving uptown. Why he'd felt so dissatisfied. Why his life felt like something was missing.

And that was another thing. He didn't have to live uptown. He could sell his grandfather's house. It didn't feel like home anyway, and it was way too big for one person. Of course, Hogan wouldn't be one person for much longer. He'd have Anabel. And, with any luck, at some point, a few rug rats to keep tabs on. Still, the Lenox Hill town house was just too much. It didn't suit Hogan. He and Anabel could find something else that they both liked. She probably wouldn't want to move downtown, though. Still, they could compromise somewhere.

The more Hogan thought about his new plans, the more he liked them. Funny, though, how the ones for the garage gelled in his brain a lot faster and way better than the ones for Anabel did. But that was just because he was sitting here in the garage right now, surrounded by all the things he needed for making plans like that. Anabel was still out there, waiting for him to make contact. But he'd be seeing her next weekend, thanks to Chloe's dinner party plans. Yeah, Hogan was *this close* to having everything he'd ever wanted.

Thanks to Chloe.

Eight

A week later, Hogan stood in his living room, wondering why the hell he'd let Chloe arrange a dinner party for him. It was for Anabel, he reminded himself. This entire situation with Chloe had always been about winning back Anabel.

Despite his recent encounter with Chloe—which neither of them had spoken about again—that was still what he wanted. Wasn't it? Of course it was. He'd spent almost half his life wanting Anabel. She was his Holy Grail. His impossible dream. A dream that was now very possible. All Hogan had to do was play his cards right. Starting now, with the evening ahead. If he could just keep his mind off making love to Chloe—or, rather, having sex with Chloe—and focus on Anabel.

He still wasn't looking forward to the night ahead, but he was relieved there wasn't going to be a large group coming. Chloe had only invited Anabel and three other couples, two of whom were friends of Anabel's that Chloe had assured him it would be beneficial for him to know, and one of whom was Gus Fiver and his date.

Hogan realized he should have been the one to plan something, and he should have been the one who invited Anabel to whatever it was, and he should be in charge of it. He also realized it should just be him and Anabel, and not a bunch of other people, too.

So why hadn't he done that? He'd been living in his grandfather's house for a month now, plenty of time for him to figure out how things were done here and proceed accordingly where it came to pursuing the love of his life. But the only time he'd seen Anabel since ascending to his new social status had been the day she came over to try and lure Chloe back to work for her. He'd thought about asking her out a lot of times over the last few weeks. But he'd always hesitated. Because he wanted the occasion to be just right, he'd told himself, and he hadn't figured out yet what *just right* was with Anabel these days.

Back when they were teenagers, they'd had fun walking along the boardwalk on Rockaway Beach or bowling a few sets at Jib Lanes or downing a couple of egg creams at Pop's Diner. Nowadays, though… Call him crazy, but Hogan didn't see the Anabel of today doing any of those things. He just didn't know what the Anabel of today did like. And that was why he hadn't asked her out.

Tonight he would find out what she liked and he *would* ask her out. Just the two of them. By summer, he promised himself again, they would be engaged.

Then they would live happily ever after, just like in the books.

"You're not wearing that, are you?"

Hogan spun around to see Chloe standing in the doorway, dressed from head to toe in stark chef's whites. He'd barely seen her since last weekend. She'd sped in and out of the dining room so fast after serving him his meals that he'd hardly had a chance to say hello or thank her.

Tonight her jacket looked like it actually fit, and she'd traded her crazy printed pants for a pair of white ones that were as starched and pressed as the rest of her. Instead of the usual spray of hair erupting from the top of her head, she had it neatly twisted in two braids that fell over each shoulder. In place of bright red lipstick, she wore a shade of pink that was more subdued.

This must be what passed for formal attire for her. Even though she'd promised him the evening wasn't going to be formal. He looked down at his own clothes, standard issue blue jeans, white shirt and a pair of Toms he got on sale. Everything was as plain and inoffensive as clothing got, and he couldn't think of a single reason why Chloe would object to anything he had on.

"You said it was casual," he reminded her.

"I said it was *business* casual."

He shrugged. "Guys in business wear stuff like this all the time."

"Not for business casual, they don't."

"What's the difference?"

She eyed his outfit again. "Blue jeans, for one thing." Before he could object, she hurried on, "Okay, *maybe* blue jeans would be okay for some business casual functions, but only if they're dark wash, and only by certain designers."

"Levi Strauss has been designing jeans since the nineteenth century," Hogan pointed out.

Chloe crossed her arms over her midsection. "Yeah, and the ones you have on look like they were in his first collection."

"It took me years to get these broken in the way I like."

"You can't wear them tonight."

"Why not?"

"Because they're not appropriate for—"

"Then what is appropriate?" he interrupted. He was really beginning to hate being rich. There were way too many rules.

She expelled a much put-upon sigh. "What about the clothes you wore to the wine-tasting that day? Those were okay."

"That guy who bumped into me spilled some wine on my jacket, and it's still at the cleaner's."

"But that was weeks ago."

"I keep forgetting to pick it up. I never wear it."

"Well, what else do you have?"

He looked at his clothes again. "A lot of stuff like this, but in different colors."

"Show me."

Hogan opened his mouth to object again. People would be showing up soon, and, dammit, what he had on was fine. But he didn't want to argue with Chloe. These were the most words they'd exchanged in a week, and the air was already crackling with tension. So he made his way toward the stairs with her on his heels—at a safe distance. He told himself he was only changing his clothes because he wanted to look his best for Anabel, not like the kid from Queens she'd chosen someone else over. He wanted to look like a part of her tribe. Because he was a part of her tribe now. Why did he keep trying to fight it?

He took the stairs two at a time until he reached the fourth floor, not realizing until he got there how far behind Chloe was. He hadn't meant to abandon her. He was just feeling a little impatient for some reason. When she drew within a few stairs of him, he headed for his bedroom and threw open the closet that was as big as the dining room in the house where he grew up. It had four rods—two on each side—for hanging shirts and suits and whatever, a low shelf on each side beneath those for shoes, and an entire wall of drawers on the opposite end. Every stitch of clothing Hogan owned didn't even fill a quarter of it. The drawers were pretty much empty, too.

Mrs. Hennessey had started clearing out his grandfather's suits and shoes before Hogan moved in and was in the process of donating them to a place that outfitted homeless guys and ex-cons for job interviews—something that probably had his grandfather spinning in his grave, an idea Hogan had to admit brought him a lot of gratification. But the housekeeper had left a few things on one side she thought might be of use to Hogan because he and his grandfather were about the same size. Hogan hadn't even looked through them. He just couldn't see himself decked out in the regalia of Wall Street, no matter how high he climbed on the social ladder.

Chloe hesitated outside the bedroom door for some

reason, looking past Hogan at the room itself. The room that was furnished in Early Nineteenth Century Conspicuous Consumption, from the massive Oriental rug in shades of dark green, gold and rust to the leather sofa and chair in the sitting area, to the quartet of oil paintings of what looked like the same European village from four different angles, to the rows of model cars lining the fireplace mantel, to the mahogany bed and dressers more suited to a monarch than a mechanic.

Then he realized it wasn't so much the room she was looking at. It was the bed. The bed that, this time last week, they were only a few hours away from occupying together, doing things with and to each other that Hogan had barely ever even fantasized about. Things he'd thought about a lot since. Things, truth be told, he wouldn't mind doing again.

Except with Anabel next time, he quickly told himself. Weird, though, how whenever he thought about those things—usually when he was in bed on his back staring up at the ceiling—it was always Chloe, not Anabel, who was with him in his fantasies.

In an effort to take both their minds off that night, he said, "Yeah, I know, the room doesn't suit me very well, does it? Even the model cars are all antiques worth thousands of dollars—I Googled them—and not the plastic Revell kind I made when I was a kid. I didn't change anything, though, because I thought maybe I'd learn to like it. I haven't. Truth be told, I don't think I'll ever stop feeling like an outsider in this house."

He hated the rancor he heard in his voice. Talk about first world problems. Oh, boo-hoo-hoo, his

house was too big and too luxurious for his liking.
Oh, no, he had millions of dollars' worth of antiques
and collectibles he didn't know what to do with. How
would he ever be able to deal with problems like that?
Even so, being rich was nothing like he'd thought it
would be.

"Then redecorate," Chloe said tersely.

"Oh, sure," he shot back. "God knows I have great
taste, what with working under cars on a street filled
with neon and bodegas and cement. Hell, apparently,
I can't even dress myself."

She winced at the charge. "I didn't mean it like
that."

"Didn't you?"

"No. I—"

Instead of explaining herself, she made her way
in Hogan's direction, giving him a wide berth as she
entered the closet.

"My stuff is on the left," he told her. "The other side
is what's left of my grandfather's things."

He hadn't been joking when he told her everything
he had was like what he had on, only in different colors. He'd never been much of a clotheshorse, and he
didn't follow trends. When his old clothes wore out,
he bought new ones, and when he found something
he liked, he just bought it in a few different colors.
He hadn't altered his blue jeans choice since he first
started wearing them, and when he'd started wearing
them, he just bought what his old man wore. If it came
down to a life-or-death situation, Hogan could probably name a fashion designer. Probably. He just didn't
put much thought into clothes, that was all.

Something that Chloe was obviously discovering,

since she was pushing through his entire wardrobe at the speed of light and not finding a single thing to even hesitate over. When she reached the last shirt, she turned around and saw the drawers where he'd stowed his, um, drawers. Before he could stop her, she tugged open the one closest to her and thrust her hand inside, grabbing the first thing she came into contact with, which happened to be a pair of blue boxer-briefs. Not that Hogan cared if she saw his underwear, at least when he wasn't wearing it. And, yeah, okay, he wouldn't mind if she saw it while he was wearing it, either, which was something he probably shouldn't be thinking about when he was anticipating the arrival of his newly possible dream. So he only leaned against the closet door and crossed his arms over his midsection.

Chloe, however, once she realized what she was holding, blushed. Actually blushed. Hogan didn't think he'd ever seen a woman blush in his life. He'd never gone for the kind of woman who would blush. Especially over something like a guy's underwear that he wasn't even wearing.

"There are socks and T-shirts in the other drawers," he told her, hoping to spare her any more embarrassment. Not that there was anything that embarrassing about socks and T-shirts. Unless maybe it was the fact that he'd had some of them, probably, since high school. "But I'm thinking you probably wouldn't approve of a T-shirt for business casual, either."

She stuffed his underwear back where she found it and slammed the drawer shut. Then she looked at the clothes hanging opposite his. "Those belonged to your grandfather?"

"Yeah," Hogan told her. "Mrs. Hennessey is in the middle of donating all his stuff to charity."

Chloe made her way to the rows of shirts, pants and jackets lined up neatly opposite his own and began to give them the quick *whoosh-whoosh-whoosh* she'd given his. She was nearly to the end when she withdrew a vest and gave it a quick perusal.

"Here," she said, thrusting it at Hogan with one hand as she began to sift through a collection of neckties with the other.

He accepted it from her automatically, giving it more thorough consideration than she had. The front was made of a lightweight wool charcoal, and it had intricately carved black buttons he was going to go out on a limb and guess weren't plastic. The back was made out of what looked like a silk, gray-on-gray paisley. It was a nice enough vest, but he wasn't really the vest-wearing type.

In case she wasn't reading his mind, though, he said, "I'm not really the vest-wearing ty—"

"And put this on, too," she interrupted, extending a necktie toward him.

It, too, looked as if it was made of silk and was decorated with a sedate print in blues, greens and grays that complemented the vest well. It was nice enough, but Hogan wasn't really the tie-wearing type, either.

"I'm not really the tie-wearing ty—"

"You are tonight," Chloe assured him before he could even finish protesting.

As if wanting to prove that herself, she snatched the vest from its hanger, leaving the latter dangling from Hogan's fingers. Before he knew it, she was maneuvering one opening of the vest over both of those and up his arm then circling to his other side to bring the vest over his other arm. Then she flipped up the collar of his shirt, looped the tie around his neck and began to tie it.

She fumbled with the task at first, as if she couldn't remember how to tie a man's tie—that made two of them—but by her third effort, she seemed to be recovering. She was standing closer to him than she'd been in a week. Close enough that Hogan could see tiny flecks of blue in her green eyes and feel the heat of her body mingling with his. He could smell her distinctive scent, a mix of soap and fresh herbs and something else that was uniquely Chloe Merlin. He was close enough that, if he wanted to, he could dip his head to hers and kiss her.

Not surprisingly, Hogan realized he did want to kiss her. He wanted to do a lot more than kiss her, but he'd start there and see what developed.

"There," Chloe said, bringing his attention back to the matter at hand.

Which, Hogan reminded himself, was about getting ready for dinner with the woman he was supposed to be planning to make his wife. He shouldn't be trying to figure out his feelings for Chloe. He didn't have feelings for Chloe. Not the kind he had for Anabel.

Chloe gave the necktie one final pat then looked up at Hogan. Her eyes widened in surprise, and she took a giant step backward. "I need to get back to the kitchen," she said breathlessly.

Then she was speeding past him, out of the closet

and out of his room. But not, he realized as he watched her go, out of his thoughts. Which was where she should be heading fastest.

Hogan was surprised at how much fun he had entertaining near-strangers in his still-strange-to-him home. The wife of one couple who was friends of Anabel's had been in the cab with her the night Hogan met her, so they shared some history there. The other couple who knew her was affable and chatty. Gus Fiver and his date both shared Hogan's love of American-made muscle cars, so there was some lively conversation there. And Anabel...

Yeah. Anabel. Anabel was great. But the longer the night went on, the more Hogan realized neither of them were the people who met on Jamaica Avenue a decade and a half ago. She was still beautiful. Still smart. Still fierce. But she wasn't the seventeen-year-old girl who flipped off a cabbie in the middle of Queens any more than Hogan was the seventeen-year-old kid who'd fallen for her.

All he could conjure up was a fondness for a girl he knew at a time in his life when the world was its most romantic. And he was reasonably sure Anabel felt the same way about him. They talked like old friends. They joked like old friends. But there were no sparks arcing between them. No longing looks. No flirtation.

It was great to see her again. He wouldn't mind bumping into her from time to time in the future. But his fifteen-year-long fantasy of joining his life to hers forever evaporated before Chloe even brought in the second course. Which looked like some kind of soup.

"*Bisque des tomates et de la citrouille*," she announced as she ladled the first helping into the bowl in front of Anabel.

"Ooo, Chloe, I love your tomato pumpkin bisque," Anabel said, leaning closer to inhale the aroma. "Thyme and basil for sure, but I swear she puts lavender in it, too." She looked at Chloe and feigned irritation. "She won't tell me, though. Damn her."

Chloe murmured her thanks but still didn't give Anabel the information she wanted. Then she circled the table with speed and grace, filling the bowls of everyone present before winding up at Hogan's spot. When she went to ladle up some soup for him, though, her grace and speed deserted her. Not only did she have trouble spooning up a decent amount, but when she finally did, she spilled a little on the tablecloth.

"I am so sorry," she said as she yanked a linen cloth from over her arm to dab at the stain.

"Don't worry about it," Hogan told her. "It'll wash out."

"That's not the point. I shouldn't have done it."

He was about to tell her it was fine, but noticed her hand was shaking as she tried to clean up what she'd done. When he looked at her face, he saw that her cheeks were flushed the same way they'd been in the closet, when she was handling his underwear. Must be hot in the kitchen, he decided.

"It's okay," he said again. Then, to his guests—because he wanted to take their attention off Chloe—he added, "Dig in."

Everyone did, but when Hogan looked at Anabel, she had a funny expression on her face. She wasn't looking at him, though. She wasn't even looking at the soup she professed to love. She was looking at Chloe. After a moment her gaze fell on Hogan.

"Your soup's going to get cold," he told her.

She smiled cryptically. "Not with the heat in this room, it won't."

Hogan narrowed his eyes. Funny, but he'd been thinking it was kind of cool in here.

The soup was, like everything Chloe made, delicious. As were the three courses that followed it. Everyone was stuffed by the time they were finished with dessert, a pile of pastries filled with cream and dripping with chocolate sauce that Anabel said was her most favorite thing Chloe made. In fact, every course that came out, Anabel had claimed was her most favorite thing Chloe made. Clearly, Chloe was doing her best to help Hogan woo the woman he had mistakenly thought was the love of his life. He wasn't sure how he was going to break it to her that all her hard work had been for nothing.

"We should have coffee on the roof," Anabel declared after the last of the dishes were cleared away.

Everyone agreed that they should take advantage of what the weather guys were saying would be the last of the pleasantly cool evenings for a while in the face of some inclement, more November-worthy weather to come. Hogan ducked into the kitchen long enough to tell Chloe their plans then led his guests up to the roof garden.

The view was the same as it was a week ago, but somehow the flowers looked duller, the white lights overhead seemed dimmer and the cityscape was less glittery. Must be smoggier tonight. He and his guests made their way to the sitting area just as Chloe appeared from downstairs. For a moment Hogan waited for her to join them in conversation, and only remembered she was working when she crossed to open the dumbwaiter. From it, she removed a tray with a coffeepot and cups, and little bowls filled with sugar, cream, chocolate shavings and some other stuff that looked like spices. Evidently, even after-dinner coffee was different when you were rich.

As Chloe brought the tray toward the group, Anabel drew alongside Hogan and hooked her arm through his affectionately. He smiled down at her when she did, because it was so like what she had done when they were kids. That was where the similarity in the gesture ended, however, because her smile in return wasn't one of the sly, flirtatious ones she'd always offered him when they were teenagers, but a mild, friendly one instead. Even so, she steered him away from his guests as Chloe began to pour the coffee, guiding him toward the part of the roof that was darkest, where the lights of the city could be viewed more easily. He didn't blame her. It was a really nice view. Once there, she leaned her hip against the balustrade and unlooped her arm from his. But she took both of his hands in hers and met his gaze intently.

"So how are you adjusting to Park Avenue life?" she asked, her voice low enough that it was clear she meant the question for him alone.

"I admit it's not what I thought it would be," he replied just as quietly. "But I guess I'll get used to it. Eventually."

He looked over at his other guests to make sure he wasn't being a neglectful host, but they were all engaged in conversation. Except for Chloe, who was busying herself getting everything set out on the table to her liking. And also sneaking peeks at Hogan and Anabel.

She was more concerned about the success of the evening than he'd been. He wished there was some way to signal her not to worry, that the evening had been a huge success, because he knew now the plans he'd made for the future weren't going to work out the way he'd imagined, and that was totally okay.

"I know it's a lot different from Queens," Anabel said, bringing his attention back to her. She was still holding his hands, but she dropped one to place her palm gently against his chest. "But Queens will always be here in your heart. No one says you have to leave it behind." She smiled. "In fact, I, for one, would be pretty mad at you if you did leave Queens behind. You wouldn't be Hogan anymore if you did."

"That will never happen," he assured her. "But it's still weird to think that, technically, this is the life I was born to."

She tipped her head to one side. "You have something on your cheek," she said.

Again? Hogan wanted to say. First the engine grease with Chloe, now part of his dinner with Anabel. Before he had a chance to swipe whatever it was away, Anabel lifted her other hand to cup it over his jaw, stroking her thumb softly over his cheekbone.

"Coffee?"

He and Anabel both jumped at the arrival of Chloe, who seemed to appear out of nowhere. Anabel looked guilty as she dropped her hand to her side, though Hogan had no idea what she had to feel guilty about. Chloe looked first at Hogan, then at Anabel, then at

Hogan again. When neither of them replied, she extended one cup toward Anabel.

"I made yours with cinnamon and chocolate," she said. Then she paraphrased the words Anabel had been saying all night. "I know it's your *most favorite*."

Hogan wasn't sure, but the way she emphasized those last two words sounded a little sarcastic.

"And, Hogan, yours is plain," Chloe continued. "Just the way I know *you* like it."

That, too, sounded a little sarcastic. Or maybe caustic. He wasn't sure. There was definitely something off about Chloe at the moment, though. In fact, there'd been something off about Chloe all night. Not just the soup-spilling when she'd ladled up his, but every course seemed to have had something go wrong, and always with Hogan's share of it. His *coq au vin* had been missing the *vin*, his *salade Niçoise* had been a nice salad, but there had hardly been any of it on his plate, his cheese course had looked like it was arranged by a five-year-old, and his cream puff dessert had been light on the cream, heavy on the puff.

He understood that, as the host, he was obligated to take whichever plates weren't up to standards, and he was fine with that. But that was just it—Chloe was *always* up to standards. She never put anything on the table that wasn't perfect. Until tonight.

Hogan and Anabel both took their coffee and murmured their thanks, but Chloe didn't move away. She only kept looking at them expectantly. So Hogan, at least, sipped from his cup and nodded.

"Tastes great," he said. "Thanks again."

Anabel, too, sampled hers, and smiled her approval. But Chloe still didn't leave.

So Hogan said, "Thanks, Chloe."

"You're welcome," Chloe replied. And still didn't leave.

Hogan looked at Anabel to see if maybe she knew why Chloe was still hanging around, but she only sipped her coffee and gazed at him with what he could only think were laughing eyes.

"So your coffee is all right?" Chloe asked Anabel.

"It's delicious," Anabel told her. "As you said. My *most favorite*. Somehow, tonight, it's even better than usual." She hesitated for the briefest moment then added, "Must be the company."

Even in the dim light, Hogan could see two bright spots of pink appear on Chloe's cheeks. Her lips thinned, her eyes narrowed and her entire body went ramrod straight.

"I'm so happy," she said in the same crisp voice. Then she looked at Hogan. "For both of you."

Then she spun on her heels and went back to his other guests. Once there, however, she turned again to study Hogan and Anabel. A lot.

"What the hell was that about?" Hogan asked Anabel.

She chuckled. "You really have no idea, do you?"

He shook his head. "No. Is it some woman thing?"

Now Anabel smiled. "Kind of."

"Should I be concerned?"

"Probably."

Oh, yeah. This was the Anabel Hogan remembered. Cagey and evasive and having fun at his expense. Now that he was starting to remember her without the rosy sheen of nostalgia, he guessed she really could be kind of obnoxious at times when they were teenagers. Not that he hadn't been kind of obnoxious himself. He guessed teenagers in general were just kind of annoying. Especially when their hormones were in overdrive.

He studied Anabel again, but she just sipped her coffee and looked amused. "You're not going to tell me what's going on with Chloe, are you?" he asked.

"No."

"Just tell me if whatever it is is permanent, or if she'll eventually come around and things can get back to normal."

She smiled again. "Hogan, I think I can safely say your life is never going to be normal again."

"I know, right? This money thing is always going to be ridiculous."

"I didn't mean the money part."

"Then what did you mean?"

She threw him another cryptic smile. "My work here is done." As if to punctuate the statement, she pushed herself up on tiptoe to kiss his cheek then told him, "Tonight was really lovely, Hogan. And illuminating."

Well, on that, at least, they could agree.

"Thank you for inviting me," she added. "But I should probably go."

"I'll walk you out."

"No, don't leave your guests. I can find my own way." She looked thoughtful for a moment before nodding. "In fact, I'm really looking forward to finding my own way in life for once."

She walked back toward the others. He heard her say her goodbyes and thank Chloe one last time, then she turned to wave to Hogan. As he lifted a hand in return, she strode through the door to, well, find her own way. Leaving Hogan to find his own way, too.

He just wished he knew where to go from here.

Nine

Tonight was a disaster.

Chloe was still berating herself about it even as she dropped the last utensil into the dishwasher. There was just no way to deny it. The evening had been an absolute, unmitigated disaster. And not just the dinner party, where every single course had seen some kind of problem. The other disaster had been even worse. Hogan's reunion with Anabel had been a huge success.

Chloe tossed a cleaning pod into the dishwasher, sealed the door and punched a button to turn it on. It whirred to quiet life, performing perfectly the function for which it had been designed. She wished she could seal herself up just as easily then flip a switch to make herself work the way she was supposed to. She used to be able to do that. She did that as efficiently and automatically as the dishwasher did for six years. Six years, nine months and...and...

She leaned back against the counter and dropped her head into her hands. Oh, God. She couldn't remember anymore how many weeks or days to add to the years and months since Samuel's death. What was wrong with her?

And why had it hurt so much to see Hogan and Anabel together tonight? Chloe had known since the day she started working for Hogan that his whole reason for hiring her had been to find a way back into Anabel's life. He'd never made secret the fact that he still wanted the girl of his dreams fifteen years after they broke up, nor the fact that he was planning a future with her.

For Pete's sake, Chloe was the one who had been so adamant about throwing the dinner party tonight so the two of them would finally be in the same room together. She'd deliberately chosen all of Anabel's favorite dishes. She'd helped Hogan make himself more presentable for the woman he'd loved half his life so he could make a good impression on her.

And she'd accomplished her goal beautifully, because the two of them had laughed more than Chloe had ever seen two people laugh, and they'd engaged in constant conversation. They'd even wandered off as the evening wound down to steal some alone time together on the roof. Alone time Anabel had used to make clear that her interest in Hogan was as alive as it had ever been.

Chloe didn't think she'd ever be able to rid her brain of the image of Anabel splaying one hand open on Hogan's chest while she caressed his face with the other, the same way Chloe had done a week ago when she and Hogan were on the roof themselves. She knew what it meant when a woman touched a man that way. It meant she was halfway in love with him.

No! She immediately corrected herself. That wasn't what it meant. At least not where Chloe was concerned.

She started wiping down the kitchen countertops, even though she'd already wiped them off twice. You could never be too careful. She wasn't in love with Hogan. Not even halfway. She would never be in love with anyone again. Loving someone opened you up to too many things that could cause pain. Terrible, terrible, *terrible* pain. Chloe never wanted to hurt like that again. Chloe never *would* hurt like that again. She just wouldn't.

She wasn't in love with Hogan. She would never fall in love again.

Anyway, it didn't matter, because Hogan and Anabel were back on the road to the destiny they'd started when they were teenagers. His hiring of Chloe had had exactly the outcome he'd intended. He'd won the woman of his dreams.

Before long Chloe would be cooking for two. She'd serve Hogan and Anabel their dinner every night, listening to their laughter and their fond conversation as they talked about their shared past and their plans for the future. And she'd bring in their breakfast every morning. Of course, Anabel liked to have breakfast in bed most days. She'd probably want that for her and Hogan both now. So Chloe would also be able to see them every morning all rumpled from sleep. And sex. More rumpled from sex than from sleep, no doubt, since Hogan's sexual appetites were so—

Well. She just wouldn't think about his sexual appetites anymore, would she? She wouldn't think about Hogan at all. Except in the capacity of him as her employer. Which was all he was. That was all he had ever been. It was all he would ever be. Chloe had reiterated that to him a week ago. All she had to do was keep remembering that. And forget about the way he—

She closed her eyes to shut out the images of her night with Hogan, images that had plagued her all week. But closing her eyes only brought them more fiercely into focus. Worse, they were accompanied by feelings. Again. Feelings she absolutely did not want to feel. Feelings she absolutely could not feel. Feelings she absolutely would not feel. Not if she wanted to stay sane.

She finished cleaning up the kitchen and poured what was left of an open bottle of wine into a glass to take upstairs with her. As she topped the step to the fifth and highest floor of Hogan's house, her gaze inevitably fell on the roof access door across from her. Unable to help herself, she tiptoed toward it and cracked it open to see if anyone was still up there. She'd been surprised that Anabel left first, until she remembered her former employer often turned in early on Saturday night because she rose early on Sunday to drive to a farm in Connecticut where she stabled her horses.

There were still a few voices coming from the roof—Chloe recognized not just Hogan's, but Mr. Fiver's and his date's, as well. She wondered briefly if she should go up and check on the coffee situation then decided against it. She'd sent up a fresh pot and its accoutrements before cleaning up the kitchen, and Hogan had assured her he wouldn't need anything else from her tonight.

Or any other night, she couldn't help thinking as she headed for her room. He had Anabel to take care of any nightly needs he'd have from now on. And every other need he would ever have again. Which was good. It was. Chloe was glad things had worked out between the two former lovers the way they had. She was. Hogan would be happy now. And Anabel was a nice person. She also deserved to be happy. Now Chloe could focus completely on her cooking, which would make her happy, too. It would.

Happiness was bursting out all over. They were all hip deep in happiness. Happy, happy, happy. Yay for happiness.

Thank God she had the next two days off.

Hogan had always loved Sundays. Sunday was the one day of the week Dempsey's Parts and Service was closed—unless there was an emergency. He loved Sunday mornings especially, because he could sleep late and rise when he felt like it, then take his time eating something for breakfast that he didn't have to wolf down on the run, the way he did during the work week.

At least, that had always been the case before he became filthy, stinking rich. Over the course of the past month, though, Sundays hadn't been like they used to be. He hadn't been working his regular shifts at the garage, so how could one day differ from any other? And he didn't have to eat on the run anymore, so a leisurely Sunday breakfast was no different from any other breakfasts during the no-longer-work-week. No, he hadn't been completely idle since leaving Queens, but he hadn't had a regular schedule to keep. He hadn't had places he *had* to be or things he *had* to get done.

Yeah, he was putting plans into place that would bring work and purpose back into his life, but there was no way his life—or his Sundays—would ever go back to being the way they were before.

The thing that had really made Sundays even less enjoyable than they were before, though, was that Chloe was never around on Sundays. She never stayed home on her days off, and the house felt even more alien and unwelcoming when she wasn't in it.

This morning was no different. Except that, somehow, it felt different. When Hogan stumbled into the kitchen in his usual jeans and sweater the way he did every Sunday morning to make coffee, the room seemed even more quiet and empty than usual. He busied himself making his usual bacon and eggs, but even eating that didn't pull him out of his funk.

Too little sleep, he decided. Gus Fiver and his date had hung around until the wee hours, so Hogan had logged half the amount of shut-eye he normally did. Of course, last weekend he'd woken having only logged a few hours of shut-eye, too, and he'd felt *great* that day. At least until Chloe had told him what a mistake the night before had been.

He stopped himself there. Chloe. What was he going to do about Chloe? The only reason he'd hired her was because he wanted to insinuate himself into Anabel's life. And the only reason he'd planned to keep her employed in the future was because she was Anabel's favorite chef. Not that he intended to fire her now—God, no—but her reason for being in his house had suddenly shifted. Hell, the whole dynamic of her place in his house seemed to have suddenly shifted. Hogan for sure still wanted Chloe around. But he didn't want her around because of Anabel anymore. He wanted Chloe around because of, well, Chloe.

He liked Chloe. He liked her a lot. Maybe more than liked her. All week he'd been thinking about Chloe, not Anabel. Even before he realized his thing for Anabel wasn't a thing anymore, it was Chloe, not Anabel, who had been living in his head. He'd had dozens of nights with Anabel in the past, and only one night with Chloe. But when he piled all those nights with Anabel into one place and set the single night with Chloe in another, that single night had a lot more weight than the dozens of others. He wanted to have more nights with Chloe. He wanted countless nights with Chloe. The problem was Chloe didn't want any more nights with him. She'd made that crystal clear.

And there was still the whole employer-employee thing. He didn't want Chloe as an employee anymore. He wanted her as…something else. He just wasn't sure what. Even by the time he finished his breakfast and was trying to decide what to do with his day—other than think about Chloe, since that would be a given—Hogan had no idea what to do about her. Even after cleaning up from his dinner that evening, he still didn't know what to do about her.

Chloe evidently did, though, because she came into the den Sunday night, where Hogan was putting together a preliminary plan for a state-wide chain of Dempsey's Garages, and handed him a long, white envelope.

"Here," she said as she extended it toward him.

She was dressed in street clothes, a pair of snug blue jeans and a voluminous yellow turtleneck, her hair in a ponytail, her glasses sliding down on her nose—which she pushed up with the back of her hand, so he knew she was feeling anxious about something.

"What is it?" he asked.

"My two weeks' notice."

He recoiled from the envelope as if she were handing him a rattlesnake. "What?"

"It's my two weeks' notice," she repeated. "Except that I'm taking advantage of article twelve, paragraph A, subheading one in my contract, and it's really my two days' notice."

Now Hogan stood. But he still didn't take the envelope from her. "Whoa, whoa, whoa. You can't do that."

"Yes, I can. That paragraph outlines my right to an immediate abdication of my current position in the event of force majeure."

His head was still spinning from her announcement, but he found the presence of mind to point out, "Force majeure only applies to things beyond our control like wars or strikes or natural disasters."

"Exactly," she said.

He waited for her to clarify whatever was beyond their control, but she didn't elaborate. So he asked, "Well, what's the force majeure that's making you give me your two weeks'—correction, two days'—notice?"

She hesitated, her gaze ricocheting from his to the shelves of books behind him. Finally, she said, "Impracticability."

Hogan narrowed his eyes. "Impracticability? What the hell does that mean?"

"It's a legitimate legal term. Look it up. Now, if you'll excuse me, I have a cab waiting."

"Wait, what? You're leaving right now? That's not two days' notice, that's two minutes' notice."

"Today isn't over yet, and tomorrow hasn't started," she said. "That's two days. And my new employers have a place ready for me, so there's no reason for me to delay starting."

She still wasn't looking at him. So he took a step to his left to put himself directly in her line of vision. As soon as he did, she dropped her gaze to the floor.

"You already have a new employer?" he asked.

"Yes."

Of course she already had a new employer. Since she'd come to work for him, Hogan had had to fend off a half dozen attempts from people besides Anabel to hire her away from him, upping her salary even more every time. He hadn't minded, though, especially now that he knew where the money went. He would have done anything to keep Chloe employed so he could keep himself on Anabel's radar. At least, that was what he'd been telling himself all those times. Now he knew there was another reason he'd wanted to keep Chloe on. He just still wasn't sure he knew how to put it in words.

"Who's your new employer?" he asked.

"I'm not required to tell you that," she replied, still looking at the floor.

"You might do it as a professional courtesy," he said, stalling. "Or even a personal one."

"It's no one you know."

"Chloe, if it's a matter of money, I can—"

"It isn't the money."

She still wasn't looking at him. So he tried a new tack.

"Haven't your working conditions here been up to standard?"

"My working conditions here have been—" She halted abruptly then hurried on, "My working conditions here have been fine."

"Well, if it isn't the money, and it isn't the working conditions, was it..." He hated to think it might be what he thought it was, but he had to know for sure. "Was it the taco meatloaf?"

She looked up at that, but she closed her eyes and shook her head.

Even though he'd assured her he wouldn't mention it again, he asked, "Then was it what happened after the taco meatloaf?"

Now she squeezed her eyes tight. "I have to go," she said again.

Hogan had no idea how to respond to that. She hadn't said specifically that it was their sexual encounter making her situation here "impracticable"— whatever the hell that was—but her physical reaction to the question was a pretty good indication that that was exactly what had brought this on. Why had she waited a week, though? If their hookup was what was bothering her, then why hadn't she given her notice last weekend, right after it happened?

He knew the answer immediately. Because of Anabel. Chloe had promised before they ended up in his bed that she would arrange a dinner party for him so he could spend time with Anabel and cinch their reconciliation. She'd stayed long enough to fulfill that obligation so Hogan would be able to reunite with the woman he'd professed to be in love with for half his life. Now she figured he and Anabel were on their way to their happily-ever-after, so there was no reason for her to hang around anymore. And, okay, he supposed it could get kind of awkward if Anabel reentered his life after he and Chloe had had sex. Maybe Chloe just wanted to avoid a scenario like that. His anxiety eased. If that was the case, it wasn't a problem anymore.

"Anabel and I aren't going to be seeing each other," he said.

At that, Chloe finally opened her eyes and met his gaze. This time she was the one to ask, "What do you mean?"

Hogan lifted his shoulders and let them drop. "I mean we're not going to be seeing each other. Not like dating anyway. We might still see each other as friends."

"I don't understand."

Yeah, that made two of them. Hogan tried to explain anyway. "Last night she and I both realized there's nothing between us now like there was when we were kids. No sparks. No fireworks. Whatever it was she and I had fifteen years ago, we've both outgrown it. Neither one of us wants to start it up again."

"But you've been pining for her for half your life."

This part, at least, Hogan had figured out. He told Chloe, "No, the seventeen-year-old kid in me was pining for her. I just didn't realize how much that kid has grown up in the years that have passed, and how much of his youthful impulses were, well, impulsive. The thirty-three-year-old me wants something else." He might as well just say the rest. He'd come this far. "The thirty-three-year-old me wants some*one* else."

Okay, so maybe that wasn't exactly saying the rest. He was feeling his way here, figuring it out as he went. Chloe, however, didn't seem to be following him. So

Hogan pushed the rest of the words out of his brain and into his mouth. And then he said them aloud.

"He wants you, Chloe. *I* want you."

He had thought the announcement would make her happy. Instead, she recoiled like he'd hit her.

But all she said was, "You can't."

Now Hogan was the one who felt like he'd been hit. Right in the gut. With a two-by-four. But he responded honestly, "Too late. I do."

Her brows arrowed downward, and she swallowed hard. "I can't get involved with you, Hogan."

"Why not?"

"I can't get involved with anyone."

"But last weekend—"

"Last weekend never should have happened," she interrupted.

"But it did happen, Chloe. And you'll never convince me it didn't have an effect on you, the same way it had an effect on me. A big one."

"Oh, it definitely had an effect on me," she assured him. Though her tone of voice indicated she didn't feel anywhere near as good about that effect as he did.

"Then why—"

"Because I can't go there, Hogan. Ever again. I was in love once, and it nearly destroyed me. I never want to love anyone like that again."

"Chloe—"

"You've experienced loss," she interrupted him. "With both of your parents. You know how much it hurts when someone you love isn't there for you anymore."

He nodded. "Yeah, but—"

"Now take that pain and multiply it by a hundred,"

she told him. "A thousand. As terrible as it is to lose a parent or a grandparent, it's even worse when you lose the person you were planning to spend the rest of your life with. Losing someone like that is so... It's..."

Tears filled her eyes, spilling freely as she continued. "Or even if you lose someone like that in old age, after the two of you have built a life together, you still have a lifetime worth of memories to get you through it, you know? You have your children to comfort you. Children who carry a part of that person inside them. Maybe they have their father's smile or his way of walking or his love of cardamom or something else that, every time you see it, it reminds you he's not really gone. Not completely. A part of him lives on in them. You walk through the house the two of you took years making your own, and you're reminded of dozens of Thanksgivings and Christmases and birthdays that were celebrated there. You have an *entire life* lived with that person to look back on. But when that person is taken from you before you even have a chance to build that life—"

She took off her glasses with one hand and swiped her eyes with the other. "It's a theft of your life before you even had a chance to live it," she said. "The children you planned to have with that person die, too. The plans you made, the experiences you should have shared, the memories you thought you'd make... All of that dies with him.

"A loss like that is overwhelming, Hogan. It brings with it a grief that goes so deep and is so relentless, you know it will never, ever, go away, and you know you can never, ever, grieve like that again. *I* can never grieve like that again. And the only way to avoid grieving like that again is to never love like that again. I have to go before I'm more—"

She halted abruptly, covering her eyes with both hands. Hogan had no idea how to respond to everything she'd said. As bad as it had been to lose his folks, he couldn't imagine losing someone he loved as much as Chloe had loved her husband. He hadn't loved anyone as much as she had loved her husband. Not yet anyway. But even after everything she'd just said—hell, because of everything she'd just said—he'd like to have the chance to find out what it *was* like to love someone that much. And if Chloe's last few words and the way she'd stopped short were any indication, maybe there was still a chance she might love that way again, too.

"I'm sorry, Chloe," he said. The sentiment was overused and of little comfort, but he didn't know what else to say. "Your husband's death was a terrible thing. But you can't stop living your life because something terrible happened. You have to do your best to move on and make a different life instead. You can't just shut yourself off from everything."

"Yes, I can."

He shook his head. "No. You can't. And you haven't."

She arrowed her brows down in confusion. "How do you know?"

He shrugged and smiled gently. "Because I think you pretty much just told me you love me."

"No, I didn't," she quickly denied. Maybe too quickly. "I don't love anyone. I'll never love anyone again. I can't."

"You mean you won't."

"Fine. I won't love anyone again."

"You think you can just make a choice like that? That by saying you won't love someone, it will keep you from loving them?"

"Yes."

"You really believe that?"

"I have to."

"Chloe, we need to talk more about this. A lot more."

"There's nothing to talk about," she assured him. Before he could object, she hurried on, "I'm sorry to leave you in the lurch. My letter includes a number of recommendations for personal chefs in the area who would be a good match for your culinary needs. Thank you for everything."

And then she added that knife-in-the-heart word that Anabel had never said to him when they were kids, the one word that would have let Hogan know it was over for good and never to contact her again, the word that, left unsaid the way it was then, had given him hope for years.

"Goodbye."

And wow, that word really did feel like a knife to the heart. So much so that he couldn't think of a single thing to say that would counter it, a single thing that would stop Chloe from leaving. All he could do was watch her rush out the door and head for the stairs. And all he could hear was her last word, with all its finality, echoing in his brain.

Ten

Chloe stood in the kitchen of Hugo and Lucie Fleury, marveling again—she'd made herself marvel about this every day for the last three weeks—at what a plumb position she had landed. Her new situation was perfect for her—something else she made herself acknowledge every day—because Hugo and Lucie had grown up in Paris and arrived in New York for his new job only a year ago, so they were about as Parisian as a couple could be outside the City of Light. They didn't question anything Chloe put on the table, so she never had to explain a dish to them, their Central Park West penthouse was decorated in a way that made her feel as if she were living at Versailles and she was using her second language of French every day, so there was no chance of her getting rusty. *Mais oui*, all Chloe could say about her new assignment was, *C'est magnifique!*

So why didn't she feel so *magnifique* after almost a month of working here? Why did she instead feel so blasé? More to the point, why hadn't a single meal she'd created for the Fleurys come out the way it was supposed to? Why had everything she put together been a little...off? And now she was about to undertake a dinner party for twelve, the kind of challenge to which she normally rose brilliantly, and all she could do was think about the last dinner party she'd put together, and how it had resulted in—

Not that the Fleurys had complained about her performance, she quickly backtracked. They'd praised everything she set in front of them, and tonight's menu was no exception. Not that they'd tasted any of it yet, but, as Lucie had told her this morning, *"Ne vous inquiétez pas, Chloe. J'ai foi en vous."* Don't worry, Chloe. I have faith in you.

Well, that made one of them.

Lucie and Hugo didn't seem to realize or care that they were paying her more than they should for a party they could have had catered for less by almost any bistro, brasserie or café in New York. But Chloe realized they were doing that. And in addition to making her feel guilty and inadequate, it was driving her crazy. She just hadn't been at her best since leaving Hogan's employ. And the whole reason she'd left Hogan's employ was because she'd feared losing her ability to be at her best.

Well, okay, maybe that wasn't really the reason she'd left Hogan. But she was beginning to wonder if she'd ever be at her best again.

He'd called her every day the first week after she left, but she'd never answered. So he'd left messages, asking her to meet him so they could talk, even if it meant someplace public, because even though he didn't understand her desire to not tell him where she was working now, he respected it, and *C'mon, Chloe, pick up the phone, just talk to me, we need to figure this out.* As much as she'd wanted to delete the messages without even listening to them, something had compelled her to listen…and then melt a little inside at the sound of his voice. But even after hearing his messages, she still couldn't bring herself to delete them. Deleting Hogan just felt horribly wrong. Even if she never intended to see him again.

I want you.

The words he said the night she left still rang in her ears. She wanted Hogan, too. It was why she couldn't stay with him. Because wanting led to loving. And loving led to needing. And needing someone opened you up to all kinds of dangers once that person was gone. Losing someone you needed was like losing air that you needed. Or water. Or food. Without those things, you shriveled up and died.

I think you pretty much just told me you love me.

Those words, too, wouldn't leave her alone. Because yes, as much as she'd tried to deny it, and as much as she'd tried to fight it, she knew she loved Hogan. But she didn't need him. She wouldn't need him. She couldn't need him. And the only way to make sure of that was to never see him again.

Unfortunately, the moment Chloe entered the Fleurys' salon in her best chef's whites with a tray of canapés, she saw that her determination to not see Hogan, like so many other things in life, was completely out of her control. The Fleurys had invited him to their dinner party.

Or maybe they'd invited Anabel, she thought when she saw her other former employer at Hogan's side, and he was her plus-one. Whatever the case, Chloe was suddenly in the same room with him again, and that room shrank to the size of a macaron the moment she saw him. He was wearing the same shirt with the same vest and tie she'd picked out for him the night of his own dinner party, but he'd replaced his battered Levi's with a pair of pristine dark wash jeans that didn't hug his form nearly as well.

As if he'd sensed her arrival the moment she noted his, he turned to look at her where she stood rooted in place. Then he smiled one of his toe-curling, heat-inducing smiles and lifted a hand in greeting. All Chloe wanted to do then was run back into the kitchen and climb into a cupboard and forget she ever saw him. Because seeing him only reminded her how much she loved him. How much she wanted him. How much— dammit—she needed him.

Instead, she forced her feet to move forward and into the crowd. Miraculously, she made it without tripping or sending a canapé down anyone's back. Even more astonishing, she was able to make eye contact with Hogan when she paused in front of him and Anabel. But it was Anabel who broke the silence that settled over them.

"Oh, yum. *Brie gougères.* Chloe, I absolutely love your *brie gougères.*" She scooped up two and smiled. "I love them so much, I need to take one over to Hillary Thornton. Talk amongst yourselves."

And then she was gone, leaving Chloe and Hogan

alone for the first time in almost a month. Alone in the middle of a crowd of people who were waiting to try her *brie gougères* and her *choux de Bruxelles citrons* and the half dozen other hors d'oeuvres she'd prepared for the evening. None of which had turned out quite right.

"Hi," he said softly.

"Hello," she replied.

"How've you been?"

"All right." The reply was automatic. Chloe had been anything but all right since she last saw him. The same way her food had been anything but all right. The same way life itself had been anything but all right.

They said nothing more for a moment, only stood in the middle of a room fit for a king, as nervous as a couple of teenagers on their first date.

Finally, Hogan said, "What are you doing after the party?"

Again, Chloe replied automatically. "Cleaning up the kitchen."

He grinned, and Chloe did her best not to have an orgasm on the spot. "What about after that?" he asked.

"I'll, um… I'll probably have a glass of wine."

"Want some company?"

She told herself to tell him no. That she hadn't wanted company for years. Lots of years. And lots of months and weeks and days—she just couldn't remember precisely how many. But she knew she was lying. She did want company. She'd wanted company for years. Lots of years and months and weeks and days. She just hadn't allowed herself to have it. Not until one glorious night three weeks, six days, twenty hours and fifty-two minutes ago, a night she would carry with her forever. Even so, she couldn't bring herself to say that to Hogan.

"Anabel is friends with the Fleurys," he said. "She told me the view from their roof is spectacular."

"It is," Chloe replied.

He looked surprised. "So you've been up there?"

She nodded. She'd gone up to the Fleurys' terrace a number of times since coming to work for the Fleurys. She didn't know why. The New York nights had turned cold and damp with winter setting in so solidly and hadn't been conducive to rooftop wanderings. But wander to the roof she had, over and over again. The view was indeed spectacular. She could see all of New York and Central Park, glittering like scattered diamonds on black velvet. But it had nothing on the view from Hogan's house. Probably because Hogan wasn't part of the view.

"Maybe you could show me?" he asked. "I mean, once you've finished with your party duties. Anabel said the Fleurys' parties tend to go pretty late, and she hates to be the first to leave."

"She was the first to leave at your party," Chloe said.

"That was because she was a woman on a mission that night."

"What mission?"

Hogan smiled again. But he didn't elaborate. "What time do you think you'll be finished?"

Chloe did some quick calculating in her head. "Maybe eleven?"

"Great. I'll meet you up on the roof at eleven."

She told herself to decline. Instead, she said, "Okay."

He looked at the tray. "What do you recommend?"

What a loaded question. All she said, though, was "Try the tapenade."

She remembered belatedly that he probably had no idea what tapenade was and was about to identify the proper selection, but he reached for exactly the right thing. Her surprise must have shown on her face, because he told her, "I've been doing some homework."

And then he was moving away, fading into the crowd, and Chloe was able to remember she had a job she should be doing. A job that would fall just short of success because, like the hors d'oeuvres and so much more, nothing she did was quite right anymore.

Instead, the party went off without a hitch, and every dish was perfect—if she did say so herself. Even the moments when she served Hogan, where she feared she would spill something or misarrange something or forget something, all went swimmingly. By the time she finished cleaning up the kitchen—which also went surprisingly well—she was starting to feel like her old self again. Like her old cooking self anyway. The other self, the one that wasn't so focused on cooking, still felt a little shaky.

She had just enough time to go to her room for a quick shower to wash off the remnants of *Moules à la crème Normande* and *carottes quatre epices*. Then she changed into blue jeans and a heavy black sweater and headed for the roof.

Hogan was already there waiting for her. He'd donned a jacket to ward off the chill and stood with his hands in his pockets, gazing at the New York skyline in the distance. The full moon hung like a bright silver dollar over his head, and she could just make out a handful of stars higher in the night sky. Her heart hammered hard as she studied him, sending her blood zinging through her body fast enough to make her light-headed. Or maybe it was the simple presence of Hogan doing that. How had she gone nearly a month without seeing him? Without hearing him? Without talking to him and feeling the way he made her feel? How had she survived without him?

Although she wouldn't have thought he could hear her over the sounds of the city, he spun around the moment she started to approach. The night was cold, but the closer she drew to him, the warmer she felt. But she stopped when a good foot still separated them, because she just didn't trust herself to not touch him if she got too close.

"Hi," he said again.

"Hello."

"It's good to see you."

"It's good to see you, too."

A moment passed where the two of them only gazed at each other in silence. Then Hogan said, "So I looked up impracticability."

She barely remembered using that as an excuse to cancel her contract with him. How could she have wanted to do that? How could she have thought the only way to survive was to separate herself from Hogan? She'd been dying a little inside every day since leaving him.

"Did you?" she asked.

"Yeah. I even used a legal dictionary, just to make sure I got the right definition. What it boiled down to is that one party of a contract can be relieved of their obligations if those obligations become too expensive, too difficult or too dangerous for them to perform."

"That about covers it, yes."

He nodded. "Okay. So I thought about it, and I figured it couldn't have become too expensive for you to perform your job, because I was paying for everything."

She said nothing in response to that, because, obviously, that wasn't the reason she'd had to leave.

"And it wasn't becoming too difficult for you to perform your job," he continued, "since you were excellent at it, and you made it look so easy and you seemed to love it."

"Thank you. And yes, I did love it. Do love it," she hastened to correct herself. Because she did still love to cook. She just didn't love cooking for the Fleurys as much as she'd loved cooking for Hogan. She hadn't loved cooking for anyone as much as she'd loved cooking for Hogan. Probably because it wasn't just cooking for Hogan she'd loved.

"So if you didn't think your job was too expensive or too difficult to perform," he said, "then you must have thought it was too dangerous."

Bingo. Because loving anything—or anyone—more than cooking was very dangerous indeed for Chloe. Loving anything—or anyone—more than cooking could very well be the end of her. At least that was what she'd thought since Samuel's death. Now she was beginning to think there were things much more harmful to her—and much more dangerous for her—than loving and wanting and needing. Like not loving. And not wanting. And not needing. She'd spent six years avoiding those things, and she'd told herself she was surviving, when, really, she'd been dying a little more inside every day. Losing more of herself every day. Until she'd become a shell of the woman she used to be. A woman who'd begun to emerge from that shell again the moment she met Hogan.

"Yes," she told him. But she didn't elaborate. She still didn't quite trust herself to say any of the things she wanted—needed—to say.

"So what was getting too dangerous?" he asked. "Were the knives too sharp? Because I can stock up on bandages, no problem."

At this, she almost smiled. But she still said nothing.

"Then maybe the stove was getting too hot?" he asked. "Because if that's the case, I can buy some fans for the kitchen. Maybe get a window unit for in there."

Chloe bit back another smile at the thought of a portable air conditioner jutting out of a window on the Upper East Side and dripping condensation onto the chicly dressed passersby below. She shook her head again. And still said nothing.

"Okay," he said. "I was hoping it wasn't this, but it's the only other thing I can think of. It was all that fresh, unprocessed whole food, wasn't it? I knew it. Someday scientists are going to tell us that stuff is poison and that boxed mac and cheese and tinned biscuits are the best things we can put in our bodies."

"Hogan, stop," she finally said. Because he was becoming more adorable with every word he spoke, and that was just going to make her fall in love with him all over again.

Then she realized that was ridiculous. She'd fallen

in love with Hogan a million times since meeting him. What difference would one more time make?

"Well, if it wasn't the sharp knives, and it wasn't the hot stove, and it wasn't the allegedly healthy food, then what was it that made working for me so dangerous?"

He was going to make her say it. But maybe she needed to say it. Admitting the problem was the first step, right? Now if she could just figure out the other eleven steps in the How-to-Fall-Out-of-Love-with-Someone program, she'd be all set. Of course, falling *out* of love with Hogan wasn't really the problem, was it? Then again, she was beginning to realize that falling *in* love with him wasn't so bad, either.

"It was you, Hogan," she said softly. "It was the possibility of falling in love with you." Then she made herself tell the truth. She closed her eyes to make it easier. "No, that's not it. It wasn't the possibility of falling in love with you. It was falling in love with you."

When he didn't reply, she opened first one eye, then the other. His smile now was completely different from the others. There was nothing teasing, nothing modest, nothing sweet. There was just love. Lots and lots of love.

"You can't fight it, Chloe," he said. "Trust me—I know. I've been trying to fight it for a month. Trying to give you the room you need to figure things out. Trying to figure things out myself. But the only thing I figured out was that I love you."

Heat swamped her midsection at hearing him say it so matter-of-factly. "Do you?"

"Yep. And I know you love me, too."

"Yes."

For a moment they only gazed at each other in silence, as if they needed a minute to let that sink in. But Chloe didn't need any extra time to realize how she felt about Hogan. She'd recognized it the night they made love. She'd just been trying to pretend otherwise since then.

Hogan took a step toward her, close enough now for her to touch him. "Do you think you'll ever stop loving me?" he asked.

She knew the answer to that immediately. "No. I know I won't."

"And I'm not going to stop loving you."

He lifted a hand to her face, cupping her jaw lightly, running the pad of his thumb over her cheek. Chloe's insides turned to pudding at his touch, and she tilted her head into his caress.

"So here's the thing," he said softly. "If we both love each other, and neither of us is going to stop, then why aren't we together?"

She knew the answer to that question, too. Because it would be too painful to lose him. But that was a stupid answer, because it was going to be painful to lose him whether they were together or not. Okay, then because she would live in fear of losing him for the rest of her life. But that didn't make any sense, either, because if she wasn't with him, then she'd already lost him. Okay, then because…because… There had to be a reason. She used to have a reason. If she could only remember what the reason was.

"It's too late for us, Chloe," he said when she didn't reply. "We love each other, and that's not going to change. Yeah, it's scary," he added, putting voice to her thoughts. "But don't you think the idea of life without each other is even scarier?"

Yes. It was. Being alone since Samuel's death had been awful. Although she could deny it all she wanted, Chloe hadn't liked being alone. She'd tolerated it because she hadn't thought there was any other way for her to live. But she hadn't liked it. The time she'd spent living with Hogan and being with Hogan was the best time she'd had in years. Some years and some months and some weeks and some days she didn't have to keep a tally of anymore. Because she wasn't alone anymore. Or, at least, she didn't have to be. Not unless she chose to.

Hogan was right. It was scary to fall in love. No, it was terrifying. But the prospect of living the rest of her life without him was far, far worse.

"I want to come back to work for you," she said.

He shook his head. "Just come back. We'll figure out the rest of it as we go."

Chloe finally smiled. A real smile. The kind of smile she hadn't smiled in a long time. Because she was happy for the first time in a long time. Truly, genuinely happy. "Okay," she said. "But I'm still not going to cook you taco meatloaf."

Hogan smiled back. "No worries. We can share the cooking. I need to introduce you to the joys of chicken pot pie, too."

Instead of wincing this time, Chloe laughed. Then she stood up on tiptoe, looped her arms around Hogan's neck and kissed him. Immediately, he roped his arms around her waist and pulled her close, covering her mouth with his and tasting her deeply as if she were the most delectable dish he'd ever had.

Chloe wasn't sure how they made it to her bedroom on the first floor without alerting the dinner guests still lingering in the Fleurys' salon, since she and Hogan nearly fell down every flight of the back stairs on their way, too reluctant to break their embrace and shedding clothes as they went. Somehow, though, they—and even their discarded clothing—did make it. He shoved the door closed behind them, then pressed her back against it, crowding his big body into hers as he kissed her and kissed her and kissed her.

By now, she was down to her bra, and the fly of her jeans was open, and he was down to his T-shirt, his belt loosened, his hard shaft pressing against her belly. She wedged her hand between their bodies enough to unfasten the button at his waist and tug down the zipper, then she tucked her hand into his briefs to press her palm against the naked length of him. He surged harder at her touch, and a feral growl escaped him before he intensified their kiss. He dropped his hands to her hips, shoving her jeans and panties down to her knees, then he thrust his hand between her legs to finger the damp folds of flesh he encountered.

This time Chloe was the one to purr with pleasure, nipping his lip lightly before touching the tip of her tongue to the corner of his mouth. Hogan rubbed his long index finger against her again, then inserted it inside her, caressing her with the others until she felt as if she would melt away. With his free hand, he slipped first one bra strap, then the other, from her shoulders, urging the garment to her waist to bare her breasts. Then he covered one with his entire hand, thumbing the sensitive nipple to quick arousal.

Her breath was coming in quick gasps now, and her

hand moved harder on his ripe shaft in response. He rocked his hips in time with her touches, until the two of them were *this close* to going off together. Just as the tightening circles of her orgasm threatened to spring free, he pulled their bodies away from the door and began a slow dance toward the bed. The moment they reached their destination, she yanked Hogan's shirt over his head, tossed it to the floor and pushed at his jeans to remove them, as well. Taking her cue, he went to work on removing what was left of her clothing, too.

When she turned to lower the bed's coverlet, he moved behind her, flattening his body against hers and covering her breasts with both hands. But when she bent forward to push away the sheets, he splayed his hand open at the middle of her back, gently bent her lower, and then, slow and deep, entered her from behind.

"Oh," she cried softly, curling her fingers tightly into the bedclothes. "Oh, Hogan..."

He moved both hands to her hips, gripping them tightly as he pushed himself deeper inside her. For long moments, he pumped her that way, the friction of his body inside hers turning Chloe into a hot, wanton thing. Finally, he withdrew, taking his time and caressing her fanny as he did, skimming his palms over her warm flesh before giving it a gentle squeeze. He tumbled them both into bed, lying on his back and pulling her atop him, straddling him. Instead of entering her again, though, he moved her body forward, until the hot feminine heart of her was poised for his taste.

His tongue flicking against her already sensitive flesh was her undoing. Barely a minute into his ministrations, Chloe felt the first wave of an orgasm wash over her. She moaned as it crested, waiting for the next swell. That one came and went, too, followed by another and another. But just when she thought she'd seen the last one, he turned her onto her back and positioned himself above her.

As he entered her again, another orgasm swept over her. But this time, Hogan went with her. He thrust inside her a dozen times, then emptied himself deep inside her. Only then did the two of them fall back to the bed, panting for breath and groping for coherent thought. Never had Chloe felt more satisfied than she did in that moment. Never had she felt so happy. So contented. So free of fear.

Loving wasn't scary, she realized then. Avoiding love—that was scary. Loving was easy. So love Hogan she would. For as long as she could. Because, *oh là là*, living without loving wasn't living at all.

It was a hot day in Brooklyn, the kind of summer day that cried out for something cold for dessert. So Chloe decided to add *tulipes de sorbet* to the daily menu of her new café, *La Fin des Haricots*. They would go nicely with the rest of the light French fare the little restaurant had become famous for in Williamsburg over the last year and a half, and it would make Hogan happy, since it was a reasonable compromise for the chocolate ice cream he preferred.

They'd compromised on a lot over the last eighteen months. He'd sold his grandfather's Lenox Hill town house, along with Philip Amherst's other properties— save the one in Paris, of course, where they planned to spend the month of August every year, starting with their honeymoon last summer. Then they purchased a funky brownstone they'd been renovating ever since, and in whose backyard Chloe had planted a small garden and built a small greenhouse. Hogan's chain of Dempsey's Garages was fast becoming reality—he was already operating three in the city and had acquired properties for a half dozen more. And *La Fin des Haricots* was fast becoming a neighborhood favorite. They worked hard every day and loved hard every night, and on Sundays…

Sundays were sacred, the one day they dedicated completely to each other. Usually by spending much of it in bed, either eating or talking or loafing or—their favorite—making love.

Hogan's other passion in life was the scholarship fund he'd set up in his parents' names for kids from both his old and his new neighborhoods. He'd also donated significantly to Samuel's fund. The losses of their pasts would help bring happiness into others' futures, and that made the two of them about as rich as a couple of people could be.

Life was good, Chloe thought as she finished up the menu and handed it off to her head waiter to record it on the ever-changing chalkboard at the door. Then she buttoned up her chef's jacket—one that fit, since she had packed Samuel's away and wore her own now—and headed back to the kitchen. Her kitchen. She might still be cooking for other people, but it was in her own space. A space where she was putting down roots, in a place she would live for a very long time, with a man she would love forever. It still scared her a little when she thought about how much she loved her husband. But it scared her more to think about not loving him.

He met her at the end of her workday as he always did, on this occasion arriving at the kitchen door in his grease-stained coveralls, since it was the end of his workday, too. They ate dinner together at the chef's table, then, hand in hand, they walked home. Together they opened a bottle of wine. Together they enjoyed it on their roof. Together they made plans for their trip to Paris in August. And then together they went to bed, so they could make love together, and wake up together and start another day in the morning together.

Because together was what they were. And together was what they would always be. No matter where they went. No matter what they did. No matter what happened.

And that, Chloe thought as she did every night when they turned off the light, was what was truly *magnifique*.

* * * * *

THE BEAUTY AND THE CEO

CAROLYN HECTOR

I would like to dedicate this book to my ambitious daughter and nieces, Haley, Kayla and Ashleigh.

I live vicariously through these talented young ladies.

Chapter 1

Morning rays of sunlight created a halo effect around the godlike body of a six-foot-four man strolling through the parting glass doors of Kelly Towers. A collective gasp of soft feminine sighs rose over the swishing sound of the automatic doors closing. With the sun behind him, the man strolled down the red carpet toward the elevator right where makeup artist Zoe Baldwin stood.

Dear Lord, Zoe began her silent prayer, *if ever there were a time to get stuck in the elevator, please let it be now and with him.*

The denim jeans he wore clung to his powerful thighs. A thin, white, long-sleeved shirt hugged the sculpted muscles of his arms and abdomen. As he came closer, everyone in the lobby turned their heads in his direction. Thick, dark brows framed his eyes.

A prominent chin jutted out from the sharp angles of his long, masculine face. Zoe cocked her head to the left and reached up to touch the signature hoop earrings she was known to wear. Instead of the cool gold circle, Zoe's fingertip brushed against heirloom pearls handed down from her grandmother. The jewels had a reputation for good luck. Perhaps with this fine-as-hell gentleman coming closer, the hand-me-down stories were true.

Though he didn't carry a portfolio, Zoe pegged her soon-to-be elevator companion as a male model. The fifty-three-story Kelly Towers was home to several of Miami's elite businesses. The local news station was housed on ten floors, while Ravens Cosmetics, Zoe's final destination, was housed on the fortieth through the forty-ninth. Modeling and a few talent agencies were sprinkled throughout the other floors. Zoe guessed he'd get off on one of those floors. For her, the only place she needed to be was at Ravens Cosmetics—the home of the oldest and most successful cosmetic line for people of color in the United States and now globally. And if today went as planned at her interview, she could call Ravens Cosmetics home as well.

In an attempt to flirt, Zoe licked her lips, tasting the hint of honey in the concoction she used for lip balm. The response she received from the gorgeous man was a lopsided, boy-next-door smile mixed with a hint of danger. The sensual curve of his full lips begged to challenge the question every makeup-wearing woman pondered: Was he worth smearing her lipstick for? His lips parted into a dashing smile and crinkles appeared at the corners of his eyes. An older model? Twenty-five? Twenty-eight? She'd heard RC was going in a new direction. It was about time they added someone more age appropriate to their ads for men. The men in the ads for shaving, lotions and other male grooming products were handsome but also extremely young—as in barely-legal-young. Under thirty as a male was far from old, but in the modeling world he might be ready to retire.

"Hello," he said.

His deep baritone touched her soul. A powerful shiver trickled down her spine while her knees weakened. "Hi," she replied.

With the limited skills she had in the flirting department, Zoe batted her lashes and damn it if her cell phone didn't ring. The old-school Prince song indicated the hotline for one of her closest friends. It was almost a bat signal, and when that song rang, Zoe picked up the phone and answered. "Hey, what's up?"

Lexi Pendergrass Reyes's cheerful voice came over the line loud and clear. "I wanted to wish you luck before your interview."

"You're so sweet," Zoe said as she offered an apologetic smile to the handsome man. Zoe stepped backward and did a little spin in an attempt to give the stranger a better view of her angles in her black pencil skirt and red silk Rochas blouse decorated with oversize magnolias. She'd received the blouse at a *Vogue* photo shoot last year, another lucky memento of her work. "Can I call you right back?"

"Of course," Lexi said, "but don't forget. On top of wishing you the luck you don't need, I do have a huge favor to ask of you."

The flashing triangle light above the elevator doors

indicated it was coming in a few seconds. "The answer is yes. I don't even have to know what it is."

"You say that now. Bye, girl."

Zoe swiped the icon on her cell to hang up the call. She took a deep breath, ready to speak to her male model again. As a makeup artist, she noticed he needed no cover-up. She'd known some models and actors who'd paid to have cheekbones as sculpted as his.

"So," he began, leaning against the marble wall near the up and down arrow-shaped buttons of the elevator.

"So," Zoe repeated.

She was prepared to have some form of meaningful conversation in the span of the few seconds provided before the elevator arrived, but that was interrupted when the doors on the first floor, leading to the building's cafeteria, opened up. It was not unusual in a place like this to run into some of the local celebrities. A gaggle of girls screamed at the sight of Zoe. Zoe and her magic beauty box kits were the reason certain faces graced the covers of top beauty magazines. She'd decorated the faces of movie stars, governors and their spouses, singers and television reality stars. Torn between not having seen these ladies in quite some time and getting to the meat of this conversation with the hot guy, Zoe offered another apologetic smile. The man stepped forward and extracted a business card from his back pocket to give to her, then winked before turning to take the door into the stairwell.

"Hey, guys," said Zoe, slipping the card into the front of her purse. "What's going on today?"

The half-dozen girls began to complain all at once about having to come in this morning for a music video which was being filmed in the cafeteria. Something about their makeup not being right and begging Zoe to ace the interview.

"Girl, that outfit is giving me life! There really should be no reason for you to interview," said Clarita Benson. She was a six-foot-three model in flats.

The next tallest was six-two, a former volleyball star turned model. Her blond hair stuck out at the ends like straw. "I heard Marcus Ravens say you were the best person for the job."

"I guess we'll see in a little bit." Zoe shrugged her shoulders and craned her neck. Thankfully, the elevator doors opened with a loud ding. "Listen, ladies, I've got to head off and ace this interview."

The doors closed as the girls chorused, "Good luck!" Zoe leaned against the back of the compartment. She smiled at her reflection, knowing she'd dressed the part.

In truth, Zoe knew she was the right person for the position as the Creative Design Director at Ravens Cosmetics. She had a BS in biochemistry and an MS in cosmetic chemistry, both from Fairleigh Dickinson University, held a license as a beautician and was the number one most-requested makeup artist at Fashion Week in New York, London, Milan and Paris. Her work with artists at Coachella over the last five years had gotten her noticed for the CDD position at several cosmetic companies.

Zoe only wanted to set roots down in the Miami office of Ravens Cosmetics. Call it a predestined destination. Her great-grandmother Sadie, affectionately known as GiGi, ran one of the largest cosmetology schools in the Southeast. As a teen growing up in Trinidad, Gigi loved getting ready for the masquerade, also known as "Mas," at Carnival. For a touch of home, she named her new school after the beloved event. Before leaving Mas Beauty School, all the students wanted to be an employee at Ravens Cosmetics, one of the oldest and most successful cosmetics companies founded by an African American woman for people of color. It would be a sign of success to join their company. Tears of pride and joy threatened to escape the corners of her eyes as she realized how close she was to following in her grandmother's footsteps.

Just last week at the after-party of a successful swimsuit fashion show, RC's president, Marcus Ravens, had told Zoe the job was practically hers. The models on both of his arms swore Zoe was the best. And modestly Zoe had agreed.

Traveling in fashion circles, Zoe had met Marcus's other board members, a group made up of siblings and cousins from the large family. Each of the directors represented shareholders, the elders of Ravens Cosmetics.

It had been hard to gauge how some of the Ravens women felt about her. In the world of fashion and cosmetics, everyone was either an enemy or an ally. For a very brief moment in Zoe's life she'd modeled. Her knowledge of the industry, inside and out, put her in a threatening position. Plenty of times she'd overstepped the bounds as a makeup artist, questioning the chemicals the other cosmetologists wanted to put on someone's face. She almost became difficult to work with. With her degree in cosmetic chemistry she could easily start her own line. But Zoe wanted stability in her life. Her parents married young before they had a chance to live out their dreams, before settling down. Seeing her parents struggle to stay together while reaching their own goals put a damper on Zoe's outlook on relationships. Things were changing now. She was established and not to mention older than her parents had been when they married. Thirty was rapidly knocking on her door and a faint biological clock was ticking in the back of her mind.

Having reaffirmed her worth, Zoe took a deep breath. When the elevator dinged to announce her presence on the fortieth floor, the doors parted and opened up to a quieter situation than on the first floor. A half-circle African blackwood desk drew Zoe's attention immediately, along with a receptionist who had curly blond hair pulled up in a frizzy ponytail at the top of her head. A headset rested somewhere in the hair, Zoe guessed, because the girl held her finger up in Zoe's direction but finished the conversation on the other end of the line before disconnecting the call.

"Miss Baldwin?" The young girl, whose foundation was poorly blended from her face to neck, rolled her eyes at the sight of Zoe. *Clearly not a fan.*

Zoe smiled and nodded. "Yes, that's me."

"Okay, so, you and the others are in the waiting room over there."

The others? Using the eraser end of a pencil, the receptionist pointed toward a glass room adjacent to her desk. A minute ago Zoe had been giving herself a pep talk. She was sure the job was hers and she knew she'd earned it. But there were others? She stood at the glass door to the conference room where just over a half-dozen women and men sat waiting at a large oval table made of the same wood as the reception desk. In an instant, Zoe recognized everyone at the table, including Titus, her nemesis.

To make it to this level of her profession, Zoe had come across several—as the young model clients had called them—haters, and Titus was not her number one fan. The one-name wonder scowled through the glass at Zoe, his long, tacky feather lashes clumping together, causing him to have to pry them apart with his loud pink fingernails. Zoe refrained herself from rolling her eyes by sighing instead. The man claimed to be the best yet can't figure out which adhesive glue for lashes worked best. At the AJ Crimson event last year, Zoe'd almost had to tell him about himself when she found her artist's kit at his station. He claimed the kit was accidentally placed there but Zoe knew better. He tried to steal it. A makeup artist's beauty kit was as important to them as a doctor's stethoscope, a police officer's badge or even a mechanic's tools. Zoe admired AJ Crimson for becoming a leader in the beauty world, bringing his popular brand of cosmetics to pop culture through hip-hop music and current top television shows. How badly did she want the Creative Design Director position? Zoe took a step backward.

"You're not leaving, are you, Zoe?"

Zoe turned around at the sound of Marcus Ravens's voice. An automatic smile spread across her face at the sight of him. Marcus was a handsome man, tall, dark and charming. Zoe returned his friendly smile. All the models who did work for RC had gushed about him. "Hello, Marcus."

"Are you going in?" Marcus nodded his head at the door. The others inside craned their necks.

"I think there's been a misunderstanding," said Zoe.

Marcus retreated a step and glanced in both directions down the hall. He stepped closer to Zoe and touched her elbow. "There is, or was," he said and shook his head. "There has been a slight change of plans. You see, my brother is here."

Zoe slowly shook her head to the left and then the right. "Okay? I spoke with Donovan last week. He assured me the job is mine. All I'd have to do is meet with the board."

"It is yours," Marcus exclaimed. "You know you're the best person for the job."

"It seems someone thinks several people are the perfect person for the job." Zoe inclined her head toward the room of other makeup artists.

"That's what I'm trying to explain." There was a panic in Marcus's deep voice. He pressed one hand on Zoe's shoulders as a vein pulsed at his temples, which he tried to cover up by scratching the back of his neck with his other hand. "My brother—my other brother, Will—is responsible."

"Will?" Zoe repeated. "I thought I knew everyone in your family."

Back in middle school, Zoe had done one of her best biography reports on the Ravens family. She'd once known their family tree like the back of her hand. The Ravens started at the turn of the century selling beauty products to the wives of the men working on the railroad. It was Marcus's grandparents, Joe and Naomi Ravens, who'd slapped a label on their business and marketed it nationally. Zoe learned all about the following generations of Ravens through the Roaring Twenties and the forties to the present. The younger generations were all connected via social media. All of the family members worked for Ravens, right?

On numerous occasions Zoe had crossed paths with the Ravens family, either in the Miami Design District or at Miami's Fashion Week.

"He's our youngest brother, and my cousins nominated him to be the CEO of RC."

"Okay?" Zoe said slowly, still not following what that had to do with her and this interview.

"Will believes he should look at everyone interested in being the CDD."

Zoe's heart ached with a surge. "I'm not understanding, Marcus. You're the president."

"The CEO has a little more pull than the president," Marcus explained. "And right now, he's our last chance at keeping RC running."

The rumors were true. Someone wanted to shut down Ravens Cosmetics. Zoe's heart ached as if she'd been wronged. How could anyone think about dissolving this company? Five minutes ago she'd pumped herself up about wanting to board the RC ship. Now it felt like the ship was sailing away while she stood on the pier watching it depart. She asked herself again, how badly did she want to be the Creative Design Director?

"This is then a waste of my time, Marcus. I am too qualified to have to go through a screening process." Zoe turned to leave. Through the glass, Zoe thought she saw Titus mouthing something to her. She was not in the mood for a fight. "Either you like my work or you don't."

With his hands still on her shoulders, Marcus clamped down firmly. He turned her to face him so her back was to the receptionist area. "I do, my brothers and sisters do, and Will is going to feel the same way."

"You guys brought in Titus." A tic began to flutter underneath her right eye. The other makeup artist was good, of course he was. But he'd copied her trademark '80s style. This was too much stress for her. Zoe sighed impatiently. Great-Grandma Sadie would have a fit if she knew Zoe got this far only to abandon her own resolve. "I just can't deal with this, Marcus."

"Will you at least listen to me first? I'll get Donovan on the phone."

"I'm right here." Donovan's familiar voice filled the hallway.

Not wanting any pity, Zoe didn't dare turn around. Like his brother, Donovan had an extremely charismatic smile. Ever the charmer, he always knew how to bring out a natural blush on any model Zoe had worked on. If she glanced at Donovan, Zoe knew she'd swoon, and right now she was too pissed off to be cheered up. She kept her angry focus on the Windsor knot of Marcus's tie.

"Tell her everything is still going on as planned," Marcus said over her head to his brother.

"The interviewing process?" Donovan asked, and Marcus nodded. "It's just a process."

"Someone too good for an interview?" Another deep voice asked.

While the voice may have been sexy, the tone was not. Zoe spun on her heels, prepared to give this person a piece of her mind when she stopped and gaped. Instead of the fitted shirt and jeans she'd seen him in earlier at the elevator, he now wore a tailored, classically cut two-thousand-dollar navy blue suit with a blue-and-yellow paisley tie. Suits made Zoe's knees weak the same way lingerie did men's.

"You?" The man brushed roughly against Donovan's shoulders without apologizing.

"You?" Zoe repeated. "I don't understand." Zoe wondered how she hadn't recognized the similarities.

"Will, this is Zoe Baldwin, the woman we've been talking about." Donovan clamped his hands on his brother's back. "Zoe, this is our baby brother, Will."

"You're a makeup artist?"

"She's the *B* in Beauty Business," Donovan interjected.

So, the man from the elevator wasn't a struggling model? Judging from the expensive suit he wore, he was far from struggling. Zoe shrugged her shoulders indifferently. "Artist, genius, whatever you want to call me is fine."

"How about we keep it simple and call you interviewee number six?" Will asked.

Gone was the charming smile from downstairs. Zoe's hand brushed against the front pocket where she shoved his business card. She extracted it and fingered the raised letters, assuming it gave the three initials of his position. CEO. Jesus Christ, this man with a dry sense of humor held her fate in his hands. Somewhere in the back of her mind Zoe heard the proverbial ship sound its horn and sail off into the ocean.

At six in the evening, Will Ravens sat back in his newly ordered chair and tried to get the feel of it and the new position. He was in over his head. As a former professional soccer player for the Texas Raiders, the only thing he knew about women was what he was attracted to. Not being raised in the family business, Will did not possess the same keen cosmetic eye as his siblings. He knew what he'd liked and what he'd seen in the portfolios from the interviews this afternoon. There was nothing to catch his eye—but that wasn't necessarily true. The woman's face from earlier this afternoon entered his mind. He thumbed through the portfolios of the potential CDDs. A silver paper clip fastened to the manila folder secured a photo of Zoe Baldwin's heart-shaped face to the outside.

How was she the woman behind the makeup and not on the runway? Her flawless sienna-and-gold skin was radiant. Her chestnut-brown hair, secured today at the back of her neck, did not do her justice as the photograph before him did. In it, her mane hung over her shoulders and she smiled for the camera with one raised brow and a playful smile across her face.

"So, what did you think of Zoe Baldwin?"

Will dropped the portfolio at the unexpected interruption and cursed under his breath. "Jesus, Donovan, don't you knock?"

"We're family."

"All the more reason to knock," Will joked. The last round of complaints from their cousins were due to Donovan's dating the models. He went through at least one on a weekly basis. They threw themselves at him. The one thing a lot of models wanted more than a modeling contract for a spread in an RC ad was to land one of the Ravens men. Having his brothers in charge of anything dealing with models was as productive as letting a fox guard a henhouse. Fortunately, Will, the youngest of the men, had more common sense.

Less than ten years ago, the new generation of Ravens had been placed on the board. Everyone owned an equal share of Ravens Cosmetics. Half of Will's cousins wanted to dismantle the company. They were tired of the meetings and responsibilities. Will knew his great-grandparents were rolling in their graves at the idea. For the cousins, even the limited time they had to spend in the office was still too much. Will and his siblings, along with a handful of cousins, wanted to keep the legacy alive. The problem was, they were a band of eight against a band of another eight.

Donovan nodded his head. "Alright, you got me there." He stepped inside Will's office and made himself comfortable in one of the matching leather seats in front of Will's desk. "So, I'll ask you again, what did you think of Zoe?"

"Which one was she?" Will needed to play dumb. When the position opened up, Will was skeptical when Donovan suggested Zoe Baldwin. Given Donovan's track record, Will didn't want to risk any form of lawsuit. Given the chemistry Will felt when he spotted Zoe at the elevator, Will did not want to admit his attraction to a potential employee.

Gossip spread like wildfires in office settings. Kelly Towers, and all the businesses housed on the floors, was not immune to the tabloids. Home to the local news station, celebrity appearances and eager folks trying to catch a break in the media world, this building was often the target of tabloid spies. Will prided himself on his discretion. He took dating a person seriously. In a building filled with scantily clad women and men representing everything Ravens Cosmetics had to offer, spotting the demure woman at the elevator had been the highlight of his life for the last few weeks. Will's days of going through women were over. He was tired of women impressed by and after his money. Will never realized how much he appreciated the classic beauty of a woman until he'd seen her. She'd worn a simple skirt, a somewhat loud red blouse and pearls at her ears, as well as around her slender neck. When was the last time a woman wore pearls around her neck as a part of an outfit—not several strands of pearls as an outfit?

Will summed up Zoe Baldwin in one word: beautiful. There had been an instant connection between them when he walked into the hallway downstairs. It had been the first time he'd actually passed out one of the business cards he was given when he took on his role of CEO. If his brothers and sisters knew Will had almost asked her out today, they'd never leave him alone about it. His cousins would never trust his decisions if he acted like Donovan or Marcus.

"Y'all talking about the interviews today?" Marcus asked, poking his head in the door.

"Yes," Donovan said, leaning back in his chair to look at their oldest brother. "And Will is trying to act like he doesn't know which one Zoe was."

Marcus chuckled and entered the room. He took the seat next to Donovan and propped his elbows on Will's desk. "The one you drooled so much over, we needed to get the cleaning crew to mop up the saliva? The one who caused the hallway to become so sexually charged when she and Will laid eyes on each other?"

It was going to take some time for Will to get used to being around his family like this. Luckily his sisters, Dana and Eva, were out of town at a convention. They would already have started planning his wedding. Will needed to get used to the idea of carrying on his grandparents' corporate legacy before he thought about adding to it.

"You ought to go into creative writing," Will said with a dry yawn.

"I've got my hands full being president." Marcus glanced down at his fingers.

As Marcus inspected his cuticles, Donovan and Will dramatically bowed down at the president, a teasing move they did every time Marcus felt the need to inform them of his title. No one *wanted* to be the president. The president was the face of the company with not as much power as people believed. But if anyone needed to be the face, it was Marcus. He was what Will considered pretty, with soft brown hair and deeply tanned skin, helped out a bit by the Miami sun.

Thanks to a car accident a few years ago, Donovan never wanted to be in the public eye. He wanted to hide the long scar down his cheek from the cameras. No matter the differences Will saw between himself and his brothers, everywhere they went, people always knew they were siblings.

"You guys are jerks, you know that?" asked Marcus with a tight smile.

"You guys nominated me, a guy with no credibility in the business other than my last name, to be the CEO while I was recuperating," Will said drily. "So sue me if I don't feel sorry for you."

"By 'recuperating—'" Donovan raised his hands for air quotes "—you mean you were at your sci-fi convention?"

Will pressed his hands on top of the portfolios. "I believe you were right there next to me in a Flash mask."

Marcus's head snapped toward Donovan. "You said you were in New York."

"I was, right after Comic-Con."

Before his brothers went off on a tangent, Will cleared his throat. "Let's talk about the interviews today. I'd like to be on a united front before we meet back with the cousins."

His grandparents carried on a long family tradition of creating products for the community. They'd raised their six kids in a modest four-bedroom home in Overtown, a predominately African American neighborhood in Miami. His great-great-grandmother had sold hair-care products to the women whose husbands worked on the railroads. Skin-care and hair-care products had helped mold the Ravens into a millionaire family back in the day. Will wanted to make sure Ravens Cosmetics made it to one hundred years in business.

Will concentrated on his brothers in front of him. "Who did y'all like?"

"Zoe," Donovan and Marcus chorused.

Will liked Zoe, but he wasn't sure it was for the same reasons as his brothers. It wasn't like Will to arrive at RC late, as he had that morning. His cousins Katie and Dixon had conveniently forgotten to remind him of the time change for the interviews. And to make matters worse, he'd worked out with Dixon this morning. No wonder Dixon had hopped off the treadmill a few miles sooner than normal. Will should have known better. These cousins were ready to dissolve Ravens Cosmetics. He frowned. Will refused to let that happen on his watch.

"I'm not sure she's what I had in mind for such a position."

"And what did you have in mind?"

Flipping open the portfolio with Zoe's face on it, Will thumbed through the photographs of all the women and men she'd worked on. "This work is too busy for me. We're here to support the everyday woman, and she paints a face like they're eighties rock stars."

"Paints a face?" Marcus snickered as if he'd said something erroneous. "What's wrong with that?"

"I want to go in a different direction. I want something more classic." Will sat back in his seat and poised his fingers like a steeple. "Like a 1940s look."

"You want to start a new retro look?" asked Donovan.

"See, that's what is wrong with you two." Will shrugged his shoulders and continued without waiting for an answer. "What's wrong with it? Everyone else is looking for these loud colors and makeup so heavy the girls resemble raccoons. I'm trying to save the company with something new this generation hasn't experienced."

"And you think you can bring classic back? Women evolved from that style, as well. Zoe is hot right now."

Will shrugged again. Yes, Zoe was hot now and if she worked here, she'd also be un-dateable. "Hey, you guys put me in this position. I can take it, but you are going to have to trust me on this. Tell me the truth, do you really want to bring your lady to Sunday dinner looking like this?" Will held up one of the jobs Zoe had done and shook his head. At the elevator she'd given off a classic vibe, but her body of work on paper did not interest him. "No, I want to take things in a new direction. Trust me."

of a conversation that he had been told an important
information about me. "Not just about me," he said
mischievously.

Chapter 2

By the time Zoe turned the lock on her door at the
Cozier Condos off Biscayne Boulevard, she was tired
and heartbroken. *Humiliated* was a better description
of her day. Never before had she expected to go through
the stressful interview process to prove her worth.
Well, maybe not never. Once she'd had to interview
for the job as a scoop girl at The Scoop's Ice Cream
Parlor back in Southwood, Georgia, when Zoe's love
for makeup had exceeded her allowance. She had to
prove to the owners she loved ice cream and all of the
flavors they had to offer. Hopefully Zoe's most stressful interviews would be her first and her last.

The set of house keys jingled with a clink into the
clear bowl on top of the credenza. The weight of the
keys shifted the bowl into yesterday's mail, nudging
the silver box with gold writing on top. The latest Ra-

vens Cosmetic Artist Kit filled with fabulous foundation colors had arrived, along with the silver tubes of lipstick. Zoe broke out one bullet-shaped container and inspected the color—No Shade. Usually these beauty boxes excited her, but today's mood rippled with disappointment.

When in doubt, Zoe always called on a hometown friend for advice. On her phone, she pressed the icon she had for Lexi—a tiara—and waited for the beauty queen to answer. While Lexi had gone to a different school during the year, she came home to Southwood for the summers and she and her friends had taken Zoe under their wing.

Lexi answered on the second ring. "How did it go today?"

"It was nothing like I expected," Zoe drawled. She set the phone on the counter and swiped the speaker button for a hands-free conversation while she fiddled around in her condo's kitchen. "I had to wait in the conference room like a person trying to..." Zoe lost her words.

"Get a job?" Lexi provided.

Even though Lexi couldn't see, Zoe rolled her eyes. "Whatever. I have a job. Several of them. Did you forget the MET Awards are coming up next in August and Fashion Week after that?"

Celebrities were already requesting Zoe's help for the big event for Multi-Ethnic Television. She had high-profile weddings in the Midwest on the schedule as well, and a few more job interviews up north. Travel was her middle name. At least the MET event was going to be held in Orlando this year.

"But you want just the one. You wanted to be in

a permanent spot." Lexi reminded her. "Or, at least, that's what you told me the last time we spoke. I bet your suitcase isn't even unpacked from your stint in Hollywood."

Since her overnight bag was still by her laundry-room door, Zoe decided not to confirm Lexi's statement. Instead, she hummed a little ditty for a moment while her eyes searched the kitchen counter for something to eat. Finding the bag of roti from Trudy's, the local West Indian market and restaurant around the corner, Zoe grabbed a piece of the bread made from stone-ground flour and went to the refrigerator for the questionable leftover curry from last week. While the food heated up, Zoe grabbed the phone, took it off the stand and headed off toward her bedroom. Her apartment had only two bedrooms, a small living room and a dinette and kitchen, but it was home—subleased, but still home.

"I can still call in some favors with RC," said Lexi.

It seemed there wasn't a person in the fashion world Lexi did not know. Her store, Grits and Glam Gowns, was renowned. As women flocked there for dresses, whether for proms, pageants or weddings, a mention of her product meant everything in the world to a company. Lexi had a lot of power.

"No." Zoe shook her head. "I want to earn this job without any favors. The president told me I'm golden. But this round of interviews is thanks to their new CEO."

"So, who is the CEO of RC now?" Lexi asked. "Donovan?"

"No," Zoe groaned. "His name is Will Ravens."

"Wait, the soccer player?"

"No." Zoe hummed a noise again, kicking out of her heels and footing them into the closet. "He's the CEO. Donovan and Marcus introduced him to us."

"Is he hot, like his brothers?" asked Lexi.

"Lexi!" Zoe gasped, wanting more than anything to elaborate on exactly how hot Will Ravens was. "You're married with a baby on the way."

"I'm married, not blind," Lexi reminded her. "If it's who I think it is, William Ravens played soccer and was hurt during a game. I want to say a broken leg."

Slipping out of her skirt, Zoe padded barefoot into the bathroom. "Since when did you become the sports fan?"

"You can thank my beautiful husband for that." Lexi giggled on the other end of the line. Zoe thought it was a nice laugh. She wanted something like that one day. A man who made her blush just by thinking of him. "I'm pretty sure he paused the match to show me the horrific leg break," Lexi went on.

The corners of Zoe's lips turned down. "Ouch. Well, this Will Ravens did not show signs of any leg injury."

As a matter of fact, Zoe thought wantonly, she thought his strut was rather sexy. At least, she had when she thought he was simply a model. As a makeup artist, Zoe was constantly around handsome men. None of them ever had her wanting to jump in a cold shower. How was it going to work out when she got the job at RC? Zoe shrugged and pushed the thought out of her mind.

"Lexi, what was it you were going to ask me earlier?"

"Oh, that. I need you to come home for an event next week," said Lexi. "I'm hosting the Miss South-wood Glitz Pageant and I need a nonbiased makeup artist. Please say you'll come. I've booked up Magnolia Palace from Monday to next Sunday. All the judges and working staff will start coming in Tuesday. I want everyone to get to know each other so they can trust their opinions when it comes time to voting and making this the best pageant ever."

The mere mention of the old hotel, Magnolia Palace, evoked a memory of Zoe's youth. She closed her eyes and heard the sound of her bare feet pounding down the wooden planks as she raced to jump off the bridge. Her parents met on that same bridge. Her mother had been a model and her father out fishing. He'd certainly snagged the biggest catch of his life that day. "Now, how am I going to say no to an offer like that?"

"You're not," Lexi laughed.

"Since I won't be starting my CDD position any time soon, I'll be there. Text me the details."

Zoe swiped her phone to the off screen and stood in the center of her bedroom, contemplating what to do next. She was hungry, but the recent talk of Will Ravens began to make her sweat—again. A shower would do her some good, then she'd eat the curry.

Fifteen minutes after her ice-cold shower, Zoe padded barefoot back into her kitchen and reheated her food. She'd slipped her cell phone into the front pocket of her fluffy pink bathrobe and felt it vibrate on her thigh as she sat at the counter.

You were great today. A decision will be made in a few weeks.

Zoe reread Marcus's text message two more times. How was she supposed to go to bed tonight knowing she hadn't secured the position of Creative Design Director? Her life was being held up by a man she knew nothing about. Where had he gone to school? Had he been a business major or something in the field of cosmetic chemistry? What had Lexi said? He'd played sports before deciding to join the family business? A feeling of dread sunk to the pit of her stomach at the thought of her life being upheld by an athlete. At least she knew that by the weekend she'd be back home in Southwood and away from the drama for a while.

Will didn't look up from the rest of the portfolios after his brothers left to pick up dinner. In soccer he'd put in his time on the field and in the locker room. He spent more time on the field finessing his skills than in the club, like some of his teammates. Will knew the odds were against him. He had no training and no experience other than on the soccer field. Since coming to RC, Will couldn't remember getting home before the sun set. Trudy's, the West Indian market and restaurant down the block, saw more of him than his own kitchen.

The grandfather clock in the corner of the office chimed eight. A smile tugged at his mouth. When they were kids, he and his brothers used to play hide-and-seek on this floor of the building. Will's favorite place was in here, where Grandpa Joe shared the office space with his wife. With a chuckle, Will realized why they'd shared an office. If Grandma was going to stay late at work, so was Grandpa. It must have been nice to have someone who stayed with you if you couldn't get home on time.

Now that he wasn't traveling full time or training, Will wondered if any of that would happen to him.

Would he have someone to share office space with, or who would sit back with a knowing smile as his children played in here? Grandma Naomi was going on ninety. So far, her six children had blessed her with over a dozen grandchildren.

The stack of portfolios in front of him moved and the top folder shifted. A knock at his door sounded and brought Will out of his daze.

Through the glass door he spotted his identical twin cousins, Joyce and Naomi. Each was beautiful enough to be the face of RC. They were easily six feet tall, with high cheekbones and perfectly arched brows that they loved to raise at Will during their meetings whenever he asked a question about their marketing department. Will considered them allies in this war to dismantle RC. He waved them in.

Joyce, the older by seven minutes, sat down first in one of the chairs in front of his desk. Naomi, however, crossed the room to admire the photographs Will refused to throw away.

"What's going on, ladies?"

"We have a great suggestion for you," said Joyce.

Will sat back in his seat and silently prayed for Marcus and Donovan to return with dinner. Whatever the girls wanted from him, they'd decided to team up.

The reason they worked so well together was they were complete opposites. Joyce was more business oriented. Naomi was more of the partying type, ironic since she was their grandmother's namesake. Joyce had more of the ninety-year-old woman's personality, business first.

"Uh-oh, do I need reinforcements?" Will teased and pretended to pick up the black office phone on the corner of his desk. "Marcus and Donovan should be back any minute now."

"What we are suggesting," said Naomi from her corner of the room, "your brothers will wholeheartedly agree to, since it will be good for business."

The deep breath he took brought in her coconut scent, a perfume he recognized from Ravens Cosmetics. "Alright."

"With you coming on as the new CEO—"

"Coming on?" Will repeated, flabbergasted. "Why does everyone say that as if I had a choice? I believe the two of you were the first ones to second the nomination, knowing good and well I'm out of my league."

Naomi rolled her eyes. "I would have nominated you first, but Charles beat me to it."

"Anyway," Naomi huffed. "If you are serious about turning things around, we think it would be a great idea for you to fly up to Southwood, Georgia, as our representative."

"Where?" Will began flipping through the paperwork on his desk. His frat brother, Dominic Crowne, recently moved his luxury car business to a town with that name.

"Exactly," said Joyce. She leaned forward, resting her elbows on the desk. "I need you to be someplace out of your element. I want you to be a judge at this beauty pageant a business associate of RC's is having."

The only thing Will could think of was some guy in a tuxedo holding a long-stemmed microphone and singing to a crowned woman. "No."

"Will," Joyce and Naomi wailed.

"What do I know about beauty pageants?"

"You're a guy, right?" Naomi asked, and answered

without waiting for a response. "You just vote on who the prettiest is."

Zoe Baldwin's smiling face at the elevator popped into his mind. He'd already met the prettiest woman. "I don't want to do it. Get Marcus or Donovan."

"Seriously?" Naomi asked drily. "There's a reason we've learned to knock on the office doors of your brothers. C'mon, Will. It's important you make a name for yourself."

"Look, Will," Joyce snapped, "Ravens Cosmetics is the sponsor at this pageant every year. If you don't do it, it will be someone like Charles or Brandon or even Dixon. You and I both know that isn't what we need right now, especially with our other choices being your horndog brothers."

"Seriously? Me?"

Joyce shrugged her shoulders. "Over the years, Lexi Reyes has been a great asset for Ravens Cosmetics." She gave a brief history about their former beauty queen and her golden touch, and how the company had been sponsoring her pageants for years. This was the first Will had ever heard of it.

"And so, if you help Lexi out, it will give RC a platform to change the way some consumers see us—we're not simply retro but classic, like you've suggested. Our brand will be the only one used for the pageant. Our gift bags of mascara, eye shadows and lotions will go to all the attendees. Do you know how many Southern women attend pageants? Our research shows most women below the Mason-Dixon Line aren't interested in the avant-garde. We can tap into this community and save RC. And that's what you claimed you wanted to do. Or was that a lie?"

"Hell, no." Will slammed his hand on the top of the portfolios. "I don't care what our cousins think. RC is not dead." Will's gut twisted with doubt. The twins made a great point. What he lacked in experience, he made up for in determination. RC was not dead and had another hundred years left. He didn't want to risk ignoring a potential market. But a beauty pageant? He hated himself for being suckered in. "Okay, fine, send me the information. What night do I have to be there?"

"Well, here's the thing," Naomi started. "In order for you to be there and be able to mesh with the other judges, you need to be there for maybe a week."

"What?" Will exclaimed.

Joyce held her hands up to calm him down. "It won't be that bad."

"I just started here last month. I don't have a week to give." He calculated the forty-plus hours a week he'd already been putting in and knew that time was still not enough. His cousins would be hovering like vultures if he left his throne for more than a few days.

"Think about how committed the family will see you are if you take the time to represent our products."

She had to go there. Will's weakness. His family's legacy was his kryptonite. Sales were down. People were losing interest in Ravens Cosmetics. They wanted something fresh and new. Well, if anyone could go to this Southwood and turn things around, it was him. "When do I leave?"

Armed with a suitcase filled with cosmetics, Zoe checked her bags at the counter at Miami International Airport on Tuesday morning and got herself cleared through security. If she was lucky, her plane would be there, allowing her to board.

This wasn't her first trip on a plane. She knew it was best to take a change of clothes in her carry-on. No matter how long or short the flight, Zoe always showered after traveling. For this two-hour flight, Zoe dressed in a pair of comfy boyfriend jeans, worn white canvas shoes and her favorite loose T-shirt, bedazzled in pink with Wear More Mascara across the chest. As she rounded the corner toward her terminal, she realized she had no such luck. And every seat in the waiting area was taken. Children pressed their faces against the windows, smudging the glass with their sticky hands as they watched the other planes taking off.

Zoe had no patience to deal with the man standing behind her she just caught checking out her rear end. The joker wasn't even embarrassed; he wiggled his brows at her and licked his lips. The only man on Earth, as far as Zoe was concerned, who was allowed to lick his lips at her was LL Cool J.

"Miss Baldwin?" Will Ravens closed the gap from the private area to where she stood. "I thought I recognized you."

For a moment, Zoe forgot how to speak. Will Ravens, the man she needed to hate right now, stood before her in a pair of jeans and a fitted green V-neck shirt, causing her to melt into a puddle as he smiled at her. Dark hairs were sprinkled across his sculpted jaw. A white sign in front of the blue terminal waiting room where he stood alone indicated the area was for passengers detoured from the hangar. Was the private area for other jets, full planes or those under construction? Zoe's mind raced with questions. Why was he here? Where was he going? How did she look? "Mr. Ravens?"

"Is everything okay?" he asked with a tilt of his head.

Blinking and then nodding, Zoe laughed lightly. "Oh, yes, sorry. I must have airport brain."

"That's a thing?" Will asked with a crooked grin.

"Yeah, you know, when you have fear of flying." Zoe inclined her head in the direction of the crowded terminal. "Not necessarily with the whole airplane thing, but who you're going to end up sitting with."

Will glanced in the direction she'd indicated and Zoe's eyes followed. Without any regard for the man currently standing next to her, another stranger blew a kiss at her. "Is it safe to assume you don't want to end up sitting next to him?"

An Elvis Presley snarl stretched Zoe's top lip as she shivered. "Exactly."

"You could end up sitting next to me," said Will.

Zoe gave her undivided attention back to the hunk before her. "Like *you* would fly commercial."

"I've flown commercial before." Will frowned. The corners of his lips turned upside down in the cutest way. "I wasn't born with a silver spoon in my mouth."

As she took a step backward, Zoe folded her arms across her chest and cocked one questioning brow. Everything about him screamed one percent.

Will pressed his hand against his heart and bowed his head. "For the record, I've been on the company plane just a few times."

"And today makes what? Your tenth time on your private plane?"

In response, Will nodded his dark head. "Every three commercial trips we get a bonus. We get to bring a guest with us. What do you say? Can I give you a lift?" The humorous tone matched the smirk on his face.

Uncrossing her arms, Zoe shook her head to the side. "What do I say to what?"

"A ride, you know, to wherever you're going."

It was as if he was asking her to share his cab with her or giving her a lift from the grocery store. So simple. So easy. *So tempting.* "You don't even know where I'm going."

At the most inconvenient time, a woman's voice came over the intercom. "All passengers heading for Atlanta, we will begin boarding in ten minutes."

"I'll take a wild guess and say you're headed to Atlanta."

The idea of squeezing into a seat next to either one of those two men, Will or the man who'd been behind her, did not sit well with Zoe. On the other hand, flying with Will might give her the chance to show off her work. "You can't be serious."

"But I am."

"I don't want to take you out of your way," Zoe said chewing on her bottom lip. So many images of having him her way entered her mind. "Where were you headed?"

"If I were to tell you, it wouldn't even matter. Just know that I am headed in the direction of Atlanta and I don't mind at all giving you a lift."

In truth, this deal had been sealed when Will broached the subject. But when one of the kids across the hall screamed he was going to be sick and proceeded to do so, Zoe was sold.

"Well—" Zoe hesitated with another gnaw on her bottom lip "—you wouldn't even have to take me all the way to Atlanta. My friend was going to pick me up and bring me down south."

Will stepped aside and waved his arm in the direction of the terminal. "Where exactly are you headed?"

Elated to not have to fly on the crowded plane, Zoe stepped forward into the blue area. "A little town called Southwood," she called over her shoulder. She walked a few more paces before she realized Will was not behind her. She turned around and found him standing in the same spot. "What's wrong?"

"Are you attending this Glitz-something pageant?"

A slow smile spread across Zoe's face. "What do you know about it?"

"My cousins, Joyce and Naomi, talked me into going. They said it would be good for business if I represented the company as a judge."

"Smart move," Zoe said with a slight nod of the head. Right now, hearing anything about the twins soured her thoughts. A month or two ago, Marcus had told her about the position at Ravens Cosmetics and got her hopes up. Zoe was supposed to have been a sure thing. Yet here she was, stuck at MIA, contemplating hitching a ride with the man who lacked the ability to see her talents. Zoe cleared her throat.

"I've got nothing but smart moves planned for the company," Will said.

Zoe felt the corners of her eyes tighten with a smirk. Her body leaned forward. She expected Will to add something along the lines of "when you join the team."

All she received was a sneer. "What do you know about the beauty industry?" Zoe boldly asked.

"I know I'm not going to let my family's legacy fail," he retorted.

Without him having to say the words, Zoe knew Will was not impressed with her work. Seemed like this week was going to turn out perfect.

When Will flashed a smile, her knees went weak again. According to Lexi's itinerary, they were going to be sequestered for almost a week. Zoe would be making over all of the contestants. One full week to prove to Will she'd be the perfect person for the CDD job.

A man wearing a dark suit and aviator glasses appeared at the entranceway of the door leading toward the plane. In a ripple effect, the man Zoe assumed was the pilot nodded his head at Will, Will returned the head nod and, in turn, inclined his head to Zoe. "There's my guy," Will said. "There's someone more important in the hangar…"

"You mean more than you?" Zoe gasped sarcastically, her hand clutched to her heart.

"Cute," he said with a sigh. "So, what's it going to be, Miss Baldwin?"

"I'll go," Zoe said hesitantly, "but understand that I am going to have to owe you a ride."

The way Will raised his brows made her shiver with wanton promise. She pressed her lips together and shook her head. Flashes of her naked body curled up in a mixture of his arms and tangled sheets entered her mind. Heat began to boil underneath her shirt. "You know what I'm talking about."

"I certainly do," Will said.

The only thing Zoe could do was pray Will hadn't

felt the dampness on her lower back as he pressed his hand there to guide her across the windy airport strip toward the plane. Once they boarded, Zoe realized they were the only ones taking up space on the twenty-two pearl-leather seats. A flight attendant, dressed in a cute thigh-length lavender button-down dress with gold and pearl accessories—staple colors of Ravens Cosmetics packaging—greeted them as they boarded. She lifted her arm effortlessly to point in the direction of all the available seats.

Ahead of Will, Zoe glanced in the direction of the restrooms. Did the mile-high club count if they were the only ones on the plane? She jumped when Will touched the back of her shoulders. His thumb circled the nape of her neck.

"We have our pick," said Will, "but these are my favorites." His gentle touch against her skin guided her to a set of seats facing one another with a round coffee table between them. She imagined all the business deals made over that table.

"Thank you again, Mr. Ravens," Zoe replied with a curt nod of her head.

The perky flight attendant came over to take their order for drinks. Both of them asked for bottled water. When they were alone again, the captain began to take off. Out of the window, Zoe watched her plane still sitting on the runway. Will sat across from her. His long legs stretched out and their knees touched. Zoe sat straighter and crossed her legs together at the ankles.

"Having doubts?" Will's deep voice brought Zoe out of her zone. She blinked into focus and he explained further. "About coming on the plane with me?"

Zoe kept a straight face and led things in a professional direction. "I do appreciate this. I'm honored to have another chance to speak with you."

"Are you now?" Will asked with a raised brow.

"Of course," said Zoe, reaching for her phone from her purse. Her fingers slid across the screen to bring it to life. "This gives me more time to show you what you may not have seen in my portfolio."

"And give you an advantage over the other artists?"

A cold chill rushed down Zoe's spine and she offered a tight smile. She slid the phone back in her purse. "Have you ever been to Southwood before?"

"Can't say that I have," said Will, crossing one long leg over the other.

Zoe inhaled deeply at the way his thighs rippled beneath the denim. "Well, you're in for a treat. It's like taking a walk into history."

"Uh," Will started, "our history in the South?"

"Just wait and see."

"I take it you've been there?"

Nodding, Zoe grinned. "I spent my summers there and the last two years of high school."

"Your parents aren't together?"

No one ever asked about her parents. When working, she did most of the talking with her clients. Zoe usually eased models' fears of being in front of a particular photographer or clients' nervousness about the events Zoe was getting them ready for. To them, she was a machine. Will made her feel like a person. "They're together in a sense," she answered, and then nodded. "They never divorced, but they never truly lived together. My mother, Jamerica, is from Trinidad and she couldn't stand being away from the islands for too long. And, well, my dad preferred to be landlocked."

The corners of Will's mouth turned down. "Does he still live there now?"

"Worried about meeting my father?"

Will uncrossed his legs and leaned forward with his elbows on his knees. "I haven't done anything to you yet to be worried about."

A chill of excitement ran down Zoe's spine. What kinds of things would he do? Just the thought of his lips on her collarbone steamed her throughout her body. Even with her last official relationship, Zoe never daydreamed about what his lips would do. Shaun Jackson had been sweet, hunky and driven, but never enough for Zoe to get distracted from her own goals. This was a perfect example of why she carried a change of clothes with her in her carry-on bag. Zoe cleared her throat and tried to stay focused on the prize. What she wanted was the Creative Design Director position. She was not going to sleep her way to the top. She'd never had to before, and she wasn't going to start now.

"Alright, I'll drop it for now," Will said, interrupting her thoughts. "Will you be staying at your father's?"

Zoe shook her head. "Dad is away this summer. But, even so, I won't be staying there."

An inquisitive brow rose on Will's face. "No?"

"I heard that everyone involved with the pageant is going to be at Magnolia Palace."

"Is it someplace special? My cousins gushed when they told me about it."

"I am biased," Zoe began, a smile touching her face at the vast memories. "My folks met there when my mother was on a photo shoot. He proposed there, as well."

A sad sigh struggled in the back of Zoe's throat. She wanted what her parents had, minus the not living together. A long-distance relationship worked for them, but not her. As much as work kept Zoe busy, she didn't have time to nurture a relationship. Soon Zoe was going to want someone she could wake up to every day. Work had always been important and the proverbial *someday* lurked around the corner. Once she got the position at Ravens Cosmetics, Zoe planned on settling down. There were a few potential men in Miami, but no one worth giving up her goals for. Zoe needed a man as driven as herself.

"Well, I can't wait to see this place," Will concluded with a dazzling grin.

"Me, either," Zoe beamed. "During high school, Magnolia Palace sort of crashed and burned. But recently it was bought and renovated. I'm excited to see the changes and I can't wait to walk along the pier."

For a moment, Zoe held her breath. Given her creative job as a makeup artist, she lived in a fast-paced world. People wanted fast-paced things. A walk along a pier on a lake was not fast-paced.

Will nodded his dark head. "Well then, I am excited to see it and take this walk, as well."

A spark went off in Zoe's heart and another heat wave of desire coursed through her veins. What she needed more than anything was a splash of cold water across her face. Maybe taking this flight had been a bad idea after all. With a combination of these close quarters, Will's sexy smiles and not having sex in six months, her senses were on high alert. Still determined to see Will as her future boss, Zoe rose from her seat and started to move around the coffee table. At the most inconvenient time, the small aircraft hit an air pocket, sending Zoe stumbling right into Will's lap.

Graciously he opened his arms and accommodated her on his lap until the turbulence ceased. One of his hands braced her back and the other secured her thighs against him. Another jolt sent Zoe's arms flailing and, rather than hit him in the face, she wrapped them around his shoulders, bringing them nose to nose. Zoe inhaled deeply. One millimeter closer and their lips would be touching.

"Ahem." The flight attendant cleared her throat from her end of the plane. Zoe scrambled out of Will's lap and headed off to the bathroom. "The captain sends his apologies and wanted to let you know we'll be landing shortly."

Zoe closed the door behind her and an overhead light turned on. A deep red tint stained her cheeks. What had she almost done? She wanted the job. But not this way. This really was going to be the longest week ever.

Chapter 3

Check-in at the Magnolia Palace started at noon. Thanks to the fact that there had been no more turbulence, Will and Zoe were able to land practically in the backyard of Southwood, Georgia, and arrive in town extra early. Dominic Crowne had moved his business, Crowne Motors Restoration, here because he wanted a quiet place in the country. Dominic restored classic cars and test-drove them on his private track; he imported foreign vehicles, as well. Dominic and Will had pledged together at Stanford. They were friends as freshmen, but brothers by graduation.

When Will had played in Germany with the Teufels, Dominic came to every match when he was in town. After Will returned to the States with the Texas Raiders, Dominic had come to his matches whenever he was close enough. In fact, Dominic was at the game when

Will had failed to qualify for the World Cup team. The limp was faint, the scar healed, but the painful disappointment of his lifelong dream being taken away from him would remain.

Will's thoughts turned to the passenger seated comfortably next to him in the shiny black 1963 Maserati 3500 Vignale Spyder, loaned to him by Dominic. Ever since Zoe had plopped down on his lap during the turbulence, Will couldn't get her out from under his skin. Even while teasing him, she dazzled him with her smile. It was too early to tell if the smile she offered was from the woman he met at the elevator or the woman who wanted the position.

"And you're telling me you don't come from a privileged background?" Zoe was saying, apparently oblivious to the way she made him feel. Her arms were folded across her chest, making her cleavage more noticeable in her V-neck T-shirt.

Will glanced over and felt the tension in his shoulders leave at the sight of her easy smile. "Hey, membership has its privileges."

Zoe's lashes fluttered against her high cheekbones. The sun spilled through the windshield and highlighted the gold tones of her dark skin. A pair of gold earrings highlighted her cheekbones. "I guess I can't complain too much. I might still be sitting on the plane in coach if it weren't for you."

"A compliment?" Will clutched his heart with his left hand before flicking the left turn signal to turn into the Magnolia Palace, as the voice from the GPS on his phone instructed.

"You're funny."

"I'm hoping you will get the chance to see I am a fun guy," Will said.

"What does it matter?"

Will slowed the vehicle down. "I am not crazy for thinking about the moment we first met at the elevator, Zoe."

"Well…" Zoe's voice was slow and hesitant. She chewed her bottom lip and cut her eyes toward the passenger-side window. "Maybe not completely crazy."

"How about I save you the trouble of trying to impress me with your work? I have major plans for Ravens Cosmetics and after our interview I believe your work is what I'm looking for. Why let our creative differences get in the way?" Will asked, and Zoe's mouth gaped open once again. A jolt of energy streamed through him. He was not his brothers, but he sure did sound like them. He didn't like the idea of mixing business and pleasure for a night or two. Will differed from his brothers that way. He wanted permanent, but was it possible Zoe was the one? "Okay, I'll back off. I'm the crazy person."

The tires crunched over the unpaved red clay driveway. Blooming magnolia trees lined the way up to the hotel.

"Please don't take this the wrong way," Zoe finally said. "But when I met you that morning, we probably could have made a go of things. Honestly, I thought you were a model and I was willing to give up my rule about dating clients."

"And now?"

Zoe shook her head from left to right. "Now, no way. You're going to be my boss."

"You don't have the job yet," Will said, raising his brows. He was turned on by her confidence.

"I will." Zoe sighed. "It was meant for me to work at Ravens Cosmetics."

"Oh, really now?" Will drawled and shook his head. "Did you see us together in your crystal ball?"

"The comedian again," Zoe retorted with a bored yawn. "I may tell you about it one day. Until I decide to share with you, you need to get used to the idea of us being nothing more than employer and employee."

That idea didn't appeal to Will. The hour and a half they'd been together already hadn't been enough. Maybe he should have flown into Atlanta to give them more time to get to know each other on the way down to Southwood. On the other hand, if by any miracle Will changed his mind about Zoe's work, they would end up working together. The last thing he needed was future tension between the two of them over a fling. With half the cousins tired of the business, and Donovan's trysts, Will didn't need the hassle. "Think you can at least settle on us being professional friends?"

There had been many times over the last month when Will resented having this CEO position. Now was one. But if Zoe only wanted to remain friends, he'd respect that. Hopefully there'd be plenty of cold water in this Magnolia Palace.

The Magnolia Palace sat on ten acres of lush green land, embraced by thick weeping willows in the back and strong magnolia trees that lined the paved circular driveway, which ended in front of the steps of the white plantation-style home. Four white columns reached from the wraparound porch to the second floor and up to where there seemed to be a balcony at the top of the roof. Someone stood at either of the long slit glass panes on both sides of the massive black double front doors.

It amazed Will how quickly the business mentality switched on in his mind. As a businessman realizing that the majority of his cosmetics were used in magazine editorial pieces, Will immediately thought this place would be the perfect background for a print layout. He scolded himself for thinking of work. Finally he understood what his parents meant by not letting it consume him. After seeing what the business did to his siblings, his father had tried to dissuade his children out of participating in the company. But it was in their blood. And when Will's brothers and sisters learned of their stake in the company, wild horses couldn't have kept them away. His parents might have sent him away to special soccer camps and facilities, but eventually, Will ended up at Ravens Cosmetics. And, yes, it was consuming his life. At least there was a bit of a break right now—sort of. He liked loud noise and the busy life. But he guessed for one week he'd be able to tough it out.

From the way his cousins described what his time in Southwood would be like, he'd assumed he would be stuck in a room watching pageants on television to get caught up. One look at the sprawling grounds and Will longed to stretch out in one of the hammocks and read a book. Although Will hated to admit it, he was looking forward to spending a week here and discovering all about the South. Even though Miami was in the south of Florida, it was not *the South*.

Relaxation called his name. As he thought about sleeping in, his attention turned toward the passenger

beside him who was wiggling in her seat with anticipation. How was he supposed to relax with her near
him? Hopefully she'd hang out with her friends and
stay out of his hair, although he fully expected her to
wear him down about his decision. Zoe was out of the
car before he placed the car in Park.

The massive doors of the B and B opened. Will expected a tuxedo-wearing butler to step out of the doors,
but instead, a tall African American woman with long
blond hair stepped onto the wraparound porch carrying
two mason jars of a brown iced beverage.

The moment the woman and Zoe locked eyes, Zoe
squealed and, out of the corner of his eye, he was sure
she pawed the ground like a bull and ran toward the
other woman. The woman turned to give the man
standing behind her the glasses and met Zoe at the
bottom step. The two embraced in a screaming hug.
Clearly they knew each other, Will thought to himself.
He'd grown up with sisters and knew how overly excited they were to see their friends. Will also knew it
was best to stand back and wait until the lovefest ended.
He clasped his hands behind his back and waited. The
man now holding the glasses stepped off the porch with
a chuckle and a shake of his head.

"I never get this kind of greeting when I come
home," he said, pushing one of the glasses into Will's
left hand.

The frosted glass cooled Will's palm. He stepped
forward and for a shake. "Will Ravens," he said.

"Hey, Will," said the man with the firm grip. "Stephen Reyes, husband of this squealing ball."

The squealing ceasing, the blonde woman stepped
to the side, and that's when Will noticed a very round

belly. Given the fact his sister had kids, Will guessed the woman was seven months along. She stood with her hand on her hip and glared at her husband. "Did you just call me a ball?"

"No, dear." Stephen winked before giving his wife his undivided attention. "Why would I say something like that?"

Zoe linked her arm with her friend's and dragged her over to where the two men stood. Stephen handed Zoe the other glass. "Will, this is one of my oldest friends, Lexi Pendergrass."

"Lexi Pendergrass *Reyes*," interjected Stephen with a dramatic roll of his *R*. "And why does she get to call you her oldest friend but I can't?"

"Because I know things." Zoe laughed. Will liked her laugh. It was light, bubbly and friendly. Zoe reached over and gave Stephen a hug. "As I was saying, this is Will Ravens."

Stephen leaned forward and whispered, loudly enough for Will to hear, "We'll have to have a real drink later, Zoe, so you can tell me what you know."

"Will Ravens?" Playfully, Lexi stepped between the pair and, instead of a handshake, gave Will a hug. "How on Earth did the two of you manage to arrive together?"

"I would have been here much later had Mr. Ravens not offered me a seat on his plane."

"The company's plane," Will clarified. "I spotted Miss Baldwin at the airport seconds before she was harassed by a…" He turned his attention to Zoe for a moment. "What would you call a wannabe LL Cool J?"

Zoe's eyes widened. A set of dimples popped up on her cheeks. "Exactly."

"Aren't you the superhero?" Stephen inquired with a humorous chuckle.

Lexi elbowed her husband in the ribs and kept talking to Will. "I cannot thank you enough for everything Ravens Cosmetics has done for the pageant. And for taking the time out of your schedule. I can't imagine coming into your position, you wanted to leave so quickly."

"Well, I'm sure you know how it is when Naomi and Joyce ask a favor," Will began with a chuckle. He took a sip of his beverage. The thick syrup coated his throat and he realized it was sweetened tea.

"Asked, or more or less forced you?" Lexi joked, hitting the nail on the head. "I know how they can be, so I have to apologize. I'm sure you're out of your element."

Beside him, Zoe snickered.

"I want to learn every nook and cranny of Ravens Cosmetics. If coming to your lovely city is one of the tasks, well, it's worth it." Will cleared his throat. "Besides, I'm always up for a challenge."

Lexi offered one last hug and pulled away. "Good. Let me show you guys to your rooms. Stephen's cousin just bought and renovated the place. I've got everyone working on the pageant sequestered here for the week, so I'm playing hostess today."

It was on the tip of his tongue to ask if that was necessary, but any words were lost as they followed Stephen and Lexi into the foyer of the Magnolia Palace. The black hardwood floors absorbed their footsteps. Adorning the walls were old pictures of a family—perhaps the people who originally owned the home. There were two large rooms, one on either side of the hallway. One appeared to be a sitting room, the other a library filled with shelves of leather-bound books. They traveled farther toward the wide-set staircase, which curled and broke off in two different directions. Light spilled in from the upstairs balcony over the crystal chandelier, creating a prism effect against the white walls.

Will's room was upstairs near the back of the house. The ceilings were high and the walls painted a pale blue. More portraits hung from the walls in gold frames. He went inside to decompress, but got caught up in the view from the balcony. The lush green backyard was neatly trimmed. A wooden path led to the docks, which jutted into the deep blue water of a round lake surrounded by more trees. Off to the side, on land, Will spotted a hammock and visualized himself in it with his shoes off and curled up with Zoe.

Will scolded himself for his obsession with Zoe. She'd made it clear she did not want to get involved with him. And she was right. Will needed to focus on the future of the company. He willed himself not to fall for the pretty smiles. Pretty faces were a dime a dozen and usually accompanied by a motive. Zoe was no different. Still, though, the confidence she'd exuded in the car was impressive as well as a turn-on.

This was not Will at all. He expected this lustful behavior from Marcus and Donovan. Will prided himself on being in control, but with Zoe, common sense went out the window. Did he dare hurt her feelings and let her know he did not see her in the future of Raven Cosmetics? Would it make her feel better to know he at least saw her in *his* future?

Thinking of her made him stiffen all over. He needed to splash some water over his face. Will moved over to the door he assumed would lead to the bathroom and yanked it open; a scream came from the other side. Upon further inspection he groaned. There stood Zoe with a fluffy blue-flowered towel wrapped around her silky dark brown skin. The sun filtering through the white-lace curtains highlighted the gold undertones of every curve.

"I guess Lexi forgot to mention the shared bathroom." Zoe recovered with an airy laugh.

Damn, this was going to be the longest week ever.

No amount of hot water could wash off the humiliation of her potential boss walking in on her almost naked body. How was she going to look him in the eyes now in a potential board meeting? After a disastrous moment before her after-travel shower, Zoe changed into black leggings and a black-and-white-checkered T-shirt long enough to cover her behind. She headed downstairs to the patio with her tablet in hand, hoping to take some amazing photographs of the setting sun. Because she and Will had gotten there early, the other guests hadn't arrived yet. Dinner was in an hour and a half, giving Zoe much-needed time to get reacquainted with the pier. She trotted barefoot across the grass to the dock, where the afternoon sun warmed the wooden planks.

Bright shades of orange, red and yellow smeared the horizon. With her breath caught in her throat, Zoe stood at the curve of the railing, in the same spot her father had knelt to propose to her mother. With the Magnolia Palace reopened, this would be the perfect spot for her father to re-propose to her mother. Zoe smiled at the horizon with excitement. She snapped a few pictures before deciding to return to the back porch.

The oversize white swings—and the fact that a producer friend had just sent her an advance copy of a superhero movie she'd worked on—helped put pep in her step. There was nothing better than the good people winning.

Zoe turned to head back to the porch, but she careened into a hard body. As she bounced backward with a prolific apology, the wooden rails creaked. The last thing she needed to do was fall into the water with her tablet. She hadn't even sent any of the files to her Cloud. She welcomed the strong arm around her waist and reached for the impeccably muscled arms.

"Whoa," a deep and now-familiar voice said into her ear.

"Mr. Ravens," Zoe gasped. Once her eyes began to focus, she narrowed in on his lopsided smirk.

"Let's see, we've shared a plane, shared a seat on a plane and I've walked in on you taking a shower."

Heat burned her cheeks. Zoe held her index finger up to stop and correct him. "Almost in the shower."

Will inclined his head. "Okay, almost. However, I do believe we are beyond the formalities. Please call me Will."

Zoe bit the right corner of her bottom lip. "Alright, Will. You have to call me Zoe."

"It's a pleasure, Zoe."

He had no idea what a pleasure it was to still be in his arms. Zoe cleared her throat. No matter what, she was going to be the Creative Design Director for Ravens Cosmetics. She needed to stop these romantic fantasies about her future boss. Taking a step away, Zoe waved her right arm at the water.

"What do you think of the view, Will?" Zoe asked with a shaky voice. "Beautiful, right?"

"You're absolutely right," Will said.

Out of the corner of her eye, she noticed he hadn't stopped looking at her. She bit her bottom lip again to keep from further blushing. The tactic didn't work and the heat from the sun was nothing compared to the flush on her face.

Will's brows rose, his left eye half winking. "Are you okay?"

"Oh, I'm fine," Zoe recovered quickly. "Were you just on an evening walk?"

"Sort of. I came to tell you your bags arrived."

"Thank you." Zoe breathed a sigh of relief. "Dare I ask how you managed that?" Zoe had been concerned about leaving her bags on the scheduled flight. But Will had said he'd take care of it and clearly he had. She'd expected to have her bags by tomorrow. This was better news. Zoe didn't like to be away from her makeup for too long.

"You don't want to know."

Zoe rolled her eyes and playfully pushed his biceps, hesitating for a moment at the way the muscle flexed. She wanted to keep her hand there, maybe let her fingers trail against his pecs, but that would be weird, especially since she'd made it clear they were not going to act on any impulse they may have. "Don't tell me you're going to have to take a pretty flight attendant out on a date all because of lil' ole me."

Why did she say that last line in her Southern belle accent? And, as her spine straightened, Zoe questioned her sanity. Did she seriously just curtsy? Judging from the strangled laugh escaping Will's throat, she guessed she did. "Sorry," Zoe coughed. "I don't know what's come over me."

"You're back home." Will provided an answer.

It wasn't the answer Zoe wanted to hear but she'd go with it. Better go with his than the naughty thoughts circling around in her mind.

"Well, thanks again for getting my bags to me."

"Not a problem," he answered.

They both started walking back toward the house. Zoe was well aware of how close they were to each other. Their forearms touched. Her fingers itched to link with his but she managed to control herself.

The only car parked off the circular driveway was the one they had driven down in. Lexi had left, as expected. She had her own home to tend to. From what Zoe gathered, Stephen's cousin had purchased the land and the Magnolia Palace and recently finished the remodeling—a job well done, Zoe thought to herself. But she had not seen the hotelier.

"Any sign of the rest of the guests?" Zoe asked.

"Stephen left to pick up someone just before I came outside. Are you starving? I'm sure I saw a basket of fruit on the kitchen table."

Zoe scrunched up her face. "I think I may have a bag of microwavable popcorn in one of my bags."

Now it was Will's turn to scrunch up his face. "Microwavable popcorn is not good for you."

"Are you telling me you happen to have popcorn kernels and an air machine in your bags?" Zoe teased, pushing his arm once more. Will's large frame didn't budge. "Leave me and my popcorn alone. I'm going to watch a movie."

"Yes," he said seriously. When her eyes shot up in

surprise, Will flashed a killer, million-watt smile. "Of course I'm kidding. What movie are you planning on watching?"

Zoe glanced down at her tablet. She preferred to keep her love of superheroes a secret. After getting teased in junior high school, Zoe learned to keep it to herself. On some websites, she'd never found anyone who shared her love but rather more or less mocked it. So she'd learned to stifle her love and watch in secret. "Oh, I did a makeup job a few years ago in college for a buddy of mine who ended up going off to the military. He finally finished putting this low-budget CGI film together and well, he sent me a copy."

They reached the back porch. Will pressed his hand against Zoe's lower back and guided her up the wide steps. Their strides matched. All too aware of the heat from his touch, Zoe prayed he didn't feel the sweat drizzling down her back.

"So, you're a movie makeup artist, as well?"

"I am extremely talented, Mr. Ravens. I can beat anyone's face," she said. Will stopped walking, clamping his hand on her shoulder. To most people, Zoe had to explain that beating a face meant putting on makeup. As CEO of a cosmetics company, he surely knew this information, which only meant his frown was for not using his given name. "Sorry, *Will*." Zoe shook her head and laughed.

"What do you mean, 'beat'?"

Zoe stood still on the top step. "You're not serious, are you?"

Will pointed his finger at her and let out a laugh. "Gotcha there."

A slow and unsure chuckle escaped Zoe's mouth.

For some reason, she didn't believe him. Was it possible for a CEO of a cosmetics company to not know what *beat* meant? In keeping up with the trends, someone should have taught Will the lingo. Maybe believing he didn't would ease her irritation at not landing the job right off the bat. Given he was going to be her boss one day, Zoe decided to take his word for it—for now.

"Why do I have a feeling I'm going to have to quiz you on cosmetics?" Zoe asked.

"What do I get when I get one hundred percent?"

With a roll of her eyes, Zoe laughed and shook her head. "Do we need to revisit our conversation in the car?"

"No, ma'am," Will said, holding his hands up in surrender.

Zoe moved over to the oversize swing. She patted the spot beside her. "Come sit. You can see my work in motion."

For the next half hour Zoe kept her tablet rested on Will's firm thigh while they watched the movie. Their breathing became synchronized and they laughed at all the right parts. A few "that's awesome work"s and "great job"s slipped out from the CEO. Zoe beamed. And then the part came where Zoe appeared on camera. She was just an extra painted in blue. The camera zoomed in on her and Will swiped his finger against the pause button.

"That's you."

"How did you know?" Zoe asked. In the film she wore a pair of yellow cat eyes.

Will's fingers pressed against her image on the screen. "I'd recognize those cheekbones anywhere."

"Nice eye," said Zoe, lips pressed together as she fought a smile.

"So, you're an actress, too?"

"Oh, no," Zoe said scooting away. "In truth, I knew this film was low-budget. It was a job for a friend, and in return I got to live out my dream to be a superhero." She covered her mouth, not believing she'd divulged her big secret.

Will turned in the bench to get a better look at her. "You're kidding me, right?"

"No, I'm not." Zoe stood up and covered her heart with her right hand and raised her left hand in the air. "I confess I am a superhero geek."

In surprise, Will stood up and took her left hand in his. He bowed his head and brought the back of her hand to his lips. Zoe's right hand moved from her heart to the back of her neck where she was beginning to sweat in this sweltering heat. "You're not going to laugh at me?"

"Laugh?" Will shook his head. "Hell, I might just ask you to marry me right here and now."

Chapter 4

The credits at the end of the film raced as fast as Will's heart had during the movie. Arms folded across his chest, Will spent the entire time trying not to make physical contact with Zoe in fear of her taking his failed attempt of a joke of a proposal too seriously. Zoe's stare, intent on her monitor, gave no indication. Will had battled himself internally. A marriage never survived on a mutual love for superheroes. His doubts of Zoe's ability to work at the company subsided, knowing about her penchant for good and evil—the epic battle in most comics. Spotting the evilness of his anti-cousins was a necessity. Will never played around with marriage. He'd managed to never lead on any soccer groupie with words implying a future with him. He planned to marry one day, just not today. Will's mild panic attack subsided with the arrival of the rest of the guests.

Lexi had made sure there were enough judges for her pageant. Will, the head of a major cosmetic company. There were two beauty queens, one former and one current. The guest celebrity judge was none other than infamous model Sasha Foxx, once a child actress, now a woman who'd grown up in front of the camera—and was someone all the men at Magnolia Palace seemed to have had a crush on at one time or another. Will was glad he wasn't the only male at this event. Kahlil Kane, heir to the Kane Diamonds empire, was serving as a judge, as well. Kahlil's family owned several high-end jewelry stores in Miami, New York City and LA.

The men bonded quickly with the new owner of Magnolia Palace, Ramon Torres, a cousin of Stephen's, over a few bottles of Torres Rum. It was nice to hang out with cousins who got along rather than fighting all the time and weren't in competition with each other. Will spent the evening in the study with the cousins instead of in the room right next door to Zoe. She was too much of a distraction and she'd made her intentions for their relationship—or lack of one—known.

Respecting what Zoe wanted was hard as hell, especially knowing she was perfect for him. How many other women who loved superheroes and knew more about the cosmetic business than him was Will going to come across who were as beautiful as Zoe? None.

So the price he had to pay for avoiding Zoe all evening long was a splitting hangover.

According to Lexi's itinerary, the judges were scheduled for a tour of the historic downtown area. With the pageant being held at the theater on the property of Magnolia Palace, the contestants needed to re-hearse without the judges around or spotting them on their way to the theater next door. Since the contestants were all local ladies from Southwood, housing was not an issue. Lexi insisted her staff enjoy the Magnolia Palace. The tour got the officials out of the place so they couldn't be accessed by the contestants or develop a bias toward anyone in particular.

As he got ready for the day, Will tried to talk himself into being excited over the tour, but he could feel the skepticism as he showered. Dressed in a pair of khaki cargo shorts and a red-and-blue-striped polo, Will thought of his family and headed out of his room.

Call him biased, but Will was partial to Overtown. His great-great-grandparents had moved down south to work on the railroads with industrialist Henry Flagler. Back then, African Americans lived separately from their white coworkers. Fanny Ravens, Will's great-grandmother, had had the great insight to bottle her mother-in-law's products and travel to Miami to sell them.

Where his grandparents were raised was a historic city. Before the big highway boom, their successful business had stood on West Second Avenue. Back in its heyday, Will's great-grandparents opened their homes to the women and men in their neighborhood. They offered a shave or beard trim for husbands and pin-curled hairstyles paired with the perfect shade of red lipstick for wives when they needed to get ready for picnics, outings or even for events held at the Lyric Theater. After World War II ended, many celebrities stayed at the Mary Elizabeth Hotel. Knowing guests at the hotel were going to need beauty supplies, Joe Ravens made a deal to have their products in every room. A round of applause brought Will out of his stroll down memory lane.

Zoe stood in the center of a group, pressing the pad of her thumb against one woman's lips. "There you go," Zoe cooed. "Now you can go all day and drink whatever. I promise that lipstick won't smear."

"And my lashes won't smear against my eyelids." The woman pressed what looked like a spoon into Zoe's hand. "You're a genius, Zoe. Thanks for this beatdown," the woman said.

The terms women used for their makeup and outfits were violent. Beatdown? *There was that word again.* Will shook his head and tried to recall the woman's name. Mack, or Makenzie, or Kenty. She'd come in with Ramon and helped out with dinner and was friendly. Will remembered her mentioning that Lexi put her in charge.

"No problem, Kenzie." Zoe stepped back to admire the work she'd done. From the back, it appeared she wore a blue flowered sundress and a pair of blue flats.

"There you are, Will," Kenzie said, eyes wide and long lashes fluttering. "Would you like some coffee or breakfast before we leave for the tour?"

All eyes turned to Will. The women and men—members of the talent search, directors, the emcee, and various coordinators—waited for him to answer, as they clearly had been waiting for him to come downstairs all morning long. Shoulder bags were hiked up on the ladies' shoulders. The men not watching Kenzie were pacing.

"I'm fine," Will said, clearing his throat. "I apologize for keeping you waiting."

"You're good." Kenzie ambled over to him and grabbed him by the elbow. "We already paired off—except for Zoe, she was a little late, as well."

The rest of the group began to move out the doors while Zoe lingered behind. This morning Will had made sure to listen for noise in their joint bathroom so he wouldn't walk in on her. What had kept her lagging this morning? Will watched Zoe as he made his way to her, taking in the perfectly round bun at the top of her head. "So, you were late also? Hmm, did you oversleep?"

Zoe shrugged her shoulders and unapologetically said, "Never question a woman with perfect winged eyeliner about being late."

"I have no idea what you just said," Will admitted, smitten with her confident voice, "but it sounds nice." He kept his voice on an even keel and made a mental note of her vast experience, which reminded him to keep his mind and hands off Zoe.

Like she often did, Zoe gawked at him, leaving him feeling either the butt of an inside joke or worse, inferior. "And you're the CEO of Ravens Cosmetics?"

At headquarters, Eva and Dana bailed him out when it came to terminology. Naomi and Joyce prepped him with flash cards before big meetings. In Southwood he was on his own. A nervous chuckle escaped his throat. "I see I'm not going to get away with much with you. What was this beatdown you gave?"

"You're representing the company as one of the judges?"

Inadequacies washed over him. The pressure reminded him of his first penalty kick. Will had eventually gotten over it and he'd get over not knowing terms. He could learn. "I am."

"Well, you'll see my beatdown there." Zoe winked. Then she let him off the hook with a shake of her head. "Okay, fine, a beatdown is when a woman's makeup is flawless, which is what my work is. Your company's products and my skills…" She shook her head again, but this time let out a low whistle.

"Ravens Cosmetics has been sponsoring this pageant for a while now."

The corners of Zoe's lips tugged upward. "You guys donate a lot of materials."

"We do."

Zoe lifted a lavender tube with RC printed in gold. "Yes. And do you know what this is?"

Confident after remembering what Kenzie said, Will nodded. "Well, it's our famous lipstick line, Much Needed. You're holding Much Needed Nude, of course."

"I…" Zoe said as she pressed the tube against her chest. The dramatic effect was to possibly show her confidence, but all Will saw was the swell of her breasts underneath the dress. "*I* am what makes this lipstick famous. When I blend this nude with a shade from RC's Get line, Get Him Back, the deep, winey red mixed with nude gives it a blackberry color that makes for a sensual lip."

"Interesting use of our products." Will grinned when she nodded in approval. He admired her. "And that's a good reason to keep you around, isn't it."

"That, and you need my insight on what products and colors to keep. You guys discontinued this merlot color last year, so I make a mental note to check out all the beauty supply stores and drug stores in every town I'm working in to buy every tube I come across."

Another reason RC needed a Creative Design Director. He needed a better idea of what needed to stay and go. "Duly noted. Low sales of Get Him Back forced us to cut back on the product. But I like your concoction."

"You need to keep that in mind when you're going over your list of interviewees. What was I? Number six?" Zoe winked.

"Actually you're a ten," Will said as he wiggled his brows at her.

A horn sounded outside and her gold hoops jingled as she bobbed her head back and forth and said, "We need to get going before Kenzie has a fit."

"She scares me," said Will. He ambled down the steps and extended his elbow for Zoe to take.

Zoe accepted his gesture, wrapping her blue-polish-tipped fingers against his skin. An image popped into Will's mind, one of Zoe touching him this same way, only with her wearing a white dress and him a tuxedo.

"You should be scared of her. Kenzie used to be the head cheerleader for Southwood High. She is used to commanding large crowds of people to having spirit."

"Ah, Southwood High," Will joked. "Will we be visiting the school today on our tour?"

"Probably."

The bright sun accosted his eyes. Will blinked several times, and while he waited for his eyes to adjust, the sweet scent of blooming magnolias filled the air. When his eyes cleared, all the faces of the guests peered out the van's window at the two of them. He felt the flex of excitement when Zoe's hand twitched.

Ramon Torres stepped out of the driver's side and lifted his aviator glasses. "You folks are welcome to ride with us, but Will, man, I think with your height you might be a little uncomfortable in the back."

The last thing he wanted to do was make someone else switch seats. Will turned his head toward the spot where the Maserati sat parked under a magnolia tree. He turned back to Zoe. "You're familiar with the area in case we get lost while following them, right?"

There was a slight rise and fall of her breasts as Zoe gulped. "What?"

"How 'bout we follow you all?" Will asked Ramon, who sent a head nod as an answer.

So much for trying to keep his distance from Zoe, Will thought. "I hope your heart wasn't set on driving in the van."

Zoe chewed on her bottom lip before rolling her eyes. "Fine, but don't try that old trick of running out of gas on a country road."

The warm air filled his lungs when he took in a deep breath at the sight of her long legs in her dress as she wiggled away. "Yeah, well, so far *every* road around here is a country road."

"Cute," Zoe called over her shoulder.

Will took a few long strides and caught up with her before she reached the passenger's side of the car. "Let me get that for you," he said, leaning down. The motion brought him closer to her ear. He was sure the sweet magnolia smell came from Zoe.

"Thanks," she said, glancing up.

And he was supposed to stay away from her? Even if Zoe earned the title of CDD, Will wasn't sure he would be able to. She was intoxicating. He inhaled once more before closing the car door after she was secured inside. Will walked around the car to get to his spot. The engine purred to life and he maneuvered down the drive to catch up with the van.

While Zoe pointed out various historic sites, Will enjoyed listening to her speak. During the interview she'd been so poised and proper. Right now, the country air relaxed her. She smiled and his world lit up. At one point while they were driving, Will almost ran off the road watching Zoe pull her thick black hair loose from the bun at the top of her head.

She asked for the top to be put down so they could enjoy the morning sun. The women he usually dated did not appreciate the top being down. And the women he'd dated in the past did not sing along with the songs on the radio. Zoe sang absentmindedly and made no apology when she got half the lyrics wrong.

Entertained, he followed the van closely and they stopped for lunch at a local restaurant. During the tour, they passed the First Bank of Southwood, which Lexi's parents owned. Like many businesses in Overtown, businesses in Southwood had begun due to the lack of support from other places. Will and Zoe passed Lexi's shop, Grits and Glam Gowns, in front of which a crowd of girls lined the sidewalk. Strange, considering it was a school day.

A lush park across the street from the shop was filled with kids kicking around a large red ball. Plastic lined a baseball diamond so the kids could slide into the bases for a large game of kickball–Slip 'N Slide. They drove by the courthouse and the town square where, according to legend, Confederate and Union soldiers decided to stop fighting and live peacefully together. The town had its history, Will thought. The best part of the tour was Zoe. She was a natural spokesperson, something to consider for the job.

After putting the car in Park under a shady weeping willow, Will strolled over to his personal tour guide's side of the car to let her out.

"Thank you," Zoe said breathlessly.

"You okay?"

"I just realized I missed breakfast this morning and got a little lightheaded." Zoe swooned and Will wrapped his arms around her waist. The move was innocent enough, but touching her evoked so much temptation. She was ill, and here he was thinking about pinning her against the car and kissing her.

They stood, eyes locked. Zoe lightly pressed her hands against his chest. She wasn't pushing him away, though, and the urge to take her hand in his to kiss the palm or her fingertips overcame him. Will closed his fingers around her left hand and started to bring it to his lips.

Some of the guests from the van were spilling out, glancing in their direction. His brain switched to business mode. If Zoe got the job, this embrace might be misconstrued. If she didn't get the job, she could sue for sexual harassment. Will finally understood her dilemma.

"Are you okay now?" Will asked her, reluctantly letting her go.

With pink cheeks, Zoe nodded. "Thanks for not letting me fall," she said.

"Never. Now let's get us something to eat before you faint."

* * *

Seated across the table from the world's most handsome man, Zoe tried to concentrate on what the other guests at the table were talking about. Most of the people invited were a part of the team Lexi had put together to help design, build and judge the upcoming Miss Southwood Glitz Pageant. Miss South Georgia opted to stay behind with her mother.

A few people included Zoe and Will in their here-and-there conversations, but Zoe was intrigued with Will's story, especially when he told the table about his former soccer career last year. Lexi was right. She stood corrected on her thoughts of him being a workaholic. It sounded like his travels were equally balanced with work and fun. Why was he still single?

"Can you sue for someone ruining your career?" Zoe asked him after a waitress came and set down a bowl of fudge brownies smothered in homemade vanilla ice cream from The Scoop. She'd originally declined dessert after having the shrimp po' boy sandwich, but seeing it on Will's plate drew her in. Using his forearms, Will pushed the bowl toward her and caused a thin wrinkle in the linen tablecloth. Picking up an unused spoon, Zoe dug in.

"Accidents happen," Will explained. "I skated by for years with no injuries to my knees. Soccer is not dangerous as, let's say, football, but we all go into the sport understanding what injuries we might incur. And getting hurt is part of the job."

The fudge from the brownie coated Zoe's tongue. She closed her eyes and slowly rolled them to the back of her head. The satisfying taste threatened to steal her senses. When she opened her eyes, Will sat across from her, amused. A grin spread across his face.

"Is it good?"

"You ought to dig in." Zoe nodded. "The Scoop makes the freshest ice cream ever, and because there are no additives, it melts quickly."

"I'm trying," Will said, scooping up a combination of ice cream, brownie, fudge and a cherry.

Their spoons played hockey for a minute over the last cherry and Zoe realized she'd been greedy. "I'm sorry. You can have my cherry."

At that, Will sat back in his seat and gave a throaty laugh. Heat warmed her face when she realized what she'd said. "Oh, my God, grow up," she ordered while trying not to laugh at her choice of words.

"Alright, I'll try."

"So tell me more about you and soccer," Zoe asked, taking another bite. "You said you played in Germany. Do you miss it?"

"I did when I first came back, but I missed my family more."

The family. Zoe knew all about them. If she told him she'd done a school project on them, would it freak him out? "Are you and your siblings close? I've hung out with Donovan and Marcus before. I never knew they had another brother."

With a scoop of brownie on his spoon, Will nodded. "We are. Not as close growing up as I would have liked."

"No?" Zoe forgot about the dessert between them. She leaned forward to listen.

"No, my folks didn't want me to fall into the RC trap of being seduced by the money, and when a coach saw the soccer potential in me, my parents pounced on the opportunity to have me trained."

"What did that mean?"

"I went to a boarding school that concentrated on sports for athletes. You know, the kind with no distractions." Will lowered his eyes to Zoe's cleavage.

Zoe sat upward. "So, no girls?"

"None."

He probably became some wild child in college, Zoe thought. "What did you do for prom?"

"What's a prom?" Will asked, and before Zoe could complete her gasp, he winked. "I'm kidding. My brothers and sisters went. I saw the pictures."

"You never went to prom?"

"What'd he say?" Kenzie asked from her end of the table.

Zoe leaned forward again and craned her neck to look at Kenzie. "He said he never went to the prom."

One of the men, a photographer named Gianluca, or Luke, as everyone called him, shook his head with an audible *tsk*. "What?"

The other staff all began to tell their stories. Prom had been a rite of passage for a lot of the men at the table. Considering the direction of the conversation, Zoe wondered about Will even further.

"It's no big deal." Even though he shook his head, the red tint creeping across Will's high cheekbones said something different.

The conversation began to turn to everyone's attire for prom. Zoe mouthed an apology and Will winked as an acceptance.

"How was your prom?" Will asked.

"Oh. I didn't go to prom." Zoe beamed. "Comic-Con was going on that weekend in California."

"I commend your priorities." Will nodded his head. She figured he would understand. Part of what she loved about her job was that pairing the right shade of lipstick with the right woman could really have that woman feeling like she had superpowers.

"My mother was not happy. She forced me to attend this party in Diego Martin called a *gradz*. It's a Trinidadian version of a prom."

Will scooped up some of the ice cream. "What happened? Didn't win prom queen?"

"That would require a tiara and a gown. The school had neither. But we celebrated the end of the year together and that counts, right?"

"This is the saddest story I've ever heard," Kenzie added.

Kathleen Royal, judge and the former Ms. Wheelchair South Georgia, nodded. "I had the best time at my prom. The best date, too."

The two ladies clinked their glasses together and Zoe shook her head. She caught Will's eye again and her heart raced.

"Do you recall your date?"

Zoe felt the coy smile spread before she could stop it. Will caught it as well, and began to grin.

"Clearly you remember him all too well."

"Now, now," Zoe said, shaking her head. Was that a bit of jealousy in his voice? "It was so long ago."

"Not that long, I'm sure," said Will. "Go ahead and tell me about you and Mr. Gradz. Let me guess, you were crowned the gradz queen."

In order to not answer, Zoe ate another bit of

brownie with the cream. Before she could take another bite, Will pressed his spoon down on hers and pinned the utensil against the white plate. "What?" Zoe asked, batting her lashes.

"No more dessert until you tell me about Mr. Gradz."

"Mr. Gradz," Zoe drawled out, "is doing just fine. I had lunch with him just the other day in LA."

"You flew out to see him?"

Zoe snickered at the frown across Will's face. "I flew out for a client's movie opening."

"Seriously?"

"I am a makeup artist, remember?"

Will shook his head as if he didn't believe her. "But you had our interview the other day."

Out of pride, Zoe inhaled deeply. "Believe it or not, I am in high demand. My job has me flying across the country on a weekly basis."

"And I thought the life of an athlete kept me on the road," said Will.

"Which is why I am looking for a permanent job." Zoe bit her bottom lip. "Sorry, I didn't mean to make that sound pitiful."

"No worries." Will's wink warmed her soul just as it had outside the restaurant. She still couldn't get over the fact she'd almost kissed him. Thank God he came to his senses. "It must be nice for your job to give you the ability to drop in on your exes."

Although she had no reason to explain further, Zoe felt she needed to. "He and his wife are lovely company."

"Wife, you say?" Will straightened up, then exhaled

a deep breath and his shoulders slumped. "That makes me feel better."

"About?"

"Never mind," Will mumbled and went back to the dessert. "Tell me how you got started in cosmetology."

Zoe licked some fudge off her bottom lip. "You have sisters, right?"

"I do, a set of twins."

"Did they ever use doll heads to practice fake makeup and hair?"

Will nodded. "I believe they each got dolls for Christmas."

"Well, I got one for Christmas as well, and by the following year I'd gone through at least twenty-five of them."

"I understand the doll's face is washable," said Will. He set his spoon down on the edge of the plate.

"They are, but after I got in trouble for using all of my mom's, I created my own makeup with food and crayons and used it on a few of them, and didn't know how to make it washable."

"Wait." Will pressed his hand on the table. "You made your own makeup as a kid?"

Didn't he read anything on her résumé? "I did get a Bachelor of Science in biochemistry and an MS in Cosmetic Chemistry." Zoe rolled her eyes. "I'd like to think my childhood products inspired the first vegan products."

"You believe in vegan products over animal-tested?" Will asked.

Didn't he know anything about cosmetology?

"I'm sure your mother was impressed and mortified. I'm imagining the ants and the smells from your food-based makeup."

A memory of her grandmother came to mind. She rarely shared personal stories, but something about being in her hometown was nostalgic. "My grandmother came to my rescue. She was so impressed with the way I perfected the 1940s eye that she brought me more doll heads and encouraged me to do everything under the sun in cosmetology, how a product is made, applied and sold."

Will shifted uncomfortably in his seat and Zoe chalked it up to their meals. They had eaten a lot this morning from a food truck. Zoe figured he would burn the meal off with the walking tour of the history of downtown Southwood later after lunch.

"Okay, so you've always loved makeup."

"I love pretty things," Zoe responded.

In his response to her, Will wiggled his brows. "What do you know? We're very similar."

It was on the tip of her tongue to remind Will she wanted him to be her boss, and that this flirting, no matter how exciting, was inappropriate. But, truthfully, she enjoyed it. She loved the thrill he gave her with each cocky grin.

"Alright, y'all—" Kenzie clapped her hands together "—it's time we get moving."

Saved by the Southern belle.

The tour ended just before dusk. Will parked the sports car in the same spot and, like earlier, came to Zoe's side of the vehicle to help her out. His Southern manners were in rare form, Zoe thought, as she watched him move in front of the hood of the car. Despite setting her own ground rules, she couldn't ignore the wave of excitement each time she got the chance to be alone with him. She'd be lying if she said she was looking forward to the barbecue this evening. It meant she'd have to share his company with the other guests and right now jealousy tingled her senses.

She'd noticed a hairstylist batting her lashes at Will after dinner. A jealous bug did bite her, but she ignored it. Zoe had an agenda. And, so far, she thought she was winning Will's favor. They stopped by Grits and Glam Gowns, and Zoe was able to point out the jobs she'd done in the photographs hanging from Lexi's walls. Will didn't say anything about her work, but he did nod his head in approval.

Zoe didn't care for Rebecca Smith, who was half trotting and half limping in her four-inch heels toward the car. Who wore heels like that on a walking tour?

A few years ago, Zoe and Titus had been at the same show. In most fashion shows, makeup was done first and then the model went over to the hairstylist. The designer collaborated with her crew to create the looks she wanted for each model. One of Zoe's models needed more attention. Titus, irritated at not getting more of the intricate work, spent his time backstage gossiping with Rebecca, who held the models in line for hair. With Zoe's models backed up and Titus's models ready, Titus had received the high praise for being professional. Rebecca never mentioned the true reason for the holdup.

"There you are, Will," Rebecca exclaimed breathlessly. Rebecca's attempt at wing-tip eyeliner was shaky at best, and in the sweltering heat, the liquid had also leaked onto her upper lid. Poor thing was oblivious. Zoe was almost tempted to pull her aside and let her know. "I was hoping to find you before we ate dinner."

Will extended his hand to help Zoe out of the car and kept a possessive hold on her hand as he spoke to Rebecca. "You found us," he said, with an emphasis on the *us*.

Rebecca gave Zoe a tight-lipped smile. Zoe dipped her head to hide her sarcastic grin. "I wanted to talk business with you."

Zoe disentangled herself from Will's grasp. "You two go on ahead. I'm going to change for the cookout." She excused herself and walked through the yard, through the hickory-scented air. What business did Rebecca have with Ravens Cosmetics? Zoe didn't realize she was stomping up the steps until Lexi, cuddled up on the hanging swing with her husband, glanced up and paused her conversation. Zoe waved an apology and headed upstairs. She had no business feeling any way over Rebecca. More than likely the hairstylist just wanted to be a part of RC, much like Zoe did. Who could knock her for trying?

Inside her room, Zoe debated whether or not to shower and erred on the side of caution. Being sweaty and standing near the lake water was a good way to get bitten by a mosquito. She slipped out of her sundress, padded barefoot into the bathroom and locked the door to Will's side of the room, just in case Will decided to do the same. Once in the shower, scrubbing her body with a loofah, Zoe thought more about what Rebecca and Will were talking about. She was in a sudsy lather and her mild rage grew as her mind wandered. What if Rebecca wanted the CDD position? What if Rebecca was willing to compromise her integrity? There was no what-if, Zoe thought bitterly.

Zoe got out of the shower, dressed in a pair of denim shorts and red crop top, and stomped down the stairs in her red flip-flops, already in a tizzy. Will stood by the grill, nursing a bottled beer, talking and watching Ramon maneuver a grilled chicken leg over to its other side. When he finished, Stephen stepped in with a basting brush and brushed a thick, deep-red sauce over the meat. Will nodded his head in approval.

"That's what I'm talking about," Will cheered the barbecuers.

"Oh, brother," Zoe groaned, walking over to them.

Kenzie came out of nowhere and linked her arm with Zoe's. "Men will bond over anything, from a sports show to meat."

"Not just meat, woman," Ramon said, puffing his chest and lifting his hands out to the sides. "We made fire." To celebrate Ramon's feat, Will and Stephen gave him high fives.

Zoe liked this side of Will. He wasn't as stuffy as he was with his brothers at Ravens Cosmetics, where he had to be the boss. He was himself…or, at least, she thought so. "What's on the grill?"

"I have some chicken now," said Ramon, "and there are burgers and hot dogs keeping warm in the oven."

"So, we're ready to eat?" asked Kenzie.

Ramon looked at the grill and nodded. "Yeah, let's start calling the guests down."

"Is there anything I can help with?" Zoe asked. "I learned from my grandmother that if I didn't bring anything to the party, the least I can do is help out."

"Yours, too, huh?" Will chuckled. "We may end up washing dishes together tonight."

Great, Zoe groaned inwardly, *a night of getting wet with Will.*

Chapter 5

The following morning, a wave of nerves washed over Zoe when she brushed her knuckles against the door to Will's room. She'd dressed in a pair of comfortable red workout shorts, a plain white T-shirt and some running shoes, and stepped out of her room into the hall to go right next door. She heard no movement but in a second Will opened the door.

Before leaving her room, Zoe had prepared a speech to coerce him into going off Lexi's daily schedule. Then he answered the door in a pair of black basketball shorts with the waistband hanging low on his hips, exposing those V-shaped muscles. Zoe's mouth went dry. She'd figured he was fine, but damn.

And the last thing she'd expected to find on his defined chest were the initials TOP over his heart. A woman? Zoe stamped down the surge of jealousy coursing through her veins.

"Hey," Will said, cocking his head to the side to catch her attention.

Zoe hadn't realized she was staring until her neck ached as she straightened it to meet his gaze. "Oh," Zoe began, "I, uh, I wanted to see if you wanted to go off course again today."

"You have something in mind?" Will asked and reached up for the top of the door frame. A natural bulge formed in his biceps. A natural moan threatened in the back of Zoe's throat.

"I thought you'd like to visit the Four Points Park today for a workout."

"A park?" A spark of excitement was in his voice.

"Well, yesterday you almost killed us while driving because you seemed so distracted by the view," Zoe teased.

Will began to rock back and forth, his arms still holding the top of the door frame. Now all Zoe could see was the way the muscles in his legs flexed. She gulped once more. Was he doing this on purpose?

"What was I doing yesterday?" Will asked.

Zoe blinked back up to make eye contact with her potential boss. If she kept saying that in her head, she'd eventually believe it. "I should have asked how your forehead was doing, considering how many times you hit your head against the window every time you saw a green pasture."

"Whatever." Will chuckled and pushed himself away from the door. "Well, all I need to do is put on my shoes and we can head out."

"And a shirt," Zoe reminded him.

From the middle of the room, Will turned around and winked. "Too much for you to handle?"

Playfully Zoe rolled her eyes and scoffed. Without stepping into his private sanctuary, she stood in the doorway and leaned against the jamb. "Whatever, I'd hate for your virginal skin to be attacked by the Southern mosquitoes—they're unlike any bug you've ever come across."

Will sat on the edge of his bed and slipped on a pair of black tennis shoes. The crumpled blankets on his king-size bed created images in Zoe's mind that she needn't think about. When he finished with his shoes, Will stood to his full six-four height. He reached for something in the covers, then stood and slipped a black T-shirt over his beautiful body. Zoe swallowed her disappointment.

"I can promise you one thing, babe," Will said. "Nothing about me has been virginal in a long time."

The only thing Zoe could do after a comment like that was choke on her words. "I wasn't talking about that."

"I know." Will crossed the hardwood floor, grabbed something off the dresser against the wall and then stood so close to her in the door frame that Zoe felt his heartbeat thump against his chest. "But I was."

At first, Zoe assumed Will was being boorish and using his size to push her out of the way. So she turned to the side with her back against the frame. Will turned to face her, and her heart raced. He lowered his lashes and licked his lips as he stared down at her. It was barely after eight in the morning and Zoe was already working up a sweat. This wasn't fair.

"Do you mind?" she asked him, hoping he'd catch on to her sarcastic tone.

"Hey, you're the one who didn't move."

In true dramatic form, Zoe sighed and took a big step to the left and into the hallway. "Better?"

"Not really," Will mumbled with a wink. "So, where are we going again?"

"To the Four Points Park."

A set of keys jingled in the palm of his hand and scraped against the brass knob when Will closed the door behind him with one hand. He placed his other hand on Zoe's lower back. She tried not to be skittish and willed herself to remain calm.

"You're dressed like you're going to work out," Will observed.

"I need to." Zoe nodded. "You keep shoving your desserts at me."

"Yeah." Will laughed. "I ordered one and you pulled it toward you."

"You pushed it toward me like you wanted to share!" Zoe gasped.

"Uh, no." Will shook his head. "I was making elbow room and getting ready to dig in when you assaulted my dessert with your spoon."

Done with this version of the truth, Zoe folded her arms across her chest and sighed.

"Then let's talk about last night and the triple-crust peach cobbler with the homemade vanilla ice cream." Will patted his stomach. "Or, at least, I believe it was homemade. I barely got some."

In jest, Zoe rubbed her belly and offered a lazy smile. "Oh, it was homemade, and it was good, too."

"So you admit you stole my dessert?"

"I was helping you out," Zoe argued. "Both desserts were too large for one person to eat. You really should be thanking me."

Bowing at the waist, Will nodded. "You're right, and thank you," he conceded. "But you must know, I'll share anything with you."

They walked along the hallway together and down the stairs. A lighting director and his assistant were the only ones awake and preparing their breakfasts. Silver-domed trays were spread out along the dining room's buffet. Fresh fruit in clear bowls stood as the centerpiece on the table. Zoe stepped in for a moment to snag two bananas before she followed Will out the door. Even though she didn't need help down the steps, Zoe wouldn't have minded Will's gentle touch again. She bit the inside of her cheek to avoid showing any emotion.

Will proved to have a good memory. They drove without her having to give any directions. The banter over who'd eaten how much dessert continued until a song from a female group Zoe had once worked with came on the radio. Without thinking, she turned the volume up and began belting out the punk-rock lyrics. At a red light, Will slowed the car and the song began to fade away. Zoe remembered her surroundings and bit the nail of her index finger.

"Sorry." She grinned.

"Don't be sorry." Will shrugged, a smile spreading across his face. "Is the band a favorite of yours?"

"In a way," said Zoe. "I did their makeup for one of their album covers. You may have seen it in my portfolio." Zoe glanced over in time to catch his fingers gripping the steering wheel.

Will cocked his head to the side. "Can we be honest here?"

"Sure."

"I wasn't a fan of your work."

The light may have turned green, but Zoe ceased to notice everything else around her. Her heart slammed against her rib cage. "What?"

Will shrugged. "You said I could be honest."

"Well, I didn't mean rip my heart out and slam it on the ground," Zoe shot back quickly. "We're talking about my life's work."

"Your work is stuck in the eighties."

"It's not stuck in the eighties," Zoe gasped. "It's an homage to the eighties. It's my signature."

"Big hair, bright colors, crazy colors." Will shook his head and frowned. "Not my cup of tea, but fortunately for you, I don't have the final say in the hiring. We do have to put it to a vote."

"And do you want to tell me what my odds are right now?"

Chuckling, Will reached over and patted Zoe's shoulder. "I have no desire to be that honest with you."

They drove along a few more miles before reaching the park. Will slipped the car into an empty spot with no cars on either side and stepped out. Zoe was still at a loss for words. He didn't like her work and he had no problem telling her so. So why *wasn't* she ready to rip his head off?

In the beauty business, there was always competition. If Zoe had a fit every time she didn't get a job, she'd be one miserable person. The only time she hated being passed over was when it came to Titus. He stole everything from her. Zoe swallowed down the bubbling irritation. No need to worry. Zoe had Donovan, Marcus and the twins on her side. Surely that was enough, right?

"Thanks," Zoe said, taking his hand as he offered to help her out. "I mean, for being honest."

Will held on to her hand to press it against his heart. "Can I be honest with you some more?"

Butterflies puttered around in her belly. How much honesty was she supposed to take in one day? "How about, if you beat me around the field," Zoe pulled herself away and took off running, "you can say whatever you want."

"No fair!" Will shouted at her backside as she left him in the dust.

Cute. She wanted to race. Will had two choices. The competitive side of him wanted to, of course, win this instant race, but winning might cause more hurt feelings than Will wanted to provide. Even though Zoe smiled at him after he gave his honest opinion, Will knew better than to push his luck. So, clearly, the other option was to let her win.

Going with that, Will jogged behind Zoe. She had great form, knees up, feet up as she paced herself. His steps were quiet, quiet enough that when he turned around to run backward alongside of her, Zoe jumped off to the side with a little scream. Her pace became a full-on dash. The light laugh she made, as if she couldn't catch her breath, was infectious. As Will caught her laugh, he made the mistake of closing his eyes and not watching where he was going. Thanks to his carelessness, he tripped over a log and fell down to the grass in a laughing heap.

"Will!" Zoe screeched and came running back. She slid into him like he was home plate. "Are you okay?"

"I'm fine," Will hooted. In truth, his pride hurt, but

as long as Zoe's hands roamed his body he wasn't going to admit anything. The damn clothes were in the way.

In a caring manner, Zoe sat and cradled Will's head in her lap. "Seriously, what were you thinking?"

"I wasn't," Will groaned. "I was just trying to make things interesting."

"Ouch." Zoe's eyes and mouth became pinched. Suddenly Will's head hit the ground as Zoe rolled onto her back. Puffs of dirt and blades of grass flew into the air when Will scrambled to her side. "Cramp. Cramp."

"Relax," Will ordered. The way Zoe grabbed the back of her right thigh, Will knew exactly what hurt and what to do. He moved her body to lie flat and wedged himself between her legs. With his right hand he lifted her right leg, his thumb grazing down her calf, roaming behind her knee; with his body, he pressed her thigh toward her. "How does this feel?"

"It hurts," Zoe whined. "I think I broke something."

"You didn't break anything. Breathe through it." His face hovered over hers and her sweet breath blew across his face. "You got this."

The way her eyes squinted at the corners did something to the blood in his head. It fueled his body. Will blinked and focused on Zoe's face. For a makeup artist, she wore very little. And yet she still radiated beauty. Zoe winced once more. Will encouraged her, stroking the hard muscle against her femur. He nearly buckled when her body melted in his arms and a moan of satisfaction oozed from her parted lips.

Zoe inhaled into the stretch. The more limber she became, the closer Will's face came to hers. He leaned his body forward and somewhere in the move Zoe's leg slipped from his hand and wrapped around his waist.

Will placed his hands in the grass on either side of her head. Once more Zoe's lips parted; this time, she arched her back toward his frame. Her eyes focused on his mouth, and with the closeness of their bodies, the pitter-patter of her heart slammed against his chest. This was it. This was going to be the moment they put their business aside. He felt it. She felt it. They both wanted it.

A pair of hummingbirds buzzed in the air in front of them. At the sound of a high-pitched whistle the birds flew off. A black-and-white soccer ball sped by them and chasing it was a group of teenage boys. Will sprang to his feet, bringing Zoe with him. He nudged Zoe behind him so the boys did not catch sight of her disheveled clothes but kept hold of her hand.

"Boys, boys," began a man with a whistle dangling from his neck and a clipboard in his hands. He wore a pair of red coach's shorts and a white T-shirt with the initials SHS across the front. A red visor shielded his freckled face from the blistering sun. "Watch where you're going. You almost knocked these people down." The man jogged to them and apologized, then backed up. "Holy crap! You're Will Ravens."

"Guilty as charged." Will extended his free hand for the coach.

"Jesus, it's a pleasure to meet you," said the man. "My name is Barney, Barney Chatman. I'm such a fan of yours."

Behind him, Zoe made some noise and stepped forward. "A fan, you say?"

Barney nodded his head eagerly and pumped Will's hand. "Am I ever. I followed your career at Stanford."

"Stanford," Zoe said, her interest piqued, and the corners of her mouth turned down.

This tidbit of information didn't need to be shared right now. Not when he was trying so hard to prove he was a regular guy. Regular guys attended regular colleges, not universities competing with Ivy League schools. Will didn't consider himself as privileged as his cousins. He'd worked hard to earn everything he had.

"And, of course, in Germany when you were with the Teufels. I was in Germany your second year with them and got the chance to watch a match."

"Thanks," Will said. "It's great meeting people who know the sport."

"Well, not like you." Barney stepped back and held up his hands in surrender. "I can't believe I've got you standing here. I can't believe my boys just ran right by you without recognizing you and paying their respects."

Will waved off the honor. "When I was young, the only thing I saw in front of me was a ball."

Barney's thick brows rose. "You don't think...could I interest you in checking out the boys? I mean, they'd really get a kick out of meeting you."

A gentle nudge from Zoe dug into his back when he looked to her for permission. "Go on and do, like, a scrimmage thing with them," Zoe encouraged him.

"You're better?" Barney asked, inclining his head toward Will's ankle.

Not wanting to appear weak in front of Zoe, Will straightened to his full height and nodded with confidence. He was. He'd recuperated. Of course, his days of playing professionally were over, but where was the harm in running around on the field with a few high school students?

"I'm not sure," said Will. "My friend and I were just getting started working out."

Another elbow, this time in the ribs, and Zoe wiggled her brows. "I'm injured, remember?" To emphasize her pain, Zoe limped in a circle. "Besides, you've seen my work. Let me see yours."

"Ravens Cosmetics is my work," Will reminded her, tipping the edge of his index finger across the slope of her nose. He offered a smile when she rolled her eyes toward the single puffy cloud in the blue sky. "But I'll go just so you can see how I give everything one hundred percent."

"Oh, man, this is the best," Barney exclaimed. He patted Will on the back of the arm. "Let me go tell the boys."

Zoe laughed as they headed for the field. Some of the boys were stretching, while others were bouncing a ball on their knees back and forth to each other. Will hated to admit he was excited to kick the ball around. He'd been far younger than these kids when a coach spotted his potential. High school was nothing but academics and sports. Judging from some teenage girls gathering on the sidelines, Will predicted a healthy balance for these high school stars.

Blood pounded in Will's ears as he came closer to the field. His heart raced with deep beats. A ref's whistle blew, signaling the start of a match. The sound evoked the auditory memory of his rapid breath when he used to run full speed toward the soccer ball. He also recalled the deafening sound at the Raiders Stadium when his opponent's cleat had sliced into his flesh. The joy he felt overshadowed the pain. This was his element. He knew everything about the game. No one questioned him on the field. No one made him lose focus. Until now.

Since it was his fault that Zoe had to sit in the silver bleachers, the least he could do was try to make it comfortable for her. He ripped off his shirt, folded it and created a comfy spot for her to sit. Will had to admit her little curtsy in thanks was cute.

"Don't hurt yourself out there," Zoe called as he trotted off to join the crowd of boys.

On a soccer field, even a makeshift one, Will always gave a hundred percent, just as he'd promised to Zoe. Every now and then, though, he did glance up to where Zoe sat and smiled. Back in the day, Will had liked to think of himself as a sports-focused man. Of course, pretty women hung on the rails and even the sidelines to catch his attention, but Will had always been focused. He'd prided himself on that. Now, distracted by Zoe, one of the kids was able to steal the ball from him.

The players were fun and energetic. He was surprised at how many kids enjoyed soccer these days. A crowd of spectators began to fill the bleachers. At one point, Will shaded his eyes to make sure Zoe was okay. He spotted her becoming the center of attention of a group of girls more intent on whatever she was saying than the actual practice. The back of his hand dripped with sweat. He hadn't realized he'd been playing that hard. He didn't even have his cleats.

The sun was high in the sky, shining brightly over the entire park, by the time practice ended. Folks from Magnolia Palace gathered around the edge of the field.

His newfound friends, Ramon and Stephen, clapped. All the boys hung around, begging for an autograph. Will signed soccer balls, T-shirts and even a pair of shoes.

But the only thing Will wanted to do was run over and swing Zoe in the air. This was the first time since the accident that he'd felt a complete fit on the field. He realized he owed it to Zoe. It had been his fear of looking bad in front of her that inspired him to keep up with the younger crowd.

The bleachers were filled with a young crowd of students, all of them holding their cell phone devices. So he held off from swinging Zoe around. Knowing how quickly things spread on the internet, Will wondered what Eva or Dana or the twins would think—or even the board for that matter. With her as a candidate for Creative Design Director, physical contact was not a good idea. It was clear Zoe wanted the position and he didn't want to jeopardize everyone else's opinion of her. Knowing where they both stood. She wanted the job Will did not want to give her. Yes, she showed signs of potential but she lacked the back-to-basics approach he needed. Will risked a sexual harrassment lawsuit with potential witnesses for Zoe.

Zoe stepped down to the bottom bleacher. Will held his hand to help her transition to the ground. Her arms stretched in the air to wrap around his neck but Will took a step back and instead raised his hand for a high five. Her brows rose in question, and Will nodded at the teenagers.

"We have an audience," he whispered into her ear, and she half turned to see where he motioned to.

Understanding, Zoe nodded her head and cleared

her throat. Their hands met in a midair high five. "I'll make sure to tell the board their CEO is a true team player."

The idea of Zoe being on his team was intriguing. But Will had to stick to his guns and make a thorough examination of all the candidates. It wasn't fair to the others that he got to spend this time with her. If he did decide to hire Zoe, there'd be rumbles from other people. The only thing he hoped was that Zoe would still want to see him after the final decision was made. If Zoe cared about the company, she would understand, right? Dare he risk sticking by his guts? Turning her down now either opened or closed the door for them to potentially date. She might try to brush it off, but there was something between them neither one of them could deny.

"Thanks for talking to us, Miss Zoe."

Thank God for the perfect timing of Lexi's niece. Kimber Reyes tapped Zoe on the shoulder, innocently interrupting a series of naughty thoughts going off in Zoe's head. Zoe took a giant step backward and away from Will's hot, sweaty body. She fanned herself with one hand and tossed him the shirt he'd allowed her to sit on with the other.

"Oh, Kimber, it was nothing," Zoe said, ignoring Will's penetrating curious glance.

"I'm going to go home and try it."

"Try what?" Will asked.

As hard as Zoe tried to will Kimber to stay strong and not fall for the dazzling smile Will flashed, it didn't work. With the game over, Zoe appreciated the modest attempt Will took to cover up his muscles. He tugged his shirt over his head. "Zoe was just teaching us a few techniques for our makeup by mixing glitter in with our gloss."

"You're stunningly beautiful," Will said to Kimber, which only made the child giggle hysterically. "Good job, Zoe."

Kimber shook her head. "No, not right now. For our pre-prom pictures we're going to take tomorrow."

"I'm so excited for you." Kenzie came over and hugged Kimber's shoulders. "You're a shoo-in to win." She tugged the side ponytail Kimber sported. "This head was made to wear the Southwood High Prom Queen crown."

Forgetting she was in the company of Will, Zoe participated in the pre-celebration, holding Kenzie and Kimber's hands to jump around and squeal. Their commotion brought over the other men from the Magnolia Palace. Everyone sobered when Stephen cleared his throat like the overprotective guardian he was. Zoe admired him and his brother Nate. They'd moved to Southwood soon after their other brother, Kimber's father, passed away in a car accident along with her mother. Immediately, they'd acclimated to the small town and both men found longtime residents to fall in love with. Zoe craned her neck to see if she could spot Nate Reyes around here somewhere. No such luck.

"Whoever heard of prom pictures the day before prom?" Stephen scowled. "When I was growing up, we took pictures the day of."

"And risk getting your dress messed up?" Kimber cringed and rolled her eyes. "No, thank you."

The uncle and niece duo could go on for hours about

their views of the world without intervention. "Where's Lexi?" Zoe asked Stephen.

Stephen groaned and shook his head. "She's on bed rest."

"Bed rest?" Zoe gasped.

Kimber huffed. "She's fine. It's Tío Stephen who is forcing Lexi to stay home in bed."

Relieved, Zoe sighed. "Did something happen to worry you?"

Patting his niece on the shoulder, Stephen shook his head. "She's been so involved with this pageant she forgot to take her prenatal vitamin yesterday."

"According to Lexi," Kenzie offered, whispering not so softly behind her hand, "she got as far as the door before he freaked out."

It was easy to imagine Stephen being so careful where Lexi was concerned. He loved her deeply and, of course, Lexi was madly in love with him. They made Zoe long for a relationship where she could settle down. For some reason, Zoe glanced over and found Will staring at her. Her heart fluttered.

Clearing her throat, Zoe tore her gaze from Will's back to Stephen. "You promise she's okay? I know she is nearing the end of her pregnancy."

"She's fine." Stephen nodded. "Feel free to stop by this evening."

"We have dinner planned for everyone tonight, don't we, Ramon?" Kenzie leaned forward to include Stephen's quiet cousin in on the conversation.

In an uncomfortable fashion, Ramon scratched at the back of his head. "I think I forgot to take it out of the freezer."

"Are you serious?"

Before they had a chance to get involved in the wrath, Zoe grabbed Will's arm and waved goodbye to Kimber and Stephen.

"I did tell you she scared me," Will said, once they were out of earshot.

"I'm scared for Ramon," Zoe laughed. "Maybe we shouldn't have left him."

Will stopped in his tracks. For a moment, Zoe wondered if he wanted to go back and rescue his new friend. He paused and looked over the hill. "Nah, I think he'll be okay."

They began to walk together in silence. Zoe wasn't sure where they were going; she just knew she didn't want to share Will with anyone right away.

"How was playing soccer again for you?" she asked when they reached the other end of the shallow lake. Their knuckles brushed against each other as she walked on the higher part of the leaf-strewn path beside the water. "Want to go back to it?"

"Not a chance." Will sighed. "I know I may not be as experienced in the makeup world as you, but there's something about doing this job for my grandmother that makes me feel honorable."

"Your grandmother, huh?"

"Yes. I promise you, I am my grandmother's favorite grandchild."

Zoe felt her lips stretch across her face as she tried to hide her smile. What would he say if he found out she did a school project on the family and never came across him? Of course, she'd done it a long time ago. "You don't say."

"Why do you sound surprised?"

"Surprised that you were spoiled by your grandmother?" Zoe made a grand gesture toward her heart. "My bad. How could I ever think such a thing?"

"You sound like my cousins."

Water rushed by an open drainage. A few birds scattered to the top of the skyscraper-tall pine trees at the sound of their footsteps. It was the perfect afternoon for a romantic stroll. *If there was a romance between us.*

"Is that a good thing or a bad thing?"

"Have you met all of my cousins?"

Zoe ticked off the cousins she knew. She was closest to the twins. "Isn't that enough?"

"There are more, and all of them are leery of me as the CEO."

"Didn't you say they nominated you for the job?"

Will nodded and hung his head. She hadn't realized he'd picked up a blade of grass until he started picking it apart. "They did. It was more an attempt to see me fail. Christmas is great in our family." He half chuckled as she mewed out a pity *aw*. "Don't feel sorry for me. At least the other group of my cousins, the loyal ones, want me to succeed, which I plan to do half out of spite."

"If you fail," Zoe breathed, "Ravens Cosmetics fails."

"Exactly." Will stopped walking and offered Zoe a half smile. "Which is why it is imperative that I choose right for the next position. I don't want to let my grandmother down."

"You won't fail if you choose me."

Chapter 6

After a family-style dinner at the table, the men cleared the table and did the dishes. Their reward was another bottle of rum. Will needed it. Though his body was tired from the exercise, his mind raced after his afternoon with Zoe and their near kiss. Lips had never been so soft. Every dream he'd had last night was of the promise of how good he and Zoe would be together. But Zoe had made herself clear she wanted to be a part of Ravens Cosmetics. The more time he spent around her, the clearer it became to Will that he wanted to be a part of Zoe.

Everything came down to the Creative Design Director position. From what he'd seen, Zoe's work still did not pop to him. The work Will had seen—not just in her portfolio but also album covers for musicians and rap artists—was more for shock value. The bold colors and designs could have been considered art. Will liked to see a woman who looked like a woman, not a walking art gallery. Will thought of the Get line. The product titles were catchy—Get Him, Get Him Back and Get Revenge—but at the end of the day, vintage colors, such as bold red, soft pinks and basic nudes, stood the test of time; meanwhile, a majority of the trendy products were discontinued and in his opinion, a waste of time and money. Will recalled old photographs of his relatives over the years in their dresses and makeup. They started off with vintage red lipstick and natural eyebrows; as the family members grew, they experimented with the trends from the seventies, from heavy, bright blue lids and oversize lashes to funky colors, then the grunge fad, and eventually returned to the basic "less is more." Zoe was a trend. He wanted classic. How was he supposed to have both?

She was *haute couture*. He smiled at his use of the phrase. Dana would be so proud of him. In just a few short weeks he'd grown. He recognized the names of the Ravens Cosmetics Zoe left in the bathroom and ignored the competitors' products.

The sleek black cell phone on the nightstand by his bed lit up. It was the first time all week it had rung. Will expected to see Marcus's or Donovan's face on the screen, but instead it was his sister. Speak of the devil. He smiled just the same. "Hey," he said, accepting the FaceTime call.

Like all of the women in the Ravens family, Dana was extremely beautiful. She'd begged their parents to allow her to be part of an RC back-to-school runway show, and her modeling career had taken off at the age of thirteen. Now, at almost forty, with three kids of her own, Dana was still as beautiful as ever.

"Hey, little bro," Dana said with a bright smile. From her position, Will could tell she was seated at the utility table in her kitchen. A bowl of fresh fruit sat on the island bar behind her and the refrigerator door opened and closed without a head bobbing over the countertop. One of the kids was sneaking their own snack. Will kept that tidbit of information to himself. "How is the country life treating you?"

"Bad news spreads fast," Will said.

"I wouldn't say bad news, more like gossip." A crash from another room sounded and distracted Dana for a moment. "Tell me about Southwood. Are you wearing overalls yet?"

"I haven't gotten that sucked in yet." Will laughed as he said it, but the small town was growing on him. The walk around the lake had sold him, or maybe it was the company he kept.

Dana narrowed her eyes and leaned in close to the screen. "You sound and look relaxed compared to the last time I spoke with you."

"It was just last week that we spoke, and that was after I had to tell a room full of interviewees that we're going to have to get back with them about the job interviews that I was late to, thanks to Dixon."

Nodding, Dana rubbed her chin. "I heard Titus was in the running. He's worked a few shows I walked in."

If his memory served him correctly, Titus was the six-foot-five artist from the interviews. Truth be told, out of everyone in the pile, Will had preferred Titus's body of work. Women looked like women, not art. On top of being a great makeup artist, Titus being a man in a female-dominated field made it fresh and new. The idea of hurting Zoe didn't sit well with Will, though.

"He is."

"And what about Zoe Baldwin? The twins told me she's at the pageant."

Will rubbed his hand over his mouth to cover the smile that the mere thought of Zoe evoked in him. "She's talented."

"And very beautiful," Dana added.

Secrecy was never at the forefront for the Ravens family. Will shook his head and sighed. "Okay, what did Donovan say to you?"

"It wasn't just Donovan," Dana said. "Marcus picked up on some sexual chemistry between you two."

"Marcus and Donovan? Our brothers who both have issues with dating women from the office?"

Another crash came from behind Dana. It sounded like a bowl with a thousand Legos falling. Judging from the way Dana rolled her eyes, Will guessed he was right. She squinted her eyes, as if pushing the noise out of her mind. "Will, they say the tension was so thick between you two. Are you sure it's wise to be working with her in a secluded town?"

Considering the way they were interrupted every time he and Zoe got close, the last thing Will would call Southwood was secluded. Someone was always around. The thought of his time with Zoe being put in jeopardy didn't sit right with Will. He sat up further and shook his head. "There's nothing going on between us."

"Are you sure? Because after going over the video surveillance from the downstairs lobby—"

"What?" Will pinched the bridge of his nose. "I

see Jerraud is taking advantage of his position at the building."

"It's not a position," Dana corrected her younger brother. "It is his job. He runs Anderson Securities and part of that requires putting out any fires at Kelly Towers."

"There was no threat."

Dana shook her head back and forth. "Judging from the heat rising between you and Miss Baldwin from the minute you two laid eyes on each other, I'd beg to differ."

Jesus, he'd forgotten about the security cameras on all the floors. He shouldn't have overlooked the sneaky lengths his sisters would go through in order to get some information on him. "So, this is how you get your gossip?" Will had to laugh. He shook his head. "You're scoping out surveillance tapes."

"Whatever, William. This isn't about me. This is about you and Zoe."

"There is no me and Zoe," Will snapped and when he did, he heard an unmistakable sneeze from the other side of the bathroom door. A jolt charged his system. While it was Zoe's idea to keep things friendly between them, he still did not want her to think he wasn't attracted to her. He desired Zoe. Will scratched the space above his heart where his TΦP, Tau Phi Rho, tattoo rested. The ink reminded him he needed to get back in touch with Dominic at some point this week. He felt bad for being in his frat brother's new hometown and not hanging out with him at any point.

"I would hate for her not to get chosen and then want to bring a lawsuit on RC. That's all the cousins need to hear before they decide to cash in their chips."

The door to Zoe's room slammed shut and footsteps shuffled down the stairs. Will cursed under his breath. "I've got this, Dana. Okay?"

"Fine. Well, I better get off this thing before the kids destroy my house."

After they said farewell, Will glanced at the itinerary on the nightstand to decide what to wear tomorrow for Lexi's last supper before the pageant Sunday. There was nothing formal until Saturday night and that was just a dinner. Since they were touring more old buildings, Will slipped into a pair of jeans, a Miami T-shirt and a pair of wheat Timberlands. He doubted they'd do a lot of running, but if they had to walk through the park or anything, Will wanted his feet protected.

Even though he knew Zoe had left her bedroom, Will knocked on the door to the bathroom they shared and opened it. The first scent was intoxicating. Magnolias. He grinned at the bottles of hair products with the Ravens Cosmetics label and wondered which ones she used. Whoever came up with the scent needed a raise. Will would never look at or smell magnolias again without thinking of Zoe.

Will understood Ravens Cosmetics, as a cosmetic conglomerate, was parent to several subsidiaries. The internet made it possible for consumers to try every product created under their umbrella. Years ago, it had helped sales skyrocket; now, beauty bloggers helped, too, but anyone with a camera phone considered themselves professional video bloggers, or vloggers, as they were known. Last Christmas, RC came out with a holiday mascara—Merry-Merry Mascara—and a customer with a cell phone reported her dislike for the makeup. Then someone purchased a tube but didn't care for the customer service she'd received and trashed the mascara. That video went viral. The bad press didn't help when the consumer named RC's competition as a better alternative. Some of these products seemed to taunt Will as he stood in the bathroom. The other products on the counter irked him. MDMFlow, PNK Digger and AJ Crimson were scattered on the countertop. Was it crazy to wish the only thing Zoe used on her body came from him or his company?

He saw a piece of jewelry Zoe wore every day. Using his index finger, he traced the hoop earring a few times, then pinched it to pick it up. Returning it to her would give him an excuse to see her—touch her, even.

Downstairs, he found Zoe seated at the head of the breakfast table draining a glass of orange juice. Though the glass covered her face, Will still caught her eyes watching him as he crossed the room. He bit the inside of his cheek trying to keep from flashing a smile at her. It seemed every time he did she would blush, and with a table filled with other guests working the pageant this Sunday, Will figured he needed to curb his flirting. What Dana had said resonated with him. He needed to keep to himself for the rest of the time here.

Kenzie carried on a light conversation with the group at the table. She kept directing the topic toward Zoe. Will snagged a biscuit and sat at the opposite end of the table from her. A silver bowl of honey butter sat in front of him. While he slathered the butter on his bread, he could only think about doing the same thing to Zoe. Her slender neck was exposed in her low-cut V-neck T-shirt with a witty picture of sparkling red lips on the front.

"Are you ready for today?"

Will turned to his left to find Rebecca sliding into the empty seat. She reached out with her right hand to stroke his forearm. Nodding, Will sat back in his chair and pulled the napkin from under his plate to wipe his hands.

"Of course," Will said. "I look forward to discovering more of Southwood's hidden charms."

"I can't wait to look at the old building," said Luke. He was the photographer for the pageant, but Will had also seen several freelance jobs he'd done for RC's digital spreads.

Will nodded his head in agreement. In one bite he consumed half of his biscuit. From across the table, Zoe stared and pressed her lips together. They'd almost shared a kiss yesterday afternoon.

Zoe had left with the girl named Kimber to check on Lexi last evening. She hadn't returned to her room until late. Will had been tempted to "accidentally" walk in on her when she was taking a shower, but he'd decided against it. Will wanted to talk about their episode yesterday.

They had been about to kiss.

He hated not being honest with Dana. In truth, he wasn't sure where he stood with Zoe. Zoe had more aspirations in life than being the wife of an athlete. Will liked the way Zoe took time to talk to the girls at the park. There were times he'd witnessed a grown woman push a child out of the way in order to get his autograph. Will could try to keep things professional like he promised his sister. The words he'd said to Dana weren't true. There *was* something going on between him and Zoe. It was only a matter of time. Because of his dedication and traveling with soccer, Will had never thought twice about getting involved in a serious relationship, yet when it came to Zoe, he wrestled with everything. Once the decision about the job was made, Will could concentrate on pursuing Zoe. Since she was from the islands, he knew the perfect place to take her on their first date when they returned to Miami.

"Alright, is everyone here who wants to go on the road trip?" Kenzie asked in her typically cheerful voice.

A chorus of yeses came from the Magnolia Palace occupants. Will looked forward to the van being overcrowded again. It would give him a chance to drive in the Maserati with Zoe. Alone.

"Okay," Kenzie went on, "Zoe, how about you sit up front with me and I'll drive."

Wait, what? Will thought quickly. This was his chance to have her alone. For a brief moment he contemplated banging his fist on the table or kicking the chair's leg in protest. But he was the CEO of a major cosmetics company. He was here on business to represent said company, but he was fighting the urge to act like a spoiled child for not getting his way. Will started to get up, but a set of hands clamped down on his shoulders. Ramon was standing behind him.

"I kind of need a favor from you, bruh," his new friend said. He slid into the seat Rebecca had left. "Kenzie is a bit upset with me and has kicked me off the tour. I figured since you have an empty seat in that car of yours, I could catch a ride."

"Sure, not a problem."

Will didn't ask what the problem was. As with he and Zoe, there was clear tension between the former cheerleader and the owner of the bed-and-breakfast.

Zoe and Kenzie were already at the doorway. Both ladies glanced back and purposely tilted their chins in the air at the men before turning fully around and leaving.

Whatever Ramon had done to piss off Kenzie, he needed to stop. This was interrupting Will and Zoe's time together.

When the van pulled up to the Mas Beauty School, Zoe's heart started fluttering. She led the tour of her great-grandmother's beloved three-story structure. They started with the old classrooms on the first floor, where the original structure was made up of four rooms. The home started off as a single level and thanks to success, they'd expanded. Sadie Baldwin used one room for teaching, and she and her husband lived in another, raised their two boys in the other, and opened their third bedroom to students coming from across the state of Georgia, and even farther away, to study the techniques of the trade.

The success of the beauty school had made it easier for the Baldwins to add on to the house. The structure grew upward with two more stories. Sadie, whom Zoe called GiGi for short whenever she came to stay, had been quite young when she gave birth to Zoe's grandfather.

Zoe retold the story of the success of the original beauty school, and pointed out that two of the other downstairs rooms were turned into classrooms, as well. During the fifties and sixties, word had gotten out about Mas, and girls traveled from as far as Chicago to come to the school where the young student's parents and grandparents attended Annie Malone's as Poro Agents. Before the internet, businesswomen signed on as Poro Agents and sold Miss Annie's products. Miss Annie went on to become a millionaire and came out with her own hair-care line for African American women in the 1900s. GiGi molded her career after Miss Annie to sell to those who could not afford to travel upstate. It was GiGi's classes that had inspired Zoe to get a degree in cosmetic chemistry.

Zoe smiled at everyone soaking in the history lesson. A lot of the women were already aware of it. Even Rebecca nodded her head with awe. Old newspaper clippings about the accomplishments of all the graduates hung in frames, and a significant number of the former students had gone on to work at Ravens Cosmetics—a little bit of news clearly interesting to Will.

Will rubbed his square jaw with his hand and stood at one of the silver-framed photographs. The picture was of GiGi with the young and successful Naomi Ravens. When girls graduated from Mas, many went back home to start their own shops and salons, but GiGi thought those who went on to Ravens Cosmetics were the ones who truly succeeded.

The tour continued through the kitchen, where GiGi once used to stand at the stove and make sure all of her students were fed and taken care of. Eventually, when the funds permitted it, she had been able to hire a cook. By the time Zoe came to live here, the number of students enrolled had begun to dwindle. With more beauty schools popping up in so many different cities, no one needed to travel to get the hands-on experience GiGi gave. At one point, everyone in Southwood came to GiGi's school for free hair and makeup treatments at the end of each semester. After the doors to the school closed, GiGi kept her shop open for local customers until the day she passed away.

A rope draped from one staircase railing to the other, warning everyone away from the third floor. That was Zoe's sanctuary. Her father still lived upstairs when he wasn't gallivanting around the world to meet up with her mother. It was probably for the best. There'd be no telling what her old room looked like now.

Kenzie took over the rest of the tour, mainly guiding everyone back downstairs and outside to the second add-on to the home. In her typically excited way, Kenzie told everyone about the back area facing into the woods known as the Firefly Forest. The covered area was meant for cookouts and party events. Kenzie and Lexi had arranged for a special late dinner the next night. It was Lexi's way of thanking everyone for their hard work. Sunday was the beauty pageant and everyone was going to be torn in different directions.

Zoe lingered behind the group, mainly to keep an eye out for Will. She hadn't meant to avoid him that morning, it just sort of happened. Not finding him in the crowd worried her a bit. Somehow she knew she'd find him on the third floor. She ducked under the tape and trotted up the steps. Of course he was standing in her bedroom with the door open. His arms were crossed over his chest; he stroked the hair on his chin and stared at the wall. In his jeans and Timberland boots he looked more like a star on a trendy hip-hop reality TV show.

"The tape over the stairwell didn't clue you in that this area was off-limits?" Zoe asked, approaching. Years ago, when her father had opened the house for tourists, the carpets were taken out and the floors stripped to reveal the original hardwood. He must have learned his lesson after having them constantly cleaned. Her father also kept the off-limits sign up to keep the family's personal belongings safe. Kenzie had a key to the house, as the town historian did with just about every historic place in town open for tours.

"I like to pick and choose when the rules suit me." Will chuckled. He dropped his hands and nodded toward the wall. "Why didn't you tell me about this?"

Walking farther into the room, Zoe found her old canopy bed still intact. The creamy veils surrounding the bed were open and held back with eggshell-colored ties. The walls were a soft beige; off-white frames holding old family photos hung on the bare wall, along with a corkboard with the framed A+ paper she'd done on the Ravens family.

Embarrassed, Zoe closed her bedroom door before another rogue tourist strayed upstairs to witness her adolescent obsession. She stood in front of Will, as if her height could actually make a difference. Not a chance. "Don't look at that."

"Why not? I want to learn about my family history." Will gently moved Zoe to the side and moved closer to the report. Zoe waved her hands in front of his face. "Wait, is this the crystal ball you were talking about that told you you belonged at Ravens Cosmetics?"

Of all the times to remember something. Zoe groaned inwardly.

"I must say, I'm quite impressed," Will continued. "You managed to include my all of my aunts and uncles, including Aunt Octavia. Most people forget about her."

"How can they forget?" Zoe gawked "Before social media, she had to have been the scandal of the decade. I mean, the eighties were a breath away from social media. Can you imagine what the rumors would have been like? From what I read, no one could believe someone could walk away like she did and disappear." As Zoe went on, Will's lips flattened together. Zoe covered her mouth and shook her head. "I'm sorry. That was probably insensitive of me."

"Nah." Will let her off with an easy smile. "Everyone else in the family seems to have forgotten about the missing heir—she's been missing for a few decades now. My siblings and my cousins never knew her. We only know her as the abstaining vote."

"She still has a stake in the company?" Zoe asked.

Will nodded. "My grandmother…"

"Ms. Naomi," Zoe provided with excitement, pointing to the spot on the Ravens family tree, where an old photograph of his grandmother was pasted.

"Yes, my grandmother Naomi still believes Octavia will come back one day."

In a way, Zoe had always thought the same thing, especially with the way everyone used some form of social media platform. Didn't Octavia want to see her family? What drove her away? Zoe had a thousand and one questions.

Will brushed his elbow against her shoulder. "Look here, you got as far as my third great-grandfather."

Zoe beamed proudly for a moment. "Well, my greatgrandmother swore by the products your family used to come up with and urged everyone to work for your grandmother once her students graduated." Then Zoe moved away, turning so he didn't see her blush. How much of a stalker did she seem right now? All her life she'd wanted to be a part of Ravens Cosmetics. "You must think I'm crazy."

"We've spent the whole week together, practically day in and day out. Why didn't you tell me about your family's links with mine?" Will asked. His voice neared her. Chills rolled down her spine. "Can't you see that's yet another thing we have in common? From what I learned today, it's as if our grandmothers aligned us to be together."

"Get serious," Zoe said as she spun around. She came face-to-face with his chest, which she stared at rather than meet his eyes. But it was useless. Will tipped her chin so she'd face him. "Will," she pleaded. "I heard you this morning on the phone with whomever. You said so yourself, there is no me and you."

"That was my sister Dana on the phone," Will replied softly. "If I gave my family any information about my love life, they'd plan a wedding before we return to Miami."

Strong hands brushed against the backs of her arms. Will's thumbs drew circles on her skin. She shivered and leaned against him.

"You're what's stopping what's happening between us, Zoe, because of one specific thing," Will said against her neck. "But you're overlooking the thousands of things we have in common with each other. You don't find that too often in two people."

Zoe bit her bottom lip and tried to fight her desires. At what point did she let go of her dream of being a part of Ravens Cosmetics? And at what point did she need to realize and give in to the temptations of the man who made her remember she was still a woman with desires? Everything about Will screamed he was the perfect man for her. She'd put all of her dating options on hold. None of the men she'd dated matched her need for success. After listening to Will's concerns with RC, she knew without a doubt they were perfect together.

Giving in, Zoe turned and found herself in Will's embrace. He cocked his head to the side and brought his lips close to hers. They'd almost kissed yesterday. The desire for a taste of him still lingered on her lips. Will finally put her out of any misery, satisfying her with a brush of his mouth against hers. A soft kiss greeted her at first, and then another one. In unison their mouths parted and their tongues danced together.

If heaven had a taste or feeling, this would be it. Will wrapped his arms around Zoe's waist and held her close as he deepened his kiss. Lost for a moment, Zoe gave in to every urge racing through her body. Her hands followed the deep muscles of his chest and wound around his neck. The tips of her fingers played with the curly hair at the nape of his neck. Will's hands roamed up and down her back, one bracing her shoulders, the other caressing her backside. Long fingers played with the hem of her shorts. The mere touch liquefied her.

A mew escaped Zoe's throat. Any common sense went out the window. The two of them found her bed and the old cushions absorbed their weight. Zoe lay beneath him, the palms of her hands embracing his face.

Will pulled his face away for a moment. His lips pressed against the curve of her collarbone and trailed along the edge of her collar. Her breasts swelled and ached for his mouth, not just the warmth of his breath.

"Will," Zoe moaned.

"Zoe," Will replied, trailing kisses back to her neck, jaw and lips.

"Zoe?" Another voice penetrated the barrier of the door.

Using all the strength she had, Zoe sat up straight. Will sat on the edge of her bed with a bewildered look on his handsome face. "Dad?" Zoe called out, and Will mouthed the same but with more questions on his face.

The brass oval door handle turned and creaked. The whole entrance took a mere few seconds, but in Zoe's mind it took forever for the door to reveal her father standing in the doorway while she struggled to sit up in the bed.

Because of the nontraditional way Zoe's parents had lived, with her having no stereotypical mom and dad to come home to every night, her maternal grandparents had been ashamed of their marriage. Zoe never wanted to do anything to cause her father embarrassment. All her life, she'd been the doting daughter. She never got in trouble in school. She went on with college and got her degrees, all without incident.

"What are you doing in here?" Frank Baldwin asked, his eyes narrowing at the sliver of space between herself and Will. "With a boy, no less?"

Zoe stood up. A cool breeze brushed against the exposed skin of her stomach. Quickly she tugged the material down. "Daddy, what are *you* doing here?"

"I thought I lived here." Frank folded his arms across his chest. "What are you doing here? Besides the obvious."

"Sir," Will said, bravely stepping forward with an extended hand. "My apologies for what you walked in on. I have nothing but the utmost respect for your daughter."

How embarrassing it was to be caught making out with a male by your father. But her father's inspection of Will's extended hand took the cake. Zoe grabbed her father's hand and pushed it at Will. "Daddy, this is Will Ravens."

"Ravens?" Frank repeated.

"Ravens," Zoe said in a clipped tone, knowing exactly where her father was about to go with this. His thick dark brows rose with curiosity and his black eyes darted between the two of them. "The Ravens family?"

"The same one on the school report." Will chuckled and pulled at her father's hand. "We were just discussing the lengthy research she did."

"Yes," Frank said drily, "because that's exactly what it looked like."

"Daddy," Zoe hissed. "Will is a guest."

"He was certainly making himself at home."

"I meant no disrespect, sir," said Will. "I got carried away and took advantage of Zoe's hospitality."

Frank eyed Will skeptically. Zoe waited for what seemed like forever for him to say something. "Zoe," he finally said, "go downstairs and let me and Mr. Ravens have a little chat."

Even though she hadn't been grounded in years, Zoe knew better than to argue with her father. She cast a pitiful glance back at Will, who winked at her. Funny how he wasn't nervous at all. The last time Zoe had had a boy in her bedroom, Frank used the kid like a punching bag found downtown at Southpaw Shaw's Gym.

"I'll meet you downstairs," Will assured her.

"We'll meet you downstairs," her father restated.

"I really came into town to finalize things for the re-enactment of my summer engagement," Frank Baldwin said, pacing back and forth in Zoe's bedroom. "I'm not sure if Zoe ever shared with you, but Magnolia Palace is where I proposed to her mother. We're still married but these things keep the spark, especially since we don't live together."

Of course Will remembered the story and the place. "Yes, sir." Will nodded, trying to focus on Zoe's father.

"No need to get all official with the 'sir' business. Call me Frank. It was kind of refreshing, knowing my daughter is not consumed with work all the time."

Never in Will's life had he ever come face-to-face with a girl's father. Sure, he'd done the proverbial sneaking out of dorm rooms back in the day. But Frank Baldwin walking in on them almost took the cake. What did take the cake was Frank shaking Will's hand and thanking him for getting Zoe out of her comfort zone.

"Excuse me, sir?" Will leaned close to make sure he'd heard correctly. "I mean Frank."

Frank Baldwin folded his arms across his chest. "Don't get me wrong. I didn't enjoy catching her being pawed all over. But it was refreshing to see Zoe act reckless. My daughter has been insanely career-driven for a while." Frank fanned his hand toward the family tree. "As you can see for yourself, she's been a fan of the Ravens."

Will held his hands in the air. "I apologize. What you saw was just a momentary lapse in judgment. I truly respect your daughter and I hold her work in high regard."

"So you're hiring her for your company and you'll be keeping your hands off her?"

There went the whole hiring matter. Uncomfortable at being faced with Zoe's father, Will cleared his throat. "I am considering it. The decision isn't final."

"I don't understand," said Frank. He crossed the room to the white-and-pink desk.

"I've already spoken with Zoe." Will explained the situation with the board.

"You can't lose if you go with Zoe."

Those words resonated with Will as the two of them headed downstairs. Will liked that her father had decorated the upstairs hallway with framed photographs of Zoe's work. If she hadn't become a makeup artist, she should have been an artist.

The rest of the group was outside, but Zoe was seated at the large wooden table in the kitchen. Her eyes darted nervously between Will and Frank. As her lips parted to say something, the sound of a song by the late Prince sounded from Zoe's cell phone.

"Hey, Lexi." Zoe's concerned look washed away. "Calm down. What? Okay, sure, I can be there in a few minutes."

After she hung up, Will stepped forward, Frank close behind. "Is everything okay?"

"There's a slight emergency at Lexi's shop. Dad, is your car here?"

Frank shook his head. "It's at the new garage downtown. I took an Uber today."

Will's chest swelled with pride with the chance to save the day. "I drove here. I can take you wherever you need to go."

Zoe looked at the house one more time. She gripped
the steering wheel and closed her eyes. She wanted to be the
woman living in...

Chapter 7

Driving through the quaint little neighborhood only reminded Zoe of the life she wanted. Children played on their neatly manicured green lawns. Husbands washed their cars in the late afternoon. Smoke billowed from lit grills in the backyards. A faint smell of hot dogs on coal filled the air.

With the car's top down, Zoe heard the unmistakable splash of people in the pools behind the homes, as well. This was so different from what Zoe saw from her condo balcony every day. There were no lawns where she lived, unless you counted the sprinkle of green nestling under the sign with the name of her building. The beaches were always covered in half-naked men and women. Tanned bodies stretched on oversize towels or beach chairs. At every corner there was always a party going on.

"What's that smile all about?" Will asked Zoe. Of the four cars at the stop sign, Will appeared to be the only experienced driver. Pimply faced boys on the left and the right of them gunned their engines, and a girl with headgear was directly across from them. All three drivers had older males, whom Zoe assumed were their fathers, seated in the passenger's seats and pointing at the stop sign. Will, being last at the stop, waited. In Miami, she would have been gone by now.

Watching the fathers with their children reminded her of her father. Zoe glanced back at Will. "Care to tell me what you and my dad were talking about?"

Will inhaled deeply, contemplating her question, and then let out his breath. "I can't. Does that negate whether or not you'll tell me what's on your mind?"

"Have you ever thought about looking for Octavia?"

"You're seriously thinking about Ravens?"

Zoe shrugged her shoulders. "When am I not?"

"I appreciate your dedication to the family," Will said. "But for the record, my grandmother looked for Octavia for years after she disappeared."

"Does anyone know why she left?"

Will shook his head. "Not to my knowledge."

"So no one even knows if she's dead or alive."

Will blew out a long breath. "No. I wish for my grandmother's sake that she would make contact with someone from the family."

"I bet anyone in the family would be interested in hearing from her," Zoe commented.

"What do you mean?"

"Well, you said there's a divide between you and your cousins, whether or not to close the company doors. Her vote could help."

"Or hurt," Will said with a nod. "So was my family really what brought that beautiful smile to your face? If so, I might need to consider keeping you around more."

"You need to keep me around because I'm what's best for Ravens Cosmetics."

"There you go. Now, why don't you tell me what else was on your mind. Are you worried about what your father said to me?"

Knowing how persuasive Frank Baldwin could be, Zoe shrugged her shoulders. "I was thinking about home."

"Miami home or here in Southwood?" asked Will.

"No," Zoe answered. "I was thinking about my place in Miami."

"Yes, your Miami address," Will nodded. "I am going to need to know that information."

It was on her résumé, but Zoe decided not to bring her future at RC up right now. They'd crossed the threshold of any work relationship they might have again just then when Will reached over and squeezed her thigh. She bit her lip to fight back the excitement. Where would things have gone between them had they not been interrupted in her bedroom? One thing was for sure, Zoe's insides were awakened and she couldn't wait to have another chance of seeing where things would lead. "I live at the Cozier Condominiums."

Will let out a long whistle and began driving again. "Swanky."

After all the teasing she'd given him about growing up privileged. "Be quiet. I am leasing it from a former client."

"Someone famous?"

Zoe shook her head again and glanced at the view.

The condo was leased to her by the Ruiz family. Natalia Ruiz was a famous reality star who grew up in the limelight. When she and her family were in Miami, she always contracted Zoe. On several occasions Natalia flew Zoe out on location for special events. But after Natalia got married, she'd shied away from the cameras. Zoe knew where Natalia lived, but she'd never betray Natalia's trust. "You must know I'm not at liberty to say."

"Perhaps you will tell me over dinner Monday night."

"Monday?" Zoe repeated.

"I figured by the time we returned Sunday after the pageant, it might be too late. Although I could try to use my, what is it you say? My influence?"

"Affluence," Zoe corrected him.

"Yeah, that's it. I can call in a few favors and see about getting Trudy's to open."

Zoe turned in her seat and placed her hands on her hips. "What do you know about Trudy's?"

"What?" Will's mouth gaped open. "It's only the best place to get roti in Miami."

As much as Zoe loved her Southern food with its savory greens, crispy fried chicken and thick, sweet tea, she missed the taste of the Caribbean. "I might just let you take me there."

"When we return home, you are coming with me, or I will pick it up and we'll eat at my place or yours."

A chill of desire ran down her spine. "You're lucky their *gulab jamun* is my kryptonite."

The reference to a superhero didn't fall on deaf ears. Will winked and shook his head. "You should try the pudding made up with sweet dough," he said. "If you're good, I'll make it for you."

Butterflies fluttered in Zoe's belly. She looked forward to holding Will to his word. She looked forward to a lot of things with him. Seeing him naked and finishing what they started this afternoon was at the top of her list. "Turn left up here. It's the house with the bars on the upstairs windows."

"Bars?" Will's right brow rose with curiosity.

"It's a long story," Zoe laughed lightly. "But that sweet kid you met at the park, Kimber, gave her uncles a run for their money when they came to live here."

If it weren't for Kimber, Lexi and Stephen might not have met. Kimber had taken a very seductive dress from Lexi's store without permission, and Stephen—assuming his niece was innocent—had arrived at Lexi's store to give her a piece of his mind. Seeing how they were about to start a family of their own, so much for that plan.

Like the rest of the homes, children were playing on Lexi's manicured lawn. Philly, Stephen's younger niece and a seven-year-old future beauty queen, ran around the front yard, tiara secured on top of her twin pigtails as she shot a pink Nerf gun at two boys. Her army, a set of twins, stood by her side. The mini-militia stopped and saluted Zoe and Will as they pulled into the driveway.

Lexi stood at the doorway, her hairstyle looking bigger than ever, if it were possible. Her signature blond hair was pulled into a ponytail at the top of her head, which she shook feverishly. "I'm so glad you came. I have no idea how this happened so quickly."

Zoe got out of the car before Will put the vehicle in Park. "Where is the patient?"

"She's locked herself in the downstairs bathroom.

I don't think she even noticed while she was getting ready—until she looked in the mirror," Lexi said, crossing her arms together and biting her fingernails.

"You guys must have florescent lights," said Zoe. "Didn't I tell you to get softer ones in the bathrooms?"

"I'm not the one who needs to be convinced." Lexi turned back and gravely nodded. "It's also motion censored in case the patient tries to sneak in late. The whole house lights up inside."

"Did she say 'patient'?" Will asked. He slammed his door shut and started to follow them inside. Before he locked the doors, Zoe reached into the backseat for her caboodle. Will jogged around the car and took hold of it.

"Let me get that for you."

"Will, I've been lugging that thing around for years now." Zoe tried yanking it from his hands but he held on tight.

"Well, I haven't been around for years. I am carrying it."

"My hero," Zoe mumbled with a sly grin.

Fortunately for Zoe, she'd brought her emergency bag with her in the van when she left this morning with Kenzie and the rest of the guests. The pink case rarely left Zoe's side. It contained everything she needed to handle emergency situations, from waterproof mascara remover and a Ravens Cosmetics product perfect for cracked lips, to other products from other favorite companies. Although, she had to admit, the majority of the items in her bag bore the lavender and cream colors.

"What kind of emergency is this?" he asked, handing Zoe the bag.

"The worst kind any teenager could face," Lexi said

gravely, as she pushed the front door open more. Cool air from inside brushed their faces.

"A pimple," Zoe explained to Will. His brows came together. "Trust me. For a girl about to take photographs that are going to last a lifetime, the last thing she wants is to have a blemish."

"It's not a blemish," Kimber cried from behind the locked bathroom door in the hallway. "It is a new life form."

Zoe tried not to smile as everyone's heels clicked on the hardwood floors. Lexi rapped the back of her hand against the closed door of the bathroom. As Kimber began to tick off her list of demands, which included none of her uncles being present, no cameras and no boys, Zoe tried not to laugh. She remembered these days.

"How bad can it be?" Will tugged on the back of Zoe's shirt and whispered in her ear.

"It's so bad it can hear you," Kimber said from between gritted teeth through the door. "Don't let him in here."

Lexi stepped between Zoe and Will. She took Will by the arm and led him off through the arched doorway. "He's going to sit with Uncle Stephen, sweetie."

"Don't let Uncle Stephen give him a shotgun."

"Gun?" Will repeated, casting a glance back at Zoe. Zoe grinned and shook her head.

"You'll be fine," Lexi told him. "As a matter of fact, I am leaving you in charge."

Zoe didn't see who was seated in the living room but she heard the boom of welcoming male voices and knew Will was in good hands. Lexi walked back down the hallway with a smirk on her face.

"Something more going on between you and the CEO?" Lexi asked. She narrowed her dark eyes at Zoe and folded her arms across her chest. "Did you forget the end game?"

"Of course not," Zoe said. Heat crept up her neck.

"The end game is you as Creative Design Director."

Before having to face Lexi's motherly attitude, Zoe turned to face the door and knocked. "Hey, Kimber, we're alone."

"Are you going to at least answer Aunt Lexi's question first?" Kimber's meek voice asked from the other side.

"Really, Kimber?" Zoe laughed.

"Inquiring minds want to know," Lexi said. She leaned against the wall.

"It would at least make this horrible day better," added Kimber.

Realizing she wasn't going to get anything done, Zoe sighed. "We're getting to know each other."

Is that what she would call it? Had they not been interrupted earlier, Zoe might have let things go a lot further. This afternoon it had been like his hands knew exactly where to go and when. His mouth was magical.

Lexi reached out with her cool hand and pinched Zoe's cheek. "You're turning beet red."

"Ohhh," Kimber sang. "Did you two kiss? He's totally hot."

"Girl, you were wailing three minutes ago about a pimple." Lexi rapped on the door. "Which is more important?"

The doorknob twisted open and the hinges squeaked. "Okay, fine."

"You started that," Zoe whispered before heading inside.

Twenty minutes later, Zoe, Lexi and Kimber emerged from the bathroom with the proper amount of foundation covering her blemish for her pre-prom photo shoot. Zoe promised to come over Saturday afternoon before prom and do Kimber's makeup before attending Lexi's dinner finale for the pageant workers. As a huge favor to Kimber, Zoe did a drastic wingtip over her lid, simply because it would show up better on film. Kimber's prom dress was a Lexi original, made up of bright yellows, oranges and peach. The colors complemented the girl's hazel eyes and golden tan. The prom might be tomorrow night, and there was no telling if Kimber had the votes to become Miss Southwood High's prom queen, but Lexi had plenty of tiaras to choose from.

They found the men in the living room. By "the men," Zoe meant she found Will, Stephen, Nate and a handsome young man dressed in a black tuxedo pinned against the wall by sheer fear. Nate, Stephen's brother, was cleaning what appeared to be a shotgun while Stephen polished his pistol. And Will, not wanting to be left out, sat in a recliner sharpening a bowie knife.

"Seriously?" Kimber wailed. "Aunt Lexi."

With one hand on her hip, Lexi pointed toward the kitchen. "I can't believe you two."

"And you," Zoe added, glaring at Will. "Put that knife down right now. We're about to leave."

"Say goodbye to Will, gentlemen."

Doing as they were told, the brothers rose from their seats. "Bye, Will," they chorused.

Nate Reyes hung his head low so he couldn't flirt

with his green eyes. Last fall Nate had met the love of his life, Amelia Marlow, when she bought him for a hefty fee at the Back to School Bachelor Auction. The "tea," or gossip on the street, was that the two shared a sexy one-night stand and then more. Whatever the truth, Amelia stayed in Southwood and Nate ceased his womanizing ways. Nate patted Zoe's arm on his way into the kitchen. The doorbell rang.

"Luke is going to be here any minute to take you guys for your photo shoot."

"And chaperone!" Stephen called out from the kitchen.

"That's right," both Will and Nate said from either side of the house.

This felt like a glimpse into any future family she might have with Will. He'd be the perfect, overly protective father to their daughter and coach to their son. *Damn it*, Zoe muttered to herself.

Beside her, Lexi cocked her head to the side. "You okay?"

"Oh, yeah." Zoe blinked and brought herself to the present. "I'm fine."

The afternoon sun spilled into the foyer at the front door. Luke stepped inside, hugged both ladies and then performed a man ritual—a handshake and half hug with Will. A few days ago they hadn't known each other. *So?* a voice in Zoe's head taunted her. A few days ago she hadn't known Will either, and now here she was, mentally planning their future.

Outside, the little pink militia saluted them once again. Will led Zoe back to the car with his hand on the small of her back and opened her door. She slid inside and unlocked his.

"That was fun," Will said with a genuine smile. The engine roared to life, just as her heart had from his constant flirting.

"Scaring a teenage boy?"

"I was helping my brethren."

"Brethren?" Zoe laughed, "Boy, you are crazy."

"Stick with me. I'll show you crazy."

Had Will not witnessed what a hurry Zoe was in to get over to Lexi and Stephen's, he would have thought forgetting her hotel key in her childhood bedroom was just a ruse to get him alone again. But since Zoe declined the offer to get to her room through his, he believed her. They arrived back at her family's old home just after dark. There were no cars in the driveway, but that didn't mean Frank Baldwin wasn't outside watching. Even though Frank wanted to encourage a relationship between Will and Zoe, Will did not want an audience. Also not wanting to be tempted to a second session in Zoe's bedroom, Will waited on the hood of the car for Zoe to return from getting her key.

Before the door to the back porch opened with a rickety creak, a light flashed on and then off. "Can you believe my key was on my bed?" Zoe asked moments later as she bounced toward him in the moon's light.

"I can believe you were preoccupied." Will straightened and opened his arms. Zoe instinctively walked into his embrace. "I'm sorry about earlier."

"What's there to be sorry about?" Zoe glanced upward.

To meet her at eye level, Will leaned against the car again. "I don't want the first time anything intimate happens between us to happen on your bed in your childhood home."

"I have to apologize about your family tree." Zoe sighed. "I was pretty obsessed when I was younger. I'm not sure why my dad put them up. I used to have cut out magazines of faces I remade using crayons and markers. Maybe those were too creepy to keep on the walls."

"Yeah," Will teased, "that doesn't sound scary." Whatever the reasons were for the old biographical report pinned on the wall, Will was glad. He was flattered. Zoe impressed him with her attention to detail, and he appreciated her dedication to Ravens Cosmetics.

"Whatever." Zoe pushed his chest. "I am an artist. Anyways, aren't you forward, thinking I was going to let anything go further?"

The key word rolled off her tongue. "Let?" Will repeated.

"Will," Zoe said, "I live a very fast-paced life, but there are some things I like to take my time with. Getting to know someone before sleeping with them is one of them."

It was on the tip of his tongue to mock her with the sleeping part, but she caught on to him and shushed him with her index finger. Will cupped her hand and stroked her finger. "I've got all the time in the world for you, Zoe. As a matter of fact, I think it would be good for us to take things slow."

A light behind the house twinkled in the air. His attention drifted for a moment.

"Because of the job?"

Focusing on her words, Will nodded. "Especially because of the job. I need to know that I'm thinking about the future of my family's company and what the right path to take is." Before Zoe could argue back, Will took his free hand and pressed it against her lips. "I don't want you to be misled about anything."

"You know what's strange?" Zoe began before he had the chance to shush her. "For the first time in my life, Will, I'm not actually thinking about work."

Zoe parted her lips. Under the moonlight he watched breathlessly as her tongue darted along his fingertip. He found his breath again when she pulled it into her mouth and sucked slightly, drawing desire from his body.

"What's on your mind, then?" Will asked, already knowing the answer. She wasn't alone in this. He wanted her. He needed her.

"You," Zoe said, resuming her position against his body. The palm of her hand rested over his heart and its fast beat greeted her. A half grin spread across her face as she looked up with her head turned slightly. Zoe pressed her hand against her own heart. Through the fabric of her T-shirt, her heartbeat fluttered.

An owl hooted and cheered him on as Will lowered his head to brush his lips across Zoe's. There was that familiar sweet taste he'd had before. They fit perfectly together, her cradled against his frame. Will deepened their kiss, his arms wrapped tightly around her waist. He could take her right here and now at the edge of the forest.

"Zoe," Will said, hating to break the kiss. "We need to stop."

"Because of my dad?" Zoe cast a glance over her shoulder, shrugged and looked back up at him. Her long lashes batted against her cheeks. "He's not even home."

"Our first time is not going to be outside."

A wrinkle appeared between her nose and brows. "There you go, thinking I'm going to do something wild with you like that. I'm not that fast."

"Fast, huh?" Will tugged on her hands.

"You know what I mean."

Even with the darkness surrounding them Will could see her cheeks redden. "I already told you, nothing more is happening between us, at least not until we get back home."

"You're so sure of yourself?" Zoe asked. Zoe pressed her hands against his chest and caressed downward across his abs to the waistband of his pants.

Humid evening air filled his lungs. "Zoe," he warned.

The warning went unnoticed. With a defiant raised brow, Zoe locked eyes with him. Her hand slipped beneath his boxers. Just from kissing her, his body went back to his adolescent days and a semi-erection already peaked. When she wrapped her small hands around the base of him, however, he stiffened to granite.

Heat rose between them. Enjoying the sweet torture, Will leaned over and captured her lips with his. Each of her strokes and grip matched the intensity of their tongues. Excitement coursed through his veins. Will broke the kiss and set a thread of kisses along her chin, jaw and neck. With his hands free, Will cupped her breasts, kneading them with his palms. His thumb and forefinger rolled her nipple. Zoe leaned closer. Her hand moved up and down as well as it could within the restriction of his damn pants. Will needed to think. This was not the place he wanted to have a hand job. Blood pounded in his ears. His vision blurred.

"Zoe," Will whispered, "we can't do this here."

Zoe stepped out of Will's embrace. Ice water poured over him. "We're not," she smiled.

Laughing, Will shook his head. "Get in the car, woman, before I change my mind."

Chapter 8

Saturday morning, after tossing and turning all night long, Zoe awoke to the sound of birds chirping outside her window. Still in disbelief of her bold actions last night, Zoe rubbed her eyes with the palm of her hands. It was safe to say there was no turning back now regarding her relationship with Will. Lines were crossed. Zoe's fingers moved from her eyes to her mouth, where her lips tingled from heated dreams of Will. Her heart raced at the thought of seeing him again. Her body shivered with the idea of seeing him alone on the alleged date he said he wanted to take her on when they returned. She couldn't wait.

Eager to see him again, Zoe kicked her comforter off her body and headed for the bathroom. She gave her side of the door a soft knock, just to be safe. No one answered. Not sure why she was disappointed,

Zoe went ahead and took her shower. Steam hung in the air and coated the mirror by the time she finished. A thick, daffodil-yellow towel soaked up the moisture on her body. She tucked it under her arms and wiped down the mirror with her bare hands.

Tonight was their last night at Magnolia Palace. Kenzie had set up a fancy dinner. Yesterday while in the bathroom fixing Kimber's emergency, Lexi had mentioned she planned on sending over a proper dress for tonight's event. Zoe trusted Lexi's taste and couldn't wait to see what her friend chose. She couldn't wait to see Will in his suit. Hell, she couldn't wait to see *him* this morning.

"Hey, Zoe," Will said, knocking on his side of the bathroom door.

Zoe, careful to tiptoe on the rugs to avoid the cold floor on her bare feet, stepped over and opened the door. What did he call her last night? A tease? She'd show him. "Good morning," she said lightly.

From the way he was dressed, in a pair of black baller shorts and a black sleeveless T-shirt, along with the sweat glazing his hard muscles, Will had already been up and working out. He held a piece of perfectly crisp bacon in his big hands.

The look of shock on his face was perfect. Will's mouth dropped open. His eyes immediately went to the droplets of water dribbling from the wet curls of her hair and to the cleavage created by the way she held the towel. The Adam's apple at his throat visibly bobbed up and down as he tried to find words to say.

"Did you need something?"

"Um," Will began. "You have…"

"I have what?" Zoe shook her hair loose with her free hand.

Will blinked several times.

She reached for the lavender bottle of body cream, courtesy of Ravens Cosmetics. "I love this stuff." Zoe held the bottle for him to read the label. He didn't, so she popped the cap open and squirted the magnolia-scented lotion into one hand. Skillfully, she held the towel tucked under her arm and cocked one leg on the counter for a better angle to smear the product on it. The towel was long enough to cover the important parts.

"Will?" She tried to snap but her moistened fingers lacked the friction.

"Sorry," said Will, finally finding his voice. His eyes glanced up to where steam billowed out into his room. "There's someone here for you."

"Someone or some*thing*?" Zoe asked. "Lexi said she was sending over a dress today."

"Someone," Will repeated. He took a bite of his bacon and closed his eyes for a moment while he chewed. Zoe's stomach began to rumble from hunger for food and the man. "Actually, several people are here for you."

Zoe's brows fused together. "What?"

"Get dressed and meet me downstairs."

Curious, it took Zoe a matter of seconds to find a pair of blue gingham shorts and a matching plain blue top. She bounced down the steps toward the sound of chatter. Lots of chatter. The moment her foot hit the bottom step, a gaggle of girls began screaming. Zoe glanced over her shoulder for the rock star who must have been behind her. There was no one. They must have been screaming for her.

"What's going on?" Zoe asked, taking a step back from the wave of practically every flowery and fruity scent possible from Bath & Body Works.

Kenzie made her way through the crowd. "The prom for Southwood High is tonight."

"Yeah, I know."

Some of the girls began wringing their hands together and bobbing at the knees. No one wore a bit of makeup. Zoe looked at all their faces like blank canvases. A twinge jolted through her fingertips as she put two and two together. "Do you guys want some help?"

"Please?" the girls all chorused.

"Did we have plans today?" Zoe asked Kenzie.

"We just have the dinner this evening."

Zoe bit the corner of her lip. She would have loved to hang out with Will today, but this was what she considered an emergency. "Alright, let's form a line. Do any of you have pictures of your gowns with you?" Everyone held their cell phones in the air. The room lit up with colorful glowing screens. "Well then, let's get started. Who was here first?"

The girls all began to speak at once, trying to figure out who was at the head of the line. Other pageant staff was trying to maneuver through the foyer. Even though Zoe didn't use the private elevator, there was another guest who did. Kathleen wheeled out and was blocked by a few of the girls. Rebecca walked out of the dining room and accidently stepped on the toes poking out from one girl's flip-flops. This was not going to work.

Reading her mind, Will sprang into action. "Okay, okay, ladies, let's assemble a line here."

"I was here first."

"No, I was," someone else cried.

There was an easy way to handle this. Zoe stepped up another stair and cupped her hands against her mouth. "Alright, if you're wearing a tube top or something easy to slip over your head, step forward."

Understanding what she was trying to do, Kenzie nodded. "Okay, if you don't have an easy top on, run back home and change into something to slip on. If you need to slip your dress over your head, come back around three." Kenzie turned to glance up at Zoe for approval. She nodded. "Okay, let's get to it."

"I don't understand what's going on," Will whispered.

She didn't expect him to. Zoe patted the center of his back. "Those girls are going to put on their dresses over their heads, so the last thing they're going to want to do is smear their makeup on the material of the gown."

"I can help." Rebecca moved toward the stairs and held on to the banister. "I can do hair."

"And I can do nails," said a pageant staffer, Lily Ortiz, from the banister at the top of the stairs. The pretty nail tech and Zoe worked together in the past at fashion expos.

"Sounds like everyone has a job," Zoe said. "Alright, let's get to it."

All the girls began to scatter. Some began forming a single-file line while others trotted out the front door. Zoe turned and found Will staring at her with awe. He stood a step above her, causing her to stare right at his chest. The muscle shirt he wore revealed the work he put in at the gym. A long vein bulged down each bicep.

Will tipped her chin toward him with a brush of his finger. "What do you need me to do?"

"Probably nothing," Zoe said honestly.

A crash came from around the corner. Some of the men from the bed-and-breakfast rushed to the rescue. Luke backed out of the room carrying a broken vase. Ramon pushed his door open and accidentally hit another girl in the back of her legs.

"I've got an idea," said Will. "How about we start an assembly line of sorts in my room? The girls can hang out in there and come through our bathroom to keep out of the way down here."

Zoe sighed with appreciation. "You wouldn't mind?"

"Not all," Will said, sliding his hands into the pockets of his shorts. "I was still at home when my sisters started dating. Our house was pure chaos."

"This isn't just a date," Zoe reminded him. They started walking up the stairs together. The girls waddled in their heels behind them like ducks. "This is the prom."

"Well, if you remember, I wasn't home for prom."

"I didn't have a prom either," Zoe said, elbowing him in the ribs, "but I at least can remember how much I wanted to get all dressed up and go."

"Ah," Will began to counter, sliding his forefinger against the slope of her nose. Her cheeks flushed with heat at the touch. "You went to Comic-Con, though."

Zoe hid the sly smile by turning her head to the side. "Dressing up as the ultimate warrior princess was worth missing my prom."

Will placed both hands on her shoulders. She glanced up into his dark eyes and a flutter rushed in the pit of her stomach. "Wait, you dressed up in a frayed leather skirt and bustier?"

Her response was a grin. She already saw the wheels in his head turning. No, she didn't still have the outfit, but Zoe did have a pair of black spikey boots and star-spangled panties. Didn't everyone?

"You two should totally come tonight," blurted out one of the girls closest to the two of them. "I'm on the prom committee and I could totally get you in. You guys would totally be the coolest chaperones."

Will paused at the top step for a moment and wiggled his brows. "I'm totally up for the after-prom," he whispered in Zoe's ear. Some of the girls giggled. Maybe not at what he said, but at the way Zoe stumbled on the step.

Later on in the afternoon, after a trip to the ice cream shop for milk shakes and the pizza parlor for pizza and wings, Will returned to the hotel. The cars had disappeared from the parking lot. The lines had thinned down to a few girls getting their hair and nails done in the dining room and living room. He wondered if Zoe was finished. Will thought of the Creative Design Director position. Zoe displayed great leadership when it came to organizing the girls. She didn't panic, and her generosity in sharing her skills with these girls in their time of need humbled him. He wasn't sure how many of the interviewees would have taken time out of their day to help.

Because he'd been running back and forth all afternoon, he never got a chance to see the prom girls when Zoe was done with them. Will hated to admit he was frightened at first to see what kind of looks she'd placed on the girls. This would have been a live résumé for her. All the jobs in her portfolio were of heavily made-up people, although there were several artistic pictures. But Ravens Cosmetics didn't need artwork displayed on its clients' faces.

What Will wouldn't mind seeing, however, was a repeat of the view from this morning when she'd opened the door after her shower. The droplets of water against her brown skin haunted his brain, in a pleasant way. Damn, he couldn't take much more of this torture.

"Oh, hey, there you are." Kenzie's voice caught Will's attention. She rounded the corner from the kitchen with a pile of black garment bags in her arms blocking her face.

Will hurried toward her. "Let me get those. What are you doing with all of this stuff?"

"Evening attire," said Kenzie. She stretched her arms, then massaged her biceps. "Courtesy of Grits and Glam Gowns."

Lexi's shop, Will remembered. He draped the bags over one arm. "Where do you want the rest of these?"

"Come with me," Kenzie said, waving her arm down the other hallway. "We start down here."

As they made their way to each female guest's door, Kenzie went on about how excited she was about tonight. Even Will started to get excited. With each delivery of a dress, the ladies all squealed with youthful excitement, much like the teenagers from this morning.

"Have you enjoyed your time here at Magnolia Palace?" Kenzie asked. They waited for the elevator. She insisted he not climb the stairs with the rest of the garments.

Will nodded. "This place has been wonderful."

"I'm kind of partial to it, myself."

"Are you and Ramon partners?"

"No!" Kenzie hissed. Her light brown cheeks reddened and her lips pressed together. Quickly she shook her head and tucked a stray hair behind her ear. "I mean, we're not partners. I just have a deep-rooted attachment to this place."

"Did your parents get engaged here, like Zoe's folks?"

"Yes, but that's not the only reason." Kenzie regained herself. "This house used to belong to my family, back before the turn of the twentieth century."

"No kidding?"

"Never would kid," said Kenzie. "But during hard times, the structure was lost by the original builders and turned over to family members who made more bad investments in wartime."

"Until Ramon Torres came along?" Will asked. The elevator arrived at the second floor. Will waved his free hand for Kenzie to exit.

"Yes," Kenzie answered, looking at him over her shoulder.

Will nodded. "Smart of him to listen to you."

"Smart of me to be the town historian."

"That's a real thing, huh?" Will asked.

"Of course." Kenzie's cell phone rang. She glanced at the caller ID and declined the call. Will wondered if the *R* he saw pop up on her screen stood for Ramon. "Enough about my family drama. I can take the rest of the dresses down the hall if you'll give this one to Zoe."

At the sound of her name, Will grew excited. The pit of his stomach shifted with an odd feeling. "I can do that," he said coolly.

"Thanks, and I'll see you later tonight."

Will headed toward his room first. He wanted to clean himself up before seeing Zoe again. Since his door was closed, he assumed the girls had disappeared. He opened the door and the smell of flowers was now faint.

"I don't want to look like all the other girls," said a young voice.

"You're not," Zoe said to whomever was in her room. "I made sure no one was exactly the same."

"Except for your signature wingtip."

Zoe's light chuckle filled the air. Will smiled as he eavesdropped. This week he'd figured out what a wingtip was and saw how Zoe *perfected* it, as she liked to boast.

"But I want to look like Lil' Get This. Your Instagram with her got the most likes I've ever seen."

Lil' Get This, Will recalled with a sneer, who'd posed basically naked on her CD cover. The only thing the young rap artist had worn was Zoe's makeup. The photo was absent from Zoe's portfolio, but that didn't mean Will hadn't seen it.

"Lil' Get This is a professional artist."

Will would use that term loosely.

"You're going to have to remember that those ladies you see on my Instagram are going for a particular look, which is why they look that way," Zoe explained. "You don't think they walk around with a full face of makeup all day, do you?"

"Yeah, well, maybe. I've seen what you did with the teen girls on BET's Black Girls Rock show."

"I see you follow my work."

"I used to collect all the different magazines your models were in, but my mom said she'd kill me if I brought in any more clutter." The girl's statement reminded Will of what Zoe's parents might have said to her. Didn't she say she used to apply beauty products to the already printed magazine pages?

"So I have a page on my blog dedicated to your work." The girl continued naming all of Zoe's accomplishments. "I love the eighties, thanks to you. Music videos were the best."

"That's so sweet," Zoe sighed.

Will imagined Zoe beaming with pride at this moment. He pictured her cheeks turning red or her biting her bottom lip and avoiding a gaze.

"You're really cool. But I still want to look like someone else. I want to look like a star."

"Lisa," Zoe said, "you don't need all that heavy makeup to make you look like a star. Think of all the faces I've done. They're like superheroes. And like all superheroes, they are wearing a mask, but when they are just being themselves, they don't need all that extra stuff to hide their beauty. Does that make sense?"

"No." The word came out more with a whine but accompanied by a laugh. "But okay."

"When you get old enough, you can put your makeup on however you like, but for now, just enjoy being a kid and enjoy your prom."

"Thanks, Miss Zoe."

When Will heard Zoe's door close, he crossed through their bathroom and leaned against the door. From this angle it appeared her bottom half was encased in a pair of tube socks with three pink stripes. Zoe wore an apron with I Love Makeup spelled out in makeup items, such as a tube of mascara for the *I*, two eyeliner pencils making the *L*, red lipstick spelling out the *O* in a heart shape, and a powder brush as the *E*. The word *makeup* was spelled out in eyeliner. Her pink apron held several pockets, each containing either a variety of lipsticks, an eyelash contraption he'd seen his sisters use, or powder brushes. Zoe's long brown hair was piled up in a loose bun. Several strands had come loose from the band securing her tresses. Different shades of powder sprinkled her face. The insides of her forearms were streaked with various pink, mauve, red, gold and brown shades. She'd never looked more beautiful.

"Long day?" Will asked. He expected Zoe to fret about her hair or her attire. But, instead, she straightened her shoulders and stood tall.

"Yes, but I had a blast."

Will crossed the room, the garment bag under his arm. "I have something for you."

It was his intent to hand her the dress, but when she opened her arms, who was he to resist? Will set the bag on the edge of her bed and pulled Zoe's body into his. Their mouths met for two or three polite kisses, just lips, but then they fed into their desire, tongues circling fiercely together. His hands dragged across her bottom, fitting underneath the cuffs of her blue-and-white shorts. The ties of her apron brushed against the backs of his hands.

"I could get used to a greeting like that every day," Will breathed, breaking the kiss and brushing the tip of his nose against hers.

"Tell me about it." Zoe stroked the side of his face. He turned his face to kiss her palm. They needed to stop.

Though he shouldn't, Will thought of being able to

kiss Zoe like this every day. Every day at the office or every day at home. If she became the Creative Design Director, he wouldn't be able to do this. There'd have to be some boundaries, and right now, Will didn't want to test those.

Zoe stepped backward with her hands on her hips. "I need to start cleaning up in here before dinner tonight."

"Speaking of dinner," Will said, remembering the garment bag. "Kenzie delivered these for you from Lexi's." Like the other ladies had at their doors, Zoe squealed with excitement. Her face lit up as she yanked down the bag's zipper. Before Will had a chance to see, Zoe pressed the dress against her chest. "What?"

"Isn't it bad luck to see the dress?" Zoe wiggled her eyebrows at him.

"I believe that's for a wedding. We haven't had our first official date," Will replied and gave a lopsided grin. "We can start things off tonight, though. Care to be my date for the dinner?"

For a moment, Zoe glanced at the ceiling and pondered his question. "It is rather late to be asking."

"Someone's already asked?" Will faked being upset—or, rather, covered the bubble in his gut. He turned toward the door. "Who had the nerve to ask after I've staked my claim to you this week?"

"Staked," Zoe laughed, grabbing Will back by the arm. "What am I? An uncharted territory?"

He liked the way her hand fit around his biceps— made it totally worth working out all the time. Will caught her hand and pulled her up to him once again. Without thinking he lowered his head and his lips to hers. "I can't wait to explore."

Chapter 9

In the end, Zoe, of course, gave in to Will's request and allowed him to take her to dinner. It didn't hurt that he knocked on her door carrying a bouquet of flowers or that he became utterly speechless at the sight of her when she let him in.

She had to hand it to Lexi and her choice of dress. The floor-length black evening gown was flawless. A diamond band cinched her waistline and the strapless sweetheart neckline helped accentuate her assets. She wished she'd thought to bring her grandmother's good-luck pearls for this evening, but settled for a pair of diamond teardrop earrings instead. For dramatic effect, Lexi had sent along a pair of black evening gloves. Thankfully, tugging the hem of the gloves over her elbows distracted her from converting into a cartoon character with her eyes popping out of her head and her jaw dropping to the floor at Will, who was amazingly handsome in his crisp black tuxedo.

What took her breath away was the way the covered area out back at Mas was set up. Someone had taken it upon themselves to put lights on the ceiling, making it seem like they were dining under the stars. Kenzie had tuxedoed waiters to serve their meals. A long, triangular table held everyone working on the pageant and was covered with white linen cloths; someone had had the foresight to bring in free-standing air conditioners and place them at each corner. Some of the tables had been taken out and in their place was a portable dance floor. Soft music pumped into the area.

Dinner was a combination of Southern battered chicken and catfish, green beans with ham, and macaroni and cheese. Sweet tea filled the glasses and laugher echoed in the air.

"I can't believe I've had such a great week," Will said, covering Zoe's left gloved hand. They were seated together, and it wasn't the first time Zoe had felt the jitters each time he accidentally brushed against her leg or her arm.

Zoe bumped her shoulder against his arm. "Are the pressures of being CEO off?"

"Not off, just on hold."

"But after tomorrow you'll be back to the grind."

Will gave her hand a squeeze. "But now I've got you in my life."

Again the butterflies returned. She couldn't wait to spend time with Will at home, walk on the beach and dine across a moonlit table—just the two of them.

"I'm sorry to break up this lovefest," Kenzie said.

"Sure you are," Ramon mumbled, loud enough for

a few people around to hear when the music was lowered via remote control.

Judging from the way Kenzie rolled her eyes, she heard it, too. She rose from her seat at the head of the table and clinked her glass with her spoon. She continued until she reached the center of the dance floor where someone mysteriously had placed a podium. "Our host, Lexi Pendergrass Reyes, couldn't be here this evening, but she wanted the night to continue."

A round of applause broke out. Zoe wondered if Lexi's absence meant Stephen had made her stay home because tomorrow was going to be a big day or because the baby was ready to make an appearance two months early. Surely Zoe would have received a text message or something.

"This week we all got the chance to get to know each other," Kenzie began. "We've seen the hard work put into making a pageant by the lighting people, stage hands, artists and even the judges." Kenzie glanced at everyone who made up part of the crew. "Hopefully we've bonded enough to trust each other's opinions come tomorrow. Whether it's with the makeup and hair, or when it comes to the judging."

Another round of applause.

Zoe glanced around at the people she'd gotten to know this week and figured everyone had some common sense. Even Rebecca had come around and performed selflessly that morning. She half expected the hairstylist to not give the prom girls the time of day. The only person Zoe thought might cause problems was the beauty queen, Vera Laing. According to Lexi, she'd invited Vera, her former student, to judge but worried their relationship had suffered irrevocable damage. Lexi trained the beauty queen from the time she was a toddler but left because of a conflict of interest. Lexi loved Vera but never knew what Vera had been told about the circumstances of Lexi's departure. Vera and her mother were the only two who had not wanted to participate in any of the activities. This was simply a free vacation for them.

"So, in order to commemorate our time together, Ramon and I have been gathering intel and we've put a lot of thought and consideration together last night to come up with a list of awards we want to hand out to you all."

Ramon stood and walked to the podium with a rolled-up piece of paper in his hands. Zoe got the feeling he didn't want to do this, but she knew how persuasive Kenzie could be. It was the first time Zoe had seen Ramon in a suit and he looked rather handsome. His black hair was slicked back and off his face, and finally Zoe saw the resemblance between him and his cousins Stephen and Nate.

"First and foremost, thanks for coming to my hotel," Ramon said, leaning into the microphone. "This has been a successful week and it's been a pleasure getting to know you."

Beside him, Kenzie cleared her throat.

"Ah, yes, we gave this a lot of thought and consideration last night."

Last night? Zoe thought with bewilderment. *Hmm, what's going on here?* She certainly knew what she'd been doing last night. Zoe placed her hand in Will's lap and squeezed his leg. His eyes darted to her. Zoe stared straight ahead and began drawing circles on his pants leg up his thigh. The bulge between his legs grew and pressed against her arm.

"...and so for the most helpful one, especially since he helped me fix all these lights up here," Ramon was saying, "I'd like to present the award of Most Handy to Tim Hernandez."

The crowd clapped again, and to Zoe's surprise, Kenzie reached under the podium and presented Tim with a gold statue.

Awards were given out left and right. Most Helpful, Most Spirit, Most Southern. Zoe entertained herself with fondling Will. She enjoyed the way he inhaled each time she cupped his crotch through his pants. His erection grew, turning her on even more. She stroked, squeezed and turned herself on with the image of herself riding him. Will's jaw twitched.

"And for the..." Ramon stopped and turned toward Kenzie. His hand covered the microphone but his muffled words were heard. "Do I really have to say it?"

"It's not going to kill you," Kenzie huffed.

Will reached for Zoe's hand and put it back on the table, wagging his index finger. He leaned so close to her ear his breath tickled her lobe. "Be careful what you start, my little tease."

"Whatever." Zoe pressed her lips together to keep from grinning.

"Whatever," Ramon said into the microphone. "We conclude this awards ceremony with the—" he cleared his throat "—with the cutest couple." He said the words as if they pained him. "Will Ravens and Zoe Baldwin."

Shocked, Zoe shook her head. "Oh, we're not..."

"Not fooling anyone," Kenzie said, pushing Ramon

away from the microphone. "Now, come on up here and get this award."

Zoe didn't get a chance to protest. After buttoning his jacket as he rose and hunched over, Will extended his hand for Zoe to take and positioned her in front of him. She obliged, knowing what she hid for him from the rest of the guests. The table clapped for them as they made their way to the podium. Ramon handed Will an envelope and Kenzie handed Zoe a gold statue of two silhouettes kissing.

"Now, let's conclude this evening with a dance."

Will took Zoe by the hand and led her to the floor. She stood against him, fitting perfectly. She took his hand and the music began, though she barely heard the melody. Others began to crowd the dance floor.

"Well, you have to admit," Will said, "we are the cutest couple."

"We are the *only* couple."

"Are we?" Will inclined his head toward Kenzie and Ramon. The two were dancing closely together, but the tight grin across Kenzie's face said something else.

Zoe turned her attention back to Will. Her heart fluttered. There was something Zoe was supposed to do or say to stop him from kissing her in front of everyone, but she couldn't think of what it was. Their bodies began to fall into perfect rhythm.

"This can't be good," Will whispered against her neck.

If things didn't cool off, Zoe was about to melt in his arms. Her eyes rolled backward with the warmth of his breath. "If it ain't good…" she began.

"Zoe, I need you," Will said, licking his lips.

The only thing Zoe heard was he needed her—that,

and her Prince ringtone going off inside the pocket of her clutch bag. Will pressed his head against her forehead. "Go ahead and answer that."

Will pressed his hands on her backside and guided Zoe back to their table where she retrieved her cell phone. She attempted to slide her finger across the screen but her gloves gave her a bit of a fit. She slipped them off her arms and swiped her finger across Lexi's face.

"Hey, girl," Zoe said, trying to sound cheerful, pushing off the feeling that a bucket of ice had doused her evening. Thank God for the portable air conditioners. Zoe glided toward one and let it cool off her body. "Are you okay?"

"I'm fine," Lexi said. "I am watching a live feed from bed."

"What?" Zoe held her phone by her side and glanced around until she spotted a red light mixed in with the faux stars. "What are you doing?"

"Saving your potential career," Lexi said. "I saw you and Will just now."

"So?"

"When I saw y'all's name on the list for cutest couple, I thought it was a joke. Jesus, Zoe, you're applying for a position in his company."

The proverbial cold water continued to fall, dousing any inkling of a hot night. "Okay, Lexi. I understand."

After a few more lines about not messing up and sleeping where you work, Lexi had drilled the message into Zoe's head. Like a child having been scolded, Zoe hung up the phone and crossed her arms over her chest.

"Is everything okay?" Will asked the question as his hands warmed her shoulders. She hadn't realized the AC had chilled her to her bones. Or maybe it was Lexi's words. Either way, Zoe stepped out of Will's embrace and turned to face him.

"I'm fine." Zoe half smiled. An ache squeezed her heart. Common sense told her she'd find someone else, sooner or later. Right now her priority was landing the Creative Design Director job with Ravens Cosmetics. "You know, it's been a long day. I probably need to head on back to the hotel and rest up for tomorrow."

Nodding, Will reached for her again, successfully pressing his hand against her lower back. "Let me tell everyone we're leaving."

"No," Zoe exclaimed, holding her hand in the air. "The last thing I need is for everyone to see us leaving together."

"I'm sorry." Will shoved his hands in his front pockets and cocked his head as if it gave him a better understanding of what she said. "Did I miss something?"

"No."

"We were having a good time just a few minutes ago." He reached for her again and in order to not make a scene, Zoe let him.

The brush against her arm sent chills down her spine. In the few seconds she tried to keep him away, his touch created such a sensation throughout her body she realized that she needed it. Zoe blinked toward the lights overhead to keep from letting a teardrop fall. She needed to focus. "We were having a good time, Will. But I need a break. I've got to go."

Foolishly, Zoe had left with no secured plan on how to get back to the hotel. She headed down Mas's driveway toward the street. In her dress and heels, she regretted her decision to leave the party. Zoe slid her phone open, searched for an Uber driver near her and placed an order for a pickup.

Less than five minutes later a car pulled up to the mailbox. But it wasn't the Uber car she'd called. Instead, it was a stretch limousine. The back window rolled down and a gaggle of girls screamed Zoe's name. In the center of the group of girls sticking out of the sunroof was Kimber Reyes, toting a crown so big it caught the moonlight across the crystals.

"Evening, ladies," Zoe said, cheering up. When she'd last checked her phone the time was close to midnight. Didn't they have curfews? "What are you doing out this late?"

"After-party!" someone yelled.

"We wanted to sneak and get a look at your party," Kimber said.

"Like, you saved all of us today," another girl said.

Someone popped the door open and Zoe sighed as she climbed in. "Well, thanks for the lift. How was the prom?"

Everyone began to talk at once. The space of the limo was filled with girls and Zoe wondered where all their dates were, but someone else mentioned again about an after-party about to get started. The story the girls gave was that they'd all been together since elementary school and they started out every party together. They'd promised each other that once they were seniors, no matter what cliques they were in, they'd all hang out together at prom. They'd managed to do the same thing for every party throughout middle and high school. Zoe liked the idea of the girls all sticking together rather than focusing on being with boys.

It was the confirmation Zoe needed to stay focused on her goals.

The limousine made its way to the front steps of Magnolia Palace. "Are you guys coming to the pageant tomorrow?" Zoe asked with her hand on the door before their chauffeur could open it.

"I'll be there all day," Kimber said with a droll roll of her eyes. "Come hell or high water, I've got to be there."

"Why the long face?" Zoe asked.

"Because y'all are starting at the crack of dawn, which limits how long I can stay out tonight."

Zoe grinned and patted Kimber's shoulder. "Behave tonight."

"I'd say the same to you," Kimber teased right back. "But considering you've gone home alone, I'm guessing you have no choice."

"You're cute."

"And you're pretty," said Kimber. "Don't waste your pretty."

Unprepared for the girl's rather grown-up response, Zoe burst out in laughter. "Get going, child. I'll see you tomorrow."

The girls went on down the road, chanting for the driver to lay on the limo's horn. Zoe headed upstairs, laughing the whole way to her room. She was glad for the peace and quiet.

Not wanting to get out of her gorgeous dress so soon, Zoe kicked off her heels and headed into the bathroom to begin her nightly rituals. A part of her felt guilty for leaving Will at the party without so much as an explanation. As she reached for Ravens Cosmetics's makeup-remover cream, Zoe realized he deserved to know why she left. But if she'd told him, he would only have tried to convince her she was wrong. What she was, was swept up with the Southern heat. After wiping the last remnants of cream off her face, Zoe heard a knock. Her heart slammed against her rib cage.

"I know you're in there," Will said from the other side of the door.

Zoe contemplated tiptoeing back to her room, but she wanted to lay eyes on him before going to bed. If she couldn't have him in real life, she could always dream about him. "Why did you leave the dinner?" Zoe asked, opening the door.

The black bowtie hung loose around Will's neck and the top three buttons of his white shirt were undone. The cut of his shirt complemented his hard jawline.

"I left because finding out what's going on with you is more important than sitting at the table watching everyone else dance."

Zoe shrugged her shoulders. "There were other people you could have danced with."

"I only wanted you." Will reached for her hand, pressing it against his beating heart. "What changed when you took that phone call?"

"What are you talking about?"

"Don't act like I don't know you by now, Zoe."

Zoe took a step backward. "No, what you know is the Zoe who has had her head fogged up in these Southern nights. Not the Zoe you met over a week ago when I applied for the director's position."

"Zoe," Will sighed.

She'd heard what he said about not liking her work. She didn't care. "Until I get an official word on Ravens Cosmetics stationery thanking me for the time but saying y'all have decided to go in a different direction, I still have a fighting chance."

"And so I have no say in this?" Will asked, letting her hand go.

"Not really. Save your say for something official, and then let's go from there. Right now I don't want to risk what I've worked so hard for."

Will's mouth dropped open. He stood in the doorway, gawking. "You're serious."

"As a heart attack."

"And what about your personal life, Zoe?" Will asked. "You want to stand here and say your career is worth more than your happiness?"

Zoe wasn't sure what the answer was. She shrugged her shoulders and stepped backward.

"You want to stand here and tell me what's been brewing between us is just some Southern spell?"

"Yes," Zoe said, finding her voice. "We'll have to wait for everything business between us to be over."

"And if you start with Ravens Cosmetics?" asked Will. "We're supposed to act like there's nothing between us?"

"Looks that way."

"So, either way I'm being punished?"

Zoe narrowed her eyes on his face. His lips were thin and his jawline twitched. It killed her to deny them what they both wanted. Her body trembled with such craving. "Will, you're utterly handsome, heir to the throne of Ravens Cosmetics. You're bothered that you're not getting your own way. And I dare say you're pouting."

"Pouting?" Will snorted out a laugh.

Zoe threw her hands in the air and backed farther away. "Whatever. I'm going to bed."

"And just like that," Will called out to her, "you're done talking?"

"Yep," Zoe yelled over her shoulder, "looks that way to me." She attempted to kick the door to the bathroom closed with the heel of her bare foot and out of the corner of her eye saw a lightning-like bolt darting toward her.

"Good, because I'm done talking, too."

Will came up behind Zoe and wrapped his arms around her waist. She had just enough time to spin around, face him and open her mouth to protest. Will braced her backside and dipped her. His mouth descended on hers and Zoe loved every moment of it. Will's left hand slid down the length of her dress and lowered the zipper, exposing her to his touch. His fingers were like feathers, tickling and caressing every inch of her. Zoe's right leg curled up and wrapped around his waist. She moaned against him.

Not breaking the kiss, Will lifted Zoe in his arms and brought her over to her bed. The soft mattress absorbed their weight. Will's magical mouth made love to hers. His hands played with skin, toyed with her nipples and rolled one between his thumb and forefinger. Juices of flat-out desire flowed through her veins.

"W—" Zoe tried to say his name when he broke the kiss, but when she pulled her head back he pressed his finger against her lips. She waited with anticipation as he moved down her body. He left a trail of sensual kisses behind her ear, neck and throat, and between her breasts. Her nipples throbbed in anticipation of the warmth of his mouth. She closed her eyes tight as she grew dizzy. Humidity hung in the air, but when Will's tongue circled her nipples, she realized how cool her flesh was. She hadn't known just how much she needed him.

Will set another trail of kisses down the curve of her belly. Warm air filtered through her black panties, and when his fingers breached the material Zoe's hips bucked forward. Zoe discovered he had at some point moved his finger from her mouth when he used both hands to slide her panties over her hips. Using his thumbs, he gently caressed the tender skin of her upper thigh. Zoe opened her legs wider for him to touch. She throbbed for him.

Will leaned forward, and as Zoe inhaled deeply, he satiated her craving for his touch by delving his tongue into the folds of her lips. Zoe gasped silently and stared upward, where their shadows danced on the ceiling. Heat lightning flashed outside the bay windows. Her toes curled. Will's tongue licked up and down, sucking and devouring. He sank his forefinger into her wet flesh, and she quivered and wantonly moved her legs over his broad shoulders. Each time she moaned, he pressed further with his ministrations. A wave of what Zoe expected to be the first of many orgasms came.

Another bolt of heat lightning flashed against Will's face. He grinned smugly and shrugged out of his shirt. Zoe didn't dare speak. She licked her lips in eagerness and scrambled to her knees. The palms of her hands itched, wanting to touch him again. Will stood, unbuttoned his trousers and shrugged out of them and his briefs at the same time. His arousal was evident, with the massive erection pointing toward her as he rolled a clear condom over it. Zoe reached her hand to take him but he gently pushed her hand away.

"Will?" she cried, her brows fusing together.

"You had your chance to talk, Zoe." Will inched closer to her. "You've told me all the reasons why we shouldn't be together and now I'm going to show you why we need to be together."

In the darkness Will reached for the back of her thigh and, in one swift swoop, landed her flat on her back. In the process, Zoe wrapped her legs around Will's waist. Will's thick shaft pressed into her with ease. They both gasped when he fully filled her. A switch went off between the two of them. Their mouths clicked together and they found their perfect rhythm. Zoe's head swam with dizziness. This was so right. So perfect. She moaned and arched her hips. Will pumped deeper. Even though she was on her back, the sensation of free-falling washed over her. Zoe clung to Will's back, and he rolled over and positioned her on top of him.

With her knees supporting her weight, Zoe rocked back and forth, grinding her body against his. She set the tempo to a ballroom foxtrot—quick, quick, slow. Will groaned and eased himself up so she sat in his lap. He feasted on her breasts and Zoe wrapped her arms around his neck again. Sweat drizzled between their bodies. Will nibbled her chin and licked her collarbone. His hands tightened their grip on her body, skin against skin, and guided the rhythm as he drove into her. Zoe bounced and called out his name. At one point, Zoe tossed her head back in the throes of another spectacular orgasm and noticed the rain coming down outside. Water poured against the glass as Zoe melted onto Will. He crisscrossed his arms across her back and pulled her down by the shoulders, then rolled with her, so her back was against the mattress.

Will covered her mouth with his. Zoe mewed against him. She didn't know where she wanted to touch him next. Her fingers splayed on his chest. Will lifted his head, offered a lopsided grin, then pulled her hands over her head and pushed against the headboard. Balancing himself on his elbows, Will stared into her eyes and made love to her visually and physically. He looked as if he was taking in an art piece. She felt exquisite and desired.

A tear threatened at the corner of her eye. She might have cried if another orgasm hadn't taken over. Will's body sped up and shivered as they climaxed at the same time. Any bit of doubt she may have had over the two of them being together was washed away.

Chapter 10

Like the rain, the power of the storm between Zoe and Will subsided. At the crack of dawn Will rose from his well-earned slumber. Zoe lay on her side facing him. Her hands were folded in a prayer position beneath her cheek. The only thing missing was a halo over her cute, messy bed head. She looked like an angel. Will smiled when her long lashes fluttered against her cheekbones.

Last night had been incredible. His heart filled with something unfamiliar. He never wanted this moment to end. Zoe belonged with him. Somehow he needed to figure things out. Since watching Zoe with the prom girls and hearing her explanation about appropriate makeup, Will's vehemence about her being over-the-top had subsided.

"Young William," a feminine voice called out.

If Will wasn't mistaken, it sounded a lot like his

sister Eva. She was the one who called him that. Will guessed from sound of the knock that she was at his door. This also meant her twin was somewhere close. This was the last thing he needed.

"Let me do it. Jerraud taught me a few tricks with locks."

So Dana was here, as well. Naked, Will slid out of the bed and trotted back through the bathroom. He locked his side for privacy and sanity.

"You and your husband have problems," Eva said.

"What? We have hobbies."

Will grabbed a pair of red ballers and slipped them on before he opened the door. Dana, on her knees, caught her balance before hitting the floor. Eva, however, tripped over her sister.

"Is spying on your brother one of them?" Will asked. He leaned over to help Eva to her feet. Though she was older by a few years, she was still a foot shorter than he was.

"Will," Eva and Dana chorused.

"Eva wanted to see the pageant." Dana brushed her hands together. "I wanted to see Sasha Foxx again. It's been a while since we walked down the runway together."

"Whatever. I came partially for the pageant," Eva said, rolling her eyes. "My other reason is to figure out what's going on between you and Zoe Baldwin."

The mention of her name made his heart jump. Will knew he wanted Zoe to be a part of his life for a while. He just wasn't sure he wanted his family to know yet. Clearly Dana already discussed Zoe with Eva. It was only a matter of time before whatever story

Dana came up with would spread to the family. "She's in her room."

"And you know this how?" asked Eva. She sauntered into the room, her head turning as she snooped in every direction. "Where were you last night?"

"I thought there was a formal dinner," Dana added.

Here came the inquisition. "There was," Will answered.

"Where's your suit?" Eva asked, opening the closet. "It's not on the floor and you never pick up after yourself."

Will trotted to the closet and closed the doors before Eva discovered it missing. "What exactly are you two doing in Southwood?"

"We wanted to watch the pageant," the girls chorused. Their sound came out in sync, with Eva beside him with her hand still jiggling the closet handle and Dana on the other side inspecting his made-up bed.

Damn. Will leaned against the closed closet and watched the twins spy. Thank God he hadn't brought Zoe in here last night. Thinking of her put a smile to his face. To be sure he didn't act on his thought, Will swiped his hand down his face. He needed to shave. Hell, he needed to shower. Along with the long list of things Will needed to do, he needed to figure out what the twins were up to. They glanced nervously back and forth at each other.

"There's more you're not telling me," he said.

"And there's something you're not telling us," Dana said, changing the subject. His sisters were nosy, but this nosy? "Like, who have you been with, Will?"

Avoidance? Will scratched the top of his head. "What's going on with the company?"

"Nothing." Dana shrugged her shoulders. "The whole board came into Southwood."

"What?" Will did a double take. The idea of his cousins, all the cousins, being there did not sit right with him. He got that RC provided the makeup. Did they make a personal trip just to deliver the goods?

"They're just here. No big deal. Don't worry about it." Eva pushed Will by the shoulder. Easy for her to say. Eva stood on her tiptoes and took a whiff of air. As Will dodged one sister by sidestepping her, the other came up behind him and inhaled. "You smell like you've been using our products."

"What's going on, Will?" Dana asked. "Why are you so jumpy?"

"I'm jumpy because you started banging on my door at the crack of dawn," said Will. "Where's the rest of the group? I know y'all don't travel too far without them." He waited a moment to hear the sound of destruction from his nieces and nephews.

"This is a business trip," they said again in unison, and giggled at themselves.

"The anti-cousins were, uh," Eva began, "not too happy when they learned from Marcus that Zoe Baldwin was here as the beauty consultant."

"Great," Will mumbled. "Which ones are here?"

"Dixon, Katie, Brandon and Charles." Eva used her fingers to tick off the names. "And Cora came."

"Cora's neutral," Will said. One of the youngest of the Ravens, Cora was too busy living her life as a college student to helm a corporation.

"She didn't think it was fair that one interviewee got special treatment."

Irritation consumed Will. His knuckles cracked as

he made a fist. This would be worse for Zoe now if she did get the position. Knowing Will and Zoe had spent time here together might bug Cora enough to side with the anti-cousins.

"I don't get why they're so quick to make a decision on the position if they are ready to call it quits. Something doesn't add up."

"Your guess is as good as mine," Dana sighed. "But you know we have your back in whatever decision you make."

"Well, if you ladies don't mind, I need to get dressed."

Dana was the first to roll her eyes. "Whatever. We used to change your diapers when you were little."

Eva punched him in the arm. "Don't be so modest."

"I'm grown now," Will clarified and puffed out his chest. "Let the record show, you two forced me to play house with you when I was walking and out of diapers."

There was a laundry list of things Will wanted to say to prove to his sisters he was a grown man but Dana's phone rang.

"No," Dana sighed. "We're up in his room. No, he's awake."

For a moment Will wondered who his sister was on the phone with, but he heard Donovan's distinct deep voice on the other end of the call. "Get out of his room so he can get ready."

"Fine, whatever," Dana huffed.

The next time he went out with his brother, Will was buying for the night. He strolled over to the bedroom door and yanked it open. "Tell Donovan I owe him."

The girls began to leave, but not before Eva sized him up. "We're not done here, mister."

And somehow Will knew they weren't. Once the

girls left, Will pressed his ear against the door to make sure his nosy sisters' voices traveled down the stairs. The first thing he needed to do was make sure Zoe was okay and, hopefully, still asleep. He pulled open the bathroom door and found Zoe leaning against the double sink with her arms folded. Long, dark strands of hair spilled over her shoulders. A yellow-and-white polka-dot towel was wrapped around her succulent brown body. Jealous of the terrycloth material, Will forgot what he wanted to say.

"So," Zoe sighed with a grin. "You wore diapers longer than the average child, huh?"

"You heard that?" Will bit his bottom lip to keep from cursing and quite possibly blushing over this re-vealed secret.

"Just the most important part." Zoe giggled. "I bet you were a cute kid. I can't wait to see pictures of you when you were younger. Did they dress you up, too?"

"My sisters are crazy."

"They sound like fun," Zoe said, "and concerned."

"That concern is called being nosy." Will reached out and stuck his finger into the crease in Zoe's towel. He tugged but she stood her ground.

Zoe shook her head. She pulled away and Will is-sued a silent prayer that the towel would fall. He didn't think he'd ever get tired of seeing her body. The curves. The softness. The wetness.

"In less than thirty-six hours..." Zoe began.

"We'll be on our first date?" Will dropped his hand and stroked his face again, remembering he needed to shave. "Or are we going for round six tonight?"

"I believe we made it to round seven," Zoe said with

a wink. "I see why you have this TOP tattoo." Soft fingers brushed against the space above his heart.

"That's my fraternity."

Her perfect lips formed an O.

"Didn't you pledge anything in college?" There was something about the striped tube socks Zoe wore that gave him the image of her in a pledge line.

More of Zoe's hair spilled over her shoulders when she shook her head. "Did you forget I was a nerd?"

A nerd was the furthest thing from his mind.

"Well, I was. There weren't too many sorority girls asking me to join or any frat guys banging on my door to date me. The Greek life didn't work out for me."

The only person who was going to bang on her door from here on out was going to be him. He couldn't wait to see what her place looked like. Did she have the same kind of posters on her walls as she did in her childhood bedroom? "I'm looking forward to our date tonight."

"Tonight?" Zoe perked up.

"We can have our first date when we return to Miami," Will clarified. "And perhaps tonight I'll keep better track of how many times you climax."

"But then again, if tonight is our first date, I ought to behave. I wouldn't want you to get the wrong impression of me."

"You've already made an impression, baby."

Zoe stepped up and gave him a kiss on his chin. The soft feel of her tongue and nibble of her teeth fueled his erection. "I'll impress you more this afternoon."

"Speaking of this afternoon," Will groaned, "I am afraid my brothers are here, as well."

"A family affair?"

"Well, we are sponsoring all the makeup." Will lifted the lavender jar of lotion and opened the top. Slowly he dipped his finger into the creamy white center and pulled out a dollop on his finger, then swiped it across her bare shoulder. "Which means the only products you can use are Ravens."

"I can make that work." Zoe leaned her head to the side and kissed his thumb.

"And it should mean the only products on you should be Ravens."

Zoe dropped the towel. "What about putting a Ravens body part in me?"

And who was he to say no?

After a quick tryst in the shower, Zoe kissed Will goodbye and headed next door to the pageant. There was a nice-sized building off to the side of the hotel that was home to small concerts. Today it held fifty girls, all aiming to win the crown of Miss Southwood. Parents and children, fans and talent scouts already filled the seats. Children in fluffy dresses practiced their dance moves in the hallway and aisles. Older teens fiddled with their cell phones as they stood around in line, waiting for hair and makeup.

Zoe waved to her new friends, the production crew. Her feet barely hit the ground on her way to the beauty room. She and Will had plans for tonight. Zoe pushed the job out of her mind for now. Their future held nothing but excitement.

"Hey, Zoe," Lily exclaimed. "We're stuck over here." She waved a metallic fingernail file with a cream-colored handle in the air to catch Zoe's attention.

All the nail accessories and products at Lily's station bore the signature cream, gold and lavender colors of Ravens Cosmetics, but the dozens of bottles were filled with various bright colors, stemming from the brightest of pinks and neon blues, to the soft classic pale pink and even to a black. It was refreshing to see Ravens stepping to the plate to meet their competitors.

"Swanky digs you've got here," Zoe said with a low whistle. Ravens Cosmetics had gone all out to make sure their name was seen.

Lily nodded her head in agreement. "As is y'all's."

"Y'all's?"

"Sorry," Lily blushed. Zoe loved the shade of red on her cheeks. She clearly did not need any makeup. "I've been in Southwood too long. I meant you guys have a nice setup over there."

"Over there" meant a long station with at least six black chairs in front of makeup mirrors. Confusion clouded Zoe's head. She was under the impression she'd be the only makeup artist today. The pageant started at noon and she would have been working nonstop until at least four. A part of her was relieved to know she'd be able to give each contestant her full attention. As a professional she could get a job done in ten minutes.

"Zoe." Rebecca waved a gold curling iron with a pearl handle in Zoe's direction. "Hey, girl."

Zoe was in midwave when the man standing next to Rebecca turned around. She snarled when their eyes locked. "Titus."

"Zoe," he mouthed with utter disdain, then turned his attention to Rebecca. "So, you two are supposed to be friends now?"

Rebecca's soft smile didn't ease the situation. "We're friends, Titus. Stop being rude."

"I'll stop being rude when she stops thinking she brought eighties makeup back by telling everyone I copied her."

Her upper lip curled, Zoe's body heated from the blood boiling in anger and with her fists clenched she stalked forward. "Why are you even here?"

"Uh, it looks like I'm about to show Ravens Cosmetics that I'm their new Creative Design Director." In usual Titus fashion, he did a dramatic spin. His black smock twirled around his large frame.

"I don't understand," Zoe snapped.

"You didn't think you were going to keep the CEO's attention all to yourself?" Titus asked with his hands on his hip. "Luckily for me, the board found out about this little trip."

Suddenly Zoe remembered what Will had told her about half the board at Ravens. They wanted to see the company fail. Bringing Titus on certainly would do the job. She needed to talk to Will. Did he know what they were trying to do? Zoe absentmindedly reached to touch her good-luck pearls and remembered again that she hadn't brought them with her.

"Don't look so lost." Titus continued to gloat. "Once I am the CDD, I may hire you to consult on the Halloween special I plan on hosting."

Rebecca elbowed Titus in the gut and offered Zoe an apologetic smile. "Go gather your girls, Titus. Let Zoe get settled in her station."

It was then Zoe realized that her station was right next to Titus's. Photographs of the contestants were taped against their mirrors, lining the frames. Zoe went over to her spot and peeked inside her beauty box. Any bit of anger washed away. Lying in the center of the lavender satin box was the soon-to-be-released glitter lipstick from Ravens Zoe had been dying to get her hands on. The lipstick was a two-part design, one containing color, the other glitter. This was the idea she'd been concocting for a while now, but it had taken using several different products for one ultimate look. Someone at Ravens had a great mind like her. She couldn't wait to collaborate. A few celebrity faces popped into mind, women who would love buying this in one tube rather than combining lipsticks. Renewed energy gushed through her veins. Zoe was armed with all the tools she needed and was headed into battle.

The girls Zoe had been given were all under the age of twenty. As with most pageants, there were age divisions. All of the makeup artists were given girls from each group. The Wee Peaches were between the ages of one and five. Everyone had at least one Wee Peach but Lexi insisted those girls be as natural as possible. The next division was the six-to-eleven age group. These girls were given full glitz makeup if they wanted it. This meant they could wear false lashes and false teeth—or flippers, as they were called. Zoe hated to admit that Titus's work was heavy but good. Zoe was not too comfortable putting her signature wingtip on. They were still little girls.

The contestants were broken down in ages somewhere between twelve and fifteen, and then sixteen to twenty-six. All were dazzled with the makeup and wanted more. Some of them were eager to sit in Zoe's chair because their sisters had gotten their makeup done for prom yesterday. Occasionally Titus stood by and sneered. It didn't help that during her downtime, Rebecca shared photographs from last night's dinner. He muttered under his breath about how, if Zoe was given the position, he was sure he knew why. Titus even commented about the time stamp on each photograph and noticed that, at some point, Zoe and Will disappeared. This was exactly the kind of thing Lexi had warned her about.

By noon, the beauty portion of the pageant was on its way for the sixteen- to twenty-three-year-olds. Zoe enjoyed getting to know her girls and learning about them. She wanted each girl's makeup to be an expression of herself, rather than a painted face. In Zoe's eyes, none of the other artists were competition. But Titus went for the kill. He didn't care about the ages of the girls. He used the glitter gloss on each girl. Zoe was tempted, but she knew the colors were too mature for clients. And, unlike Titus, Zoe's groups of contestants were all under the age of sixteen. She overheard one of Titus's girls say she was twenty-six. A part of her wondered if this was part of the competition. Was Ravens Cosmetics looking for a way for the interviewees to integrate their new makeup line?

Everyone was able to take thirty to forty-five minutes for lunch. Everyone who worked backstage gathered around the long buffet table. Riddled with guilt, Zoe decided to give Lexi a call. She needed to know what she should do. Did she go against her morals of keeping young girls looking young or did she go full out to get the job? The cell service in the back was horrible.

Zoe went outside to get better reception. She headed over to the bridge for privacy and clarity. Lexi's phone went straight to voice mail, so Zoe decided to finish her walk, then she'd try again. She wondered if her father had ever made it out here to check out the view. At any point now, Zoe expected a call from him to give the go-ahead to bring her mom back. It wasn't like her mother didn't know about the proposal. He did it every year, just in different places.

The summer sun felt good on her face. Freezing air conditioning blasted in Zoe's station. It had to, in order to keep the girls from melting. Green leaves littered the walkway of the bridge over the lake. With everything there was to do this week, there hadn't been a lot of time for long strolls over the water. A low limb of a weeping willow blocked part of the way. As she grew closer the clear sound of a conversation grew louder. Zoe hesitated and wondered if she should turn around or try to walk through the group talking.

"So, how did Will take it when he found out we're backing his choice for the director by whomever he votes to win the pageant?"

Will? Zoe decided to stand still. Whoever was talking about Will—*her Will*—did not have a caring pitch to his tone. Through the leaves she spied three people: two men and a woman. All three had the height of the Ravens family. She wondered if these were some of the cousins Will warned her about.

"Charles, can you believe he told me and Dixon it was fine?" the woman said. She spoke as if her head were held high in the air, very snooty. "As if he has things under control. I can't stand him."

"Katie," the man named Charles answered, clapping his hands together, "we are so close to being done with this company, once and for all. We just need to focus."

"I promise you guys—forcing Will to choose this quickly is going to throw his game," said the man Zoe guessed was Dixon.

"I can't believe he has no idea we found Octavia." Charles rubbed his hands together manically.

A row of hairs rose on the back of Zoe's neck. Octavia Ravens? The missing heir?

"We'll just keep her under wraps until after the final vote. Grandma will be upset with the company, but we'll be the ones softening the blow when we bring our long-lost aunt home." Charles chuckled. "Let Grandma's favorite continue thinking he knows what he's doing."

"And we owe this to my fabulous sis." Dixon gave a silent round of applause. "If you hadn't broken your nail after trying to negotiate things at Pink Stilettos Cosmetics, we might never have had this opportunity." He gave a harrumph. "Will ain't the only one who can play hero."

"Oh, my God, don't get me started," Katie gasped. "Did you hear him talking about beat-faces and winged eyeliner? You would have thought he took a class."

Through the seething anger, Zoe's heart swelled with pride. So Will had been listening to her all this time.

"Whatever," a male voice said. "He still thinks he's going to be Grandma's savior."

"That's because he never had to work hard a day in his life," the woman sneered.

Well, Zoe shrugged, before knowing Will, she might have agreed there. But that didn't mean she agreed with whatever these people were saying. They truly were trying to ruin the company. Zoe turned around and headed back toward the pageant. She spied Will's broad shoulders immediately. He sat heads above the rest of the judges at their own booth with his back to her. A red velvet rope separated them from everyone else roaming around. If she had superpowers right now she'd use telepathy to get Will to turn around.

"You know I can't let you get any closer," said a security guard.

Zoe read the name tag of the man-wall. "I'm sorry, but Mr. Anderson, it's imperative that I speak with Will Ravens."

"And you can," the giant man turned Zoe around, "*after* the pageant."

"Fine." Zoe scooted off and realized she didn't have Will's cell phone number. She had last week, but was sure she'd thrown it away after her interview. Zoe swam upstream in the sea of mothers and daughters. A cloud of hairspray choked her and she had to stop and catch her breath for a moment.

"Zoe, right?"

Zoe glanced down at the beefy hand on her shoulder. She glanced up and tilted her head to the side, trying to recall the name of the man who'd let Will land his plane on his property. When she had met him he was wearing a pair of greasy overalls and now he wore a tailor-made dark-blue suit. Sharp, Zoe thought to herself.

"Dominic," he offered. "Will's frat brother. You guys were at my place earlier this week."

Earlier this week seemed more like a lifetime ago. "Hi, yes. How are you?"

"A bit out of place." Dominic chuckled. He slid his hands into his pockets and looked around. "This isn't really my speed."

"Yet, here you are." Zoe widened her eyes. She decided to skip the obvious. The man was here supporting his friend and checking out the women. "Are you enjoying yourself?"

"It's a bit insane," Dominic admitted with a quick nod of his head. He fanned away another cloud of hairspray from a mother spraying her young daughter as they rushed by. "I can't believe people willingly put themselves through an ordeal like this."

"All in the name of the crown," Zoe offered.

"That is the end game, right?"

"Say, how much do you know about what Will's going through at his company?"

Dominic extracted his hand from his pocket to scratch his chin. "You mean, about half the family wanting to shut down the operations?"

"That would be it," said Zoe. "Well, his cousins are here and I just overheard them plotting about his decision for today's contestant." She relayed the story, and Dominic listened with fierce intent. Clearly he cared for his friend. "And I can't get close enough to warn him."

"So you're afraid if he doesn't select your work as the overall winner, he's going to lose the company?"

The tone of his voice changed more into an accusation. Zoe took a step back. "Well, I…"

"Sounds to me like you may care more about your future job than his."

A jolt of embarrassment shocked Zoe's system. "I care a lot about Will."

"As long as you're in the running for this position he has to fill?"

It was then that Zoe realized Dominic's eyes were

a fiery light brown that practically glowed red with anger. "Hey, I think we got off on the wrong foot here. If you're asking me if I want the job as Creative Design Director, well, the answer is hell yes. I'm sure you're just looking out for your frat brother here, but I can assure you I could get any job that I want."

Dominic crossed his arms across his wide chest, making him look even larger. "So you wouldn't care if he doesn't pick you today?"

"He's already picked me," Zoe snapped.

"Well then, you have nothing to worry about."

A set of identical twin women were returning to their seats and stopped at the sound of Zoe's declarations. She had no doubt in the world these were Will's sisters. The lights dimmed. So much for trying to get hold of Will.

Chapter 11

Will glanced down at the score sheet once again. He had no idea what in the hell half the items on the lists meant. He was supposed to rate these ladies and young girls on a scale of one to ten in several categories. Evening gowns, hair, smiles, makeup, talent and technique. What did he know about any of those?

Technique? No one fell off the stage. A few girls tripped while tap dancing and some hit the wrong note while singing, but other than that, Will didn't know what he was supposed to do. Sasha, who sat beside him on the right, scribbled over her sheets with each contestant. Vera, on his left, did the same. She made notes, smiley faces and even drew the devil on one girl's page. Kathleen, at the very edge of the table, already had her paperwork stacked together with her hands folded on top. Kahlil leaned forward and gave him a head nod. They were in the same boat. Sort of. Will knew what was at stake.

According to the meeting held after he left Zoe's side this morning, his scores determined who received the Creative Design Director position. Zoe's future was in his hands. Besides his immediate family coming to Southwood for the pageant, the anti-cousins had arrived, as well. They were tired of the position lingering unfilled and wanted him to make a quick decision. Katie and Dixon were smug with their demands, stating that as members of the board, they had a right to make him choose.

So far he hadn't seen anything too crazy and over-the-top to make him think any of the numerous girls walking across the stage were done up by Zoe. He studied the eyeliner, but it seemed as if every other girl wore the winged look. It wasn't until a contestant blew a kiss into the crowd that Will found his winner. The crowd loved her. Will liked her makeup. And to add icing to this cake, the girl wore the glittered lipstick the same way Zoe had applied it to the prom girls at Magnolia Palace and most importantly, the dramatic wing tip. He teetered on the contestant with the modest beauty, but after last night and this morning, Will set aside his morals. He needed Zoe near him.

To be sure he chose right, Will glanced at the other score sheets whenever the other judges came across the same girl. Everyone gave her high scores, except for the beauty queen seated next to him. Vera had been generous, even to the girl who dropped her baton, which was on fire, giving her a higher score than she did Will's favorite. He was more confident that the other beauty queen, Kathleen, liked the same girl, too.

"Are we all settled on who the winner is?" asked Kathleen.

Will, along with everyone else at the table, nodded. The houselights dimmed. There were girls and parents seated beside him at the judges' table. Will doodled on a piece of paper as the names were called for each category and age range. The young girls went first. Winners were called by special titles. Everyone got a small trophy for participation and then crowns were given to the winners in those groups. There were awards for the prettiest smile, friendliest contestant and most helpful. The runner-up princess of each category received a sizable tiara. But they had to go through this for each group. At this rate, Will wasn't going to get back to Miami until late, and he still had plans to be with Zoe tonight, with or without her as Ravens Cosmetics's newest employee.

Finally it was time to crown Miss Southwood Glitz. The top three women stood dressed in sparkling ball gowns—pink, blue and yellow—on the stage, clutching hands. They'd changed into their evening gowns. The winner, as the emcee explained, would travel across the county and represent Southwood in the official Miss South Georgia pageant in December.

The pageant contenstants were narrowed down from fifty to ten girls, and then down to five left on the stage. Each girl drew questions written by one of the judges from a clear fishbowl. The five were slimmed down to three final contestants. Will was glad his question wasn't chosen. He'd wanted to know if any of the ladies had a superpower, what it would be. He would definitely wish for the power of transportation. He'd be anywhere else but here—with Zoe.

December. Will zoned out with the idea of Zoe. He wondered what he'd get Zoe for the holidays. Would they stay in Miami or visit someplace cold? Without thinking, Will wiggled his eyebrows at the idea of stretching out in front of a fireplace with Zoe.

"And the second runner-up…" the emcee said into the microphone.

Second? Leaning forward, Will shook his head and blinked into focus and realized there were just two girls on stage. His daydream of Zoe had caused him to miss the final three going to answer the same question from the emcee. They faced each other, clutching hands for dear life.

"Second runner-up is Miss Cupcakery."

The audience screamed with applause. Miss Cupcakery was whisked away by a few ushers. The reigning Miss Southwood placed a crown on top of Miss Restoration's head and the queen began her walk across the stage. His choice won.

The applause of the audience was deafening. The other judges at the table mouthed congratulations and shook hands. Will glanced around the stage. The other contestants surrounded the new Miss Southwood. The behind-the-scenes staff peered through the curtains. Will shifted in his seat for a glimpse of Zoe and her purple smock. The spotlight caught her golden hoop earrings, visible beneath her hair, piled on top of her head in a messy bun. Will's heart seized.

"Zoe," he breathed her name and began to rise from his seat.

A set of heavy hands clamped down on Will's back. At the moment, the only person Will wanted to see was Zoe and perhaps the person she was about to hug. He needed to make sure she hugged the winner and held her hand in the air like a true boxing champ and coach. Every step she took agonized Will. Mothers and little girls were stopping her to take selfies. Teens stopped her for a photograph. Beauty queens who hadn't won covered their faces with their hands and Zoe helped each one stop their mascara from running. All he needed to see was who Zoe had teamed up with, just to make sure she was the one who'd secured the spot at Ravens Cosmetics.

He needed her to win to prove his cousins wrong. Zoe had been right. She was the best thing for the company.

"Young William!" Eva screamed in his ear as she came up behind him and wrapped her arms around his shoulders.

"Will," Charles said, strolling into his line of view. An annoyed sigh escaped Will's throat. It came out more like a growl and with the crowd's applause slowing down, it was apparently heard by his cousin. Charles's eyes stretched wide. "Let's see your score sheets."

"No need," Will retorted, still shoving his paper-work in his cousin's direction. "She's about to hug the winner now." Sure of himself, Will cocked his head to the side and nodded toward the stage…and that's when he realized he'd been too sure too quickly. Zoe stood off with the second runner-up, dabbing underneath the girl's lashes with a tissue.

"Rather rude of you," Charles said, looking toward the stage where a large bald man in a lavender smock and white boots hugged the new Miss Southwood.

What the hell? Will asked himself.

"Fantastic," Charles said, clapping his hands. "I'll go let him know right now."

Will rose again to get to Zoe, but another hand clapped onto his shoulder. Will shrugged off the grip and turned around. For a moment he didn't recognize his frat brother, Dominic. At least there was one friendly face, someone who didn't want something from him. "Hey, man."

"Hey, great job." Dominic nodded his head at the commotion on stage.

"Why didn't you tell me you were into pageant shows? Is this your way of picking up women now?"

Dominic shrugged his shoulders. "It's not what you think." At the same time, a few ladies waved like schoolchildren in his direction. Dominic turned to watch them leave, and when he turned back, Will gave him a raised brow. "I swear," Dominic laughed. "I am sponsoring a contestant."

The questions flooded Will's brain. He started with the first one. "What?"

Dominic rubbed his chin. "Well, Alisha suggested I bond with the community better. Apparently, my upscale shop matches my attitude."

One thing Will had enjoyed when Dominic's family came to visit them. Dominic was the oldest and his baby sister followed them around. Will, never having had a younger sister, found her charming. If Alisha thought Dominic needed to change things, she was probably right.

"In other words, the town thinks you're stuck-up." It couldn't have been further than the truth, but Will understood how Dominic might give the wrong impression. Maybe if his frat brother showed off more of his tattoos, the people would find him down-to-earth. "So, which one did you sponsor?"

"The winner, Miss Restoration, as in Crowne's Restoration."

Will raked his hands over his head. Blood pounded in his ears. "I didn't even put two and two together."

Dominic's girl had won; meanwhile, his lost. Jesus, what had he done?

From Zoe's vantage point on the stage she watched Will and his best friend shake hands. She tried to focus on the girls wanting to take a picture with her, but her mind was spinning. If what she'd overheard was true, she'd just lost her opportunity for the position she most desired. Titus, clearly knowing what was at stake, hugged his winning contestant and gave Zoe a smug wink. Through it all, Zoe kept a smile on her face. She had to. Everyone kept asking for a photograph.

With each picture her mind wandered. How did this happen? She had no Plan B. After the last of the girls and their mothers finished taking pictures, a man dressed in a suit approached her. She'd seen him before. There was something familiar about him. His features were very Ravens-esque and then it hit her. This was Charles, whom she'd spied on through the weeping willow leaves.

"Miss Baldwin," the man said, with his hand outstretched. "Allow me to introduce myself."

The badge around his neck already told her who he was. "Mr. Ravens."

"Charles Ravens," he replied. "We haven't had the pleasure to meet."

"No, we haven't." Zoe tried. She wanted to be

friendly, but this man's vendetta against his cousin had cost her a job. Her dream job.

"I've been a fan of yours for a while now." Charles held on to Zoe's hand for a few seconds too long.

Zoe pulled her arm back and shoved her hands into the front of her smock. She fiddled with the tube of lipstick from the beauty box. Her downfall. Maybe she should have used it like Titus had.

"I wanted to come over here and let you know that we at Ravens Cosmetics appreciate you applying to our company and we'll keep your name on file," Charles went on.

"That's kind of you." Zoe glanced over at Will. Electricity jolted her body when their eyes locked. He stopped his conversation with Dominic and made his way toward her, not caring who he bumped into. "I appreciate the opportunity."

What else was she supposed to say? What else was she supposed to do? Fall on the ground like one of the younger contestants who hadn't gotten the trophy she wanted? The redeeming factor in all of this was Will. Her heart swelled with…love. Love? The room spun. How had this happened? It was too fast, right? She couldn't believe it. All the noise around her ceased. The only thing she heard was the beating of her heart…the beating of her heart and Will's footsteps as he neared her. She needed to tell him. She loved him.

"I hope I'm not interrupting anything." Will reached Zoe with arms outstretched. He took hold of her forearm, then wrapped her against his frame.

Zoe blinked him into focus. "Not at all."

Charles's eyes darted toward the tender touch. His lips pressed together and Zoe was sure he *hmm*ed under his breath. "I was telling Miss Baldwin about her wonderful work and how we'll keep her résumé on file."

The grip around her waist tightened and Will cleared his throat. He wasn't letting her go. "Once again, thanks, Charles, for doing my job for me."

"Well, you were busy with your frat brother. Ah, here he comes now."

In the brief moment when Charles lifted his head above Will's shoulder, Will leaned over. "Zoe, I need to explain something."

"Don't worry about it." Swallowing past the lump in her throat, Zoe shrugged her shoulders. "I second-guessed myself and Titus was better today when it counted."

"I'll figure something out," Will whispered with a kiss at her temple.

More than anything she wanted to tell Will what she'd realized, but her words were lost when Dominic came over, Titus and the new Miss Southwood Glitz in tow. Zoe remembered the woman's name was Waverly. She was a former Miss Something who'd lost her other crown due to bad behavior.

"Zoe, you remember Dominic Crowne?" Will asked, his hand on her lower back.

For a millisecond, Zoe and Dominic stared each other down. He gave a lopsided smirk and a head nod.

Waverly stepped forward and shook Zoe's hand. "You're awesome, Miss Zoe. It was a real pleasure to meet you this afternoon. I am a huge fan."

"But you work better with me." Titus brought up the rear. His smugness was enough to knock Zoe off the stage.

Zoe's eyes darted between the four of them standing in front of her. The dots began to align. Now she recalled why Will hadn't cared about her getting the Creative Design Director's position. He already had something in mind.

"This is cozy." Charles cleared his throat. "Titus, you must be familiar with Zoe Baldwin."

"We've met," Zoe and Titus belted out with the same amount of animosity in their voices.

"I can't thank you enough for this opportunity, Mr. Ravens," Waverly gushed, shaking Will's and then Charles's hands. "And Mr. Ravens."

Zoe stepped backward but Will's hold on her waist kept her from leaving. "Everything okay?"

"No," Zoe whispered.

"Dom was just talking about all of us getting together for a celebration," said Will. "What do you say we hang back here for one day?" He leaned close to whisper in her ear. "Tonight can still be our first date."

Pain ached in her ribs. "Honestly," Zoe began slowly, "I'm all packed. I might as well head back tonight and I already have my ticket."

"So you'll fly back with me on the company plane." Will moved closer. "Like when we came here."

A lifetime ago, Zoe thought. She shot a glance at Dominic, not sure why he made her so nervous. Probably because he already knew what Zoe wanted and knew the plans he'd already made with Will for the winner. How long had they been conspiring? Did Will plan on making Waverly a winner before he learned of the company's plans to hire the makeup artist who did the winner's face?

A piercing pang pinched the bridge of Zoe's nose. Tears were threatening. She needed to get away from here. Disappointment hit her harder than she expected. She needed to go home and made up a lie. "No, forgot I have things I need to do tomorrow."

"Zoe?" Will questioned her with a raised brow. He was confused, as he should be. Zoe knew he had no idea she was aware of his plans for hire. But, then again, she'd known all along he didn't want her. Zoe choked out a sob. After he met with his cousins, did he meet up with Dominic and make plans for his contestant to win? This is what fraternity members did, right? Help each other out? How easy had it been for Will to come up with a decision on the position after swearing he needed to think long and hard? Will's face softened, his lips frowned. "What is it?"

"I've got to go, Will." Zoe stepped backward. "I've got to get back. Please excuse me. And congratulations, Waverly. You were truly lovely."

At some point after midnight Zoe returned to the comfort of her home. Usually she wasn't on the verge of tears when she returned, but dropping her keys on the ground nearly set her off. The extra weight of emotions drained her. This was clearly not her day, her month— hell, even her year. Zoe rushed inside her apartment before her sobs could wake the Dohertys next door.

Even though she had only been on the company plane one time, Zoe already missed it. She wondered what would have been better, flying last week seated next to the fake LL Cool J or being seated tonight with someone who could have been a heavyweight wrestler. Zoe's bones ached from being wedged against the window.

Leaving her suitcase by the door, Zoe trotted over

to the kitchen, kicking out of her red flip-flops. Before leaving for the airport she had been able to change out of her smock and slip into a red-and-white-striped maxi dress. As much as she wanted to shower after her flight, Zoe's stomach growled. She was famished and the refrigerator had no answers for her. Like déjà vu, Zoe's cell phone rang and Prince came over the speaker. This was the same scenario as when Lexi had invited her to come back to Southwood. Zoe had been heartbroken over Ravens Cosmetics and she was starving. The two differences this time were that Zoe let the phone ring and she had no food in her fridge. Zoe closed the refrigerator door and let the call go to voice mail.

No one on the van ride to Atlanta could believe Zoe hadn't stayed in Southwood for one more evening with Will. Kenzie, the main person rooting for a union between Will and Zoe, asked everyone to cut Zoe some slack. Luke sat in the van and ticked off a list of the places he freelanced for that were interested in her work for the same position. Zoe needed to come up with a new plan, and this time it might include having to move and try resettling someplace else. She sighed heavily and reached for the stack of mail on her counter, still hating the idea of leaving. Where else would she find a neighbor willing to drop off her mail while she was out of town?

A soft knock came at the door. She figured it was either Mr. or Mrs. Doherty, coming to check on her after all the noise she'd made coming inside. Without thinking, she opened the door. It took several blinks for her eyes to adjust to the image in front of her.

On top of her heart breaking, it now melted. Will, still in his suit, leaned against the jamb. The first three buttons at his neck were undone and the tie hung loose. A rustle of plastic caught her attention. Down by his side he held a takeout bag sporting the red, black and white of the Trinidad and Tobago flag.

"You went to Trudy's?"

"I called it in. We were supposed to have our first official date when we got back to Miami, Zoe," Will said with a calm voice. "We couldn't decide on Monday or tonight, so I chose now."

"I'm not hungry," she lied. The delicious scents caused her mouth to water.

"I don't understand. I didn't peg you for a sore loser."

Of all the audacity in the world! Zoe's mouth widened as a few choice words came to mind about Will and his nerve. "Sore loser?" she hissed. "How did you even know what apartment I live in?" The locks on her neighbor's door clicked and Patrick Doherty poked his red head out. "Sorry to wake you, Patrick."

"Everything okay?"

For a moment Zoe wondered if she needed to get rid of Will. He may have arrived with dinner but the way his eyes bored into her soul unnerved her. "I'm okay, thanks for asking."

After a reluctant few seconds, filled with five-foot-eight Patrick sizing up Will's six-four frame, her neighbor nodded and went back inside his place. Zoe stepped back and allowed plenty of space for Will to enter her apartment.

"Your address was on your résumé," Will answered her. As he passed, she couldn't help but be mesmerized by his powerful stride. He went straight to the open kitchen and set the bag down. Fragrant aromas from the Trinidadian chicken stew filled the air.

Despite the rumble in her stomach, Zoe leaned against the counter and folded her hands. "Why are you here?"

"We have a date." Will helped himself to a view inside her refrigerator and shook his head. "This is funny."

"You're mocking the contents of my fridge?" Zoe squared her shoulders.

"I'm laughing at yet another thing we have in common." Will widened the door. "We have matching contents."

Zoe rolled her eyes to keep from grinning.

Will closed the door and turned to lean over the counter. He covered her hands with his. "I'm sorry with the way things ended with the CDD position, Zoe."

"It is what it is. And you warned me you weren't interested in my work." The key word in there was "work." There was no doubting his attraction to her. Zoe thought about her newly discovered feelings. Somehow, this was not the moment to confess she was in love with him. Anger and disappointment still seethed within.

"Don't act like that," said Will. "The board put the restrictions on me this morning. They specified that the makeup artist who did the winner would get the position. I've watched you work with the staff and crew at Magnolia Palace and I've learned to appreciate your work. I even was sure I knew your work. I looked for all the ladies with the drastic winged liner you do. I was sure Waverly was yours."

"Well, she wasn't," Zoe snapped. "She was Titus's. Of all people, she was Titus's."

"So are you mad at me for not voting the right person?" Will asked, squeezing her hand. His dark eyes pleaded with hers.

Zoe tried to jerk her hand away but he held on to her. "Oh," she chuckled sarcastically, "I believe you picked the person you wanted to pick."

"Zoe, I looked for everything you taught me over the past few days." He let go of her hand and ticked off on his fingers the things he'd learned. "She even had the glittery mixed-matched lipstick thing you've been doing."

"That was from Ravens Cosmetics," Zoe grunted. "I thought you gave that to us on purpose. The products were great for women, but not the group of young girls I was assigned."

Will shook his head. "How in the hell was I supposed to do that? I wasn't allowed to see you all day."

"It was in the beauty box from your company," she gritted through her teeth. Realizing this wasn't going anywhere, Zoe took a step backward. "You know what? It doesn't even matter anymore. Titus won and your frat brother won. That's why you knew all along I wasn't going to get the position."

Will stood back as well and held his hands in the air in surrender. "Hold up. I had no idea Titus and Waverly would be paired up or that Dominic decided to sponsor a beauty queen. The whole point of the separation from the contestants was so that we didn't fraternize."

"Funny you mentioned frats. That's not the vibe I got from Dominic."

"Wait, when did you talk to Dom?" Will rushed to Zoe's side. "Did he say something that bothered you?"

"He didn't have to." Zoe avoided Will's touch. "He alluded to it enough. I just wish you would have told me."

Will didn't take her attempt to brush him off well. He stepped even closer. So close, she backed up against the archway leading into the living room. Using the back of his knuckles he caressed her cheek. "I'm not sure what's going on here. I didn't know Dom was sponsoring anyone until after the pageant. Talk to me."

Zoe hated herself for melting. There were plenty of jobs she had gotten in the past and she didn't need anyone to comfort her like this. But being here with him was different. If what he said was true, then there was no moment of conspiring against her or favoritism. Zoe's eyes stung from the overwhelming sensation of feeling foolish. "Look, I get not getting the job. I can handle it. It just stings that it's to someone like Titus. I'm bitter."

"You're not mad at me?" Warm breath brushed against her nose when Will chuckled. "But bitter over Titus?"

Not appreciating his laughter, Zoe pushed his chest away. "You're laughing at my pain?"

"No. Just your honesty."

Zoe moved toward the living room, all too aware of Will hot on her tail. She tried to focus on the bookshelves across the room on the wall, but only thought strangely of future photographs of the two of them, like at Lexi's from her and Stephen's wedding. "Something I figured you would appreciate."

Will wrapped his arms around her from behind. The

bitterness slowly thawed. His forearms were cradled beneath her breasts and lifted the stress of their weight and her emotions. Zoe leaned into him, willingly allowing him to lead her to the sleet-gray couch. Chills ran down her spine from the feathery touch of his fingertips. "What can I do to make it up to you?"

Zoe turned in to him. "Hire anyone else but Titus."

"What is the deal with you and Titus?"

"Nothing other than the man not having an original thought in his brain." Zoe wrapped her arm around Will's shoulders. Her fingers splayed against the curly hairs at the nape of his neck. She pushed out an irritated sigh. "You say a lot of the contestants had the same winged eyeliner and the glitter lips, right?"

"Yes."

"Titus has been stealing every design I do. That's why my designs on certain celebrities are so elaborate. I make them impossible for Titus to copy without getting caught, but as you know, no everyday woman walks around with a couture face."

"Why didn't you tell me any of this before?" Will stroked Zoe's thigh.

"And sound like I'm a complainer?" Zoe shook her head, letting it rest on his shoulder. The beat of his heart comforted her pain. "I respect your decision. I'm resilient. I'll make other plans."

Will pulled his head back, and wrinkles marred his perfect face. "Other plans?"

"The reason I went after the Creative Design Director position is because I wanted something permanent in Miami."

Will stroked Zoe's left arm and trailed it down to

her hand where they locked fingers. "You're not thinking about leaving here, are you?"

"I don't know," Zoe said with a shrug. "I have a few weeks to think about it."

"Good," Will said, maneuvering Zoe so her back rested against his chest. "I have a few weeks to convince you to stay in Miami."

Large hands stroked the swell of her breast and moved down toward her belly. Zoe moaned. The material of her dress crept up her legs as Will pulled it up. "I have a few jobs out of town," Zoe moaned in between sharp breaths. "But if I want to do anything in beauty, I've got to go somewhere else. Ravens Cosmetics holds the monopoly on practically everything in South Florida."

"You're leaving me?"

"Well, not right now." Zoe turned to tilt her face to his.

Something about their mouths meeting, something felt right. Something felt like home. Zoe purred. His hands stirred at the apex of her legs. The panties she wore were instantly wet. Slightly embarrassed, Zoe—as much as she hated to—pushed Will's hand away. "Will," she moaned. "I just got off the plane. I haven't showered."

Instead of listening to her, Will's index finger circled her nub. The length of his middle finger slipped deep inside. Zoe bucked her hips forward and, obliging, Will pressed his palm against her, grinding against her flesh. The other hand slipped the through the V of her dress and freed her breast.

Ecstasy consumed her. Heated blood boiled her bones. Zoe tried to get her thoughts together but it was hard, as hard as the erection pressing against her back. Will rubbed deeper, harder. His mouth skillfully worked hers and branded him on her. Their tongues reunited with a spark. Will used his legs to keep her legs spread wide. Moisture dripped from her body. She heaved, bounced and eventually rested her feet against the coffee table for leverage. Will hit the right spot over and over. Zoe broke the kiss. Her hands gripped the fabric of her couch and steadied herself with the right rhythm. Will pressed his lips against her earlobes and began to suck, and Zoe's body went crazy. She cried out for him over and over with each orgasmic wave.

"And now we shower," Will whispered into her ear before sweeping her up into his arms.

Chapter 12

In the few weeks after Zoe and Will returned to Miami, they tried to have a normal relationship, but it was damn near impossible for Will to have Zoe to himself for more than a couple of days at a time. She'd flown out to LA for a celebrity wedding right after they returned from Southwood. Then they had two full days together, which they spent in her apartment without ever leaving the facilities. Right after that she drove up to Orlando for the annual MET Awards, where she was surrounded by celebrities, all of whom gave Zoe a shout-out when they won an award or gave her name when interviewed on the red carpet. Will hoped her excessive traveling while they developed their relationship would make her want to stay. According to Zoe, her parents maintained a long-distance relationship. Zoe swore she never wanted that for herself.

"I feel like I haven't seen you in forever," Zoe wailed on her side of the FaceTime connection.

Will glanced down at his blotter calendar. After this Labor Day weekend, Zoe would be in New York for Fashion Week. If she felt like they hadn't seen each other much since they returned from Southwood, it was going to be even busier in the next few months.

"Me, too." Will tried to sound excited, when deep down inside he was equally frustrated. She'd warned him that her life was hectic. He understood now why she wanted something more permanent and he hated himself for not being the one to give it to her. "You don't have my face as the screen saver on your phone?" The moment he said that, the five-minute timer on his computer screen expired and the selfie Zoe had taken of the two of them together out on her balcony filled the screen. Will pressed the space bar and brought up the projected figures in spreadsheets for Ravens Cosmetics.

"You're cute," Zoe said drily.

"And even cuter in person," Will added. "Speaking of which, when do I get to see you?"

"You're seeing me now." Zoe laughed and blew him a kiss.

"I meant naked in my bed."

A pretty shade of red brushed across her cheeks. Someone near her laughed. A flutter shook his heart with the idea of her on the Fisher Island Ferry, heading toward his home on the barrier island neighborhood. She was close. "Where are you?" he asked, looking at the images behind her. She must have been sitting with her back against a wall.

"I'm not alone but I was heading toward your place."

Knowing she was this close, he felt excitement flush him. The hands on the grandfather clock in his office slowly ticked away toward five, but since it was Friday, why the hell *not* kick the weekend off early? Half the support staff had left already, including Will's secretary. So keeping up with everyone else, Will pulled his briefcase out from under his desk. This weekend they were going to have time together. Will had made arrangements to have everything they needed at the tips of their fingers in his home. He toyed with the idea of having a personal masseuse but broke the pencil in his hand in half at the idea of someone else touching her body.

"Give me forty-five minutes and be naked when I get there."

"Will—" Zoe pleaded.

Not wanting to hear a protest, Will slid his finger to the red icon and disconnected the line just in time. The door to his office pushed open without a knock. Donovan and Marcus entered.

"Hey, little brother," Marcus said, taking a seat. "Zoe must be in town."

Since the pageant, there had been no way to keep his relationship with Zoe quiet. Eva and Dana were already hounding him about when to have a wedding and whether he and Zoe wanted it in spring or summer. In his last email from Dana, she'd wanted permission to contact Jamerica Baldwin, Zoe's mother. It wasn't quite permission but more of a reminder that Dana still had modeling contacts she could use to get in touch with her. Right now, Will found the way his sisters teased him amusing. Nothing was set in stone. Will hadn't even broached the idea of marriage with

Zoe. Hell, compared with the intimate time at Magnolia Palace, the two of them barely spent any time together.

"What makes you think Zoe's in town?" Will asked.

Donovan snorted and elbowed Marcus in the ribs. He leaned back in his seat and propped his feet on Will's desk. "You're about to pack up and leave for the day."

"It's so cute," Marcus mocked. He lifted his fingers in the air and pretended to pinch Will's cheeks from across the room. "Don, you remember a few months ago when Will burned the midnight oil every night?"

"Is there something the two of you wanted?" Will asked. He kicked his briefcase back under his desk.

"We don't want to alarm you," said Donovan, "but the board just called an emergency meeting."

Will swore under his breath. "What now?"

"I couldn't get anything out of Charles or Brandon," Marcus began, "but Dixon's secretary has been pulling the data for the online work from Titus."

The online magazine was Titus's field. The new CDD of Ravens Cosmetics had sunk a lot of money into technology for people to order their cosmetics and products via their website. Because Titus held a tech degree, Will trusted him to sweeten the site.

"And you know this how?" Will asked with a slow drawl. What ran through his mind was a potential lawsuit. They were beginning to run out of single women working at Ravens.

As usual, Marcus smiled smugly and leaned back in his chair. "Don't you worry your pretty little head over that. Your big brother is handling things."

Will decided to ignore the mental list of corporate crimes sounding off in his head with the illegal implications of what Marcus said. The last thing they needed was a lawsuit. "I'll buy you a drink for taking one for the team."

"No worries. It was actually my pleasure." Marcus shrugged his shoulders. "She was pretty hot and flexible. I think she only missed the Olympics in Brazil due to a hurt back. But her back is fine now," Marcus concluded with a sheepish wink.

Rather than listening to his brother's escapades, Will preferred hearing the news. He cleared his throat and gained his brothers' attention. "What did you find out about the data she'd been collecting?"

"It was data on the Creative Design Director, the one *you* handpicked," said Marcus, reminding Will of a choice he would never live down. "What were you thinking?"

"Me?" Will gasped. "You were at the impromptu board meeting where they said whoever styled the winner of the pageant I voted for would get the CDD position."

"Which you still got wrong," Marcus reminded him—something he reminded Will of every time they got together. This included the moment before Titus had attended his very first meeting. "Zoe was perfect for the job."

"And now she's perfect for Will." Donovan chuckled.

"Can we get back to this meeting?" Will asked, resisting the urge to pinch the bridge of his nose to ward off an oncoming headache.

"Let's try more like, go to the meeting."

Tonight's plans were inevitably going to be put off. Will sent Zoe a text, pushed himself away from his desk and decided to dial Zoe's cell to let her know he would be running late.

Zoe's voice filled the screen before her face. "Are you trying to find out if I'm naked or not?"

Donovan and Marcus playfully leaped over the table. Will stood back against the window behind his desk. He held on to the phone while warding off his brothers with one hand. "Sorry, Zoe, I'm not alone now."

"Zoe," Marcus yelled out.

"When are you saving Ravens Cosmetics?" Donovan asked.

"Who needs saving?" Zoe bantered back. "I'm the one running around here from coast to coast. Need I remind you that one or both of you told me that Creative Design Director position was mine?"

"Sorry," both men sang.

"But it was Will's fault," Donovan blurted out.

Zoe's easy smile proved why Will loved her so much. She didn't hold a grudge and had wished Titus well on his first day. Zoe made it clear she didn't want to hear too much about how great Titus was or wasn't doing, but she supported the company because she genuinely wanted what was best.

"I was calling," Will said, shrugging away from his brothers' grasps, "to let you know I am going to be late. The board has called some emergency meeting."

"Everyone's here," Marcus called out.

"Including the young ones," Donovan finished.

"Sounds ominous," Zoe said, breaking eye contact with Will. He wondered for a moment if this was something she wished, but pushed the thought away. "Well, try to stay positive. I'll see you in a little bit."

The three brothers headed off toward the corner office of Ravens Cosmetics. This reminded Will of walking through a stadium ready to hit the field for a match. In soccer he'd prepared himself by working out and doing a lot of strength training and conditioning. Will readied himself for a match by studying his opponents. This meeting was far worse. His opponents were family members out for blood.

The glass walls of the conference room gave a clear view of the board: the Ravens. His blood. Will straightened his red tie with tiny magnolia flowers sprinkled on it. The tie was a gift from Zoe so he wouldn't forget about her. Not a chance. Will resisted smirking. He didn't want the anti-cousins, all facing him when he walked in, to get any sense of his emotions.

Instead of the stoic faces Will expected to see, most of the anti-cousins sat with knowing smirks. Katie, Dixon, Charles, Oscar, Mari, Thea and Brandon looked like the cats who'd devoured the canaries. This didn't worry Will. What bothered him, as he, Donovan and Marcus took their seats, was seeing Cora and J.J., Uncle Charles's wayward son. School should have already started and they needed to be in their dorms. Cora avoided eye contact with Will, and J.J. drummed his fingers on the glass cover of the black oak table. The beat stopped once the three brothers sat down on the same side as both sets of twins. Seven against seven.

"So, what brings all of us here today?" Will asked.

Dixon spoke first. Well, rather shoved a thick, legal-sized binder toward the center of the table. "This has been the data for the last twelve weeks of our e-commerce with your Creative Design Director in place."

A twitch threatened at the back of Will's jawline. "Alright?"

"Your golden choice failed to bring in tweaks, changes," said Dixon, referring to Titus once again. Nothing had improved after bringing Titus on board. The fans Will thought would follow Titus failed to support the hire. "As a matter of fact, our online sales have been cut in half and we've been steadily losing our subsidiaries left and right."

"What is this supposed to mean?" Marcus asked. "If these smaller companies are buying back their titles, we're still making money."

"For the love of God, you guys," Thea hissed, "we're getting off this sinking ship. It's time you all faced the truth."

"What truth?" Dana scoffed "That you guys are a bunch of lazy, entitled brats who don't know a thing about hard work?"

Thea's purple sculpted nails scraped against the glass and she rolled her eyes and fluttered what Will had come to know were wispy, catlike false lashes. "Said the prima donna model who used the company plane to get lobster from Maine." Thea paused for a moment, long enough for everyone to hear the audible sound of Dana closing her mouth. "Yeah, I saw the books. You're not modeling anymore, so there's no reason for the flight other than your sister's Key West lobsters not being good enough for you."

"Hey," Eva drawled with a scowl.

"You don't have the votes to shut Ravens down," Donovan declared with his intimidating, booming voice.

Cora squeaked, her face turning bright red. She

turned to look away but a tear fell down her face. Will knew at that moment it was over for Ravens Cosmetics. His heart fell. His shoulders slumped and a knot formed in his throat. He'd failed.

"Why are we bothering with conversation?" Charles asked. His gloating smirk was enough to make Will want to leap over the table and punch it off his face. "We're demanding a vote right now."

"How can you do this to Grandma?" Naomi asked. Her voice cracked with a hint of crying. Her twin reached over and patted her back. Will and his brothers clenched their fists.

Joyce spoke up. "It's plain and simple," she began. "Tell us how much it would take to buy you guys out."

With a quick calculation in his head, Will already knew they couldn't come up with the funds to buy them out at what he expected to be their inflated going rate. But Brandon surprised him the most with his response.

"We're done having our name attached to the sinking ship," said Brandon. "You think we want to stay if for some strange reason you guys pull a rabbit out of your hats and turn this around?"

"And if we even thought about selling the company to you guys," said Mari, another anti-cousin, "how do you think you'll look in the eyes of Grandma Naomi? We want to present it to her as if we made a group decision."

"That's not our concern," Donovan said. "We're the ones here on a daily basis."

"We're not selling to you," said Oscar. "We're dissolving the company. We have the votes."

The only thing Will could do was close his eyes and pray for a miracle. They needed to be saved. Grandma's birthday was next week. Was the family truly going to sit in the same room and tell her they'd dissolved the company? Her child? Her baby? How was he supposed to look his grandmother in the eyes and tell her he failed? The news was sure to kill her.

Will couldn't breathe. The air around him became stagnant. All he wanted to do was jump across the table and break one of their faces. If he moved to do so, he wasn't sure he'd be able to stop.

Before anyone had a chance to speak their minds, the conference door opened. Zoe entered. Confused, but still a gentleman, Will rose to his feet. All the men did. The receptionist from the front desk stormed breathlessly after Zoe.

"I'm so sorry for barging in like this," Zoe said.

"I tried to tell her y'all were in a meeting."

"It's okay, Tracey," said Donovan.

Will moved around the table to greet Zoe with a kiss on the cheek while she and Tracey faced off in the war of smirks. "What's going on, Zoe?"

"We're in a meeting," said Katie, rising to her feet with her arms across her chest. "A family meeting."

"Key word, 'family,'" Dixon enunciated.

In true Zoe-dramatic form, Zoe pressed her hand to her chest and took a bow. Will bit back a proud grin. "Well, I do apologize for interrupting this family meeting, but since you said it's a family thing..." She waltzed back over to the door and opened it.

Though the walls were glass, Will's angle didn't allow him to see who she was ushering inside. He was more caught off guard by the gasp coming from anti-cousins Katie, Charles and Dixon.

"Zoe?" Will asked, focusing back on the door. An

older woman close to his father's age stepped inside. She was tall like a Ravens, with silky gray hair like his grandmother's and almond-shaped eyes like his grandfather Joe's. Blood pounded between his ears. He knew the answer of her identity before Zoe introduced the guest.

"I figured you would want another shareholder here," Zoe said, giving Will a wink. His heart fluttered back to life. "Everyone, in case you didn't realize it, this is your Aunt Octavia."

"How in the hell?" Dixon growled.

"Hello, everyone," Octavia said. Her voice was like a melody. "Katie, how nice to see you again."

"Again?" the pro-cousins cried.

Katie sat back in her seat as her face turned beet red. "I was going to send for you."

"What is going on here?" Marcus asked. He came over and extended his hand to his aunt. "I'm Marcus Ravens, Mark's son."

One by one everyone introduced themselves to their long-lost family member. Will stood off to the side, his arm wrapped around Zoe's waist. "How on Earth did you find her?"

"Actually your cousins did," Zoe beamed. "I overheard them at the pageant a few weeks back. I knew your cousin Katie found your aunt at a nail shop in Pennsylvania."

"I thought you flew to Pennsylvania for an interview at Pink Stiletto Cosmetics in Aston." Will distinctly recalled the trip. It was the first time he'd become nervous about Zoe moving farther away for a job.

"I was," Zoe nodded, "but I recalled the conversation I overheard and went out to find your aunt. When

I heard how your cousins wanted to reintroduce her to the family after a vote had been made, I thought I'd better see if she was interested in coming back and visiting before anything happened to the company."

Will bent down and kissed Zoe. His lips locked with hers and there was no way he wanted to let go. He cupped her face, breaking only to remind her of what he'd said every day since they returned from Southwood. "I love you."

"Uh, it still doesn't matter," Charles began, knocking his knuckles against the tabletop. Everyone surrounding Octavia turned to give him their attention. "No offense, Aunt Octavia, but your generation only acts to advise the board, and we're the board."

"Aunt Octavia's vote still counts," Eva announced as she wrapped her arm around their aunt's shoulders. "Grandma still has her down as a shareholder. Our folks still have their shares, which we control, and we also have shares, as well."

"Be sure to explain how her vote has counted. You know, the abstaining kind," Katie sneered with glee. "Even if she voted, you're still outnumbered since J.J. and Cora have agreed with us."

"You're short," said Brandon.

Spunky as Grandma Naomi, Octavia frowned. "Oh, dear," Octavia's voice dripped with sarcasm. "I worked close with my father. I understand any grandchildren would be given shares at their birth. I'm sure we'll have to get the lawyers in here to double check. But I know it's fact. If you guys want a rough vote right now, I wonder if I can advise my son, Joseph, to vote to keep Ravens Cosmetics running." She tiptoed to the glass door and ushered in the damn-near splitting image of

Donovan, minus the scar. "This is my son, Joseph. I kept him away from the family for a reason and clearly I was wrong. Y'all need each other."

"It's still just one vote," said Katie.

Will began to groan but Zoe patted his back. When he glanced down to read her face, she nodded at the closed doors, which Aunt Octavia opened again.

"Allow me to introduce you all to your other cousins, my twins, Amber and Audra."

"Guess y'all should have done a little more investigating," Eva laughed.

Joyce and Dana both leaned across the table toward Katie. "We outnumber you now."

Whatever bickering went on, Will didn't care. Legally, the pro-cousins had won this round. Will wrapped his arms around Zoe again. "You are my hero, you know that?"

Zoe pressed her lips together and nodded. "Given that I'm a nerd, I'll take that as a compliment."

After the hustle and bustle of New York Fashion week, Zoe was excited to finally get back to Southwood to meet up with her parents to witness their reproposal. Because of everyone's busy calendars, they kept having to reschedule their vacation. It was a shame Will couldn't make it this weekend, but given the excitement of the return of Octavia Ravens, Ravens Cosmetics was constantly in the news, and that was a good thing. Titus resigned and the position was still open.

"How does she look?" Dressed in a dark suit similar to the one he'd worn over twenty-five years ago, Frank Baldwin met Zoe as she came down the walkway of the backyard of Magnolia Palace.

The "she" would be her mother, Jamerica. "She's beautiful and ready for you to propose again." Zoe added the last bit with a teasing eye roll. She enjoyed her parents involving her with this re-creation. This made her feel more of a family, since they were already so nontraditional. How many children got to witness their parents' engagement? But that was something Zoe had learned over the last few weeks. Family—no matter where they were or how close or far they were from each other—was family.

Last week Zoe had had the time of her life at the Ravens compound celebrating Grandma Naomi Ravens's ninetieth birthday. Away from the company, the anticousins were not as intimidating. Octavia was there, along with her three kids, and she shared the reason why she'd left. She'd been too afraid to face her parents. Back then, teen pregnancy was not popular. Either way, Zoe thoroughly enjoyed her time with Will and his family, but she just wished she and Will could have had more time together.

"It's important to create memories, Zoe," her father said, tugging her arm. "Most people like to renew their vows."

"But we're not most people." Zoe nodded and laughed. Her canvas shoes hit the front step of the boards to the dock. The cooling weather called for a long, pumpkin-colored sweater layered over a cream camisole and cuffed denim shorts. She figured she'd take the sweater off after her father proposed. Later on today, Ramon Torres would fire up the grill and Zoe secretly hoped she'd get a chance to see Kenzie once again. With everything going on in her mind, Zoe tripped over the raised wood of the dock.

"My clumsy daughter." Frank chuckled.

"Whatever."

Frank patted Zoe's hand. "Just remember, I'll always be here to catch you."

"Uh, thanks," Zoe said slowly. Her father quit walking and Zoe raised a brow. "What are you doing?"

"I think I forgot the ring," he began, backing up. "Can you do me a favor and make sure your mother doesn't come around that corner and find the spot empty?"

Zoe rolled her eyes. "Fine." How could he have forgotten the important part of the day? Zoe shook her head and laughed at the craziness of her parents. While her father fretted over the ring, her mother was in the bathroom scrutinizing the beauty work Zoe had done on her.

While hurricane season was still in full effect for Florida, Southwood was in line for the powerful weather. The magnolia leaves were gone but the wood of the docks was still slippery. Zoe kept her head down to make sure she didn't slip. Not looking ahead, she nearly walked into an unexpected figure on the dock.

"Whoa, sorry," Zoe exclaimed. Then she locked eyes with Will. "Oh, my God, what are you doing around here?" She threw her arms around his neck. Will spun her around two times before setting her down. She placed her hand against his chest. He still wore a light-blue button-down Oxford shirt with a pair of khakis. "Did you leave work early?"

"Sort of," Will said, visibly gulping.

With her hand still on his shirt, she felt his heartbeat pounding against her palm. "What's wrong? Is someone hurt? Did something happen with your grand-mother?"

"Zoe." Will chuckled and pulled her hands down to her sides. "Everything at home is fine."

"Then what are you doing here?"

"I came…" he began, letting go of her hand. With his fingers he began to unbutton his shirt. "Zoe, since laying eyes on you in Kelly Towers three months ago, you have been an intricate part of my life. You've been my best friend, my confidant and the woman I have fallen in love with."

"Will?" Zoe cocked her head to the side and watched Will get down on one knee. Tears sprang to her eyes. A drop clung to her bottom lash, blinding her. Once she wiped it away, Will had completely taken off his Oxford and underneath he wore a blue cape.

"Zoe, a few months ago you asked me to choose you, and I am down here on bended knee, asking—no—" Will shook his head "—I'm begging you to choose me and be my wife."

"Are you serious?" The words barely got out of her mouth. She couldn't swallow past the lump in her throat. She knelt down with Will and began kissing him without a care in the world for her lipstick.

Will broke the kiss first. His thumbs wiped away the happy tears. "I've never been more serious in my life, Zoe. Please save me one last time and tell me you'll marry me."

All her life Zoe had wanted to be a part of Ravens. Before falling in love with Will, she thought it was the business she wanted to be a part of, but after getting to know everyone, Zoe realized she wanted to be a part of his life and his family. She'd known about their history and now she had the chance to be a part of the future. "Oh, my God, yes, a thousand times over, yes."

"I have this ring," Will said. His hands nervously reached into his pocket. The pear-shaped diamond sparkled in the afternoon sun. It was the ring she'd spied in picture after picture during her research on women marrying into the Ravens family tree. The heirloom was passed on from generation to generation. "It belongs to you, Zoe. You were meant to be a Ravens."

* * * * *

HIS PREGNANT
SLEEPING BEAUTY

LYNNE MARSHALL

This book is dedicated to the two paramedics who
helped me make my character, Joe, a true hero.

Thank you, John-Philip Maarschalk and
Rick Ochocki, for your expert input and help.

What would the world be without our first responders?

CHAPTER ONE

CAREY SPENCER HAD never felt more alone in her life than when she got off the bus in Hollywood.

Joseph Matthews, on that night's shift for the prestigious Hollywood Hills Clinic, had just delivered one of the industry's favorite character actresses to the exclusive twenty-bed extended recovery hotel. It was tucked between Children's Hospital and a smaller private hospital on Sunset Boulevard, and the common eye would never guess its function. Joe had agreed to make the Wednesday night run because James Rothsberg himself had asked. After all, the lady *had* won an award for Best Supporting Actress the year before last.

As the lead paramedic for the ambulance line he owned, Joe had attended the not-to-be-named-aloud patient during the uneventful ride to the recovery hotel. She'd been heavily sedated, her IV was in place, her vitals, including oxygen saturation, were fine, but she'd had so much work done on her face, breasts and hands she looked like a mummy. When they'd arrived, you'd have thought he'd delivered the President to Walter Reed National Military Medical Center the way the abundant staff rushed to the ambulance and took over the transfer.

Now, at nine p.m., back sitting in the front of the private ambulance, Joe switched on some music. Jazz, his favorite station. Yeah, he owned this bus—hell, he owned all six of them—so he could play whatever music he wanted. But that also kept him thinking about work a lot. It was the first of the month and he'd have to make copies of the June shift schedule for the EMTs and paramedics on his team before they showed up for work tomorrow morning.

"I'm hungry," Benny, his EMT, said from behind the wheel.

Why was Joe not surprised? The kid had barely turned twenty and seemed to have hollow legs.

Restless and out of sorts, a state that was nothing new these days, Joe nodded. "How about that Mexican grill?" They'd just made their last run on Friday night, without plans for later, so why not?

"You read my mind." Benny tossed him a cockeyed grin, his oversized Afro flopping with the quick movement.

He turned off Hollywood Boulevard and up N. Cahuenga to the fast-food place by the cross-country bus depot, where a bus had just arrived from Who Knew Where, USA. Benny had to wait to pull into a larger-than-average parking space. Joe mindlessly watched a handful of people trickle off the bus.

A damn fine-looking young woman wearing oversized sunglasses got off. Sunglasses at night. What was up with that? She was slender and her high-heeled boots made her look on the tall side. She wore jeans and a dark blue top, or was it a sweater? Her thick hair was layered and long with waves and under the bus depot lights looked brown. Reddish? He wondered what her story was. Probably because of the shades at night. But he didn't bother to think about ladies these days. Yet, still, dang, she was hot. And stood out like a rose in a thorn patch.

Benny backed the private ambulance into the space at the farthest end of the restaurant lot, and Joe got out the passenger side, immediately getting hit by the mouthwatering aroma of spicy beans and chipotle chicken. He stretched, eager to chow down. A sudden movement in his peripheral vision drew his attention. Someone sprang from behind a pillar and snagged a lady's purse strap and wrist, pulling her out of the crowd and toward the nearby alley. It was the woman he'd just been gawking at! The other travelers had mostly dispersed. She put up a fight, too, and squealed, yet the few people left lingering didn't seem to notice…but he did.

Joe ran to the mouth of the alley. "Hey!" Then sprinted toward the young woman, who was still fighting to hold on to her purse.

The tall but skinny, straggly-haired dude dragged her by the shoulder strap and wrist deeper down the alley. *Why doesn't she just let go? Ah, wait, it's one of those over-the-torso jobs.*

"Hey!"

This time the guy turned and whacked her with his fist, knocking the young woman to the ground. Her head hit with a thud. He ripped off the purse, hitting her head on the pavement again, then stepped over her to get to Joe with a wild swing.

Joe blocked the first punch with little effort—the dumb punk didn't know what he was dealing with as he boxed for his workouts—but the guy pulled a knife and lashed out. Joe threw another punch and landed it, even while feeling a hot lightning-quick slice across his ribs. Now he was really ticked. The guy ran deeper into the alley with Joe in pursuit, soon disappearing over a large trash bin and tall crumbling brick wall. Joe skidded to a brief stop and watched in disbelief. For a scumbag the man was agile. Probably from a lot of practice in assaulting innocent people.

The girl! Holding his side, he sprinted back to where she lay. Out cold.

Benny met up with him. "I called the police. You okay?"

"Just a superficial wound." Still, he checked it briefly since an adrenaline rush could mask pain. The last thing he wanted to find out was that the cut was deep enough to cause evisceration and he hadn't noticed. Fortunately the only thing he saw was oozing blood, nothing gushing. He'd throw a thick absorbent pad over his middle as soon as Benny got back with the trauma kit, oxygen bag and backboard. He didn't want to bleed all over the poor lady. "Bring our equipment, okay?" He grabbed a pair of gloves from Benny's belt, and knelt in front of the young woman as Benny took off for the ambulance. "I'm a paramedic, miss. Are you okay?" he said loudly and clearly. She didn't respond.

She'd hit her head hard when she'd fallen—correct that, had been punched to the ground. He tried to rouse her with a firm hand on her shoulder. "Hello? You okay, you awake, miss?"

He watched the rise and fall of her chest. At least she was breathing normally. He felt her neck for the carotid pulse and found it. Rate and strength normal. Good. He scanned her body for bleeding or other signs of obvious injury. Maybe the scumbag had stabbed her too. Then he used the palms of his gloved hands to sweep the underside of her arms and legs to check for bleeding, and did the same beneath both sides of her back. So far so good.

There was a fifty-cent-sized pool of blood behind her head, but he didn't move her neck, not before he and Benny had placed a cervical collar on her. Her assailant had run off with her purse and she didn't appear to have any other form of ID. He checked her wrist and then her neck to see if she wore any emergency alert jewelry. No such luck. They'd have to wait until she regained consciousness to find out who she was.

Even under the dim lights in the alley she had an obvious black eye, and because the dirtbag had yanked off her torso-anchored purse strap the sweater she'd been wearing had been pulled halfway down her left arm... which was covered in bruises. She'd just been mugged, but these marks weren't fresh. Anger surged through him. She'd been beaten up long before today.

What kind of guy treated a woman like that?

He shook his head. Of all the lousy luck. She hadn't stepped off the bus five minutes ago and had already gotten mugged and knocked unconscious. The only thing she had going for her on this nightmare of a Friday night was him. He shuddered for the young stranger over what might have played out if he hadn't been here.

Maybe it was those thick eyelashes that seemed to glue her eyes shut, or her complete vulnerability, being unconscious in an alley, or maybe it was the obvious signs of abuse, but for whatever reason Joe was suddenly struck with an uncompromising need to protect her.

From this moment on tonight he vowed to take responsibility for the out-of-luck Jane Doe. Hell, if anyone had ever needed a guardian angel, she did.

Benny had moved the ambulance closer, and brought the backboard and equipment. Joe let Benny apply a large sloppy dressing around his middle as he checked her airway again, noting she had good air exchange. He worried, with the head injury, that she might vomit and wanted to be near if she did to prevent aspiration.

"We're going to give you some oxygen and put a collar round your neck," Joe said calmly, hoping she might already be regaining consciousness and hear him explain everything they did to her. They worked together and soon had Jane on the backboard for stability. Joe secured her with the straps, never taking his eyes off her. She had definitely been knocked out cold, yet still breathed evenly. A good thing. But he knew when unconscious people woke up they could often be combative and try to take off the oxygen and cervical collar. Hell, after what she'd just been through, could he blame her if she woke up fighting?

With her long dark auburn hair spread over her shoulders and her hands strapped to the transport board, she made the strangest image.

An urban Sleeping Beauty.

"Ready for transfer?" Joe said, breaking his own thoughts.

"Don't you want to wait for the police?"

"If they're not here by the time we get her in the back of the van, you call them again and tell them to meet us at the clinic. She might have a skull fracture or subdural bleed for all we know, and needs medical attention ASAP." He knew the next forty-five minutes were all she had remaining in the golden hour for traumatic head injury. "I'm going to call Dr. Rothsberg and let him know what we've got."

He jumped into the back of the van first to guide the head of the gurney on which they'd placed the long spine board and patient as Benny pushed from the back, then he rolled the gurney forward and locked it in place with sprung locks on the ambulance floor.

He'd ride in the back with her. If she woke up, confused and possibly combative, he wanted to be there. Plus it would be his chance to do a more thorough examination.

Joe did another assessment of Sleeping Beauty's condition. Unchanged. Then he made the call. Unexpectedly, Dr. Rothsberg said to bring her to the clinic instead of county. Which was a good thing, because Joe would have taken her home before he'd consider delivering a Jane Doe to county hospital to potentially slip through every conceivable crack due to their overstretched system.

He stripped off the makeshift dressing and his shirt to assess his own wound, which was long and jagged, still wept blood and would definitely need stitches. Now that he was looking at it, it burned like hell. Benny had a short conversation with the police, who'd just arrived. Great timing! He showed them where they'd found her and where the attacker had fled over the wall then left them to look for witnesses as Joe cleaned and dressed his own wound. Damn, the disinfectant smarted! One of the policemen took a quick look inside the ambulance, saw the victim and Joe with his injury, nodded and took off toward the alley.

Benny closed the back doors of the van, got into the driver's seat then started the ambulance. "They'll take our statements at the clinic later."

"Good," Joe said, taping his dressing, constantly checking his patient as he did so.

As Benny drove, with their lights flashing, Joe checked her vital signs again, this time using a blood-pressure cuff then a stethoscope to listen to her lungs.

He opened her eyes, opening the blackened eye more gingerly, and used his penlight to make sure she hadn't blown a pupil. Fortunately she hadn't, but unfortunately he'd had to move a clump of her hair away from her face in order to do so. It was thick and wavy, and, well, somehow it felt too intimate, touching it. It'd been a while since he'd run his fingers through a woman's hair, which he definitely wasn't doing right now, but the thought of wanting to bothered him.

By the status of her black eye, it'd been there a few days and definitely looked ugly and intentional. Someone had punched her. That was a fact. There was that anger again, flaming out of nowhere for a woman he knew zero about.

He decided to insert a hep-lock into her antecubital fossa so the clinic would have a line ready to go on arrival. A head injury could increase cranial pressure and so could IV fluid. He didn't want to add to that, and so far her blood pressure was within normal limits. While he performed the tasks he thought about everything that had happened to his patient prior to winding up in that alley.

She'd gotten off the bus and hadn't waited to collect a suitcase, which meant all she'd carried with her was in that large shoulder bag. And that was long gone with the punk who'd knocked her cold and jumped the wall. He tightened his fists. What he'd give to deck that guy and leave him in some alley.

If Joe added up the clues he'd guess that the lovely Sleeping Jane was running from whoever had bruised her arms and blackened her eye. She'd probably grabbed whatever she could and snuck away from…

"Who are you?" Joe asked quietly, wondering if she could hear him, knowing that unconscious people sometimes still heard what went on around them. "Where did you come from?"

He lifted one of her hands, that fierce sense of protectiveness returning, and held it in his, noticing the long thin fingers with carefully manicured but unpainted nails, and made another silent vow. *Don't worry, I'll look out for you. You don't have to be afraid where I'm taking you.*

They arrived at The Hollywood Hills Clinic, nestled far beneath the Hollywood sign at the end of narrow winding roads with occasional hairpin turns. The swanky private clinic that hugged the hillside always reminded him of something Frank Lloyd Wright might have designed for the twenty-first century, if he were still alive. The stacked boxy levels of the modern stone architecture, nearly half of it made of special earthquake-resistant glass, looked like a diamond in the night on the hillside. Warm golden light glowed from every oversized window, assuring the private clinic was open twenty-four hours. For security and privacy purposes, there were tall fences out front, and a gate every vehicle had to clear, except for ambulances. They breezed through as soon as the gate opened completely.

Benny headed toward the private patient loading area at the back of the building. Joe put his shirt back on and gingerly buttoned it over his bandaged and stinging rib cage.

He still couldn't believe his good fortune over landing the bid as the private ambulance company for James Rothsberg's clinic only two short years after starting his own business. He'd been an enterprising twenty-three-year-old paramedic with a plan back then, thanks to a good mind for business instilled in him by his hard-working father. James must have seen something about him he liked when he'd interviewed him and Joe had tendered his bid. Or maybe it had had more to do with the nasty info leak the previous ambulance company had been responsible for, exposing several of the A-list actors in the biz on a TV gossip show, making Joe's timing impeccable. He used to think of it as fate.

James's parents—Michael Rothsberg and Aubrey St. Claire—had had enough info leaks in their lives to fill volumes. Everyone, even Joe, remembered the scandal, and he'd only been in his early teens at the time. Their stories had made headlines on every supermarket rag and cable TV talk show. Everyone knew about their private affairs. After all, James's parents had been Hollywood royalty, and had been two of the highest-paid actors in the business. Watching them fall from grace had become a national pastime after a nasty kiss-and-tell book by an ex-lover had outed them as phonies. Their marriage had been a sham, and their teenage children, James and Freya, had suffered most.

James had told Joe on the day he'd hired him that loyalty to the clinic and the patients was the number-one rule, he wouldn't tolerate anything less, and Joe had lived up to that pledge every single day he'd shown up to work. He'd walked out of James's office that day thinking fate was on his side and he was the luckiest man on earth, but he too would soon experience his own fall. Like James, it hadn't been of his own making but that didn't mean it had hurt any less.

These days Joe didn't believe in fate or luck. No, he'd changed his thinking on that and now, for him, everything happened for a reason. Even his damned infertility, which he was still trying to figure out. He glanced at the hand where his wedding ring had once been but didn't let himself go there, instead focusing on the positive. The here and now. The new contract. His job security.

The clinic had opened its doors six years ago, and two years later, right around the time James's sister Freya had joined the endeavor, Joe's private ambulance service had been the Rothsbergs' choice for replacement. Having just signed a new five-year contract with the clinic, Joe almost thought of himself as another Hollywood success story. Hell, he was only twenty-eight, owned his own business, and worked for the most revered clinic in town.

But how could he call it true success when the rest of his life was such a mess?

James Rothsberg himself met the ambulance, along with another doctor and a couple of nurses, and Joe prepared to transfer his sleeping beauty.

A little bit taller than Joe, James's strong and well-built frame matched Joe's on the fitness scale. Where they parted ways was in the looks department. The son of A-list actors, James was what the gossip magazines called "an Adonis in scrubs". Yeah, he was classy, smooth and slick. He was the man every woman dreamed of and every man wanted to be, and Joe wasn't afraid to admit he had a man crush on the guy. Strictly platonic, of course, based on pure admiration. The doctor ran the lavish clinic for the mind-numbingly affluent, who flocked to him, eager to pay the price for his plastic surgery services. Well, someone had to support the outrageously luxurious clinic and the well-paid staff. In fact, someone on staff had recently commented after a big awards ceremony that half of the stars in attendance had been through the clinic's doors. A statement that wasn't far from the truth.

"James, what are you still doing here?"

"You piqued my interest," James said. "I had to see Jane Doe for myself."

Joe pushed the gurney out of the back of the ambulance, and Rick, one of the evening nurses, pulled from the other end.

James studied Jane Doe as she rolled by. "She didn't get that shiner tonight."

"Nope," Joe said. "There's a whole other story that went down before she got mugged."

James nodded agreement. "That reminds me, I got a call from the police department. They'll be here shortly to take your statement." He tugged Joe by the arm. "Let's take a look at your injury before they get here, okay?"

Joe was torn between looking after Sleeping Beauty or himself, but knew the clinic staff would give her the utmost medical attention. Besides, it wasn't every day the head of the clinic offered to give one-to-one patient care to an employee.

"Thanks, Doc. I really appreciate it."

"It's totally selfish. I've got to look out for my lead paramedic, right?" James said in a typically self-deprecating manner. That was another thing he liked so much about the guy. He never flaunted his wealth or his status.

Joe glanced across the room at the star patient of the night, Ms. Jane Doe, still unconscious but breathing steadily, and felt a little tug in his chest, then followed James into an examination room.

After the nursing assistant removed Joe's dressing, James studied it. "So what happened here?"

Joe explained what had transpired in the alley as the doctor applied pressure to one area that continued to bleed.

"Oh, you're definitely getting a tetanus shot. Who knows what was on that guy's blade."

"Well, he *was* a scumbag."

"Good thing you've got a trained plastic surgeon to stitch you up. I'd hate to ruin those perfect washboard abs."

Joe laughed, knowing his rigorous workout sessions plus boxing kept him fit. Boxing had been the one thing he could do to keep sane and not beat the hell out of his best friend during his divorce. "Ouch," he said, surprised by how sensitive his wound was as the nursing assistant cleaned the skin.

"Ouch!" he repeated, when the first topical anesthetic was injected by James.

The doctor chuckled. "Man up, dude. I'm just getting started."

That got an ironic laugh out of Joe. *Yeah, sterile dude, man up!*

"You won't be feeling much in a couple of minutes."

Joe knew the drill, he'd sutured his share of patients in his field training days, but this was the first time in his entire life he'd been the patient in need of stitches. Hell, he'd never even needed a butterfly bandage before.

"So, about the girl with the black eye," James said, donning sterile gloves while preparing the small sterile minor operations tray. "I wonder if she may have had any prior intracranial injuries that might have contributed to her immediately falling unconscious."

"I was wondering the same thing, but she hit that pavement really hard. I hope she doesn't have a subdural hematoma."

"We're doing a complete head trauma workup on her."

"Thanks. I know this probably sounds weird, but

I feel personally responsible for her, having seen the whole thing go down, not getting there fast enough, and being the first to treat her and all. Especially since she doesn't have any ID."

"You broke a rule, right? Got involved with your patient?"

"Didn't mean to, but I guess you could say that. I know it's foolish—"

James turned back toward him. "And this might be foolish too, but when the police come we'll tell them we'll be treating *and* letting our Jane Doe recover right here."

Touched beyond words, as the cost for staying at this exclusive clinic would be astronomical, Joe wanted to shake the good doctor's hand but he wore sterile gloves. "Thank you. I really—" He was about to say "appreciate that" but quickly went quiet, not used to being the patient as the first stitch was placed, using a nasty-looking hooked needle, and though he didn't feel anything, he still didn't want to move.

"If I stitch this up just so, there'll hardly be a scar. On the other hand, I could make you look like you've got a seven pack."

As the saying went, it only hurt when he laughed.

A couple of hours later, the police had taken a thorough report, and also told Joe they hadn't found anyone matching the description a couple of witnesses had given for the suspect, they also said they hadn't recovered Jane Doe's purse.

Joe sighed and shook his head. She'd continue to be Madam X until she came to. Which hopefully would be soon.

"We do have one lead, though."

He glanced up, hopeful whatever that lead was it might point to Jane's identity.

"The clinic staff found a bus-ticket stub in her sweater pocket. If she used a credit card to purchase the ticket, we might be able to trace it back and identify her."

"That's great. But what if she paid cash?"

"That might imply she didn't want to be traced."

"Probably explain those bruises, too."

The cop nodded. "The most we could possibly find out is the origin of the ticket. Which city she boarded in, but she's bound to wake up soon, right?"

Joe glanced across the room. Jane was now in one of the clinic's fancy hospital gowns and hooked up to an IV, still looking as peaceful as a sleeping child. "It's hard to say with concussion and potential brain swelling. The doctors may determine she needs surgery for a subdural hematoma or something, for all I know."

The young cop looked grim as he considered that possibility, and Joe was grateful for his concern. "Well, we'll be in touch." He gave Joe his card. "If she wakes up, or if there's anything you remember or want to talk about, give me a call. Likewise, I'll let you know if we find anything out."

"Thanks."

An orderly and RN rolled Jane by Joe. "Where's she going?"

"To her room in the DOU. She's in Seventeen A."

The definitive observation unit was for the patients who needed extra care. Dr. Di Williams ran the unit like a well-oiled machine. Jane would be well looked after, but… He made a snap decision—he wasn't going home tonight. If James and Di would let him, he'd wait things out right here.

Fifteen minutes later, Sleeping Beauty was tucked into a high-end single bed in a room that looked more like one in a luxury spa hotel than a hospital. The only thing giving it away were the bedside handrails and the stack of monitors camouflaged in the corner with huge vases and flower arrangements. The tasteful beige, white and cream decor was relaxing, but Joe couldn't sleep. Instead, he sat in the super-comfy bedside chair resting his head in the palm of his right hand, watching *her* sleep. Wondering what her story was, and pondering why he felt so responsible for her. He decided it was because she was completely vulnerable. He knew the feeling. Someone besides a staff nurse had to look out for her until they found out who she was and could locate her family.

Sporting that black eye and those healing bruises on her arms, it was likely she had been in an abusive relationship. Most likely she'd been beaten up by the man she'd thought she loved.

His left thumb flicked the inside of his vacant ring finger, reminding him, on a much more personal level, how deeply love could hurt.

CHAPTER TWO

A FIRM HAND sent Joe out of a half dreaming, half awake state. He'd been smiling, floating around somewhere, smiling. The grip on his shoulder made a burst of adrenaline mainline straight to his heart, making his pulse ragged and shaky. He sat bolt upright, his eyes popping open. In less than a second he remembered where he was, turned his head toward the claw still grabbing him, and stared up at the elderly night nurse.

Cecelia, was it?

"What's up?" he said, trying to sound awake, then glancing toward the hospital bed and the patient he'd let down by falling asleep. Some guardian he'd turned out to be. She'd been placed on her side, either sound asleep or still unconscious, with pillows behind her back and between her knees, and he hadn't even woken up.

"Your services are needed," Cecelia said with a grainy voice. "We have a helicopter transfer to Santa Barbara."

"Got it. Take care of her."

"What I'm paid for," Cecelia mumbled, fiddling with the blanket covering her patient.

Joe stood, took one last look at Jane, who still looked peaceful, and walked to the nearest men's room to freshen up, then reported for duty in the patient transitioning room.

Rick, the RN from last night, was at the end of his shift and gave Joe his report. "The fifty-four-year-old patient is status post breast reduction, liposuction and lower face lift. Surgery and overnight recovery were uneventful. She's being transferred to Santa Barbara Cottage Hotel for the remainder of her recovery. IV in right forearm. Last medicated for pain an hour ago with seventy-five milligrams of Demerol. Dressings and drainage tubes in place, no excess bleeding noted. She's been released by Dr. R. for transfer." The male RN, fit and overly tanned, making his blue eyes blaze, gave Joe a deadpan stare. "All systems go. She's all yours." Then, when out of earshot of the patient, Rick whispered, "I didn't vote for her husband."

Joe accompanied the patient and gurney to the waiting helicopter on the roof and loaded the sleeping patient onto the air ambulance. He did a quick head-to-toe assessment before strapping her down and locking the special hydraulic gurney into place. He then made sure any and all emergency equipment was stocked and ready for use. After he hooked up the patient to the heart and BP monitor, he put headphones on his patient first and then himself and took his seat, buckling in, preparing for the noisy helicopter blades to whir to life then takeoff.

After delivering the patient to the Santa Barbara airport and transferring the politician's wife, who would not be named, to the awaiting recovery hotel team, he hoped to grab some coffee and maybe a quick breakfast while they waited for the okay to take off for the return trip.

Two hours later, back at the clinic, Joe's only goal

was to check in on Jane Doe. He hoped she'd come to and by now maybe everyone knew her name, and he wondered what it might be. Alexis? Belle? Collette? Excitedly he dashed into her room and found her as he'd left her...unconscious. Disappointment buttoned around him like a too-tight jacket.

The day shift nurse was at her side, preparing to give her a bed bath. A basin of water sat on the bedside table with steam rising from the surface. Several towels and cloths and a new patient gown were neatly stacked beside it. A thick, luxurious patient bath blanket was draped across her chest, Sleeping Beauty obviously naked underneath it. He felt the need to look away until the nurse pulled the privacy curtain around the bed.

"No change?" he asked, already knowing and hating the answer.

"No. But her lab results were a bit of a surprise."

"Everything okay with her skull?"

"Oh, yeah, the CT cranial scan and MRI were both normal except for the fact she's got one hell of a concussion with brain swelling. Well, along with still being unconscious and a slow-wave EEG to prove it."

Joe knew the hospital privacy policy, and this nurse wasn't about to tell him Jane Doe's lab results. Theoretically it wasn't any of his business. Except he'd made a vow last night, and had made it his business to look after her. As he hadn't signed off on his paramedic admission notes for Jane last night, he suddenly needed to access her computer chart to do so.

He headed to the intake department to find a vacant computer, but not before running into James, who looked rested and ready to take on the day. Joe, on the other hand, had gotten a glimpse of himself in the mirror when he'd made a quick pit stop on arriving back at the clinic a few minutes earlier. Dark circles beneath his eyes, a day's growth of beard… Yeah, he was a mess.

"What are you still doing here?" James asked.

"Just got back from a helicopter run to Santa Barbara for one of your patients."

"Cecelia told me you stayed here last night."

Damn that night nurse. "Yeah, well, I wanted to be around if Jane Doe woke up."

He didn't look amused. "This is an order, Joe. Go home and get some sleep. Don't come back until your usual evening shift. Got it?"

"Got it. Just have to sign off my charting first."

Several staff members approached James with questions, giving Joe the chance to sneak off to the computer. He logged on and quickly accessed Jane Doe's folder. First he read her CT scan results and the MRI, which were positive for concussion and brain swelling, but without fractures or bleeding, then he took a look at her labs. So far so good. Her drug panel was negative. Good. Her electrolytes, blood glucose, liver and kidney function tests were all within normal limits. Good. Then his gaze settled on a crazy little test result that nearly knocked him out of the chair.

A positive *pregnancy* test.

His suddenly dry-as-paper tongue made it difficult to swallow. His pulse thumped harder and his mind took a quick spin, gathering questions as it did. Did the mystery lady know she was pregnant? He wondered if the father had been worried out of his mind about her since she'd gone missing. Or was the guy who beat her up the father…because she was pregnant?

Had she been running away? Most likely.

Shifting thoughts made bittersweet memories roll through his mind over another most important pregnancy test. One that had changed his life. He wanted more than anything to make those thoughts stop, knowing they never led to a good place, but right now he was too tired to fight them off.

He'd once been on that pregnancy roller-coaster ride, one day ecstatic about the prospect of becoming a father. Another day further down the line getting a different lab test irrefutably stating there was no way in hell he could have gotten his wife pregnant. Any hope of becoming a father had been ripped away. The questions. The confrontations. The ugly answers that had finally torn his marriage apart.

Hell.

He needed to leave the clinic. James had been right. He should go home and get some sleep because if he didn't he might do something he still wanted to do desperately. Give his best—strike that—*ex*-best friend the beating he deserved.

On the third day Joe sat in his now favorite chair at the mystery lady's bedside, thumbing through a fitness magazine. Di Williams, the middle-aged, hardworking head of DOU, had shaken him up earlier when she'd explained Sleeping Beauty's condition as brain trauma—or, in her case, swelling of the brain—that had disconnected the cerebral cortex circuits, kind of like a car idling but not firing up the engine. She'd also said that if she didn't come around soon, they'd have to consider her in a coma and would need to move her to a hospital that could best meet her longer-term needs.

The thought of losing track of the woman he'd vowed to look after made his stomach knot. The doctor had also said she'd be getting transferred to a specialist coma unit later that afternoon for an enhanced CT scan that would test for blood flow and metabolic activity and they'd have to go from there, which kept Joe's stomach feeling tangled and queasy.

Time was running out, and it seemed so unfair for the girl from the bus. What about her baby?

Jane moved and Joe went on alert. It was the first time he'd witnessed what the nurses had said she often did. He'd admitted, when no one had been around, to flicking her cheek with his finger from time to time to get some kind of reaction out of her, but nothing had ever happened. The lady definitely wasn't faking it. She moved again, this time quicker, as though restless. A dry sound emitted from her throat. He held his breath and felt his heart pump faster as he pushed the call light for the attending nurse.

Jane Doe was waking up.

Tiny sputtering electrical fuses seemed to turn on and off inside him as his anticipation grew. He stood, leaned over the hospital bed and watched the sleeping beauty's lids flutter. Instinctively, he turned off the overhead lamp to help decrease the shock of harsh light to her vision as her eyes slowly opened.

They were dark green. And beautiful, like her.

But they'd barely opened before they snapped shut again as her features contorted with fear.

Carey fought for her life, flailing her arms, kicking her feet. Someone wanted to hurt her. It wasn't Ross. Not this time. She ran, but her feet wouldn't move. She tried to scream, but the sound didn't leave her throat. Fear like she'd never felt before consumed her, but she couldn't give up, she had to protect herself in order to protect her baby.

Someone shouted and ran toward her. She knew he

wanted to help. Broad shoulders, and legs moving in a powerful sprint. "Hey!" His voice cut through the night. That face. Strong. Determined. Filled with anger over the man trying to take her purse. She fought more. She had to break away from the smelly man's grip.

"Hey!"

Fight. Fight. Get away.

"Hold on, everything's okay. You're safe." Did she recognize the man's voice? "I've got you." Hands gripped her shoulders, kept her still. She held her breath.

More hands smoothed back her hair. "It's okay, hon." A woman's voice. "Calm down. You're in the hospital."

Hospital? Had she heard right?

Carey shook her head. It hurt. She was hit by a wave of vertigo that made her quit squirming. She lay still, waiting for the hands to release her. It felt like she was in an extremely comfortable bed. She relaxed her tight, squinting eyes and slowly opened first one then the other. She turned her head to a shadow looming above her. It had features. The face she remembered from her dreams. Strong. Brave. Was this *still* a dream?

She stared at him, her breathing rapid, waiting for her eyes to adjust to the light. He was the man who'd taken on her attacker. She scanned his face. Kind brown eyes. Short dark hair. A square jaw. Good looking.

"You're in the hospital and you're safe," he said in a low, comforting voice.

She looked beyond him to a gorgeous room. A hospital? It looked more like an expensive hotel with muted colors and modern furniture, chic, classy, a room she'd never been able to afford in her life. Was she still dreaming? Since she'd stopped protesting, it was quiet. Oh, and there was an IV in her arm. Being an RN herself, she recognized that right off. A catheter between her legs? And she wore a hospital gown. But this one was silky and smooth, not one of those worn-out over-starched jobs at the hospital where she worked.

Everything was so strange. Surreal. As she gathered her senses she couldn't remember where she was other than being in a hospital. She couldn't figure out why she'd be here. Wait. Someone had attacked her. She'd been pushed down. *Oh, no!* Her hand flew to her stomach, and she gasped.

"My baby!" Her voice sounded muffled and strange, as if her ears were plugged.

"Your baby's fine," the woman said. "So you remember you're pregnant."

Her hearing improved. She nodded, and it hurt, but she smiled anyway because her baby was fine.

The attractive young man smiled back at her, and the concern in his eyes was surprising. Did she know him?

"My baby's fine," she whispered to him, and a rush of feelings overcame her until she cried.

Then the strangest thing happened. The man that she wasn't sure if she knew or not, the man with the kind brown eyes...his welled up, too. "Your baby's fine." His voice sounded raspy.

She cried softly for a few moments, his eyes misty and glistening as he gave a caring smile, and it felt so good.

"Where am I?"

"You're in the hospital, hon," the nearby nurse said.

"But *where* am I?"

"Hollywood," he said. "You're in California."

She thought hard, vaguely remembering getting on a bus. Getting off a bus. It was all too much to straighten out right now. She was exhausted.

"What's your name, honey?" The nurse continued.

"Carey Spencer." At least she remembered her name. But she needed to rest. To close her eyes and…

"She's out again." The kind man's voice sounded far, far away.

"That's what happens sometimes with head injuries," the nurse replied.

Dr. Williams cancelled the plan to transfer her to a coma unit since it was clear Carey Spencer was waking up. Joe assigned another paramedic to cover his shift and stayed by her bedside, hoping to be there when she woke up again. The next time, hopefully, would be permanently. He had dozed off for a second.

"Where am I?" Her voice.

Had he slept a few minutes?

He forced open his eyes and faced Carey as she sat up in the bed, propped by several pillows. Her hair fell in a tangle of waves over her shoulders. Those dark green eyes flashed at him. She'd already figured out how to use the hand-held bed adjuster. "Where am I?" she asked more forcefully.

He'd told her earlier, but she'd suffered a head trauma, her brain was all jumbled up inside. Because of the concussion she might forget things for a long time to come. She deserved the facts.

"You're in the hospital in Hollywood, California. You got off a cross-country bus the other night. Do you remember where you came from?"

"I don't want anyone contacting my family."

He rang for the nurse. "We won't contact anyone unless you tell us to."

"I'm from Montclare, Illinois. It's on the outskirts of Chicago."

"Okay. Are you married?"

She shook her head, then looked at him tentatively. "I'm pregnant." Her eyes captured his and he could tell she remembered they'd gotten emotional together earlier when she'd woken up before. "And my baby's okay." She gave a gentle smile and odd protective sensations rippled over him. Those green eyes and the dark auburn hair. Wow. Her blackened eye may have been healing, but even with the shiner she was breathtaking. In his opinion anyway.

"Yes. Everything is okay in that department. How far along are you? Do you know?"

"Three months."

"And you came here on the bus for...?"

She hesitated. "Not for. To get away." She lifted her arms, covered in fading bruises. "I needed to get away."

"I understand." The uncompromising need to protect her welled up full force again. "Are you in trouble?"

She shook her head, then looked like it hurt to do so and immediately stopped.

The nurse came in, and asked Joe to leave so she could assess her patient and attend to her personal needs. He headed toward the door.

"Wait!" she said.

He turned.

"What's your name?"

"I'm Joseph Matthews. I'm the paramedic who brought you here."

"Thank you, Joseph. I owe you my life. And my baby's," she said from behind the privacy curtain.

He stared at his work boots, an uncertain smile creasing his lips. She certainly didn't owe him her life, but he was awfully glad to have been on scene the night she'd needed him.

The police were notified, and Joe didn't want to stick

around where he had no business, though in his heart he felt he deserved to know the whole story, so he went back to work. Around ten p.m., nearing the end of his shift, James approached. "Did you know she's a nurse?"

"I didn't. Interesting."

"She won't tell us how she got all banged up, but the fact she doesn't want us to contact the father of the baby explains that, doesn't it."

"Sadly, true."

"So, since she's recovering, if all goes well after tonight, I'm going to have to discharge her."

Startled by the news, Joe wondered why it hadn't occurred to him before. Of course she couldn't live here at the clinic. Her identity had been stolen along with her purse and any money she may have had in it. She was pregnant and alone in a strange city, and he couldn't very well let her become homeless, too. Hell, tomorrow was Sunday! "I've got an extra room. I could put her up until she gets back on her feet."

Joe almost did a second take, hearing himself make the offer, but when he thought more about it, he'd meant it. Every word. Even hoped she'd take him up on it.

"That's great," James said. "Though she may feel more comfortable staying with one of our nurses."

"True. Dumb idea, I guess."

"Not dumb. Pretty damn noble if you ask me. I'll vouch for you being a gentleman." James cast him a knowing smile and walked away.

Joe fought the urge to rush to Carey's room. She'd been through a lot today, waking up after a three-day sleep and all, and probably had a lot of thinking and sorting out to do. The social worker would be pestering her about her lost identification and credit cards and helping straighten out that mess. The poor woman's already bruised brain was probably spinning.

He needed to give her space, not make her worry he was some kind of weird stalker or something. But he wanted to tell her good night so he hiked over to the DOU and room Seventeen A, knocked on the wall outside the door, and when she told him to come in, he poked his head around the corner.

"Just wanted to say good night."

She seemed much less tense now and her smile came easily. She was so pretty, the smile nearly stopped him in his tracks. "Good night. Thanks for everything you've done for me."

"Glad to be of service, Carey."

"They're going to let me go tomorrow."

"Do you have a place to stay?"

"Not yet. Social Services is looking into something."

He walked closer to her bed and sat on the edge of his favorite chair. "I…uh… I have a two-bedroom house in West Hollywood. It's on a cul-de-sac, and it's really safe. Uh, the thing is, if you don't have any place to go, you can use my spare room. It's even got a private bathroom."

"You've done so much for me already. I couldn't—"

"Just until you get back on your feet. Uh, you know. If you want. That is." Why did he sound like a stammering, yammering teenager asking a girl on a date? That wasn't what he'd had in mind. He just wanted to help her. That was all.

She was the vision of a woman trying to make up her mind. Judging him on whether she could trust him or not, and from her recent experience Joe could understand why she might doubt herself. "Um, Dr. Rothsberg will vouch for me."

"I'll vouch for who?" James walked in on their awkward moment.

"I was just inviting Carey to stay in my spare room, if she needs a place to stay for a while."

James nailed Carey with his stare. "He's a good man. You can trust him." Then he turned and faced Joe and looked questioning. "I think."

That got a laugh out of Carey, and Joe shook his head. Guys loved to mess with each other.

"Okay, then," she said, surprising the heck out of Joe. "Okay?"

"Yes. Thank you." The woman truly knew how to be gracious, and for that he was grateful.

He smiled. "You're welcome. I'll see you tomorrow, then." It was his day off, but he'd be back here in a heartbeat when she was ready for discharge.

He turned to leave, unusually happy and suddenly finding the need to rush home and clean the house.

CHAPTER THREE

JOE HAD WORKED like a fiend to clean his house that morning before he went to the clinic to bring Carey back. He'd gotten her room prepared and put his best towels into the guest bathroom, wanting her to feel at home. He'd stocked the bathroom with everything he thought she might need from shampoo to gentle facial soap, scented body wash, and of course a toothbrush and toothpaste. Oh, and a brush for that beautiful auburn hair.

Aware that Carey only had the clothes on her back, he'd pegged her to be around his middle sister Lori's size and had borrowed a couple pairs of jeans and tops. Boy, he'd had a lot of explaining to do when he'd asked, too, since Lori was a typical nosy sister, especially since his divorce.

Once, while Carey had been sleeping in the clinic, he'd checked the size of her shoes and now he hoped she wouldn't mind that he'd bought her a pair of practical ladies' slip-on rubber-soled shoes and some flip-flops, because she couldn't exactly walk around in those sexy boots all the time. Plus, flip-flops were acceptable just about everywhere in Southern California. He was grateful some of the nurses had bought her a package of underwear and another bra—he'd heard that through the grapevine, thanks to Stephanie, the gossipy receptionist at The Hollywood Hills Clinic, who'd said she'd gone in on the collection of money for said items.

Now he waited in the foyer for the nurse or orderly to bring Carey around for discharge, having parked his car in the circular driveway. Careful not to say anything to Stephanie about the living arrangements, knowing that if he did so the whole clinic would soon find out, he smiled, assured her that Social Services had arranged for something, and with crossed arms tapped his fingers on his elbows, waiting.

She rounded the corner, being pushed in a wheelchair—clinic policy for discharges, regardless of how well the patient felt, but most especially for someone status post-head injury like her. She was dressed the way he'd first seen her last Wednesday night, and she trained her apprehensive glance straight at him. Even from this distance he noticed those dark green eyes, and right now they were filled with questions. Yeah, it would be weird to bring a strange lady into his home, especially one who continuously made his nerve endings and synapses react as if she waved some invisible magnetic wand.

He wanted to make her feel comfortable, so he smiled and walked to pick up the few things she had stuffed into a clinic tote bag, a classier version of the usual plastic discharge bags from other hospitals he'd worked at. It was one of the perks of choosing The Hollywood Hills Clinic for medical care, though in her case she hadn't had a choice.

It was nothing short of a pure leap of faith, going home with a complete stranger like this, Carey knew, but her options were nil and, well, the guy *had* cried with her that first day in the hospital when she'd woken up. The only thing that had mattered to her after the mugging was her baby, and when she'd been reassured it was all right, she'd been unable to hold back the tears. Joseph Matthews was either the easiest guy crier she'd ever met or the most empathetic man on the planet. Either way, it made him special. She had to remember that. Plus he'd saved her life. She'd *never* forget that.

When Dr. Rothsberg had vouched for him, and she'd already noticed how everyone around the clinic seemed to like the guy, she'd made a snap decision to take the paramedic up on his offer. But, really, where else did she have to go, a homeless shelter? She'd been out of touch with her parents for years and Ross was the reason she'd run away. She had zero intention of contacting any of them.

Recent history proved she couldn't necessarily trust her instincts, but she still had a good feeling about the paramedic.

When they first left the clinic parking lot Joseph slowed down so she could look back and up toward the hillside to the huge Hollywood sign. Somehow it didn't seem nearly as exciting as she'd thought it would be. Maybe because it hurt to turn her head. Or maybe because, being that close, it was just some big old white letters, with some parts in need of a paint touch-up. Now she sat in his car, her head aching, nerves jangled, driving down a street called Highland. Having passed the Hollywood Bowl and going into the thick of Hollywood, she admitted to feeling disappointed. Where was the magic? To her it was just another place with crowded streets in need of a thorough cleaning.

It was probably her lousy mood. She'd never planned on visiting California. She'd been perfectly happy in

Montclare. She'd loved her RN job, loved owning her car, being independent for the first time in her life. She still remembered the monumental day she'd gotten the key to her first apartment and had moved out once and for all from her parents' house. Life had been all she'd dreamed it would be, why would she ever need to go to Hollywood?

Then she'd met Ross Wilson and had thought she'd fallen in love, until she'd realized too late what kind of man he really was.

Nope. She'd come to Hollywood only because it had been the first bus destination she'd found out of Chicago. For her it hadn't been a matter of choice, but a matter of life and death.

Back at his house, Joe gave Carey space to do whatever she needed to do to make herself at home in her room. She'd been so quiet on the ride over, he was worried she was scared of him. He'd probably need to tread lightly until she got more comfortable around him. He thought about taking off for the afternoon, giving her time to herself, but, honestly, he worried she might bolt. Truth was, he didn't know what she might do, and his list of questions was getting longer and longer. All he really knew for sure was that he wanted to keep her safe.

The first thing he heard after she'd gone to her room had been the shower being turned on, and the image that planted in his head needed to be erased. Fast. So he decided to work out with his hanging punchbag in his screened-in patio, which he used as a makeshift gym. He changed clothes and headed to the back of the house, turned on a John Coltrane set, his favorite music to hit the bag with, and got down to working out.

With his hands up, chin tucked in, he first moved in

and out around the bag, utilizing his footwork, warming up, moving the bag, pushing it and dancing around, getting his balance. With bare hands he threw his first warm-up punches, *slap, slap, slap*, working the bag, punching more. The stitches across his rib cage pulled and stung a little, but probably wouldn't tear through his skin. Though after the first few punches he checked to make sure. They were healing and held the skin taut that was all.

As his session heated up, so did the wild saxophone music. He pulled off his T-shirt and got more intense, beating the hell out of the innocent bag where he mentally pasted every wrong the world had ever laid at his feet. His wife sleeping with his best friend, the lies about her baby being his. The divorce. He worked through the usual warm-up, heating up quickly. Then he pounded that bag for women abused by boyfriends and innocent victims who got mugged after getting off buses. *Wham*. He hit that bag over and over, pummeling it, his breath huffing, sweat flying. *Thump, bam, whump!*

"Excuse me, Joseph?"

Jolted, he halted in mid-punch, first stabilizing the punchbag so it wouldn't swing back and hit him, then shifted his gaze toward Carey. She had on different jeans, and one of his sister's bright pink cotton tops, and her wet hair was pulled up into a ponytail, giving her a wholesome look. Which he thought was sexy.

"Oh. Hey. Call me Joe. Everything okay?" he asked, out of breath.

"That music sounds like fighting." She had to raise her voice to be heard over the jazz.

"Oh, sorry, let me turn it off." That's why he liked

to work out with Coltrane, it got wild and crazy, often the way he felt.

Her gaze darted between his naked torso and his sweaty face. "I was just wondering if I could make a sandwich."

"Of course. Help yourself to anything. I've got cold cuts in the fridge. There's some fruit, too."

"Thanks." Her eyes stayed on his abdomen and he felt the need to suck it in, even though he didn't have a gut. "You know you're bleeding?"

He glanced down. Sure enough, he'd tugged a stitch too hard and torn a little portion of his skin. "Oh. Didn't realize." He grabbed his towel and blotted it quickly.

"Did you get hurt when you helped me?"

"Yeah, the jerk sliced me with his knife." Still blotting, he looked up.

Her eyes had gone wide. "You risked your life for me? I'm so sorry."

"Hey, I didn't risk my life." Had he? "I was just doing my job."

"Do paramedics usually fight guys with blades in their hands?"

"Well, maybe not every day, but it could happen." He flashed a sheepish grin over the bravado. "At least, it has now."

Her expression looked so sad he wanted to hug her, but they hardly knew each other.

"Thank you." He sensed she also meant she was sorry.

"Not a problem. Glad to do it." He waited to capture her eyes then nodded, wanting to make sure she understood she deserved nothing less than someone saving her from an alley attacker. They stood staring at each other for a moment or two too long, and since he was the one who always got caught up in the magic of her eyes, she looked away first. Standing in his boxing shorts, shirtless, he felt like he'd been caught naked winning that staring match.

"So... I'm going to make that sandwich." She pointed toward the door then led into the small kitchen, just around the corner from the dining area and his patio, while he assessed his stitches again. Yeah, he'd taken a knife for her, but the alternative, her getting stabbed by a sleazebag and maybe left to die, had been unacceptable.

The woman had a way of drumming up forgotten protective feelings and a whole lot more. Suddenly the house felt way too small for both of them. How was he going to deal with that while she stayed here?

Maybe one last punch to the bag then he promised to stop. *Thump!* The stitches tugged more and smarted. He hated feeling uncomfortable in his own house and blamed it on the size. He'd thought about selling it after Angela had agreed to leave, but the truth was he liked the neighborhood, it was close enough to work, and most of his family lived within a ten-mile radius. And why should he have to change his life completely because his wife had been unfaithful? Okay, one last one-two punch. *Whump, thump. Ouch, my side.* He grabbed his towel again and rubbed it over his wringing-wet hair.

One odd thought occurred to him as he dried himself off. When was the last time a woman had seen him shirtless? His ex-wife Angela had left a year ago, and was a new mother now. Good luck with that. He hadn't brought anyone home since she'd left, choosing to throw himself into his expanding business and demanding job rather than get involved with any poor unsuspecting women. He was angry at the world for being sterile, and angrier at the two people he'd trusted most, his wife and his best friend. Where was a guy supposed to go from there? Ah, what the hell. He punched the bag again. *Wham thud wham.*

"Would you like a sandwich?"

Not used to hearing a female voice in his house, it startled him from his down spiraling thoughts. A woman, a complete stranger no less, was going to be staying here for an indeterminate amount of time. Had he been crazy to offer? Two strangers in an eleven-hundred-square-foot house. That was too damn close, with hardly a way to avoid each other. Hell, their bedrooms were only separated by a narrow hallway and the bathrooms. What had he been thinking? His stomach growled. On the upside, she'd just offered to make him a sandwich.

Besides everything he was feeling—the awkwardness, the getting used to a stranger—he could only imagine she felt the same. Except for the unwanted attraction on his part, he was quite sure that wasn't an issue for her—considering her situation, she must feel a hell of a lot more vulnerable. He needed to be on his best behavior for Carey. She deserved no less.

"Yes, thanks, a sandwich sounds great." Since the bleeding had stopped, he tossed on his T-shirt after wiping his chest and underarms, then joined her in the kitchen.

"Do you like lettuce and tomato?"

"Whatever you're having is fine. I'm easy." His hands hung on to both sides of the towel around his neck.

"I never got morning sickness, like most women do. I've been ravenous from the beginning, so you're getting the works."

She was tallish and slender, without any sign of being

pregnant, and somehow he found it hard to believe she ate too much. "Sounds good. Hey, I thought I'd barbecue some chicken tonight. You up for that?"

She turned and shared a shy smile. "Like I said, I'm always hungry, so it sounds good to me."

He got stuck on the smile that delivered a mini sucker punch and didn't answer right away. "Okay. It looks like it'll be nice out, so I thought we could eat outdoors on the deck." He needed to put some space between them, and it wouldn't feel as close or intimate out there. *Just keep telling yourself she's wearing your sister's clothes. Your sister's clothes.*

He'd done a lot with his backyard, putting in a garden and lots of shrubbery for privacy's sake from his neighbors, plus he'd built his own cedar-plank deck and was proud of how it'd turned out. It had been one of the therapeutic projects he'd worked on during the divorce.

The houses had been built close together in this neighborhood back in the nineteen-forties. He liked to refer to it as his start-up house, had once planned to start his family in it, too. Too bad it had been someone else's family that had gotten started here.

Fortunately, Carey interrupted his negative thoughts again jabbing a plate with a sandwich into his side. He took the supremely well-stacked sandwich and grabbed some cold water from the refrigerator, raised the bottle to see if she'd like one. Without a word she nodded, and put her equally well-stacked sandwich on a second plate. As he walked to the dining table with the bottles in one hand and his sandwich in the other, he called out, "Chips are on the counter."

"Already found them," she said, appearing at the table, hands full with food and potato-chips bag, knocking him over the head with her smile—how much could a lonely man take? Obviously she was ready to eat.

It occurred to him they had some natural communication skills going on, and the thought made him uneasy. Beyond uneasy to downright uncomfortable. He clenched his jaw. He didn't want to communicate with a woman ever again. At least not yet, anyway, but since he'd just had a good workout and he was hungry, starved, in fact, he'd let his concerns slide. For now. Carey proved to be a woman of her word, too, matching him bite for bite. Yeah, she could put it away.

After they'd eaten, Carey asked to use his phone to make some calls.

"What'd I say earlier? *Mi casa es su casa.* It's a California rule. Make yourself at home, okay?" Though he said it, he wasn't anywhere near ready to meaning it.

"But it's long distance."

"I know you've got a lot of things to work out. All your important documents were stolen." This, helping her get her life back in order, he could do. The part of living with a woman again? Damn, it was hard. Sometimes, just catching the scent of her shampoo when she walked past seemed more than he could take.

"The clinic social worker has been helping me, and my credit cards have been cancelled now. But I couldn't even order new ones because I didn't have an address to send them to."

"You've got one now." He looked her in the eyes, didn't let her glance away. He'd made a promise to himself on her behalf that he'd watch over her, take care of her. It had to do with finding her completely helpless in that alley and the fierce sense of protectiveness he'd felt. "You can stay here as long as you need to. I'm serious."

She sent him a disbelieving look. In it Joe glimpsed

how deeply some creep back in Illinois had messed her up and it made him want to deck the faceless dude. But he also sensed something else behind her disbelief. "Thank you."

"Sure. You're welcome." Though she only whispered the reply, he knew without a doubt she was really grateful to be here, and that made the nearly constant awkward feelings about living with a complete stranger, a woman more appealing than he cared to admit, worth it.

Later, over dinner on the deck in the backyard, Joe sipped a beer and Carey lemonade. Her hair was down now, and she'd put on the sweater she'd worn that first night over his sister's top. In early June, the evenings were still cool, and many mornings were overcast with what they called "June gloom" in Southern California. She'd spent the entire dinner asking about his backyard and job, which were safe topics, so it was fine with him. Since she'd been asking so many questions, he got up the nerve to ask her one of the several questions he had for her. Also within the safe realm of topics—work.

"I heard at the clinic that you're a nurse?"

She looked surprised. "Yes. That was the call I made earlier, to the hospital where I worked. I guess you could say I'm now officially on a leave of absence."

"So you'll probably go back there when you feel better?" Why did this question, and her possible answer, make him feel both relief and dread? He clenched his jaw, something he'd started doing again since Carey had moved in.

She grimaced. "I can't. I'll have to quit at some point, but for now I'm using the sick leave and vacation time I've saved up and, I hope you don't mind, I gave them your address so they could mail my next check to me here."

"Remember. *Mi casa es tuya.*" He took another drag on his longneck, meaning every word in the entire extent of his Spanish speaking, but covering for the load of mixed-up feelings that kept dropping into his lap. What was it about this girl that made him feel so damn uncomfortable?

His practiced reply got a relieved smile out of her, and he allowed himself to enjoy how her eyes slanted upward whenever she did. It was dangerous to notice things like that and, really, what was the point? But having the beer had loosened him up and he snuck more looks than usual at her during dinner. "The clinic is always looking for good nurses. What's your specialty?"

"I work, or I should say worked, in a medical-surgical unit. I loved it, too."

"See…" he pointed her way "…that would fit right in. When you feel better, maybe you should look into it. I can talk to James about it if you'd like." *Yeah, keep these interactions all about helping her, and maybe she'll skip the part about asking you about yourself.*

"James?"

"Dr. Rothsberg."

"First I have to get my RN license reissued from Illinois since it was stolen along with everything else."

So maybe she did have plans to stay here and seek employment. Now he could get confused again and try to ignore that flicker of hope he'd kept feeling since she'd walked into his life. He ground his molars. "Would your license be accepted in California?"

"I did some research on the bus ride out and I'll have to apply here in California. That'll take some time, I suspect."

"Well, I'm working days tomorrow, so you can spend the whole day using my computer and phone and maybe start straightening out everything you need to."

She nodded. "I do have some people I owe a call." Deep in thought, she probably went straight to the gazillion things she'd have to do to re-create herself and begin a new life for her and her baby in a new state. He wouldn't want to be in her shoes, and wished he could somehow help even more. Would that go beyond his promise to watch over her?

At least the social worker and the police department had started the ball rolling on a few things. But, man, what a mess she had to clean up, especially since she hadn't wanted her family notified of her whereabouts. Why was that?

Joe wanted to ask her about her living situation back home, but suspected she'd shut down on him like a trapdoor if he did this soon, so he tucked those questions into his "bring up later" file. With an ironic inward laugh, he supposed they had a lot in common, not wanting to bring up the past and all. "You feel like watching a little TV?" He figured she could use something to distract her from all the things she'd have to tackle tomorrow.

"I'd like that but only after you let me clean up from dinner."

"Only if you'll let me help." Hell, could they get any more polite?

She smiled. "So after we do the dishes, what would you like to watch?"

"You choose." Yeah, he'd let his guest make all the decisions tonight. It was the right thing to do.

"I like that show about zombies."

"Seriously?" He never would have pegged her as a

horror fan. "It's my favorite, too, but I didn't think it would be good for your bambino."

"Ha," she said, picking up the dishes from the bench table on the outdoor deck. "After what this little one has been through already, a pretend TV show should be a walk in the park." She glanced down at her stomach while heading inside and toward the kitchen. "Isn't that right, sweetie pie."

There he went grinding his molars again. He followed her in and watched her put the dishes on the counter and unconsciously pat her abdomen then smile. That simple act sent a flurry of quick memories about Angela and how excited they'd once been when she'd first found out she'd gotten pregnant. They'd been about to give up trying since it had been over a year, had even had fertility tests done. They'd rationalized that because they were both paramedics and under a lot of stress, and he worked extended hours trying to make a good impression with Dr. Rothsberg, that was the reason she'd been unable to get pregnant.

So they'd taken a quickie vacation. Then one day, wham, she magically announced she was expecting. Joe had practically jumped over the moon that night, he'd been so happy. They'd finally start their own version of a big happy family. Since Angela's body had gotten the hang of getting pregnant, he'd planned to talk her into having a few more kids after this one. He'd walked on air for a couple of months…until his fertility report had dropped into the mailbox. Late. Very, very late.

What a fool he'd been.

Trying to give his overworked jaw a break, Joe went to town scrubbing the grill from the barbecue as if it was a matter of life and death. By the time they'd finished with the cleanup, he didn't know about Carey any more, but he definitely needed the distraction of some mindless TV viewing.

She sat on the small couch, passing him along the way, and he caught the scent of her shampoo again. It was a fresh, fruity summer kind of smell with a touch of coconut, which when he'd bought it for her had never planned for it to be a minor form of torture.

Mixed up about his feelings for the smart and easy-going nurse from Illinois, he intentionally sat on the chair opposite the couch, not ready to get too close to her again tonight. It brought up too many bad memories, and he so did not want to go there. There was only so much boxing a guy could do in a day. Torture sounded better than reliving his failed marriage. He clicked on the TV right on time for the show they both liked to escape to. If zombies couldn't make him forget how attracted he was to the lovely stranger living in his house, nothing could.

Carey put her head on the pillow of the surprisingly comfortable guest bed, thinking it was the first time she could remember feeling safe in ages. Things had gotten super-tense living with Ross those last few weeks, and, talk about the worst timing in the world, she'd gotten pregnant right around the time she'd known she had to leave him.

She didn't want to think about that now, because it would keep her awake, and she was really tired. It'd felt so normal and relaxing to sit and watch TV with Joe. He'd made the best barbecue chicken she'd ever eaten and she'd made a pig out of herself over the baked potato with all the toppings, but she chalked it up to his making her feel so welcome. The only problem was she couldn't get the vision of him in his boxing shorts, working out with the punchbag, out of her mind. Wow, his lean body had showcased every muscle in his arms and across his back as he'd punched. His movements had been fluid and nothing short of perfection. Not to mention his washboard stomach and powerful legs. The guy didn't have an ounce of fat on him.

What on earth was she thinking? Her life was in a shambles. She had an unborn baby to take care of. The last thing she should be thinking about was a man.

A naturally sexy man with kind brown eyes and a voice soothing enough to give her chills. She squeezed her eyes tight and shook her head on the pillow.

When she finally settled down and began to drift off to sleep she realized this was the first day she'd ever felt positive about her and the baby's future in three months. Things would work out for her, she just knew it. Because she, with the help of Joe, would make sure they did.

A slight smile crossed her lips as a curtain of sleep inched its way down until all was dark and she peacefully crossed into sweet dreams. Thanks to Joe.

CHAPTER FOUR

On Monday, after working all day, Joe insisted Carey come out with him for dinner, which was fine with her because she'd felt kind of cooped up. They ate at a little diner, then he showed her around Santa Monica, like the perfect host. She got the distinct impression it was to get them, and keep them, out of the house, because sometimes things felt too close there.

At least, that's how it felt for her, and sometimes she sensed it was the same for him. The guy seemed to bite down on his jaw a lot! But she soon ignored her worries about him not wanting her around and went straight to loving seeing the beach and the Pacific Ocean, and especially the Santa Monica pier.

On Tuesday Joe had the day off, and he dutifully took her shopping for more clothes at a place called the Beverly Center. They checked the directory and he guided her to the few stores she'd shown interest in, then he stood outside in the mall area, giving her space to shop. Clearly he wanted nothing to do with helping her choose clothes, rather he just did what he thought he should do out of courtesy to her situation. She protested all the way when he insisted on paying for everything. She sensed his generosity was based on some sense of charitable obligation, and she only accepted his offer when he'd agreed to let her repay him once she was back on her feet. She'd be sure to keep a tally because things were quickly adding up!

Wednesday morning, before he started an afternoon shift, he chauffeured her around to the Department of Motor Vehicles for a temporary driving license, and since she'd received a check from her old job he also helped her open a bank account. She decided the guy was totally committed to helping her, like he'd signed some paper or made some pact to do it. And she certainly appreciated everything he'd done for her, but...

Even though he was easy enough to be around, she felt it was out of total obligation to treat people right in life. Far too often she sensed a disconnect between his courtesy and that safe distance he insisted on keeping between them. Well, if that's what he wanted, she knew exactly how to live that way. Her parents had, sadly, been perfect role models in that regard.

Joe got home on Wednesday night to a quiet house. Carey had said hello, but now kept mostly to herself in her room. It made him wonder if he'd done something to offend her. He'd been trying his best to make her feel at home, though admittedly he may have been going about it robotically. But that seemed the only way he could deal with having a woman in his life again. Since he worked the a.m. shift the next day, he didn't get a chance to ask Carey if he'd put her off or if her withdrawal had nothing to do with him. Something was definitely on her mind, and under the circumstances, being battered, bruised, mugged, homeless, and completely vulnerable, not to mention living with a stranger, he could understand why.

Maybe he'd come off aloof or unapproachable at

times. But she had no idea how nearly unbearable it was to fix meals with her when it reminded him how much he missed being married. And having Carey there twenty-four seven, with her friendly smile and naturally sweet ways, was nearly making him come unhinged. She deserved someone to share things with, to talk to, but it couldn't be him. Nope. He was nowhere near ready or able to be her sounding board. All he'd signed up for was offering her a place to live.

Maybe he could arrange for some follow-up visits with the social worker at the clinic. That way she could get what she wanted and needed and he wouldn't have to be the person listening. Because when a woman vented, from his past experience with Angela, he knew she always expected something in return. Nope, no way would he unload his lousy past on Carey, no matter how much she might think she wanted him to. The lady had far too much on her plate as it was, and, truthfully, re-living such pain was the last thing he ever wanted to do. The social worker was definitely the right person to step in, and he planned to ask Helena to follow up the next day.

On Thursday evening, Joe came home to find Carey scrubbing the kitchen floor. From the looks of the rest of the house, she'd been cleaning all day.

"What's up?" he asked.

She was so focused on the floor-scrubbing she didn't notice him. He stepped closer but not onto the wet kitchen tiles.

"Am I that much of a slob?" he tried to joke, but she didn't laugh. Something was definitely eating at her. "Carey?"

Finally she heard him and shook her head as if she'd

been in a trance and looked at him. "Hi." Not sounding the least bit enthusiastic.

"Everything okay?"

She stopped pushing the mop handle. "Just trying to pay you back for all you're doing for me."

Damn. She may as well have sliced him with a knife. "You don't have to be my house cleaner, you know."

"What else can I do?" The obvious "else" *not* being to sleep together.

Why was that the first thought to come to his mind? Cripes, she had him mixed up. He used her clear frustration as a springboard to what his latest mission on Carey's behalf had been. "I, uh, spoke to the social worker today—the one who helped you while you were in the hospital—and she said she'd love to keep in touch." He'd totally reworded their true conversation, trying to make it sound casual, not necessary, but the truth was he'd talked at great length with Helena at work about Carey's precarious situation. The social worker wanted to keep connected with Carey and promised to call her right away.

"Yes. Thanks. She called earlier today. I'm going to have a phone appointment with her on Monday."

"That's great." He almost said, *I hope it helps you snap out of your funk,* but kept that thought to himself because a sneaky part of him worried he'd put her there. He knew too well how unhelpful being told to snap out of it could be, especially when a person was nowhere near ready. He would protect Carey in any way he could, and felt she shouldn't be nervous all the time. But he'd never been in her shoes, and…

Then it dawned on him. Why hadn't he thought of it before? The woman was a nurse. Nurses were always busy on the job. She was used to helping people, not the other way around. She was probably going crazy with so much time on her hands and nothing to do but watch TV or read while he was away every day. But she'd had a head trauma and needed to heal. "Do you feel ready to go back to work?"

She shifted from being intent on cleaning to suddenly looking deflated. "That's the thing, I can't until the California RN license comes through. Plus I still feel foggy-headed from the concussion. At this point I'd worry I might hurt some poor unsuspecting patient or something. But on another level my energy is coming back, and I'm feeling really restless."

That damn mugger had not only stolen her identity and money but also her confidence. He thought quickly. It was early summer, people went on vacations. "I think there might be some temporary slots to fill in while people go on vacation. Jobs that don't require a nursing license."

She stopped mopping and looked at him, definite interest in her eyes.

"For instance, I know of a ward clerk on the second floor who's getting ready to visit her family back east for two weeks. Maybe you could fill in on something like that. Sort of keep your hand in medicine but in a safer position until you feel back to your old self."

She rested her chin on the mop handle. "How can I just walk in off the street and expect to get a job in a hospital like The Hollywood Hills Clinic?"

He flashed an overconfident grin he hadn't used in a long time. "By knowing a guy like me? I could put in a good word to Dr. Rothsberg for you. What do you say?"

The fingers of one hand flew to her mouth as she thought. "That would be great. But it would also mean

I'd have to quit my job back home." Worry returned to her brow.

Joe was sure he was missing out on another story, probably something huge. Like, who she was running away from, and would they come after her? If only he could get her to open up. This was stuff he needed to know if he expected to protect her. Rather than press her right then, he let her finish her task and went to his room. Besides, he needed time to figure things out for himself, like the fact that he both totally looked forward to seeing her each day but dreaded how it made him feel afterwards.

After he changed into workout clothes, he headed to the back porch for some boxing, since it was the one sure way to help him blow off steam. Well into his usual routine, while she was in the other room, watching TV, he wondered if, in fact, the guy who'd given Carey her shiner might come after her, and an idea popped into his head. "Hey, Carey, come out here a minute, would you?"

Within seconds she showed up looking perplexed, and maybe like she'd rather be watching TV. Yeah, she'd probably already had it with living with him.

"Since you were mugged recently, and I'm sure you never want to go through that again, would you like me to show you a couple of moves?"

She looked hesitant, like learning a few self-defense maneuvers might bring back too many bad memories.

"Maybe it's too soon," he quickly.

"No, I can't keep hiding out at your house. I know there's a bus stop right down at the end of your street, and I shouldn't be afraid to use it." She nodded, a flicker of fight in her eyes. "Yeah, show me how I could have kept that creep from dragging me into the alley that night."

"That's the attitude," Joe said with a victorious smile. She smiled back, that spirited flash intensifying.

"Okay." He clapped his hands once. "I saw the guy grab you by the wrist and pull you away that night. So, first off, a lot of the information that's on the internet for ladies' self-defense is bogus. Here's something that works. When that guy grabbed your wrist, you could have used your other hand to push into his eyes, or, if he wore glasses, you could have gone for his throat. With either move you also could have included a knee to the groin. That stuff hurts the attacker and surprises them. Knocks them off balance. Let me show you."

He grabbed Carey's right wrist and immediately felt her tense, making him think maybe he was right and it was too early to do this lesson with her. But he was committed now and pressed on, and she had enough anger in her eyes to put it to good use.

"Okay, use your left hand and go for my face," He showed her how to make an open, claw-like spread with the fingers and how to jab it at a person's face to do the most damage. "Get those fingers on my eyes and press with all your might."

She followed his instructions and went for his eyes.

"Ow!" He reacted and pushed her hand back to keep her from injuring him.

"Sorry!"

"Don't be sorry, fight for your life. It's up to me to keep you from hurting me. You just caught me off guard. Got it?"

She gave one firm and committed nod.

"That's the spirit. If the guy foils that move with his other hand, like I just did, make sure you put your knee to his groin at the same time." He flashed a charming grin. "Don't actually do that one now, okay?"

She laughed, and it felt good to get her to relax a little.

"Just knee him in the groin area and later you can practice kneeing the heck out of that boxing bag."

"Got it, boss." Yes, she was really into this now.

He said, "Go!" and grabbed her left wrist this time, and she moved like lightning for his face and eyes, driving her knee into his groin at the same time. Being prepared for the move, in case she got overzealous, which she obviously had, he brought his own knee up and across to protect himself, letting her full force hit his thigh. If he hadn't, he'd have been on his hands and knees, riding out the pain, right now.

He didn't want to discourage her efforts but, damn, that could have hurt! "Good." Up close, their eyes locked. He could hear her breathing hard and felt the pulse in her wrist quicken. The fire in her green-eyed stare made him take notice. He stepped back, releasing her wrist. "That was good."

She rubbed her wrist and searched the floor with her gaze, making a quick recovery. This wasn't easy to relive, he understood that, but keeping the same thing from ever happening again was more important than her current comfort zone.

"Now do the same thing, going for my throat." He showed her the wide V of his hand between the thumb and index finger and demonstrated how to drive it into the Adam's apple area of the attacker's neck. "Since most guys, like that scumbag the other night, will be taller than you, force your hand upward with all you've got. Okay?"

Carey agreed and he immediately grabbed her hand, trying to catch her off guard. Something clicked, like she'd gone back in time. She went into attack mode and because he wasn't ready for it she got him good in the throat. He coughed and sputtered and backed away to recover, and only then did she realize she'd shifted from demonstration to true life.

"I'm sorry!" she squealed, grabbing her face with her hands, as if just snapping out of a bad dream.

He swallowed, trying to get his voice back. "That's the way. See how it works? I dropped your hand, and that means you could have run off screaming for help at that point."

"Oh, Joe." Carey rushed to him. "I'm so sorry I hurt you." She touched his shoulder and, without thinking, he reacted by opening his arms. Carey threw her arms around him and squeezed. "Can I get you some water? Anything?"

"Maybe a new throat," he teased, though he really liked having her arms around him, the realization nearly making him lose his balance. She smelled a hell of a lot better than he did, and up close, like this, her eyes were by far the prettiest he'd ever seen in his life, though fear seemed to have the best of them right now.

Surprised, no, more like stunned by how moved she'd been when grappling with Joe, Carey held him perhaps a second too long. Fear still pounded in her chest. At first the lesson had brought out all the bad memories she'd been trying to force down a few months before leaving home and definitely since coming to Hollywood. Ross had changed from attentive boyfriend to jealous predator. He had frightened her. He'd also grabbed her by the wrist like that on several occasions, each time scaring her into submission. Then the creep at the bus station must have seen her as an easy mark, sensed her fear, and grabbed her the same way, pulling her into the alley.

She hated feeling like a victim!

Anger had erupted as horrible memories had collided with Joe's grip on her wrist. She'd never be a victim again, damn it. Never. Suddenly fighting for her life all over again, she'd switched to kill mode and had practically pushed his larynx out the back of his neck. Darn it! She hadn't meant to hurt him, not the man who'd saved her and taken her in, but she clearly had.

Now, being skin to skin with her incredibly fit and appealing roommate had changed the topic foremost in her mind. Being in Joe's arms wiped out her fear and she shifted from fighting for her life to being completely turned on. What was it about Joe?

So confusing. It wasn't right.

Obviously her concussion was still messing with her judgment.

In a moment of clarity she broke away and strode to the kitchen to get him a glass of water, trying to recover before she brought it to him.

"What about pepper spray?" She schooled her voice to sound casual, completely avoiding his eyes, as if she hadn't just survived a flashback and had flung herself into Joe's arms. There was nothing wrong with a decoy topic to throw him off the scent, right? The man had turned her on simply by touching her. Pitiful. Blame it on the head injury.

"First you have to get it out of your purse, right?"

She nodded, quickly realizing the fault in her premise. He stood shirtless, damp from his workout, skin shiny and all his muscles on display. Cut and ripped. A work of art. She handed him the glass. Thought about handing him his T-shirt so he'd cover up and make her life a little safer for the moment, or less tempting anyway. At least it seemed easier for him to swallow now and that made her grateful she hadn't caused any permanent damage. Could she have? If so, he'd just given her a huge gift of self-protection. No way would she let herself be a victim. By God, she'd never let anyone hurt her again.

"Plus, I've heard about guys who've been sprayed and didn't even react," he continued. "Also, when you're scared or nervous, you might spray all over the place and not hit the eyes."

She kept nodding, watching him, completely distracted by his physique, unable to really listen, wishing she'd brought herself a cool drink too. Surely her head injury had left her brain unbalanced, taking her back to the worst moments in her life one second and then the next rushing into the realm of all things sensual.

"Your hands and your knees are your best defense. Want to practice again?"

She sucked in a breath and shook her head quickly. This was all too confusing. "I think that's enough for tonight."

He put down his glass on the nearby table, folded an arm across his middle, rested the other elbow on it and held his chin with his thumb and bent fingers, biting his lower lip and nailing her with a sexy, playful gaze. "Chicken, eh?"

Joe had saved her life. He'd also just given her a great gift of learning self-defense. And there *was* that sexy sparkle in his eyes right now...

"Are you challenging me?" Suddenly awash with tiny prickles of excitement again, she moved toward him and grabbed his wrist with all her might. "Let's see you fight your way out of this one, buddy." She knew she didn't have a chance in hell of keeping hold but enjoyed the moment, and especially grappling with the hunk. When was the last time she'd had fun horsing around with a man and not felt the least bit afraid or vulnerable?

She trusted Joe not to hurt her.

He swung his free arm around behind her and pulled her close, pretending to get her in a head lock but quickly moving into a backward hug. "I don't suggest you ever let your attacker get you in this position," he said playfully over the shell of her ear.

"There won't be any more attackers," she said through gritted teeth. "Because I'll kick their asses first."

He tightened his hold, but in a good way, a sexy way. She went limp in his arms, feeling his closeness in every cell and nerve ending, confused by the total attraction she had for him. This was the worst time in the world to fall for someone. She was pregnant with another man's baby, for crying out loud. He must have felt the shift of her mood from fight to flight, or in this case to catatonic, and he quickly backed off. They'd gotten too close. Too soon. That sexy, challenging gaze in his eyes from a second before disappeared and he reached for his water to take another drink as a distraction.

"So," he started again, sounding nonchalant, "another good idea, if a bad guy only wants your wallet, is to reach into your purse, grab your wallet and throw it as far away as you can. He probably wants your money, not you, and will go after it. Then scream like hell and run for your life. Of course, if he has a gun you may want to reconsider that move."

She gave the required light laugh over his obvious smart-aleck attempt to change the focus of what had just gone down. But their eyes met again, his honey brown and inviting as all hell, and it seemed they both knew some line had just been crossed. Though she couldn't tell from Joe's steely stare how he felt, and wasn't about to guess because the thought made her get all jittery inside, she hoped he couldn't tell how shaken she was.

She watched him with a mixture of shame and longing, but mostly confusion. Damn that concussion. "Thanks for the lesson," she whispered. "I'd better get some rest now."

They'd gotten too close, that was a fact.

She turned to head for her room, but a sense of duty stopped her. The man had saved her life then offered to share his home with her. Where did a guy like that come from? The least she could do was tell him what she'd been through, why she'd run away from home. He deserved to know how she'd ended up smack in the middle of his life. And if she shared, maybe she'd find out something about him, too.

"Joe?" She circled back to face him.

"Yeah?" He'd gone back to throwing punches at his punchbag and stopped.

"I ran away from a man who wanted to possess me. Completely. Little by little he clipped away at my life. Half the time I didn't even notice, until one day I realized he'd isolated me from everything I liked and loved other than him." She picked at a broken fingernail. "He wanted to control my life, and when I got pregnant he acted like that would ruin everything and got abusive with me." Carey stared at her feet rather than risk seeing any judgment on Joe's face. "I ran away the night he handed me a wad of money and told me to take care of 'it', as if my baby was a problem that needed fixing. He didn't want to share me with anyone, not even our kid."

She finally glanced up to find nothing but empathy in Joe's eyes. "I fought him and he roughed me up. So when he gave me the money I grabbed whatever I could without being obvious, acted like I was going to do what he wanted, then ran for my life."

Joe stepped toward her but she backed up, needing the distance and to tell him her entire story.

"I came to California because it was the next bus out of Montclare, and I didn't have time to pick or choose. I must have looked like a sitting duck because I stepped off the bus and immediately got dragged into that alley." Frightened to relive that night, and frustrated by the emotion rolling through her, she dug her fingers into her hair. "At first I thought maybe Ross had somehow found me and he was taking me back home. Then I realized I was getting mugged, but it was too late. I didn't know how to protect myself." She removed her hands from her hair and held them waist high, palms upward, beseeching Joe to understand. "If it wasn't for you I don't know where I'd be.

"I owe my life to you, and I've got to be honest and say it's strange to feel that way." She sat on the edge of the nearby dining table chair. "Yet here you are day after day watching over me, making my life better. I'm grateful, I am, but please understand that I'm confused and scared and..." Her voice broke with the words. "And I don't know what the future holds for me. Whether I stay here or go somewhere else, I just don't know, but the only thing that matters right now is my baby." Her forearm folded across her stomach and she blinked.

"I get it," Joe said. "Believe me, I understand how life-changing a baby can be."

"You do? Are you a father?"

"Uh, no." He immediately withdrew.

"So how do you know, then?"

"Look, forget I said that. Right now, all I want is for you to be healthy and safe." He came to her and crouched to be eye level with her. "I'm sorry if I've made you uncomfortable. I can't help but find you attractive, so there, I've said it, and I know that's not acceptable."

How was she supposed to answer him? "It may not be acceptable but I feel the same way." Oh, God, she'd put her secret thoughts into words. "It's just the worst timing in the world, you know?"

"I know. Like I said, I get it." He made the wise decision not to touch her but instead to stand and step back.

"Thank you for understanding."

"Of course."

She stood and started walking, this time without looking back, and headed on wobbly legs to her room. Had she just admitted she found Joe Matthews as attractive as he'd just confirmed he found her?

This was nuts! So she'd blame it on the head trauma.

Joe stood perfectly still, watching Carey make her exit. He half expected to hear her lock the door to the bedroom. He hoped he hadn't made her feel creepy about him. It hadn't been his intention to get her in a hug, but he'd been showing her ways to get out of predatory attacks and had inadvertently become a predator himself.

Great going, Joe. You made your house guest think you wanted to crawl into her bed.

He went back to the porch and punched the bag. "Ouch!" He hadn't prepared his fist and it hurt like hell. And what had gotten into him to let slip that he'd known how it felt to be an expectant parent? That wouldn't happen again. He wound up, wanting to punch the bag again, this time even harder, but stopped himself.

Regardless of how awkward he may have made Carey feel, she'd just opened up to him. Man, she'd had it tough back in Chicago. He couldn't remember the name of the suburb she'd come from, and right now that didn't matter. What mattered was that she shouldn't feel like she'd run all the way across country only to find herself in the same situation again.

She needed to get out of the house. To begin something. To get that job and start some money rolling in before she got so pregnant she wouldn't be able to. His head started spinning with everything that needed to be done for her. He needed to help her get her independence back.

From personal experience he knew about a special class at The Hollywood Hills Clinic. A class that would be perfect for where she was right now in her life. He knew the right people to talk to about it, too. And he'd move ahead with her getting that job, so if she wanted, in time, she could move out.

Maybe he couldn't erase what had happened between them just now, but he sure as hell could make some changes for the better happen, starting tomorrow.

He flipped off the light and headed to his room to take a cold shower and hopefully catch a little sleep.

On Friday afternoon Carey sat on the backyard deck in the shade of the huge jacaranda tree, the flowers falling into piles of light purple and scattering across the wood planks like pressed flowers in a painting. She'd been reading an article about early pregnancy on the internet on Joe's tablet when she heard his hybrid SUV pull into the garage and shortly after he came through the gate in the backyard.

Did he know she was out here? Or, more likely after last night, maybe he wanted to avoid her by coming through the back way, hoping she'd be inside.

"Hey," he said, all smiles, as if nothing monumental had occurred between them last night.

"Hi. You're home early."

He came toward the deck but didn't come up, keeping a safe distance between them, placing a foot on the second step and leaning a forearm over his knee. "One of the perks of owning your own business is that I call the shots. It was a slow day, so I took off early."

"Lucky you." His smile was wide, giving her the impression he had some good news. Maybe he had found somewhere for her to move to? If she was honest, that would give her mixed feelings, though the social worker Helena had said she'd look into housing for her, too, and she'd agreed to it at the time. "But I know you've worked hard to get where you are and at the ripe old age of twenty-eight you deserve your afternoon off. Twenty-eight, that's right isn't it?"

He nodded proudly. Yeah, he'd made something out of himself and he wasn't even thirty yet. "And you are?"

"Twenty-five."

"A mere child." He smiled, pretending to be the worldly-wise older man, but his gaze quickly danced away from hers. Yeah, he was still mixed up about last night, too. "So, listen, about you feeling isolated and stuck here and everything…"

"I didn't say that."

"You didn't have to. I figured it out after you went to your room last night. But let's not rehash that, because I've got some good news."

She shut down the tablet and leaned forward in the outdoor lounger. "Good news? They found my stuff?"

He wrinkled his nose and shook his head. "Sorry, I wish. But here's the deal—the clinic has this prenatal class, they call it Parentcraft and it's starting a new session tomorrow. I hope you don't mind, but I put your name in, and Dr. Rothsberg gave me the okay. I thought you could ride into work with me in the morning, and check it out."

"You signed me up? Isn't there a fee? I…uh…can't—"

"Like I said, James took care of everything. He's a generous man. There's a spot for you and the first session starts tomorrow at ten."

"Joe, I'm really grateful for you doing this, but you're helping so much, I don't think I'll ever be able to repay you."

"Carey, I'm not doing any of this to make you feel indebted to me. Please, don't feel that way. My parents taught me a lot of stuff, and helping folks was big in our family. When you're back on your feet you'll find a way to help someone else in need. That's all. No debt to me, just pay it forward."

"Joe…" She stared at him, trying her hardest to figure him out. Was he a freak of nature or her personal knight in shining armor? She leaned back in the lounger and looked into the blue sky dotted with its few wispy clouds. "It's just hard to take in all this goodness after the way my life had been going this past year." She heard him step up the stairs and walk toward her.

"Well, get used to it." He sat on the adjacent lounger then reached out to touch her hand. "That man you ran away from is ancient history. It may not have been your plan, but Hollywood is your new beginning. Just go with the flow, as my yoga-brained sister likes to say."

Carey laughed, wondering about Joe's family. They must be some special people to produce a gem like him. "Okay. Thanks. I'm excited about the class tomorrow."

"Great, and while you're at the hospital you can fill out the papers for the temporary ward clerk job, too."

"What?"

"I know, too much goodness, right?" He laughed, and she thought she could easily get used to watching his handsome face. "James, uh, Dr. Rothsberg, has taken care of everything. Hey, not every clinic can boast their very own Jane Doe. We just want to help get you back on your feet."

"This is all too much to take in."

"Then don't waste your time." He stood. "Come on, I'll take you to my favorite deli on Fairfax. You like roast beef on rye? They make their sandwiches this thick." He used his thumb and index finger to measure a good four inches.

Well, come to think of it, she was hungry. Again! And what better way to keep her mind off the whirlwind of feelings gathering inside her about that man than stuffing her face with a sandwich. Otherwise she'd have to deal with her growing awareness of Joe, the prince of a guy who had literally come out of nowhere, protecting her, saving her, taking her in, changing her life in a positive way, and, maybe the most interesting part, forcing her to remember pure and simple attraction for the opposite sex.

Saturday morning Carey was up and dressed in one of the new outfits Joe had bought her, a simple summer dress with a lightweight pastel-green sweater that covered the tiny baby bump just starting to appear. She was nervous about applying for a job, though she knew she really needed to get out among the living again, to prove to herself she was getting back on her feet. Also, having something to do after a week of lying low since being discharged from the clinic was a major reason she looked forward to applying for the job. As for the parenting class, with her huge desire to be a good mother she was eager to start.

Joe had dressed for work, his light blue polo shirt with The Hollywood Hills Clinic logo above the pocket fit his healthy frame perfectly and highlighted those gorgeous deltoids, biceps and triceps. The cargo pants, though loose and loaded with useful pockets, filled with EMS stuff no doubt, still managed to showcase his fine derriere. She felt a little guilty checking him out as he walked ahead to open the door to the employee entrance. How much longer would she be able to blame her concussion for this irrational behavior? In her defense, there was just something so masculine about a guy wearing those serious-as-hell EMS boots!

He glanced at his watch. "You should have enough time to get your paperwork done for the job application first. I'll walk you over to HR."

"HR?"

"Human Resources."

"Ah, we call it Employee Relations back home."

"Yeah, same thing, but first I'm going to show you where your parenting class will be so you'll know where to go when you're through. Follow me."

Carey did as she was told, clutching her small purse with her new identification cards and temporary driving license, while walking and looking around the exquisite halls and corridors with vague memories of having been there before. Though the place seemed more like a high-end hotel than a hospital. And this time she had money from her last pay check from the hospital back home, instead of being completely vulnerable, like before. Ten days ago she'd arrived on a stretcher, and today she was applying for a job and starting a new parenting class. She was definitely getting back on her feet. Who said life wasn't filled with miracles?

"Oh, Gabriella," Joe said, to a pretty woman walking past, "I'd like to introduce you to Carey Spencer. She'll be starting your class later." He turned to Carey. "Gabriella is the head midwife and runs the prenatal classes."

The woman, who looked to be around Joe's age, with strawberry-blonde hair and a slim and healthy figure, smiled at Carey, her light brown eyes sparkling when she did so. They briefly shook hands, then all continued walking together, as the midwife was obviously heading somewhere in the same direction. As Gabriella was just about Carey's height, their eyes met when she spoke. "Oh, lovely to have you. How far along are you?"

"A little over three months."

"Perfect. We're beginning the class with pregnancy meal planning trimester by trimester, plus exercises for early pregnancy."

This was exactly what Carey needed. Just because she was a nurse it didn't mean she knew squat about becoming a mother or going through a pregnancy. "Sounds great." Her hopes soared with the lucky direction her life had taken. Thanks to Joe and Dr. Rothsberg.

"Yes, I think you'll love it." Gabriella cut off into another hallway. "Be sure to bring your partner," she said over her shoulder. "It's always good to have that reinforcement."

And Carey's heart dropped to her stomach, pulling her pulse down with it. Was having a partner a requirement? Obviously, Gabriella didn't know her circumstances.

Joe gave her an anxious glance. "That won't be a problem. Trust me, okay?"

Surely, Carey hoped, in this day and age there were

bound to be other women in the class without partners. Joe was probably right about it not being a problem. But, please, God, she wouldn't be the only one, would she?

Forty-five minutes later, after submitting her job application for the temporary third-floor medical/surgical ward clerk in HR and feeling very positive about it, Carey had found her way back to the modern and pristine classroom and took a seat. Several handouts had been placed on the tables. A dozen couples were already there, and more drifted in as the minutes ticked on. She glanced around the room, seeing a sea of couples. Oh, no, she really was going to be the only one on her own. How awkward would that be?

Fighting off feeling overwhelmed but refusing to be embarrassed, she glanced at the clock on the wall—three minutes to ten—and thought about sneaking out before the class began. She could learn this stuff online, and wouldn't have to come here feeling the odd man out every week. But Joe had gone out of his way to get her enrolled, and Dr. Rothsberg was footing the bill. She went back and forth in her mind about staying or going, then Gabriella entered and started her welcome speech.

She'd sat close to the back of the room, and it would still be easy to sneak out if she wanted or needed to. But, wait, she wasn't that person anymore, the one who let life throw her a curveball and immediately fell down. Nope, she'd turned in her victim badge, and Joe had helped her. She could do this. She forced her focus on the front of the class to Gabriella, who smiled and brightened the room with her lovely personality. The last thing Carey wanted to do was insult anyone, especially after Joe and Dr. Rothsberg had made special arrangements to get her here. But, oh, she felt weird about being the only single mom in the class.

"Why don't we go around the room and introduce ourselves?" Gabriella said.

Soon everyone else would notice, too.

The door at the back of the class opened again. Feeling nervous and easily distracted, Carey glanced over her shoulder then did a double take. In came Joe, his heavy booted steps drawing attention from several people in the vicinity.

"Sorry I'm late," he said to Gabriella, then walked directly to Carey and took the empty chair next to her. "If you don't mind," he whispered close to her ear, "I'll pretend to be your partner today." For all anyone else knew in the class, he could have told her he loved her. The guy knew how to be discreet, and from the way her heart pattered from his entrance he may as well have just run down a list of sweet nothings.

He'd obviously picked up on her anxiety the instant Gabriella had told her back in that hallway to be sure to bring her partner. He was here solely to spare her feelings.

Joseph Matthews truly was a knight in shining armor! Or in his case cargo pants and work boots.

As he settled in next to her his larger-than-life maleness quickly filled up the space between them. Warmth suffused her entire body. Being this close to Joe, having access to gaze into those rich brown eyes, would definitely make it difficult to concentrate on today's lesson.

"You're next, Carey. Introduce yourself and your partner," Gabriella said, emphasizing the *partner* part.

Joe hadn't meant to put Carey on the spot, but after seeing the panic in her eyes earlier, when Gabriella had told her to be sure to bring her partner, he couldn't let her go through this alone. At first he'd wanted to run like hell when he'd shown her the classroom. Coming here had brought back more awful memories. He and Angela had actually started this class before she'd moved out.

Feeling uneasy as hell when he'd dropped Carey off earlier, he'd gone back to his work station, but had soon found he'd been unable to concentrate on the job. His mind had kept drifting to Carey sitting here alone, feeling completely out of place, and he couldn't stand for that to happen. Besides, wasn't it time for him to move on? Determined to put his bad memories aside once and for all—his divorce hadn't been his fault—he'd made a decision. She shouldn't have to attend this class alone. If offering her support could ease her discomfort, he'd take the bullet for her and be her partner. The woman had been through enough on her own lately.

"Oh," she said, as if she'd never expected to have to introduce herself, even though everyone else just had. "Um, I'm Carey Spencer, I'm a little over three months pregnant, I, uh, recently moved to California." She swallowed nervously around the stretching of the truth. Joe reached for her hand beneath the table and squeezed it to give her confidence a boost. "I'm a nurse by profession, a first-time mother, and…" She looked at Joe, the earlier panic returning to those shimmering green eyes. He squeezed her hand again.

"I'm Joe Matthews," he stepped in. "Carey's friend. *Good* friend." He glanced at her, seeing her squirm, letting it rub off on him a tiny bit. "A really close friend." Overkill? He gazed around the room, having fudged the situation somewhat, and all the other couples watched expectantly. "We've been through a lot together, and we're both really looking forward to taking this class and learning how to be good parents."

Okay, let them think whatever they wanted. His

statement was mostly true—in fact, it was ninety-nine per cent true, except for the bit about being "really close" friends, though they had been through a lot together already. Oh, and the part about him ever getting to be a parent. Yeah, that would never happen. The reality hit like a sucker punch and he nearly winced with pain. Why the hell had he willingly walked into this room again? Carey's cool, thin fingers clasped his hand beneath the table, just as he'd done to support her a few seconds ago. The gesture helped him past the stutter in thought.

He'd come here today for Carey. She needed to catch a break, and he'd promised the night he'd found her in the alley that he'd look out for her. If she needed a partner for the parenting class then, damn it, he'd be here.

"I'm a paramedic here at the clinic, so if I ever need to deliver a baby on a run, I figure this class will be good for that, too." He got the laugh he was hoping for to relieve his mounting tension as the room reacted. "It's a win-win situation, right?"

He shifted his eyes to the woman to his left. If taking this class together meant having to really open up about themselves, well, he was bound to let her down because he was far, far from ready to talk about it.

Carey didn't know squat about his past, and if he had his way, she never would. Why humiliate himself again, this time in front of a woman he was quickly growing attached to, when once had already been enough for a lifetime?

CHAPTER FIVE

ON THE SATURDAY after the next Parentcraft class, Carey stood in the kitchen, using her second-trimester menu planner for dinner preparation. She'd had to stretch her usual eating routine to include items she'd never have been caught dead eating before. Like anchovies! Why was Gabriella so big on anchovies? Obviously they were high in calcium and other important minerals, plus loaded with omega three and six fatty acids, but Carey didn't think they tasted so great and smelled really bad. Carey practically had to hold her nose to eat them.

Fortunately this Saturday-night menu included salmon—yay, more omega fats—which Joe was dutifully grilling outside on a cedar plank. Dutiful, yeah, that was the right word for Joe. Everything he did for her seemed to be done out of duty. Sure, he was nice and considerate, but she never sensed he was completely relaxed around her.

She diligently steamed the broccoli and zucchini, and in another pot boiled some new red potatoes, grateful that Joe seemed okay to eat whatever she did. So far she'd managed to keep her occasional junk-food binges to herself. Nothing major, just items that had definitely been left off the Gabriella-approved dietary plan for a pregnant lady, like sea salt and malt vinegar potato chips, or blue corn chips, or, well, actually, any kind of chip that she could get her hands on. She rationalized that if occasionally she only bought the small luncheon-sized bags she wouldn't do the baby any harm. Or her hips.

Her weight gain was right on target, and when she'd seen Gabriella in clinic for a prenatal checkup, thanks to Dr. Rothsberg, she'd complimented her on how well she was carrying the baby. The ultrasound had been the most beautiful thing she'd ever seen, and the first person she'd wanted to share it with had been Joe, and since he'd brought her to the appointment, once she'd dressed she'd invited him back into the examination room. He'd oohed and aahed right along with her, but she'd sensed a part of him had remained safely detached. She could understand why—he was a guy and it wasn't his baby.

It made sense…yet he'd gotten all watery-eyed that day in the clinic when she'd found out her baby was okay, and he'd made that remark that one time about knowing how life-changing a baby could be. She'd asked him point blank if he was a father, but he'd said no and had powered right on. What had that been about? Heck, she'd only just recently found out how old he was, and the only thing she knew beyond that, besides he had a big, kind family, was that he was divorced.

The thing that kept eating away at her thoughts was that Joe didn't seem like the kind of guy who'd give up on a marriage.

Carey popped the top from another beer can and carried it outside to Joe. Being so involved together in the parenting class had definitely changed their relationship for the better, yet she knew Joe held back. She'd opened up about Ross in the hope of getting Joe to share whatever it was that kept him frequently tense and withdrawn.

At first she'd written off that always-present slow simmer just beneath the surface as being due to his demanding job as a paramedic, and also the fact he ran the business. But he clearly thrived on being in charge. It was obvious he loved the challenge. No, that wasn't the problem, it was when they were in the house together, her occasionally indulging in baby talk to her stomach, or discussing the latest information from the Parentcraft classes that she noticed him mentally slip into another time and place. Granted, another person's pregnancy wasn't exactly riveting to the average person, but Joe had volunteered to attend the class with her. If it was an issue, why had he signed on?

Now outside, she smiled and handed him a second beer. "Ready for another?"

His brows rose. "Sure. Thanks." As he took it, their eyes met and held, and a little zing shot through her. The usual whenever they looked straight at each other.

She turned and headed back toward the kitchen, feeling distracted and desperately trying to stay on task.

"You trying to get me drunk?"

"Maybe." She playfully tossed the word over her shoulder then ducked inside before he could respond.

Tonight was the night she hoped to get him to open up. If she had to ply him with beer to do it, she would.

Later over dinner… "Mmm, this is delicious," Carey said, tasting the cedar-infused salmon. "That lime juice brings out a completely different flavor." They sat at the small picnic table on the deck under a waxing June moon.

"Not bad, I must say. What kind of crazy food do we have to prepare tomorrow?"

"Watercress soup with anchovies, what else?" She laughed. "That's lunch, but for dinner we get chicken teriyaki with shredded veggies, oh, and cheese rolls. Can't wait for the bread!" She leveled him with her stare. "I have to thank you for putting up with this crazy diet."

His gaze didn't waver. "I've enjoyed everything so far." He reached across the table and covered her hand with his. "Since I'm your prenatal partner, the least I should do is help you stay on the diet. Your baby will thank me one day."

Sometimes he said the sweetest things and she just wanted to throw her arms around him. But she'd made that mistake once already during the self-defense training and it had mixed up everything between them for days afterwards. Since then he seemed to have shut down like a spring snare, and she'd carefully kept her distance. But he'd just planted a thought she couldn't drop. Would her baby ever know him?

Right now his hand was on top of hers, and she couldn't for the life of her understand why such a wonderful man wasn't still happily married with his own assortment of kids.

She lifted her lids and caught him still watching her, both totally aware of their hands touching, so she smiled but it felt lopsided and wiggly. She stopped immediately, not wanting him to think she was goofy looking or anything. Things felt too close, it nagged at her, and she knew how to break up that uncomfortable feeling pronto. "You mentioned once that you were divorced." She decided to get right to the heart of the conversation she'd planned to start tonight.

He removed his hand from hers and sat taller as ice seemed to set into his normally kind eyes. "Yeah." He dug into his vegetables and served himself more fish, suddenly very busy with eating. "My wife left me."

Why would any woman in her right mind leave Joe? "That must have hurt like hell."

"It was not a good time." He clipped out the words, with an emphasis that communicated it would be the end of this conversation. And why did she know without a doubt that he wasn't telling her anywhere near the whole story? Because he'd hinted at "getting it" and knowing how babies changed lives. Things didn't add up. Had he lost a child?

So she pressed on, hoping that talking about herself some more might help him to open up. "Sometimes people *should* get divorced." She pushed her empty plate away and sipped from her large glass of iced water.

"For instance, my parents were a train wreck. My dad was out of work most of the time, and my mother was always taking on whatever odd jobs she could to make up for it. Instead of being grateful, my typically belligerent father went the macho route, accusing her of thinking him not good enough to take care of the family. Occasionally he'd haul off and hit her, too. I swore I'd never, *never* put myself in the same position."

Joe protested, shaking his head. "You didn't."

"Didn't I? After working my whole life to be independent, I fell for the exact same kind of guy as my dad. A man so insecure about his masculinity that he kept me isolated, insisting it was because he loved me so much. Then he turned violent whenever I stood up to him, and especially when I told him we were going to have a baby. What a fool I was. I didn't learn a thing from my parents' lousy marriage." If she hadn't already finished eating she wouldn't have been able to take another bite, with her stomach suddenly churning and contorting with emotion.

"He must have had a lot going for him to get you interested at first, though. I'm sure he hid his insecurities really well." His hand came back to hers. "Don't call yourself stupid. You have a big heart. You just didn't see the changes coming."

"You give me a lot of credit." She squeezed his hand. "I'm still mad at myself for winding up in this position."

"As crazy as it sounds, I'm kind of glad you did." He squeezed back then let go completely, keeping things safe and distant. "You're better off here."

With you? She wanted to add, *I am better off here but where do we go from here?* "What are we, Joe?"

He screwed up his face in mock confusion. "What do you mean?"

"Are we friends? You can't call me a tenant because I'm not paying you rent." She tried to make an ironic expression, but fell far short because the next pressing question was already demanding she ask it. "Am I one huge charity case that you, in your kindness, the way your parents taught you, just can't bring yourself to send away?"

"God, no. Carey, come on." He wadded up his napkin and tossed it on the table. "You're overthinking things, making problems where there aren't any. We're friends." He shrugged.

"We can't call ourselves friends if you won't open up to me." She stood and started clearing the table. "Friends share things."

Joe shot up and helped to pick up dishes, as usual, and they headed to the kitchen and washed the plates in silence. A muscle in his jaw bunched over and over. Not only had she *not* gotten Joe to open up, she'd made sure he'd keep his distance and would probably never let her close. Major fail.

But what should she expect, being pregnant with another man's baby?

Early on Monday morning the phone rang. Sunday evening had been strained but tolerable between them, and Joe had withdrawn more from Carey by working during the day and later by working out while listening to that aggressive jazz saxophone music while he did so. It made her want to put on headphones. Carey didn't know if she could take much more of him distancing himself from her, but under the circumstances she felt trapped for now. Which felt far too familiar, considering her past.

Joe had the day off and answered, then quickly handed the phone to Carey.

"This is Mrs. Adams from social services. The police department told us about your current situation, and Helena from The Hollywood Hills Clinic Social Services also contacted us. Sorry it took so long, but there is quite a backlog. Anyway, we have found a temporary apartment in Hollywood where you can stay for now."

"Well, that's wonderful. When can I have a look?"

"You can move in this weekend, if you'd like. Or today if you need to. We have a voucher worth a month's rent and this unit has just become available. Would you like me to bring the voucher by?"

"Yes. Of course. Thanks so much."

Carey hung up having made arrangements with Mrs. Adams, glancing up to see Joe watching her skeptically. She owed him an explanation and told him exactly what Mrs. Adams had just said.

"So, if all works out, I'll be out of your hair, maybe as soon as tonight."

"Where is this place? Will you be safe?" There went that jaw muscle again.

"I don't know anything, but would social services send me somewhere unsafe?"

"They're just trying to put a roof over your head." His fingers planted on and dug into his hips, his body tensed. He wore an expression of great concern, making his normally handsome face look ominous. "Safety might not be their number-one goal. I'm going with you."

Every once in a while, thanks to her recent experience with Ross, Joe seemed too overbearing. Yeah, she'd messed up lately, but she was a big girl, a mother-to-be! And she would be in charge of her life from here on. "I can take care of myself. Thanks."

His demeanor immediately apologetic, he came closer. "I didn't mean to come off like that, dictating what I intended to do, but please let me come with you. I'd like to see where you'll be living. I know all the areas around here."

Since he sounded more reasonable, she changed her mind. "Okay, but I make the decision. Got that?"

"Got it. But first off you've got to know that you don't have to move out. You're welcome to stay here as long as you need to."

"Thank you, but as a future single mother I've got to prove to myself I can take care of things. I got myself into this situation, I should get myself out. Besides, I'll be starting the temporary job next Monday, and—"

"Your salary won't be enough to rent an apartment in any decent neighborhood. I'm not trying to throw a wet blanket on your plans, I'm just being honest."

She refused to lose hope. "I'm going to go see that apartment with Mrs. Adams and then I'll decide."

"Can you at least call her back and tell her I'll drive you over there?"

"Okay, but only because it will be more convenient for her."

"Fine."

That afternoon Joe parked on North Edgemont in front of an old redbrick apartment building that was dark, dank and seedy-looking as hell. He clamped his jaw and ground his molars rather than let Carey know what he thought. She'd made it clear it would be her decision, and he'd honor that. The only thing the area had going for it was a huge hospital a couple of blocks down on Sunset Boulevard.

If they'd offered the rent voucher the first week she'd moved in, he would have encouraged her to jump on it. Having a woman in his house again, especially a pregnant woman, brought back a hundred different and all equally awful memories. Having to do things together, like shopping for groceries and fixing meals, was nearly more than he could bear. Plus, with Carey living with him, it seemed Angela had moved back in, just in a different form. So he'd concentrated on Carey being a victim and he was her protector. Keeping it clinical and obligatory had been the key.

Best-laid plans and all, he'd gotten involved with her anyway. Why had he taken it on himself to teach her self-defense, and why in hell had he volunteered to be her prenatal class partner? The problem was there was too much to like about Carey. So he glanced at the dreary apartment building and felt a little sick.

If she decided to take this place, he'd have to find her

a car. Which wouldn't be a problem with his father's business. No way did he want her walking these streets at night, coming home from work and getting off the bus. Pressure built in his temples just thinking about it.

He stood back and let Carey introduce herself to Mrs. Adams, who showed her inside. The term *flophouse* came to mind, but Joe kept his trap shut. Damn, it was hard.

The single room had a tiny alcove with a half-refrigerator, a small microwave and a hot plate. How would she be able to continue with the nutritious meals from Gabriella's class? He'd throw out the mattress from the pullout bed and burn it rather sleep on it, and the rusty toilet in the so-called bathroom made his stomach churn. Not to mention that the constant dripping from the kitchen sink would keep her awake at night.

Caution was as plain as day on Carey's face as she glanced around the place. But he already knew her well enough to know she'd try to make the best out of a lousy situation. Hell, she'd been putting up with him withdrawing every time they'd gotten too close. Probably walked on eggshells around him. But was living with him so bad that she'd choose a dump like this just to get away?

Last night she'd said a real zinger, not realizing it, of course, but nevertheless her comment had hit hard. When she'd talked about her ex being insecure about his masculinity to the point of taking over her life, it had made Joe cringe. He could relate, especially since getting the lab results about him being sterile, and following up later with a urologist as to the reasons why. Was that part of him wanting to protect Carey? Was it some twisted way of making himself feel like a complete man again?

"And you said you have a voucher for the rent here for the next month?" Carey asked.

Mrs. Adams, a tiny African-American woman with short tight curls and wearing a bright red blouse, looked serious. "Yes, we can also provide food stamps and you can move in now or this weekend if you'd like."

Carey was about to say something, and damn it to hell if it meant he was waving around his insecure masculinity or whatever, Joe couldn't let this fiasco continue another second. "What's the crime rate in this neighborhood?" he butted in.

An eyebrow shot up on Mrs. Adams's forehead. Was she not used to being asked that question by people desperate enough to need county social services assistance? "I honestly don't know. It's a busy neighborhood. There's a church right up the street, a hospital down on Sunset. There's a small family-run market on Hollywood Boulevard and the apartment building is really well situated for all of her needs."

Carey stood still, only her eyes moved to watch him. Was it trust or fear he saw there? Was his being concerned coming off as overbearing? He hoped she saw it a different way, the way he'd intended, that he was worried for her safety. He subtly shook his head but she quickly glanced back at Mrs. Adams. "Thank you so much for showing me this place. Do I have to sign anything?"

Joe understood she'd been trying to be a good soldier, stiffening her lip and all, but all it had done was turn her to cardboard. She obviously wanted to make the offer from social services work out, but Joe strongly suspected that in her heart she was scared. And he was pretty sure he saw it in her eyes, too. Those lush meadow-green eyes seemed ready for a storm. How could she not be afraid? Now that he'd identified what was going on with her, he could practically smell that fear. He just hoped it wasn't directed toward him.

She didn't belong here. She belonged with him. Safe. Protected. That's all there was to it. Was he being crazy, like Ross? With all his heart he hoped not, but right at this moment it was hard to evaluate his motives because the lines had blurred and there was no way in hell he'd let this happen.

Joe stepped forward, unable to let the scene play out another moment. He reached for and gently held Carey's upper arm, pleading with his eyes, hoping she wouldn't see a crazed, insecure man. He fought to keep every ounce of emotion out of his voice. "Stay with me." Making the comment a simple suggestion. Then he stumbled, letting a drop of intensity slip back in. "Please."

Carey hadn't given in, though she'd wanted to. Mrs. Adams had gone on alert when Joe had taken her arm in his hand. The poor woman had probably thought he was the guy she needed to get away from. Carey had made sure she knew otherwise. No, Joe wasn't scary, but he had a rescue complex and she needed to help him get over it.

They drove back toward West Hollowood mostly in silence. True, the last thing she wanted was to move into such a depressing place, but rather than cave just because Joe wanted her to she'd asked Mrs. Adams to give her twenty-four hours to make her decision. It had also seemed to calm the woman's sudden uneasy demeanor over the battle of wills between Carey and Joe about moving.

And this had been where Joe had proved he was nothing like Ultimatum Ross. Trusting her decision, he'd agreed that was a smart idea, and Mrs. Adams had smiled again. Inside, so had Carey.

The man was too good to be true, and she couldn't trust her instinct to believe he was what he was, a great guy! She'd thought she'd fallen for a great guy back home, a man who'd gone out of his way to charm her and make her laugh, and above all who'd wanted to take care of her. Look where that had led. But the last two weeks of living with Joe had been little short of perfection. He was patient and friendly, didn't have mood swings, like Ross, had just mostly kept his distance. Sometimes that had been maddening. Joe was tidy and helpful and—oh, she'd tried long enough to avoid the next thought—sexy as hell! The male pheromones buzzing through that house had awakened something she'd tried to put on hold since long before she'd gotten pregnant. Desire.

When she'd taken off her blindfold and finally seen who Ross truly was, she hadn't wanted to be engaged to him anymore. But he was such a manipulating and suspicious guy that she'd pretended to be sexually interested just enough to keep him off the scent. She'd intended to leave him. Had made plans for it, too. Then the unthinkable had happened and she'd gotten pregnant. The only thing she could figure was she'd missed a birth-control pill. Ross had hated hearing that excuse, and he'd accused her of wanting to ruin everything they'd had together. He'd even accused her of being unfaithful.

And he'd gotten violent.

How could she ever trust her instinct where men were concerned?

She needed Joe to open up to make sure he wasn't hiding something awful. Maybe she could use him wanting to rescue her all the time as a bargaining chip to get him to share something personal. She'd been kind of forced to tell him about Ross, what with her bruises and black eye and being pregnant and running away. But her attempt to get him to tell her about his failed marriage Saturday night had fallen flat. Maybe his divorce still hurt too much.

"If you expect me to continue to live with you, we have to actually be friends, not just say we are."

"Of course we're friends." He kept his eyes on the road.

"No, we're not. I've shared some very personal stuff with you, and yet you're nothing but a mystery to me. Friends know things about each other."

"What do you want to know?" He sounded frustrated.

"Why did your wife leave you? What happened? What broke up your marriage?"

He braked a little too hard for the red light, then stared straight ahead for a couple of moments. "If you're thinking I was a player you'd be wrong. In our case it was the other way around."

Carey nearly gulped in her shock. What woman in her right mind would be unfaithful to a guy like Joe? What in the world was she supposed to say to that? "She left you for another man?" She admitted she sounded a little dumbstruck.

"As opposed to a woman?" He gave an ironic laugh and glanced at her with challenge in his eyes. "I guess that might have hurt even more, but yes to your question. It was another man." He could have been testifying in court by his businesslike manner. Just the facts, ma'am.

So Joe was one of the walking wounded, like her.

"I'm so sorry." It was probably a lot easier for him to assign himself the role of protector than to open the door to getting involved with another woman. Especially a vulnerable person like her. Joe had proved to be wise on top of all his other wonderful assets.

Though she knew without a doubt what had gone down today, looking at the apartment, was on a completely different level. Joe had asked her to stay. She'd seen from that touch of desperation in his eyes that he'd meant it, too. She didn't have a clue if once upon a time he'd asked his wife to stay and she'd left anyway, but right at this instant Carey made a decision.

No way would she be another woman walking out on Joseph Matthews. "May I borrow your cell phone?"

While driving, he fished in his pocket and handed it to her. She looked in her purse for the business card. "Hello, Mrs. Adams? This is Carey Spencer. Yes, hi. About that apartment, I am so grateful for the rent voucher and the offer of food stamps, but I have decided to stay where I am."

Not another word was spoken on the drive home, but Carey could have sworn the built-up tension in the car had instantly dissipated as if she'd rolled down the window and let the Santa Ana winds blow it all away.

The following Monday Carey started her new job as a substitute ward clerk and couldn't hide her elation over working again. More importantly, the California Board of Registered Nurses assured her she'd get her RN license in a couple more weeks, just in time to apply for another job, this one as an RN, after the vacationing ward clerk came back. Life was definitely looking up.

The evening shift on the medical/surgical unit was nonstop with admissions and discharges, and she was grateful she'd spent a couple of afternoons learning the computer software and clinic routine with the current ward clerk the week before she'd left.

Joe had offered to rent her a car, but she didn't feel ready to drive the streets of Los Angeles, especially those winding roads in the Hollywood Hills, just yet, so Joe had reworked things and scheduled himself on evening shifts so he could bring her to work and back.

She sat transfixed before the computer at the nurses' station, deciphering the admitting orders from Dr. Rothsberg for a twenty-eight-year-old starlet who'd been intermittently starving and binging herself then herbal detoxing for the last several years, until now her liver showed signs of giving out. She'd been admitted with a general diagnosis of fever, malaise and abdominal tenderness. Though bone thin everywhere else, her abdomen looked to be the same size as Carey's, but the actress wasn't pregnant.

Carey had arranged for the ultrasound and CT studies for the next day, and had moved on to requesting a low-sodium diet from the hospital dietary department, which had a master chef. She could vouch for the great food with a couple of memorable meals she'd had during her stay. The patient would probably never notice the lack of salt amidst a perfect blend of fresh herbs and spices. Then she reminded the admitting nurse that her patient was on total bed rest. She went ahead and read Dr. Rothsberg's analysis and realized therapeutic paracentesis was likely in the petite Hollywood personality's future.

Deep in her work, she glanced up to find Joe smiling at her. "I brought you something," he said, then handed her a brown bag with something inside that smelled out of this world.

She stood to take the bag over the countertop, inhaled and couldn't resist. "Mmm, what is it?"

"Your dinner. I was on a call in the vicinity of Fairfax, so I got you one of those deli sandwiches you gobbled down the last time we were there."

"Turkey salad, cranberries and walnuts with bread dressing?"

"Yup."

"Including the pickle?"

He nodded, as if offended she'd even suggest such an oversight.

"Well, thank you. I'll be starving by the time my dinner break rolls around."

"You're welcome." He got serious and leaned on his forearm, making sure to hold her gaze. "I've been thinking. We'll have to get more organized now that you're working and pack a lunch for you every day. We can still use Gabriella's guidelines."

"Sounds good." Totally touched by his concern for her well-being, she fought that frequent urge to give him a hug. Fortunately the nurses' station counter prevented it this time. "But please let me splurge on things like this once in a while." She held up the deli bag.

He winked, and it seemed a dozen butterflies had forced their way into her chest and now attempted to fly off with her heart. Since she'd decided to keep living with him, he'd changed. He'd become easier to talk to, and though he still hadn't opened up he'd quit grinding his teeth so much. Truth was, the man could only suppress his wonderful nature for so long. Now she was the lucky recipient of his thoughtfulness and loving every second of it.

"See you later," he said, making a U-turn and heading off the ward. The perfectly fitting light blue polo shirt showed off his broad shoulders, accentuating his trim waist, the multi-purpose khaki cargo pants still managing to hug his buns just right, and those sexy-as-hell black paramedic utility boots... She guiltily watched his every move until he was out of sight. Wow, it looked like she didn't have to worry about her sick relationship with Ross at the end before she'd run away, and ruining her natural sex drive. She'd faked interest and excitement with him for her safety. Now, with Joe, without even trying, the most natural thoughts of all had awakened some super-hot fantasies. Like the desire to make love and really mean it. What would that be like with Joe?

"Uh-huh. Nice." One of the other nurses in the area had joined her in staring at the masculine work of art as he'd swaggered out the door. How could a guy *not* swagger, wearing those boots?

Getting caught ogling Joe made Carey's cheeks heat up, especially after what she'd just been thinking, so she tossed a sheepish look at the nurse then delved back into the admission packet for the actress.

Joe went straight to the clinic's paramedic station just off the ER to check on the EMT staff. He knew the emergency nurses sometimes got upset if the guys didn't help out when things got busy. Joe was always prepared to intervene and explain that wasn't their job, and the RNs didn't need to get all worked up about the EMS guys sitting for half a minute, waiting for the next call. On the other hand, he'd insisted to his guys that if a nurse said she needed more muscle, and they weren't doing anything at the time, they should jump to it and help out with lifts and transfers. Keeping RNs happy was always a good idea. He'd also taken to suggesting the guys hang out in their truck on downtime rather than at the tiny desk with two computers designated as their work station, so as not to complicate things in the ER.

Not taking his own advice, he took a seat and brought up the evening's schedule, and in the process sat in the vicinity of James, who was conferring on the phone about a patient he'd just admitted to Carey's floor with liver issues. James nodded and smiled at Joe, and Joe returned the courtesy.

Soon James hung up. "How's that scar doing? Any more tearing with your workouts, you beast?"

Joe laughed. "I'm all healed. Thanks." Joe saw James's sister, Freya, appear across the ER, obviously looking for someone.

"There you are," she said over the other heads, immediately making her way toward James.

James ducked down in an obvious fashion. "Oh, boy. Here we go," he said jokingly in an aside to Joe. "What does she want this time?" He raised his voice to tease his younger sister.

Knowing from their rocky history that the brother and sister's relationship had never been better since Freya had come to The Hollywood Hills Clinic as a sought-after public relations guru, Joe chuckled at James's wisecrack.

"There you are," Freya said, her dark blue eyes sparkling under the fluorescent ER lights. "I know you've been avoiding me, but I need a firm date for when you'll visit the Bright Hope Clinic. Here's my calendar, I've highlighted the best days and times for me and them. What works for you?" She shoved her small internet tablet calendar in front of James, making it impossible for him not to pick a day and time.

Her long brown hair was pulled back into a simple

ponytail that waved down her back, nearly to her waist, yet she still looked like she could be royalty. Hollywood royalty, that was. Joe had heard rumors about her once having had to go to rehab for anorexia, but from the healthy, happy-looking pregnant woman standing before him he'd have never guessed.

James took a deep inhale and scrolled through his smartphone calendar, matching day for day, saying, "No. Nope. Not that one either. Hmm, maybe this one? September the first or the second?"

"Let's take the first." Freya quickly highlighted that day. "It is now written in stone. Do you hear me? There's no getting out of it. You'll show up and do those publicity photos in the clinic in South Central and smile like you mean it."

"Of course I'll mean it. I'm going for the children."

"I know, but you know." They passed a secret brother-sister glance, telling an entirely different story than the simple making of plans for publicity shots. Joe deduced that since Dr. Mila Brightman ran Bright Hope, she was the issue. She happened to be Freya's best friend, and also the woman James had stood up on their wedding day. Or, at least, that was the scuttlebutt Stephanie the receptionist had told Joe one day on a break over coffee in the cafeteria. It had happened before Joe had started working there, she'd said, so all he could do was take Stephanie's word for it. The woman really was a gossip. But, damn, if that was the case, no wonder James hesitated about going. How could he face her after dumping her on the day of her dream wedding?

Having achieved her purpose, Freya rushed off, no doubt wanting to end her day and get home to her husband Zack.

"The last thing I want to do is upset a pregnant lady,"

James said to Joe in passing, "but, hey, you know all about that, right?"

The casual comment took Joe by surprise. At first he thought James was referring to his ex, Angela, but then realized he must have been referring to Jane Doe, aka Carey, who lived with him and happened to be just shy of four months pregnant.

"Tell me about it," Joe said, hoping he'd recovered quickly enough not to seem like a bonehead, and pretending that pregnant ladies were indeed unpredictable and demanding, while knowing for a fact Carey was anything but.

On Friday night, at the end of the first week on the job for Carey, Joe insisted they stop for a fast-food burger on the way home. How could she have been in California for three weeks and not tried one? They didn't even bother to wait to get home but devoured them immediately on the drive. Even though it definitely wasn't on her second-trimester diet list, she'd never tasted a better cheeseburger in her life.

"My parents are having a barbecue on the Fourth of July," Joe said, his mouth half-full, one hand on the steering wheel, the other clutching a double cheeseburger.

A national holiday had been the last thing on her mind lately. Plans seemed incomprehensible. She thought of that dreary apartment she'd almost taken and shivered at the thought of being on her own there, especially on the Fourth of July, grateful to have Joe's sweet house and lovely garden in the back to look at. She'd be just fine.

"Do you want to come? They'd love to have you."

What? He was inviting her to his parents' home?

Why? Out of his usual sense of obligation? "Oh, you don't have to—"

"I want to, and my whole family's going to be there so you can meet my sisters and brothers, too."

"Do they know about me?" Why was he pushing to take her?

"I have a prying mother and a loose-lipped sister. Mom's got this sixth sense about changes in my life, no doubt recently fueled by Lori loaning out some clothes."

"The whole story?" She really didn't want her personal failures shared, especially with Joe's family.

He shook his head and took another bite of his burger. "I wouldn't do that. You know better. But you said you wanted to be friends, and I take my friends to family barbecues."

She'd put her foot down when she'd decided to stay with him. He'd agreed to consider her a friend. If this was his way of proving it, as confusing as it would be for her, not to mention nerve-racking, she really shouldn't refuse to meet his family. It might set things back if she didn't.

"Then I guess I'll have to go." She played coy, but cautious contentment she hadn't felt in ages settled in a warm place behind her breastbone. This was more proof that Joe was *nothing* like Ross. He pushed her to get out and do things, got her a job, and now he wanted her to meet his family on Independence Day no less. Wow, what did it all mean?

Joe finished his hamburger as they neared his house. It'd tasted great, as always, but now his stomach felt a little unsettled. He'd tried not to think about the ramifications of what he'd just done, but couldn't avoid it. Trust, or lack thereof, in women in general and Carey, by reason of her gender, made him have second thoughts about the invitation. The gift of Angela's infidelity just kept on giving.

Maybe he'd jumped the gun in asking her to his parents' Fourth of July party. It was too soon. She might get the wrong impression and he wasn't anywhere ready to get close to her. He pulled into the driveway and rather than pull into the garage he parked under the small carport instead. It wasn't like he could change the date of Independence Day, and for the record he wondered if he'd ever be in a place to trust a woman again, whether next week or two years from now.

But the damage had been done. He'd asked Carey to go along, and he couldn't very well take the invitation back. He'd just have to live with it.

Once home, Carey went directly to her room to change her clothes, planning to watch a little TV to unwind after another busy evening shift at the end of her first week. But not without noticing a shift in his mood since he'd issued, and she'd accepted, the invitation to his parents' Fourth of July barbecue. When she came back, Joe was already working out on the patio, hitting his punching bag like it was a full-out enemy. For someone who'd just wolfed down a double-double cheeseburger, French fries and a large soda, he looked the picture of health.

Feeling a bit guilt-ridden, she wandered into the dining room to have a better look, wondering if he'd taken his T-shirt off for her benefit. She particularly loved watching the muscles on his back ripple whenever he landed a good punch. She stood quietly, taking in the whole workout, admiring every inch of him.

Before she'd run away, she'd worried about ever having normal desire for a man again. Faking love with Ross had scarred her more than she'd ever dreamed.

But it hadn't stopped there. Ross had dominated her entire existence to the point of making her fear for her life. How could she ever desire a man who'd treated her like that?

Yet Joe, without even trying, brought out her most basic feelings. He turned her on. So confusing. Maybe she could blame that on the concussion or the pregnancy. Yet what a relief to know she was still a red-blooded woman with a normal sex drive.

With his back to her, he grunted and huffed as he punched the bag, and she could swear the muscles on his shoulders and arms grew more cut by the moment. Needing to either bite her knuckle to keep from groaning or do something to cool herself off, she chose to head to the kitchen for a bottle of water. When she opened the refrigerator, she grabbed one for Joe, too.

This time making her presence known, she went out onto the patio, setting his water near him. "You're making me feel very guilty about having that burger and not intending to do my preggers exercises tonight, you know."

Joe laughed, and because of it messed up his timing and the punch nearly missed the bag altogether. He went for the bottle. "Thanks." Carey enjoyed watching his Adam's apple move up and down his throat while he gulped the water. A few drops dribbled down his chest. Yeah, she noticed that, too.

Her eyes drifted to the jagged scar running across his ribs, still red and tender-looking. He'd been stabbed rescuing her. The thought seemed surreal and sent a barrage of intense feelings ranging from gratitude to lust to guilt rushing through her. On impulse she walked toward him, reached out and gingerly ran her fingers across the scar. His skin was damp, smooth and…

She slowly lifted her gaze from the fit washboard abs to his chest and the pumped pecs lightly dusted in dark hair, then onward to his strong chin and inviting mouth and last to his intensely brown, almost black with desire, eyes.

The moment, when they were up close and locked into each other's stare like that, shuddered through her.

Feeling absurdly out of character in general, and especially because she was four months pregnant, she ignored her insecurities, focusing only on the consuming pull between them, making a trail with her fingertips across the expanse of his muscled torso, along the broad rim of his shoulder, then upward to his jaw.

She swallowed lightly in edgy anticipation.

He didn't move, just kept willing her into the depth of his eyes, and she knew without a doubt he was as into this moment as she was. So she edged closer, lifted her chin and, though feeling breathy from nerves, she went for it, covering his mouth with a full-on kiss.

CHAPTER SIX

IF JOE LET Carey's kiss continue, he'd have to take her all the way and probably scare her half to death with his need. The mere touch of her lips had unleashed pure desire, like a lightning bolt straight down his spine.

But he knew Carey well enough now, and the woman was trying to show her gratitude for his saving her and taking her in. He didn't want gratitude, or, if she knew his whole story, pity, or anything else. All he wanted was to get lost in her body, to make love.

He broke off the kiss to get things straight. "I don't expect anything from you. You don't have to—"

She didn't listen or give him a chance to call her out, she just kissed him again, and, damn it, those lips he'd so often admired on the sly felt better kissing him than he could ever have imagined. He quit fighting his need and pulled her near, devouring her mouth, half hoping she'd get scared and back off so that what was otherwise inevitable wouldn't happen. But the hard and desperate kiss only seemed to fan her need as much as his as she pressed her body flush with his.

He could handle this, wouldn't lose control. They'd just make out for a while then call it quits. But then there was the feel of her lips, smooth, plump, that inviting-as-all-hell tongue, and the touch of her fingertips at the back of his neck and on his shoulders. The sound of her deep breathing, the scent of coconut in her hair, and especially those little turned-on sounds escaping her throat made it so hard to not completely let go. And, damn, that wasn't the only thing that was hard. Yeah, he was pumped, horny, and making out with a woman who seemed to want him as badly as he needed her.

This was about sex. Against a wall. He needed to look into her eyes, to see if she really was as into this as he was, because he wouldn't take her if she wasn't. Electricity seemed to run through his veins, maybe partly because he was worked up from boxing, but most definitely from holding and kissing her. Surely she felt that electricity too. If she was just looking for some comforting necking, she'd come on way too strong, so it was best to check things out. Figure out where she was at before he let loose. He placed his thumbs in front of her ears, his fingers digging into that thick and gorgeous auburn hair, and though hating to separate their mouths he moved her head back.

Carey seemed dazed and was breathless, so it took a moment for her to connect with his stare. Her eyelids fluttered open and maybe Joe's interpretation was skewed from wanting her so much, but her eyes were on fire. For him.

Her nostrils flared and she breathed quickly. "Please don't stop," she whispered. "This has nothing to do with gratitude, believe me." She kissed him again, and the dam of unspoken longing, secret desire, and flat-out need totally broke.

She wanted him. He wanted her. Tonight he'd have her.

He walked her backwards, reached under the back of

her thighs and lifted her as he did so. She wrapped her legs around his waist, and soon her back was against a well-secluded wall in the corner of the patio. She'd already pulled her top over her head by the time they'd gotten there, and once at the wall, just as quickly, she released her full breasts from the constraints of the bra.

He looked down. The view of their chests mashed together exhilarated him, the hot, soft feel of her breasts even better. But she was hungry for his mouth and wanted all his attention there. So he obliged. He wedged her tight against the wall, sitting her on the edge of a book case, leaning into her, weaving his fingers with hers and lifting her arms flush to the plaster so he could be closer still. She moaned, enjoying the full body contact every bit as much as he did. He inhaled her sweet-scented neck and nuzzled it deep with kisses. She liked it, moaning again and bucking her hips just above his full erection, causing more lightning bolts along his spine.

Soon Carey wiggled off his hips, standing just long enough to tug down his boxing shorts and her yoga pants. She took the time to run her hand along his glutes and give them an appreciative squeeze as she stepped up close and hugged him again.

His erection landed between their bodies and the surge of sensation from her skin to his nearly sent him over the top. God, he wanted her. And she obviously wanted him. Right then.

He may be sterile and she pregnant, but he still knew the purpose of protected sex, and it wasn't all about birth control. Any guy his age had a stash of condoms, even though lately he hadn't been in the least bit interested in getting involved enough with a woman to use them…until Carey.

Living with Carey these past few weeks had made him very much aware of where those condoms were, too. "One second." He stopped pressing her to the wall, and regretfully removed himself from between her gorgeous thighs. "Don't move." He stepped back and his eyes took her in, in all her lush splendor. God, he wanted her.

Joe zipped around the wall to his bedroom and returned in record time, afraid she might have already changed her mind.

She wasn't there. His heart sank.

"I'm in the bathroom. I'll be right there!"

The wall was looking less and less appealing so he went into his bedroom and pulled back the covers on his king-sized bed, finding it hard to believe he'd soon be making love to Carey.

Carey never had expected to be having sex with Joe tonight, but now that she'd started it, and sex was definitely on the table, or nearly against the wall in their case, she wanted to freshen up. Ross may have scarred her but Joe could heal her. She didn't expect anything more than tonight, just the chance to find out she could let go and be with him, someone new, different, better than toxic Ross. If she didn't take this opportunity, she might never get over her past or feel normal again.

She stepped into the hall to find Joe waiting for her, having made the mistake of glancing at her pregnant abdomen just before she did. A wave of insecurity nearly made her back out, but the instant she saw his Adonis-like form, and the unadulterated desire in his eyes, every insecure thought left her mind. She wanted Joe more than she'd ever wanted to be with any man.

She rushed to him and he picked her up again, her

cooler skin crashing with his hot damp flesh. She inhaled his musky scent and grew hungrier for him. He carried her to his bed and, probably because she was pregnant, laid her down gently. Frantic for him, she'd have none of that, pulling him firmly toward her, and impatiently bucked under him.

He had other plans, though, and took his time exploring her body, figuring out what excited her and what drove her wild. Just about everything at this point! On his side, facing her, he rested on one arm, lowering and lifting his head to kiss her mouth, her neck, her breasts, while his free hand cupped her and explored her most intimate area. Breathless with longing, sensations zinging every which way through her body, she never wanted the intensified make-out session to end. Until, very soon, the mounting desire was too much and she needed him, all of him, inside her.

She rolled onto her side, throwing her leg over his hip, straddled him and pushed him back onto the mattress. From his firm feel she had zero worries whether he was ready or not. She slid her awakened center, thanks to his earlier attentions, along his length, thrilling at the feel of it and the thought of him soon being inside her. He'd already made her wet so she skimmed along his smooth ridge with ease, several times, stimulating herself more than she thought she could take. He definitely liked it.

But stopping her in mid-skim, as if he might lose control, he sheathed himself in record time then, taking control, placed her on her side with her back to his chest. One arm was underneath her and that hand cupped her breast while the other dipped between her thighs and opened her, rubbing the amazingly sensitive area, and she was soon straining at the onslaught of arousal. She moaned in bliss and Joe, being definitely ready, tilted her hips back, making her swaybacked, then entered her.

The culmination of sensations as he pressed into her took her breath away. She rolled with him, taking in every electrifying thrust. His hands remained attentive in those other strategic places as friction built deep inside, knotting behind her navel and lower. Heat lapped up the base of her spine, across her hips and over her breasts, flooding the skin on her chest and cheeks. She could feel the fully ignited body flush nearly burning her skin. If possible, he felt even harder now and an absurd thought occurred to her. She was making love with him, Joe! It wasn't a wish or a fantasy or a secret dream anymore. It was really happening.

Maybe it was the added hormones of pregnancy, and more probably it was the undivided attention from Joe, but she'd never, *ever* been this turned on in her life. With her entire body tingling and covered in goose bumps, running hot with sensations—not to mention the involuntary sounds escaping her throat—there would be no guessing on his part about how he made her feel. *Freaking amazing.*

She couldn't take more than a few minutes of the intense sensory overload without completely giving in to it. His pumping into her, slowing down and drawing out every last response, then speeding up at the perfect moment to drive her near the flashpoint soon became her undoing. She turned her head and found his mouth. They kissed wildly, wet and deep.

When she came, her center seemed to explode with nerve endings lighting up, zinging and zipping everywhere as they relayed their ecstatic message deep throughout her body. She gasped and writhed against him, riding the incredible wave for all it was worth, while sensing his time was near. Soon his low, elongated moan became the sweetest music she'd ever heard.

It had taken several minutes for things to settle down between Joe and Carey. He'd briefly jumped out of bed for the bathroom to take care of business, returning to find she'd probably done the same. He smiled when she came back with the fresh flush of lovemaking on her face and across her chest. Though she'd run a brush through her hair, it was still wildly appealing. He continued floating on the post-sex euphoric cloud when she crawled back into bed beside him. He'd just had mind-blowing sex with an amazing lady and he felt great. Beyond great. He pulled her close, delivered a sweetheart kiss then snuggled in, savoring the afterglow between them. But it was late and they'd worn each other out.

Within a few short minutes Carey fell asleep. She'd gone still, wrapped in his arms, then her breathing shifted to a slower, deeper rhythm. It felt right, holding her, breathing in her scented hair, touching her soft skin and womanly body. But sleep wasn't ready to come to Joe.

His hand dropped over her abdomen and the noticeable early second-trimester bump. It jolted him. His mind raced with comparisons with another woman and another time. He'd avoided the thought long enough, now it wouldn't let him go.

What the hell had he just done? He'd ruined everything.

The battle in his mind continued with rival thoughts. He had to be honest, he'd wanted this more than anything, and being with Carey had been on his mind for longer than he cared to admit. She'd knocked every sensible thought out of his head just by being the wonderfully appealing, sweet woman she was. The sexy-as-hell—and who'd just proved it beyond a doubt—mother-to-be.

Yes, she was pregnant with another man's baby, and though the circumstances were totally different, the scenario seemed too damn familiar.

Also, Joe worried that Carey was confusing gratitude with desire. She'd denied it when he'd bluntly asked her, but they were both obviously under some voodoo spell when it came to each other. He wouldn't dare call it love. Hell, she'd just escaped a toxic, abusive relationship. Any decent guy, and Joe considered himself one of the good guys, would be an improvement.

Back and forth he silently argued, feeding his confusion rather than solving anything. He'd essentially been acting like a partner to Carey in all but name—how had he not seen that before? It'd started with the staggering need to protect her and moved on to bringing her home. They'd lived together for almost a month, sharing the little everyday things that true couples did. He was the first person other than the midwife to see Baby Spencer in the ultrasound. He'd secretly teared up, seeing how the fetus already sucked its thumb and had a tiny turned-up nose in the profile. She'd even asked him to go to the next doctor's appointment with her, too, joking she was worried she'd forget something, and he'd been following her pregnancy like an auditor.

Just like he'd done with Angela at the beginning of her pregnancy.

What had possessed him to step into the role of being Carey's partner in the parenting class? He squeezed his eyes tight, avoiding the answer, holding her a little tighter than before. It wasn't out of pity for her being the only one enrolled without a significant other—no, he had to be honest. It was because he'd wanted to. Maybe even needed to.

Did he enjoy getting kicked in the teeth?

Damn it, for one of the good guys he was really screwed up. Losing Angela had nearly done him in, along with getting hit by the hardest dose of reality in his life. He was sterile. He'd never be a father. And Angela had cheated on him, taking the task of getting pregnant to his best friend, Rico.

In time he'd lose Carey and her baby, too, once she got back on her own two feet again. Just like he'd lost Angela and the baby he'd once thought was his for a brief but ecstatic period of time.

He slipped out of bed, unable to stay close another second to the woman who'd just thrown his entire world on its head. He pulled on his boxing trunks, went to the kitchen and drank a full glass of water, then walked to the couch and sat. Being away from her spell helped his body settle down. His mind was another story altogether, though. He folded his arms across his chest, plopped his feet on the coffee table and, using the TV controller, turned to an old black and white movie with the sound muted. Fortunately it dulled his thoughts and little by little, as the dark drama unfolded and minutes passed, he finally drifted off to sleep.

"Joe? What are you doing out here?"

Sunshine slipped through the cracks in the living-room window blinds on Saturday morning. Joe eased open one eye from where his face was mashed against the armrest cushion on the couch. "Huh? Oh, I couldn't sleep and I didn't want to wake you so I came out here."

"I was worried I'd snored or something." She'd obviously tried to lighten the mood, so he laughed easily, as if nothing was wrong at all. She looked nearly angelic, standing with the window behind her, her silhouette outlined by bright morning light. She was wearing an oversized T-shirt with those long, slender legs completely bare. It made him want her all over again, but that was the last thing he should ever do.

"No." He scrubbed his face, trying to wake up, realizing she hadn't bought his explanation, and he needed to be straight with her. "You didn't snore." Yeah, he had to nip this in the bud and, though it might sting today, she'd thank him later for sparing her more pain.

"What's up, Joe? I don't have a good feeling about us having sex and then you sneaking off to the couch."

He wasn't ready to look at her, and when he told her his thoughts she deserved his undivided attention. "I need some coffee." He stood and she followed him into the kitchen. He glanced at her before he got on the job of filling the coffeemaker and saw the frightened and forlorn woman he'd first seen at the bus station. It made him feel sick to do that to her so he stopped avoiding the moment and grabbed one of her hands. "Look." He shook his head. "I'm sorry we crossed the line last night. It was fantastic, amazing, and a huge mistake."

"No. It was totally okay with me. Couldn't you tell?" She searched his eyes, looking for answers. It made him look down at the hand he held. "In fact, it was an incredible night. I never dreamed making love with you could be so wonderful."

He glanced upward, finding those eyes…greener in the morning light. "It was great, but things are too confused between us. You need time to heal from your lousy relationship with Ross, and the most important thing in your life right now should be your baby. Focus on the baby, instead of getting all involved with me. Not that I didn't love what we did in there last night, it's just that we're dangerous for each other right now. I shouldn't take time and energy away from you focusing on what you want to do with your life. I'll just interfere, and you need to think what's best for you, not anyone else."

Who was he kidding, laying all the excuses at Carey's feet? He still wasn't ready to trust another woman, to open up about the pain of his wife's infidelity. And that's what he'd need to do in order to be with someone new. Her. It was why he'd been living like a workaholic hermit all this time. What would she think of him if she knew how scared he was to tell her the truth, and if he wasn't ready to be completely honest, what was the point of being with her?

He pulled her close and held her, and it hurt to feel her stiffen when he wanted to love her. But now he had to push her away because she deserved better. She deserved a future of her own making. All he'd do was mess things up. "We both have a lot going on in our lives right now and it isn't a good time to confuse things even more with sex." He pulled back to engage with her eyes, but she was now the one avoiding eye contact. "And, believe me, that was incredibly hard to say, because I wanted you like I've never wanted anyone else last night."

It seemed she'd stopped breathing, a dejected expression changing her beauty to sadness. He felt queasy, like he'd already finished the pot of coffee and the acid lapped the inside of his stomach. But he forged on because he had to.

"It's not right for us to be together now. Our timing

is off. We just have to face that. And no one is sorrier than me."

Something clicked behind those beautiful eyes. Her demeanor shifted from tender and hurting to world-weary chick. "Yeah, you're right. It really was stupid." She pecked his cheek with a near air kiss. "Now I need to shower."

He watched her walk away, her head high and shoulders stiff. In that moment he hated more than anything having given her a reality check, and the thought of drinking a cup of coffee made him want to puke.

CHAPTER SEVEN

CAREY STOOD UNDER the shower, hiding her tears. Joe's rejection had stung her to the core. She'd given him everything she had last night yet this morning he had closed the door.

She lifted her head and let the water run over her face. He'd made her remember her shameful past, and she wanted to kick herself for trying to forget. If there was one lesson she should have learned by now it was not to ever let herself get close to any man again. Yet here she was a month after running away from Ross, opening her heart to Joe. Could she have been more stupid?

Joe wasn't out to hurt her. It had just turned out that way, and it was her fault. She'd suspected from the beginning that he carried heavy baggage. It may have taken a near stranglehold to get him to reveal one small fact—the tip of the iceberg—that his wife had screwed him royally, and what the rest of the story was, Carey could only guess. One thing was certain, he was hurting and afraid of getting involved again.

Truth was she wasn't the only one with a past not to be proud of. Joe belonged in her league. All the more reason the two of them were a horrible match.

Yet she'd trudged on, defying the truth, letting his

kindness and charming personality, not to mention his great looks, win her over little by little. She'd let him take care of her and he'd quickly earned her trust. She still trusted him. But she couldn't let herself fall any deeper in love with him. Something in her chest sank when she inadvertently admitted she'd fallen for him. No. That couldn't be. She needed to stomp out any feelings she already had for Joe beyond the practical, and she needed to do it now. She lived here because she couldn't afford her own place. Yet. In time she'd be free of him, wouldn't have to be reminded daily how wonderful he'd been at first. Then how tightly he'd shut her out. Yet how much she still cared for him fanned the ache in her chest.

She diligently lathered her body, aware of more tears and that sad, sad feeling nearly overtaking her will to go on. Then her hands smoothed over her growing tummy and she knew she couldn't let anything keep her from the joy of becoming a mother. Her baby deserved nothing less than her full attention. Wasn't that what Joe had said, too?

From now on she'd concentrate on getting her life together and becoming a mother, and forget about how being around him made her feel as a woman. Really, how stupid was it, anyway, that fluttering heart business. It never paid off.

After showering and hair-drying and dressing, with her mental armor fully in place, she marched into the kitchen where she heard Joe puttering around. "I've decided to take you up on that offer to rent a car for me."

"Sure, we can do that this afternoon since my dad owns a rental franchise." He responded in the same businesslike tone she'd just used on him.

"Thanks. In the meantime, may I borrow *your* car? If I don't leave now I'll be late for the Parentcraft class."

He was dressed. He stopped drying the coffee carafe, turned and looked at her dead on. "I'm going too, but you can drive if you want."

He tossed her the keys, and in her profound surprise she still managed to catch them. "Uh, I don't think so."

"Well, I know so, because you forget things. And two sets of ears are better than one, especially since you're probably already distracted from everything I pulled on you this morning."

"It would be totally awkward for both of us. You know that."

"No, I don't because I've never done this before. Besides, no one else needs to know."

He was making her crazy with this line of thinking, and so, so confused. "I can't just give myself to someone then forget about it. What's wrong with you?"

"You're right, I'm totally screwed up, I admit it, but I started this class with you, and I intend to be there for you all the way to the end."

Why was he being so unreasonable? But, honestly, how could she hold against him what he'd just acknowledged? He was the first guy in her life who insisted on sticking something out with her. It seemed a very unselfish thing to do.

Now her head was spinning, and it wasn't because of the recent concussion. "This is all too complicated. I'd rather just go myself." He'd hurt her enough for one day. She couldn't possibly sit next to him in a class for two hours and not think about what had happened. Surely he knew that. What was wrong with the man?

He touched her arm and she went still. Something told her he was about to convince her to let him go, and right this minute—*thanks a million, armor, for abandoning me*—she felt too confused to argue.

"Carey, I know how it feels to be let down by someone. I know you've been let down a helluva lot lately, and I respect you too much to do that with this class on top of everything else I've already fouled up."

She felt like grabbing her head and running away. "Let's just drop this. I'm going now." She turned to leave, but he stopped her again.

"Listen, I may have totally screwed up by letting my body do the thinking instead of my brain last night, but long before that… I'll be honest and say I made a promise to myself about you. That first night I promised I'd look after you. And once I found out you were pregnant, I vowed to be there for the baby, too."

He took her by the shoulders, leveling his gaze on hers, delving into her eyes. She couldn't bring herself to look away. "This class is important. You need to know what Gabriella has to say. I signed on to be your partner, and I intend to stay on. We may have made a huge mistake, sleeping together so soon, but in this one thing I'm going to be the only person in your life right now who won't bail on you. Please let me go with you."

Damn her eyes, they welled up and she had to blink. The man was too blasted honorable, and she hated him for it. Hated him. "I won't be able to concentrate with you there." It came out squeaky, like she needed to swallow.

"You wouldn't be able to concentrate if I didn't go either. All the more reason for me to be there." He patted her stomach. "Little baby Spencer needs us to pay attention. Now, let's go."

He gently turned her by her shoulders then nudged her in the small of her back through the door, and because she couldn't stop the stupid mixed-up tears she handed back the keys. "You'd better drive."

Carey finished the temporary job as ward clerk just in time to interview for a staff RN position in the same ward at the clinic. Having seen her work ethic already, and now that she had her RN license straightened out, they hired her on the spot. Carey was thrilled! Life was looking up. Except for that messy bit of being crazy about Joe Matthews and him being adamant about living by some code of honor. He was so damn maddening!

Ever since they'd made love, and especially after he'd explained how he'd made a promise to look after her, she'd thought she'd figured him out. Basically, he was the guy of her dreams but didn't know it yet. The next big test was to get him to realize that. The guy followed the rules, maybe hid behind them, too. She could live with that for now, but it sure was hard! No deep, dark Joe secret would scare her away. Nothing he exposed could deter her. He was a good man, and she didn't want to lose him, no matter how stubborn he was. But she had to be careful not to let on about her continued and growing feelings for him or she'd blow it. The big guy needed to be handled with the utmost care. For his own good.

Things had been very strained at the West Hollywood house since they had "faced the facts" a little over a week ago. It seemed they'd both bent over backwards to be polite and easy to get along with since then, taking the art of being accommodating to a new extreme, but simmering just beneath the surface was the tension. Always the tension. There was nothing like confusing love with kindness and one spectacular "crossing the line" event to create that special brew. Now she'd clearly seen the error of her ways.

He thought he'd convinced her to only look out for herself and the baby, and she was! But she was also letting her heart tiptoe into the realm of love, the kind she'd never experienced before. The problem was, she couldn't let her champion paramedic know or he'd run. So the question remained, was she being the world's biggest fool or the wisest of wise women?

Only time would tell.

The nursing recruiter spent the entire first day on the new job orienting Carey and preparing her for the transition to the floor. From this day forward she'd remember July the first as her personal almost-Independence Day in California. But first she had to get through the holiday weekend, which included meeting Joe's family at their annual barbecue celebration. Why? Because he was the kind of guy who would never retract an invitation once made. Hadn't he proved that already by continuing with the prenatal classes?

Man, he irked her…in a good way.

Another reason was that purely out of curiosity she wanted to meet the family that had spawned such a unique guy as Joe. If she played her cards right, she might find out a lot more about him. As she'd predicted, so far he'd yet to renege on the invitation, but she thought she'd test the waters anyway.

"Listen," she said, on the night of July third, "I think I'll skip the barbecue tomorrow." Her heart wasn't into the excuse by a long shot. After his incredibly lame but amazingly touching reason for continuing with the parenting classes, she was curious to see how compelling he could be over Independence Day.

"But you've got to come. Mom will hound me for weeks if I back out now."

"You don't have to back out. I'm just not sure I'll go."

"If you don't go, I won't either."

"You can't play me like that."

"Play you? I just gave us both a way out. I'll tell her you don't want to come."

"So I get blamed? Oh, no. It's not that I don't want to go, it's our weird relationship I'm worried about. How would we hide that?"

"By acting like friends. We are still friends, right?"

"In some crazy bizarro-universe sort of way, yes, I guess we are. Besides, your mother would be horribly disappointed if you didn't go."

"Exactly my point."

Darn it, his logic had outsmarted hers once again. "You are so frustrating!"

"So you're saying you want to spend your first Fourth of July in California by yourself? Really?"

She couldn't argue with that line of thinking. He'd invited her into his family, an honor for sure but one that wouldn't come without questions. Probably most of the questions would come from his mother. Did she want to open herself up to that? And, more importantly, why did he? But, on the other hand, did she really want to spend the holiday by herself? "Honestly, I'd rather not be alone, but I don't want to feel on the spot either."

"Trust me, I know how to handle my family, and I promise you'll have a good time. You'll like them."

That's what she was afraid of.

"My parents live close enough to the Hollywood Bowl to see the fireworks there," he said, driving to his boyhood home. "When I was a kid I used to lie flat on my back in the yard so I wouldn't miss a thing."

Carey wasn't sure she'd be able to handle anything about today, but she smiled and pretended to be interested in his story and happy he felt like talking about it. No way would she let on to Joe how tough each and every minute spent with him was for her. She did it to hold out for a bigger reward, but so far he wasn't showing any signs of opening up or changing. Holiday Joe was still By-the-Book Joe.

Carey sat in the car, wearing red board shorts with a string-tie waist to accommodate her growing tummy, a white collared extra-long polo shirt and a blue bandana in her hair. Joe wore khaki shorts and a dark gray T-shirt with an American flag on the chest in shades of gray instead of in color. Still, the point was made. They were celebrating the Fourth of July. With his big family. Oh, joy. Cue butterflies in stomach.

Although they'd made love and had opened up to each other that one night, Carey hadn't learned one bit more about Joe's broken marriage. Evidently he was determined not to ever let her know the whole story. Because of that, she felt stuck in a holding pattern, unable to be a real friend even though he'd insisted they were, definitely not a lover but merely a person who needed a place to stay, biding her time until she could move out. Every agonizing day, since things hadn't changed, it became more evident it was time to make her break.

In the back of her mind she kept assuring herself that with her new RN salary she should be able to save up enough fairly soon to rent a small but decent apartment somewhere and then get out of Joe's hair once and for all. Yet the thought of *not* seeing him every day sent a deep ache straight through her chest. Because she still cared for him.

He glanced at her, taking his eyes off the road briefly and giving a friendly yet empty smile. If only she could read his mind. She returned the favor with a wan smile of her own. What a pitiful pair they'd become. They'd both taken to wearing full mental armor since the morning after their one perfect night. Politeness was killing them. And it hurt like hell.

Joe's parents' home turned out to be in the Hollywood Hills area, not far from Joe's house. He explained while they snaked up the narrow street that he'd grown up in a neighborhood called Hollywood Heights. She could see the Hollywood Bowl to the north and some huge and gorgeous estates to the west, wondering if he might have grown up there and was secretly rich. The thought amused her. Hey, the guy had owned his own business since he'd been in his early twenties. Hadn't he said his father owned a car rental franchise? Maybe his dad was a CEO of one of the major chains. But then they turned into a long-standing middle-class neighborhood instead, and, to be honest, Carey was relieved.

Joe had never mentioned much about his family before, beyond the sister who'd loaned some clothes. Carey thought about that as they pulled into the driveway of a beautifully kept older Spanish Revival home. The front of the one-story, red-tile-roofed house was covered in ivy with cutouts where the living-room windows were and a well-maintained hedge lined the sprawling green yard in front of two classic arches on the porch. The fact that rows of palm trees stood guard on each side of the house made her smile. So Californian.

She had no idea how long his family had lived there,

but he'd just said he'd been a kid here. That made her wonder what it would be like to always have a family home where you went for holiday celebrations.

Joe introduced Carey to his parents, who clearly adored him, and she could see that he'd gotten his soft brown eyes from his mother, Martha, and his broad shoulders and dark hair from his dad, Doug. They both grinned and immediately made Carey feel welcome, though there were questions in their gazes. She wondered if they assumed she and Joe were a couple.

The sister who'd loaned Carey clothes turned out to be named Lori, and she made a point to put it out there right off—Joe was the nice guy he was only because she'd been his middle sister by two years and had often insisted he play dress up and dolls instead of cowboys and Indians. Carey laughed and watched Joe blush, something she'd never seen before. She'd bet a fortune he'd always looked out for his kid sister and younger siblings, too.

Being an only child herself, she'd never experienced the power of a sibling, in this case to put a macho guy like Joe in his place in front of his mysterious new woman friend—who'd once been so desperate as to need to borrow Lori's clothes. Now she was dying to find out who they thought she was and, more importantly, what they thought she was to Joe.

Andrew—Drew to his family and friends—was the taller but younger brother to Joe by four years, and was a fairer version of Joe but had the narrower build of his mother. Where Joe was a muscled boxer, Drew looked more like a long-distance runner. Both looked fit but in different ways.

"We're waiting for Tammy and Todd to arrive before

we begin making ice cream," Martha said, as she gave Carey a quick tour of the house.

Carey soon found out they were the babies of the family at twenty-two, fraternal twins who still seemed to hang out with each other all the time and therefore would be arriving together. Interesting. This family believed in togetherness. Another foreign idea to Carey. Maybe that had something to do with Joe insisting they continue the parenting classes together?

The rest of the four-bedroom house gave the appearance of being lived in but with obvious recent upgrades, like a state-of-the-art kitchen and a family-friendly brick patio and neatly manicured lawn, complete with a small vegetable garden. Now she understood where Joe had probably gotten his idea for his own inviting patio and backyard. He hadn't fallen far from his family tree.

Being in this home, sensing the good people who inhabited it, caused nostalgia for something Carey would never have to sweep through her, pure bittersweet longing. She'd be all the family her baby would ever have. Their home would be each other, small but loving. She vowed her child would always feel loved, no matter where they lived. Seeing good people like Joe's parents with such love in their eyes when they looked at their adult kids gave her hope for her and the baby. She wanted it more than anything for herself, that parent-child relationship.

The moment the twins walked in with a couple of bags of groceries, everything stopped and it was clear they were the wonder kids. The light of their mother's life. Martha made over them as if they were still in their teens, and Joe raised his brows and half rolled his eyes over her ongoing indulgences. *Wow, would you look at that, the babies have just managed to go to the market all by themselves*, he seemed to communicate with that look. Since she and Joe had a strong history of nonverbal communication, she was willing to bet on it. Come to think of it, Lori and Drew had exactly the same expression, and it made Carey smile inwardly. Nothing like a little friendly sibling rivalry, something she couldn't relate to. She also found it interesting that Tammy had dark hair like her father and Todd was nearly a blond—the only one in the family.

"Let's get that ice cream going," Doug said, clapping his hands, reminding Carey of Joe. He grabbed Todd, since his shopping bag contained the essential ingredients, putting him immediately on ice-cream duty. Joe was assigned to grill the burgers on the gorgeous built-in gas stainless-steel barbecue on the patio, and Lori enlisted Carey to help put together some guacamole dip and chips to go along with cold sodas and beers for those partaking, as an appetizer. Except, coming from Illinois, Carey didn't have a clue how to make guacamole, so all she actually wound up doing was mashing the avocados and letting Lori take over from there. With Martha overseeing the condiments and side dishes, already made and waiting in the refrigerator, the early dinner preparation seemed to run like a well-oiled machine.

Carey felt swept up, like a part of the family, and she cautioned herself about enjoying it too much. These were Joe's people, she'd never be a part of them. Today was simply a gathering she'd been invited to take part in rather than be left alone on a huge national holiday. If there was one thing to be sure of in these otherwise confusing days, Joe was way too nice a guy to let that happen. Yet, curiously, no one else had brought a date.

His mother loved to tell tales about her kids, embarrassing or not, she didn't care. It was clearly her privilege to share as their mother. Carey learned a whole history of childhood mess-ups and adventures for all five of the Matthews kids as the afternoon went on. Then Lori took her aside and asked her a dozen questions about what it was like to be unconscious for three days. They wound up having a long conversation, just the two of them, and Carey could see herself making friends with Lori if given the chance. It made her feel special to be taken in so easily, and closer to everyone—a sad thing since she understood there would never be a chance to really be close to any of them beyond today. Unless Joe came to his senses.

Later, as they ate, Carey found out that Drew's lady friend was in the navy and was currently deployed in Hawaii. Poor thing, he'd said with a grin, and just as quickly notified his parents he was planning to take a trip to see her in August if his dad would be willing to give him the time off. Hmm. Carey wondered if anyone else worked for their dad.

Just as Carey prepared to take a bite of her thick and delicious-looking home-grilled cheeseburger, which required both hands to hold the overfilled bun, a gust of wind blew a clump of hair across her face. Before she could put down the burger to fix it, Joe swept in and pulled the hair out of her face, tucking it behind her ear, a kind but cautious glint in his eyes. The simple gesture was enough to give her shivers and make her once again long for that dream she'd had to tuck away. Fact was, the guy couldn't resist coming to her rescue. Plus at his parents' house they couldn't very well hide out in their separate bedrooms, avoiding each other.

Why did things have to be the way they were? Why couldn't they just go for it? She took the bite of seriously delicious burger, Joe having cooked them to perfection, her mind filled with more secret wishes. But even as she wished it she knew that between the two of them, with all the baggage they held on to, the fantasy of being Joe's woman would probably never be.

Lori, a yoga instructor, soon explained that her significant other was a resident at County Hospital and couldn't get the day off. Martha mentioned that Todd and Tammy would be seniors at the University of Arizona and were living at home for the summer. It made Carey feel like a special person to have the entire family to herself. And they all truly seemed to enjoy having her there.

"This is the most delicious peach ice cream I've ever tasted," she said later to Todd when the homemade dessert was served.

"It's my dad's secret recipe. He wants to make sure I carry on the family tradition."

It made Carey wonder if only the men got to learn the peach ice-cream recipe and she glanced at Joe, her unspoken question being, *Do you know how to make it, too?*

Incredibly, he gave a nod. She looked at Lori, who shook her head. Then she glanced at Drew, who'd made eye contact with her and nodded. Cripes, this intuitive communication business must run in the family, and evidently only the guys got the ice-cream recipe.

"Before you call me sexist." Doug spoke up, obviously noticing all of the subtle communication going on. The mental telepathy gift was beginning to creep Carey out! "I have my reasons," Doug continued. "It's to make sure that once a lady tastes this ice cream, she'll love it so much she'll never be able to leave one of my boys." He gave a huge, self-satisfied grin over the explanation that Carey couldn't argue with. Obviously it had worked with Martha. And from the taste of it, she understood perfectly well why. It was also very apparent Joe had never thought to make any for her.

Then it hit her that Joe's wife had left him, peach ice cream or not, and putting her own feelings aside she worried that Doug had inadvertently brought up a touchy subject for Joe. She glanced at him as he studied his bowl of dessert, though he'd stopped eating it. Martha seemed uncomfortable, too, and sent those unhappy feelings Doug's way through a terse look.

The family was well aware of Joe's heartache, and that was probably why they'd been so delighted he'd brought her over today. Oh, if they only knew how disappointed they'd soon be, but that would be nothing near what she already felt. If only...

As the afternoon wore on into evening one by one the siblings made excuses to leave, and soon it was only Joe and Carey hanging out with Doug and Martha.

"Over the years the trees in the neighborhood have grown so high they block out a lot of the view of the Bowl fireworks." Martha seemed compelled to give Carey a reason.

"I thought you said you could watch the fireworks from your backyard?" she said when she had Joe alone at one point.

"The really big ones we still can, but everyone has plans, you know how that goes."

She guessed she understood, but the thought of families, like trees, outgrowing themselves made her feel a little sad. It didn't seem to faze Martha and Doug, though. After all, the twins would be home for the entire summer.

It amazed Carey that after spending only one afternoon with the Matthews clan she already felt she knew more about their open-book world than she did about Joe, having lived with him for over a month.

"We're staying, though, right?" To be honest, Carey looked forward to seeing those famous Hollywood Bowl fireworks from his family's backyard.

"We sure are." His beeper went off and he checked it. "Excuse me." He got up, walked toward some bushes and made a return call.

She figured it was work related and suspected she might not get to see any fireworks at all today. Her sudden disappointment quickly dissipated when Joe smiled at her.

"Guess what? I've just received a special invitation."

"To what?"

Joe winked. "I must be doing really well at the clinic because James himself just invited me and a guest to his private fireworks viewing tonight."

"At his house?" A flash of pride for Joe made the hair on Carey's neck stand on end, further proving she was still far too invested in the guy. "Why so last minute?"

A satisfied smile stretched Joe's lips, the ones Carey had secretly missed kissing. By the way she'd longingly glanced at them just now, she'd probably just given herself away. "Well, apparently someone cancelled, and I was the first person he thought of."

"So you're a replacement?"

"I'd rather not put it like that but, yeah, I guess I am."

She wanted to hug him. "I didn't mean to burst your bubble. It's really a big honor."

"I know. I've heard that every year he invites a handful of employees to share the evening with him. It's sort of his way of giving a pat on the back to his best-performing department heads." Pride made his smile bright, and Carey quickly realized how rarely he grinned. If only she could put a smile like that on his face again. She had, that one special night.

"That's fantastic, Joe." Without thinking, she touched his arm, immediately being reminded of and missing the feel of his strength. "You're a hard worker and it's good that Dr. Rothsberg has noticed."

He covered his pride with a humble shrug. She wanted to throw her arms around him, but he'd made it very clear that he was never going to let her near again. Yet she'd had a wonderful afternoon and evening with his family and really liked every single one of them, feeling closer to him because of them, and a secret dream to be a part of his life rose up, refusing to get brushed aside again. Stupid, stupid girl.

Joe knew better than to push things any further than they already had, after spending the entire afternoon with Carey and his family. But he'd had a great day. Carey had fit right in with everyone, and they all clearly liked her. It made him wonder if he'd made the right decision to never let anything further happen between them. In so many ways she was right for him. It was all the stuff from before that kept both of them hung up. He hated to admit how scared he was, because it seemed so damn wussy, but he was. And Carey had wounds and scars of her own, yet she seemed more willing to move beyond them than he was. Being here with her made him feel confused again. Needing to keep his distance but not wanting to completely let go.

And here she was, in his old backyard, smiling at him. The Tiki torches lining the patio emphasized the red in her beautiful auburn hair and made her eyes look as green as the lawn. He couldn't seem to stop himself from making another big mistake where Carey was concerned. Knowing he really shouldn't open the door for more, James had told him to bring Carey along when he'd mentioned where he was and who he was spending the holiday with. And right now he couldn't think of a single reason not to.

Letting the moment take control, Joe made a snap decision. "Will you come with me?"

At a quarter to nine Joe pulled into the designated employee parking lot at The Hollywood Hills Clinic, the huge, lighted building as alive with activity as ever. Hospitals never got to take days off, but Carey was grateful she had this one Monday before she started her new job.

He directed Carey to a mostly hidden employees-only elevator by putting his hand at the small of her back. His touch made her tense with longing. *Stop it! Don't get your hopes up.*

Soon they were on the top floor, walking down a long, marble-tiled hallway. Joe opened huge French doors at the end and they stepped onto a balcony. She immediately heard music and loud talking coming from above. In the corner of the small balcony was a spiral staircase leading to the roof. Joe took her hand to show the way. Again, touching him like this set off a million unwanted feelings and emotions with which she wasn't ready to deal. Fortunately, the spectacle of a group of highly gorgeous people on the roof quickly took her mind off that.

Wow! The panoramic view of the entire city of Los Angeles was spectacular from up there, too.

Dr. Rothsberg, the tall and handsome, blue-eyed blond, golden boy of medicine, immediately came to greet Joe. "Hey, great, you could make it." He turned to Carey. "I'm so glad you could come, too."

"Thanks for having me." Carey tried to hide her fascination with the incredible specimen of a man but was worried her dazed stare may have given her away.

Dr. Rothsberg kept smiling as though he was used to people looking at him like that. "Make yourselves at home. There are drinks over there." He glanced at Carey. "No alcohol for you, young lady."

She laughed, perhaps a little too easily, wondering if all women acted this way around the guy, then figuring, *Hell, yeah*.

Joe led her to the bar and got her a root beer, already knowing her weakness for that particular soda, while he grabbed an icy IPA because it wasn't everyday he got a chance to enjoy an imported Indian pale ale.

"See that lady over there?" Joe pointed out a beautiful woman with hair a similar color to Carey's. She nodded. "Her name is Dr. Mila Brightman and she runs a clinic in South Central L.A. It's called Bright Hope. She used to be engaged to James." He'd lowered his voice and moved closer to her ear so she'd better hear him say the last part.

Carey's eyes went wide. It was hard enough being around Joe after only spending one incredibly beautiful night with him, so what must it be like to be on the same rooftop as an ex-fiancé? "What happened?"

"I don't like to spread gossip, but I heard from Stephanie the receptionist that he stood her up at the altar."

Holy moly! Why would she come close to the man if that was true?

"She's best friends with Freya, James's sister," Joe continued.

"Oh, I met Freya one day in the recruiter's office. She's our PR lady, right?"

Joe nodded.

"That should make for some heavy family tension. Wow."

"You've got that right."

He'd moved closer to bring Carey up to date without sharing the info with anyone else, and she'd moved in because of the music and talking, and now they huddled together, sipping their drinks and taking in the incredibly romantic skyline of L.A., and it suddenly overwhelmed her. They'd gotten too close. She couldn't handle it.

"I'm going to get one of those delicious-looking cookies I saw over there." She pointed to a dessert table in a secluded corner that promised to be both a delight and a nightmare for a woman monitoring her baby weight. "Can I bring you one?"

Joe shook his head, a look she couldn't quite make out covering his face. Was he sorry she'd stepped away? Or was he shutting down again? After such a great day, she hoped not.

She crossed to the spread of goodies and wound up having a harder time than she'd thought, making a decision. There was so much to choose from!

On the walk over she'd noticed Dr. Rothsberg surreptitiously watching Mila, who was across the roof, talking to Freya. Then Mila wandered over to the dessert table and stood next to Carey, and though she gave a friendly enough greeting, the woman seemed totally preoccupied with the group where James stood. As Carey continued to decide which two goodies to choose—she'd increased her limit upon seeing all the choices—Dr. Rothsberg also headed for the table.

Not having anything to do with the couple but now knowing their history thanks to Joe via Stephanie,

Carey got nervous for both of them as well as for herself. Yikes. What would happen when they faced each other? She kept her eyes down, studying the huge display of desserts, unable to make a choice or move her feet, willing herself to become invisible.

"Mila," James said, all business, "I'm sure Freya has told you I'll be coming to your clinic for a personal tour in early September."

Carey had wound up being between the two of them but on the other side of the table, and didn't dare move. They didn't seem to notice her anyway, as their eyes had locked onto each other. She chanced a glance upward to see for herself. *Yowza*, she could feel the tension arcing between them, so she distracted herself by first choosing a huge lemon frosted sugar cookie.

"Yes, Freya mentioned it. So thoughtful of you to tear yourself away from your girlfriend to make the trip."

Could the woman have sounded *more* sarcastic? But who could blame her? She'd been stood up on her wedding day. He was lucky she didn't pull a dagger on him! Carey worked to keep her eyes from bugging out and began to slice a large piece of strawberry pie in half so as not to feel too guilty about gobbling it all down. It had whipped cream topping with fresh blueberries sprinkled over it, so it was definitely a patriotic pie. Really, she *should* eat it. For the holiday's sake.

James moved dangerously close to Mila, a woman who looked like she'd claw out his eyes if he got even an inch nearer, and yet he leaned down with total confidence, his mouth right next to her ear. "In case you're interested, I've broken up with her."

Carey couldn't help looking up, but only moved her eyes so they wouldn't see body movement, still praying she was invisible, but the couple didn't seem to see her or care that she could hear their entire conversation. Mila was clearly flustered by his comment. She obviously hadn't known he'd broken up with the other woman. Wow...oh, wow.

Practically impaling Mila with his piercing blue eyes, now that he'd noticed her surprised reaction, he went still. "In the future, why don't you ask me personally how things are going in my life, instead of relying on the gossip pages as your source of information?" The sarcasm was sprinkled over every single word, yet Carey got the distinct impression that a pinch of hurt had been mixed in. She wanted to gasp over their hostile encounter but kept her mouth shut rather than draw attention to herself.

Then she accidentally dropped the knife. They both noticed. "Sorry," she said as she grabbed the pie, put it on the plate with the cookie and rushed away, wondering why Freya hadn't told Mila that James had broken up with his girlfriend, since they were best friends.

She arrived back where Joe stood, casually talking to another employee she'd seen around the clinic over the last couple of weeks. Frank, was it? They said hello and the man seemed friendly enough. Her hands shook as she took the first bite of the cookie. She glanced over her shoulder back to the dessert table but Mila and James had moved away to their respective groups. Even while trying to hide, she'd felt their sexual chemistry.

James may have stood Mila up, an unforgivable thing to do, but Carey could've sworn she'd glimpsed lingering love in his eyes. And though Mila had come off like a hurt and still angry woman toward him, Carey was pretty sure she'd seen relief on her face when James had told her he'd broken up with whoever that other woman was. Then again, Carey did have a huge imagination where love was concerned and may have seen what she'd wanted to see. She glanced at Joe, still chatting with Frank, remnants of her own lost before it ever started love driving home the point.

She promised to keep everything she'd just heard to herself. No way would she want that gossip Stephanie to get hold of this juicy information.

At exactly nine, as if some great force had waved a magic wand, fireworks started popping up all over the valley from the Hollywood Bowl, all the way out to Santa Monica beach. Someone shut off the outdoor lights as the magical display continued. Amazing and mesmerized, having never seen anything as spectacular in her life, Carey stood closer to Joe, and his arm soon circled her waist, and her arm wrapped around his. So natural. And right now there was no fighting her attraction to the man. The constant effort from living with him, plus spending all day long with him today, and especially now with a night filled with sparkles and shimmering colors dripping down the sky, had worn her down. She secretly savored his sturdy, steady build.

Carey gazed up at Joe, who beamed like a kid, nothing like that dutiful mock smile he'd given on the drive to his parents' house earlier today. She offered a bite of the fabulous cookie and was surprised when he took it greedily. Knowing this moment would only complicate things further between them, she ignored caution and leaned into his strength. His fingers gripped her side the tiniest bit tighter and her own version of pyrotechnics exploded in her chest. Yes, this would definitely confuse things. Their eyes locked for an instant. Along with seeing the reflection of fireworks in his darkened gaze, she was pretty sure she saw some regret.

Oh, who was she kidding? She'd just read her own

feelings into those wonderful brown eyes, just like she'd done with Mila and James. She really needed to stop projecting her thoughts and feelings onto everyone else. It would never get her anywhere, just make her feel disappointed. Because no matter how much she might want a second chance with Joe, it didn't matter. He wasn't open to it. But why did he keep glancing at her during the fireworks show? And now his fingertips lightly stroked her side. Funny how holidays could do that to people.

She went back to watching the dazzling and dizzying display of colors across the night sky and became aware of a strange sensation inside her. Had she eaten too much sugar? Or were the gunshot-like sounds of the rainbow-colored rockets popping and crackling through the night causing the reaction?

The feeling was very subtle, yet she couldn't deny it. This had to be *quickening*. She'd learned in her class with Gabriella that primigravida mothers often didn't realize it the first time their babies moved. Who knew? Maybe it had happened before and she'd missed it. But not this time! *Oh. My. God.* Her baby was alive and moving. *Inside. Her.*

"Joe." She nearly had to yell for him to hear her.

Grinning from the bright chaos playing out before them, he glanced down at her. When she knew she had his full attention, she was so excited she could hardly get out the words. "I just felt the baby move for the first time." Her throat tightened with emotion as she admitted it, and the unrelenting firework display went blurry in the background.

His eyes widened and his childlike grin from the fireworks turned to an amazed smile, as if she'd just told him "their" baby had moved. There she went, projecting again. But, in her defense, they had just gone over the information at the last prenatal class. Joe had been there with her, like he'd promised.

He grabbed her full on, pulling her close, then squeezed. "That must feel amazing."

Thankful for his goodness, and her good fortune of feeling her baby move for the first time on the Fourth of July, the blurriness turned to tears. "It did. Oh, my God. How strange and wonderful." She sucked in a breath, feeling like she was floating on air, then pulled away from his shoulder.

His eyes had gone glassy and the dazzling lights sparkled off them as he turned serious. She could have sworn she'd seen a flash of pain, but he quickly covered it up. He shook his head as if amazed and unafraid to show it. Just like the day in the clinic when she'd come to and nearly the first thing she'd asked had been if her baby was all right, and the nurse had assured her it was. She'd cried with joy. So had Joe. The stranger who'd saved her.

He was anything but a stranger tonight. He was the greatest guy she'd ever met.

She hugged him again and promised herself she'd remember the priceless expression on Joe's face for the rest of her life. Then she cried once more as a pang of longing for what she could never have set in deep and wide.

CHAPTER EIGHT

THEY DROVE HOME from the party in silence, still riding the high from the fireworks. Joe kept his confusion to himself. He'd held her in his arms again, and the longing had dug so deep he'd been unable to completely hide it. He was pretty sure she'd noticed his reaction, too. He couldn't continue with Carey like this. She didn't belong to him, her baby wasn't his. She deserved some guy who could love her and give her more children. Not him.

Yet she'd fit in so well with his family, and it had been clear they'd all liked her. It'd made him wonder about possibilities, and he thought he'd given up on those ages ago. Could he actually get over being cheated on by his wife and best friend, or the fact he was sterile? Was he ready, maybe, to finally move on? In his usual rut, the answer came glaring back. No.

Holding her, watching the fireworks together had been a huge mistake. Hell, ever letting her into his life had been a mistake. He'd been the one to point out how much they both had going on personally, and how important it was not to confuse things between them any further. Yet he hadn't had the heart to un-invite her for the Fourth of July celebration with his family. He'd resorted to using the lame excuse of protocol as the reason. Yeah, he was a guy of his word. Besides, his mother wouldn't have let him, and if he hadn't brought Carey, Mom would have spent the entire afternoon badgering him.

Carey's baby had moved, and the truth had knocked him sideways. She had a life to look forward to and she didn't deserve having a guy like him hold her back. Maybe one day he'd be able to forget and move on, but he wasn't there yet, and most days he doubted he ever would be. Their timing sucked. She pregnant. He like one of those zombies on the show they liked to watch together.

If he insisted on continuing to look after her, his job from now on would be making sure she became independent of him. Not to get swept away and continue to confuse and complicate things by grabbing her under the fireworks and holding her like she belonged to him. What the hell had he been thinking? From now on he had to act logically and realistically. It was his only defense for survival. And he really needed to stay out of her way.

Getting her the car from his father's lot had been a start. She could have it as long as she needed it. Now that he knew she'd be working from seven a.m. to three p.m. at the clinic, he'd go in tomorrow and change his schedule to work the evening shift.

The less time he spent near Carey, the better. The alternative was too damn painful.

"Thanks for everything," Carey said once they'd gotten home. She lingered in the living room, a dreamy smile clinging to her face.

He'd been so wrapped up in his thoughts he'd almost forgotten she was there. "Oh. Sure. You're welcome. It was fun." He shoved his hands in his back pockets and kept his distance.

"The best fireworks I've ever seen."

His attempted smile came nowhere near his eyes. "Me too." Empty words. He may as well be talking to a stranger, and she obviously felt his detachment because her expression turned businesslike.

"Well, I'd better get right to bed since tomorrow is my first day on the new job."

He tried a little harder to be part of the human race. "I'm glad you had a good time."

Her eyes brightened. "I loved your family."

That's what he'd been afraid of. "I could tell they really liked you, too." It didn't matter, he needed to step back and let her move on. Without him. "Oh, and good luck tomorrow."

She flashed that genuine killer smile and it took him by surprise. Why did it always do that? Taking every single crumb he offered, she struck him as beautiful and innocent. The sharp pang of longing nearly made him grimace. All he wanted to do was grab her and kiss her, and let his body do the thinking for the rest of the night, so he stayed far across the room, hands shoved in his pockets, and worked on making his smile look halfway real. She noticed his awkwardness and pulled back.

"So good night, then." She turned and headed for her room, her beautiful auburn hair forcing him to watch every step of her departure. That constant ache inside his chest doubled with the inevitable thought.

"'Night," he muttered. *Get used to it, buddy, soon enough she'll be walking right out of your life.*

At the end of the first week of Carey's new job, Joe, after agonizing over how best to handle the situation, told her he had to work on Saturday and would have to miss the next Parentcraft class. His intention was to let her down easily, yet he still dreaded it.

In truth, he'd scheduled the extra shift after he'd talked to Gabriella about helping Carey find a birth coach. He couldn't be the one. The thought of going through labor with her, being there for her at the toughest time, seemed beyond him. He worried he might have an emotional setback because of it, and fall apart on her. Angela and Rico had really done a job on him. He also understood how important it was for a mother-to-be to bond with their birth coach when it wasn't the husband or partner. They'd gone over that very topic the Saturday before. The sooner she found one, the better.

When he got home late that afternoon he saw Carey out on the patio deck, napping on one of the lounging chairs. Though he knew he shouldn't, he tiptoed to the screen door and studied her up close, afraid to breathe so as not to wake her. A real sleeping beauty. It brought back memories of sitting by her hospital bed, watching her, when she'd been unconscious for those three days.

Joe remembered trying to imagine who she was and where she belonged then. Now he knew exactly who she was, how wonderful she was, and how much he wanted her for himself. What a stupid fantasy. He may as well try to sprint to the moon.

She must have felt his presence or she'd been playing possum all along because he turned to leave, then heard her stir.

"Joe?"

"Yeah." He stopped in mid-step. "Didn't want to disturb your nap."

She stretched and yawned, and he didn't dare go out there, just stayed bolted to the floor, wishing things could be different. Knowing they never could be. Yearning to make it so anyway.

"What time is it?"

"Almost five. Want me to get dinner started?"

She swung her legs around and sat, feet on the wooden planks, facing him. "I missed you in class today. We started practicing relaxation techniques and special exercises. She had us work with our partners, but Gabriella worked with me."

"I had to accompany a transfer patient on the helicopter to Laguna Beach today." He'd volunteered. Would he have been able to function getting up close and personal with her in class? He'd definitely made the right decision to work, but he wondered when he'd started becoming a coward.

"The thing is, I talked to Gabriella about our situation, and she said she has access to the local doula registry. Those women love to be birthing coaches, so I asked her to give me some names." She stood and walked toward the screened-in porch door, each standing on opposite sides of the thin barrier. "Bottom line, you don't have to come anymore." With sadly serious eyes, she watched and waited.

He'd wanted to let her down easily because he was a coward. Now she'd beaten him to the task, officially releasing him. He didn't have the right to feel hurt, hell, he'd wanted a way out, but the casual comment—*you don't have to come anymore*—cut to the bone. An ice pick could have done the job just as well.

He resisted reacting, but his skin heated up anyway. He wondered how much she'd told Gabriella about them, if her story fit in any way, shape or form with his. He hadn't expected to feel upset, but he was really bothered, and definitely sad now that she'd come out and said it. Ah, hell, truth was it killed him to stand aside, even though he'd already set the ball in motion to arrange this very thing. He hadn't expected to feel like the air had been kicked out of his lungs and feel a sudden need to sit down. He steadied himself, because he knew one fact that couldn't be denied. "I guess that's for the best."

Clearly feeling let down, if he read her sudden drooping shoulders right, she covered well, too. Just as he had. "Yeah. I guess so, but thanks for being there for me all these weeks."

They'd been reduced to communicating in robotic trivialities.

"You're welcome. It was fun." *While it lasted, which he'd known from the beginning couldn't be long.* He'd just never fathomed the profound pain that would be involved. He'd gotten swept up in emotion and carried away that first Saturday, letting his feelings for Carey blur reality. He couldn't let her be the only one without a partner. He'd let down his usual guard, acted on a whim, and had paid for his mistake every single week since. Sitting beside her, acting like they were a couple, wishing it was so, scaring himself with the depth of desire for it to be so, but knowing, always knowing, it could never be.

His mouth went dry with unexpected disappointment. He needed to get away from her now. "Hey, listen, I'm going to the gym. Don't hold up dinner for me, okay? I'll grab something on the way home."

He left without before he could see her reaction.

The next Friday, Carey admitted a late-afternoon patient. The forty-eight-year-old male had a face everyone who'd ever gone to a movie or watched a TV show might recognize, but no one would know his name. The character actor had been admitted with the diagnosis of severe acute pancreatitis. Basically the guy's pancreas was digesting itself thanks to an overabundance of enzymes, in particular trypsin. His history of alcohol abuse—according to Dr. Williams, the doctor who'd been the attending doctor for Carey, and who she had enormous respect for—had made a major contribution to his current condition. However, according to the doctor's admitting notes, they would do studies to rule out bacterial or viral infection as a possible source as well.

Carey found the computer notes fascinating, and Dr. Williams had left no stone unturned. She'd even commented on the fact the man was almost fifty and still extremely buff. Probably because of his need to stay fit for the action/adventure roles he normally took, Carey decided. But getting back to the doctor's notes, she intended to consider his possible use of steroids as well.

To add another angle, when Carey did the admitting interview, the actor, who also did his own stunts for most movies, told her he'd had an accident on the job and had sustained blunt abdominal trauma. Well, that wasn't how he'd put it—*I got kicked in the gut*—but Carey's notation was worded that way. She put a call in to Dr. Williams to inform her.

Carey often thought how the practice of medicine was like a huge mystery where patients arrived with symptoms and the doctor's job was to gather all the evidence and figure out what was going on. Carey knew the clinic staff's job with this patient would be to watch for fluid and electrolyte imbalance, hypotension, decrease in blood oxygen, and even shock. This guy with the affable smile but pained brow was not to be taken lightly. Like many in the clinic, he was fit and healthy looking on the outside but a mess on the inside. These days, Carey could relate perfectly to that, too.

He'd been complaining of severe abdominal pain for a day or two, and had assumed it was because he'd been kicked in the gut, as he'd described it. Carey noted his abdominal guarding when she made a quick but thorough admitting physical assessment, and found his abdomen to be harder than usual. Of course, that could be due to the fact the man looked like he did hundreds of crunches a day. He'd said his symptoms had gotten worse in the last twenty-four hours, and had told her he felt "sick all over" so he'd come to the clinic's ER. After a few more questions he'd also admitted to going on a drinking binge a few days back. Yet somehow the guy was tanned and youthful looking for his age, until she looked closer. The saying about the eyes seemed true, and they were the mirror to, if not his soul, his health. There she could see the lasting effects of his living extra-large for many years.

His admitting labs showed his amylase and lipase levels were over the top, and that alone could have gotten the guy admitted. Add in the bigger picture, and this actor's next gig turned out to be the role of a hospital patient.

Carey inserted an IV to be used for medications as well as parenteral nutrition since he was on a strict NPO diet. Next she needed to perform a task no patient ever wanted to go through, at least from her experience as an RN. She had to insert a nasogastric tube.

"This is more to help relieve your nausea and vomiting than anything else," she said calmly. "You'll thank me for it later."

He gave her a highly suspicious stare, especially when she gave him a cup of ice chips.

"Suck on these when I tell you," she said as she manipulated the thick nasogastric tube with gloved hands and approximated externally how deep it would need to go to reach his stomach. "Okay, now."

He took a few ice chips and sucked at the exact time she used his nostril to insert the well-lubricated tube and push past the back of his throat and down into his esophagus and all the way to his stomach. His sucking on the ice would prevent her from going into his lungs. He gagged and protested all the way but didn't fight her. He gave no indication of the tubing mistakenly going into his lungs by having shortness of breath or becoming agitated, but she did the routine assessment of the placement anyway. She listened through her stethoscope as she inserted a small amount of air with a big syringe into a side port of the NG tube, hearing the obvious pop of air in his stomach when she did so.

"You did great," she said as she taped the tubing in place on his cheek and attached the external portion to his hospital gown, then connected the end to the bedside suction machine. He gave her the stink eye, but she knew he was playing with her so she crossed her eyes at him. "It's one of the perks of my job. You know most nurses have a tiny sadistic side, right?"

That got a laugh out of him, and she figured she'd tortured the guy enough for now, even though she knew he was lined up for all kinds of extra lab work and additional tests in the next twenty-four hours. So she made sure the side rails on his bed were up and the call light was within his reach, then prepared to leave. "Get some rest."

"Like I can!" he managed to say.

"Carey?" Anne, the ward clerk she'd covered for while she'd gone on vacation called her name just as she exited the patient room.

"Coming." Carey marched to the nurses' station to see what her co-worker needed, only to find a huge vase of gorgeous flowers sitting on the counter. Lavender asters, golden daisies, orange dahlias, and roses, oh, so many perfect roses! "Wow, where'd these come from?"

"They're for you!"

"What?" Joe? What was he trying to do, make up for bailing on the parenting class? Why go back and forth like this, mixing her up even more? Ever since he'd said all those things about not confusing their living situation by getting involved with each other, and especially after the Fourth of July when he'd introduced her to his family, and especially later when they'd shared that significant moment during the fireworks, he'd been avoiding her like crazy. It'd stung and confused her, and she was only just getting her bearings back, thanks mostly to having the new job and not seeing him nearly as often. Was he feeling guilty for leading her on or letting her down? Both? She wanted to pull her hair out over his inconsistency.

Carey searched for a card, but all she found was an unsigned note.

These flowers are as lovely as you.

Sorry, Joe, but that is just inappropriate. Either you want to be involved with me or you don't. You can't have it both ways!

Hadn't he learned in the parenting class that hormones during pregnancy made every emotion ten times stronger? This tug-of-war with her feelings had to stop.

"Do you mind if I take a short break?" she asked one of the other nurses who'd begun to gather around the spectacle of colorful blooms, admiring them. The more she thought about those flowers, the more upset she got.

"Sure. I'll cover for you."

"Thanks." Carey marched to the elevator and pressed the "down" button, got off on the first floor and headed toward the ER. It was after two, and she knew Joe had been avoiding her by working the afternoon shift from two to ten p.m. in case he actually thought he was fooling her. Her eyes darted around the room until she spied him over by the computers, so she trudged on, determined to get some things straight.

"You got a second?" she asked.

"Sure. What's up?" His hair was a mess. Had he not even combed it? Her first thought was how endearing it made him look, but she stomped it out the instant she thought it. There was no point.

She had to admit the guy didn't have the self-satisfied look of a man who knew he'd just surprised a lady with flowers. "Did you send those flowers?"

He pulled in his chin, brows down, nose wrinkled. "What flowers?" He wasn't an actor and, honestly, he couldn't have made up that reaction.

"Are you horsing around with me?" Her frustration growing, she needed to be sure.

He raised his hands, palms up. "Honest. I don't have a clue what you're talking about. It wasn't me." Now he looked curious. "You got flowers and no one signed their name?"

She nodded, racking her brain to figure out who besides Joe would do such a thing.

Now he looked perturbed. "You must have an admirer."

"Oh, come on." Where did he get off, making such crazy statements?

"You don't think guys watch you?"

"I'm *pregnant*, Joe."

"You wear those baggy scrubs, and you're only just now starting to really show."

"You've got to be kidding. I don't encourage anyone. I mean I smile at people, I'm nice, but that's just being polite." If not Joe, then who? And, honestly, she was disappointed they hadn't been from him, and, she wanted to kick herself for even allowing the next thought.

Was that a look of jealousy on his face?

Joe hadn't felt this jealous in a long time. He'd skipped the jealous part with his wife, going directly to fury once he'd found out she'd gotten pregnant with Rico. But this was different. This feeling eating through his gut right now was good old-fashioned jealousy.

Who the hell had sent Carey flowers?

He looked suspiciously around the department. He'd introduced Frank to her at the party on the roof, but surely he could tell Carey and Joe were more than roommates. Plus they hadn't spoken two words to each other beyond, "Hi, how are you?"

It was time to get honest with himself. What could he expect? Carey was stunningly beautiful and he'd noticed admiring glances around the hospital whenever she passed by. At first it had given him great satisfaction to know she was living with him, and no one knew about it. It had been his big, fun secret. The gorgeous woman who'd come in as Jane Doe was his housemate. Now someone had the nerve to make a move on her. And it really ticked him off.

If—no, *when* he found out who it was he'd have an in-your-face moment and straighten out any misunderstanding. Carey was off-limits. Got that? Did he have the right to do that? No. But he felt unreasonable whenever things involved her, and he was being honest with himself. He. Was. Jealous.

"Um, I've got to get back to work. My shift's almost over," she said.

"Sure. Okay. If I find out anything, I'll let you know."

"Thanks."

He watched her leave, her hair high in a ponytail that swayed with each step. When he noticed one of the ER docs also watching her, he wanted to cuff the back of the guy's head. Carey was off limits. Was he being territorial when he had no right to be? Yes. Hell, yes. He folded his arms across his chest, the anger soon turning to self-doubt. How could he honestly expect loyalty from Carey when he wasn't even prepared to come clean with her about the truth of his past?

In a frustrated fit he flung his pencil across the desk. His EMT lifted a single brow at him.

Don't dare ask, if you value your job.

Back home that night, the more Carey thought about it, the more upset she got about the flowers. She tried to remember giving anyone the slightest misconception that she was interested. Beyond Joe, that was. But what bothered her more was that Joe seeming to run hot and cold with her. She still didn't put it past him to send those flowers and pretend he hadn't. Surely he'd noticed how down she'd been lately, since they'd been forced to change their relationship. But wait, they hardly saw each other anymore. Maybe he hadn't noticed anything about her mood swings.

One thing she knew for a fact, she'd gone and ruined everything by kissing him and coming on to him that night. She was a runaway, pregnant with another man's baby. Did she expect Joe to be a saint on top of everything wonderful about him and welcome her into his life with open arms? She should have left well enough alone.

She took the bouquet home and put the vase on the coffee table in the center of the living room. Might as well enjoy them since someone had spent a lot of money on them. She chewed a nail and stared at the flowers. Had their one incredible night together been worth all the confusion and heartache it had caused?

She thought for a couple of seconds and shivered through and through with some incredible memories. Hell, yeah!

Dejected, she went to the bathroom and washed her face and was getting ready for bed when she heard Joe let himself into the house.

There was no way Joe could avoid those flowers when he came in. They may not have been from him, but they sure would be a perfect catalyst to force them to have a long-overdue conversation about a few things.

She needed answers to the question that wouldn't stop circling through her mind, especially since seeing how jealous he'd been earlier: *Where do we stand?*

He'd said he didn't know who had given the flowers to her, and had seemed not to care. He'd even suggested that she'd unknowingly flirted with someone and might have encouraged the gift, which really annoyed her. Like it was her fault. And come on, she was pregnant! Why the hell would she want to get involved with a new guy now?

Precisely! That was what he'd hinted at the night he'd leveled with her. They had no business getting involved.

But she couldn't get Joe's expression out of her mind from when she'd confronted him at work and he'd sworn he hadn't been the one to send the flowers. It had been a look of pure jealousy, until he'd quickly covered it up. He still had feelings for her, as she did for him.

What a mess.

All revved up, she headed straight for the living room and the man who'd just come home. "You know what I don't get?"

"Well, hello to you, too." He looked more tired than he usually did, coming off his shift, like maybe he hadn't been sleeping well. Join the club! Or maybe work had been more stressful than usual.

"If you don't want anything to do with me anymore, why were you jealous?"

"Jealous? What are you talking about?" Now, on top of looking tired, he looked confused.

"I saw your eyes when I told you about those flowers." She didn't need to point them out. He'd obviously seen them the instant he'd walked in. His demeanor shifted, having more to do with her accusation than the flowers.

"I'll admit, it took me by surprise. And I still don't like the idea of some guy hitting on you in such an obvious way."

"But you have no right to." She folded her arms across her chest, having just then remembered she was in her pajamas. "You made it very clear we aren't allowed to have feelings for each other. It's for the best. Remember?"

He went solemn, watching her, and she made it clear she intended to have it out right then and there. Too bad if he was tired or jealous or whatever else. Now was the time. Finally. "If you don't care about me, why were you jealous?"

In an instant he'd covered the distance between them, and his hands were on her shoulders, pulling her toward him. Time seemed to stand still for a moment as they looked deep into each other's eyes and both seemed to know—without the benefit of a single word, just using that damn communication thing they had going on—that once again they were about to do something they'd regret. But it didn't stop Joe from planting a breathtaking kiss on Carey. And it didn't stop Carey from kissing him back like it might be the last kiss she'd ever get in her life. From Joe.

The kiss extended for several seconds, turning into a getting-to-know-you-all-over-again kind of thing. Her breasts tingled and tightened as she felt the tension from Joe's fingers digging into her shoulders while he continued to claim her lips. With them, a kiss was *always* more than just a kiss. She sighed over his mouth, searching with her tongue, soon finding his.

Joe's breathing proved he was as moved as she was, but then just when they were getting to the really good part he stopped. And stared into her eyes, a combination of desire and seething in his.

"Because I *am* jealous. Damn it." He'd finished with her, and now gently pushed her away.

She felt foolish standing there, her breasts peaked and pushing against the thin material of her pajama top, exposing exactly what he'd just done to her. "You can't do this to me, Joe. I don't understand why you act this way. It's not fair to keep me all mixed up like this."

He looked back at her, considering what she'd just said, and then, as if he'd made a huge decision, his expression changed to one of determination. "Then you'd better sit down, because if you want to know why I'm the way I am, it's a long story."

The comment sent a shiver through her. He finally intended to open up to her, and she was suddenly afraid of what she might find out. But she cared about Joe, and if it meant helping her understand him, she'd listen to anything he needed to share. No matter how bad it was or hard to hear.

She took a seat on the edge of the small couch. Joe chose to pace the room.

"How far back do you want me to go?"

"To the beginning, if that helps explain things."

He stopped pacing, stared at his feet for a second or two, as if calculating how far back he needed to go to get his story told once and forever. Then he started. "I met Angela, my ex-wife, when I took my paramedic training in an extension course at UCLA. We started a study group and things heated up pretty fast. Within the year, once we both got our certifications and got jobs, we got married." He glanced up at Carey, who hadn't stopped watching him for an instant. "You know how I love my family." She nodded. "Well, since I was married I wanted to start having kids right off. Like my parents did. I'd launched my business and things were going well, so I figured, let's go for it."

He started moving around the room again, turning his back on her. "After a year she still hadn't gotten pregnant, and we wondered if our stressful jobs might have something to do with it. So we took a two-week vacation to Cancun. Still nothing." He cleared his throat and glanced sheepishly back at Carey. She continued to train her gaze on him, so he turned around and faced her. "We decided to get fertility tests done. But I've got to tell you, things were really tense between us around that time, too." His hand quickly scraped along his jaw. "You know how you hear stories all the time about people who can't have kids, then they adopt a kid and the woman gets pregnant?"

Carey nodded, her heart racing as he came to what she suspected would be a key part of his story.

"Well, Angela got pregnant." He lifted his hands. "Great, huh?"

Somehow she knew it hadn't been great.

"I was thrilled, of course, and we went on our merry way, planning to be parents."

She read anything but happiness in his words, and especially with the tension of his brows and tightening in his jaw she understood he was in pain. Wait a second, she also knew Angela had left him for his best friend. He'd told her that much. But with his baby? Oh, my God, how horrible. And here she'd been dragging him to her parenting classes! If she'd only known.

Making him repeat the entire history for her benefit was cruel. "Joe, you don't have to—"

"Nope. I said I would, and I want you to hear the whole mess. Okay?" He looked pointedly at her, like it was her fault for making him begin and she needed to hear him out.

Carey tried to relax her shoulders but felt the tension fan across her chest instead. "Okay. Go on, then." She could barely breathe in anticipation.

"So we're all thrilled and planning for our baby and five months into the whole thing, out of the blue my fertility results show up in the mail. We'd completely forgotten about them because we were pregnant!" He made a mocking gesture of excitement, and it came off as really angry. "Where they'd been all that time, I didn't have a clue, but, bam, one day the results were there. Angela wasn't home when I opened them." He stopped, needing to swallow again. "And the thing is, it turned out..." He glanced up quickly, if possible looking even more in pain, and then, dipping his head, his eyes darted away. "I'm sterile."

How could that be? He was a healthy, magnificent specimen of a man, but she knew to keep her thoughts to herself.

"I did some research after I got that diagnosis because, honestly, I couldn't believe it. Evidently my sperm ducts are defective from multiple injuries in high-school baseball and from kick boxing. It's the only explanation the doctor could come up with when I finally followed up. Who knew high-school sports could do a guy in?"

Carey stared hard at Joe as she bit her lip, hoping her eyes wouldn't well up. Angela had been pregnant and living a lie under his roof. Of course, now she understood why her being pregnant seemed difficult for Joe. Oh, God, what he'd been through. And she'd rubbed his nose in that memory every single day she'd lived here. She wanted to cross the room and hug him then apologize, but every unspoken message he sent said, *Stay away. Leave me alone. Let me get this out once and for all. You asked for it!* So she stayed right where she was, aching for him and crying on the inside.

"My life stopped right then. All the happy future-parents hoopla came crashing down. My wife was pregnant—but not by me." His words were agitated and the pacing started up again. Carey understood how hard this must be for Joe, but he insisted he needed to tell the entire story. So he paced on, and she waited, nearly holding her breath. "I thought it had to be a mistake. I called the fertility clinic, suggesting they'd mixed things up. They'd obviously lost my results, since it had taken so long to mail them. But, nope, I was one hundred per

cent sterile. Said so right there on that piece of paper."
He flashed her a sad, half-dead excuse for a smile.

"So I had to confront my wife." He'd lowered his
voice as if this part was solemn, or someone had died.
"Angela insisted it was a mistake, because I hadn't
told her I'd already called to make sure. I watched her
squirm and avoid looking at me. I never felt so sick in
my life." Joe gave a pained, ironic laugh. "Oh, she swore
the baby was ours, that it had to be. I listened to her
lie. Then she finally broke down and confessed that if
the baby wasn't ours it was Rico's." Joe's fist smashed
into the palm of his other hand. Carey started to understand the importance of his punching bag. Yet all she
wanted to do was rush to him, hold him and kiss him.
He'd been betrayed by the two most important people
in his life after his family.

"My best freaking friend." A hand shot to his forehead, fingers pinching his temples as if he'd suddenly
gotten a headache, reliving the story. He sucked in a
ragged breath. "Evidently, just before we'd gone to Cancun, when things had gotten really intense here, she'd
gone to him to cry on his shoulder, but a hell of a lot
more than that wound up happening. Turns out my *best*
friend had an unusual way of consoling *my* wife."

Anger and sarcasm mixed as his agitation grew. She
wanted to tell him to stop, not say anything else, but
kept silent, sensing his need to purge the full story at
long last.

"Angela swore she'd been too racked with guilt to
tell me, especially when she didn't know who the real
father was. Can you believe it? If she could have gotten away with it, she would have tried. And I got to
think I was the future father of a beautiful baby for five

months before we were forced to face the facts. What a fool I'd been."

Carey shook her head, feeling responsible for his pain right now. "You don't have to say anything else, Joe."

"But wait, it only gets better! Angela told Rico and he wanted her to get a paternity test! Yeah, he turned out to be a real prince. So there I was looking at this stranger who was supposed to be my wife, and she's telling me about this bastard who was *supposed* to be my best friend, and the only thing I could think of saying was, 'You can leave now. You're welcome to each other.' Yet part of me couldn't bear to kick out a pregnant woman, and I was about to take it back when she got up and called Rico." A look of incredulity covered his face. "Right in front of me she told him I knew everything, and she needed a place to stay."

Joe nailed Carey with his tortured expression. "They've been together ever since. Have a baby girl and seem to be doing fine. Or at least that's what I hear from other people I used to know."

Carey's hand flew to her chest. Joe had lost his wife, child and best friend in a single moment. And to make matters worse, he also knew he'd never be able to have a child of his own. What torture that must have been for a guy who'd wanted a big family. Yet when she glanced at him she saw a man suddenly at peace.

"As you can imagine, relationships have been off-limits for me for a while now. I mean, what's the point? I'm not into one-night stands, and I can't give a woman what she'd want most if we got serious—children of her own. Not unless I send her over to Rico."

"That's not funny, Joe." Carey had heard enough, and she'd realized why Joe was the distant man he was for so many reasons. Why he blew hot and cold. It went against his natural personality to be bitter, though, which had always confused her, but now she understood why. "I'm so sorry this happened to you. Now I see why you overreacted to me getting those flowers. I mean, it makes perfect sense…"

"Nothing *ever* makes perfect sense, Carey." He sounded desperate, tired and defeated. He went into the kitchen and filled a glass with tap water, then drank. She followed him there, wishing she could love away his sadness and anger, yet understanding why he deserved to feel that way. Why he needed to keep her at a distance.

"Then I show up on your doorstep pregnant and homeless, and you're too nice a guy to toss me out. I get it. The last thing I should have done was come on to you, but I believed and still believe that it's mutual attraction. There's something real between us, Joe. You couldn't have faked that night."

He swung around, some of the water slopping out of the glass. "It doesn't matter what happened that night. It can't ever happen again. There's no point. Besides, you're all set up now. You've got a job, an income, you're back on your feet—hell, someone even sent you flowers."

"Joe, that's uncalled for."

"Is it? Ever heard the phrase 'been there done that'? I can't do it again. Won't."

Pain clutched her chest when she realized what he intended to do. Every secret hope she'd held on to was about to get dashed by a guy who'd been beaten up by love and never wanted to open his heart or life to love again.

"Look, Carey, you're a strong woman who knows

what's best for you and the baby." Now he sounded like he was pleading for her to let him go. For her not to torment him by dangling love and sex in front of him by living under his roof. "You'll be an amazing mother. Truth is, you don't need me anymore. You're ready to move on."

"Please don't push us away..." her lip trembled as she spoke from being so racked with emotion "...because you're afraid you'll get pushed first. I'm not that girl. I'm not Angela."

"And I'm not the guy for you. Sorry."

He'd shut down completely, going against every single thing she knew in her soul about him. He wanted to be the scarred guy who could never feel again, but he lied. She'd seen and felt his love firsthand. He hated that his wife had once lied to him, but now he was lying to *her*. He wanted her to leave, and she couldn't argue with a man who'd just turned to stone in front of her eyes.

"Please listen, Joe."

Something snapped. Anguish mixed with fury flashed in his stare. "Don't you get it? Every time I look at you I'm reminded what I can never have for myself. I may be stuck in the Dark Ages, but I can't get past that."

She'd heard his deepest hurt. Joe had pretended, but he really hadn't survived his wife cheating on him with his best friend, on top of finding out he was sterile. That was a total life game changer; he was broken and she couldn't fix it. He'd just said her presence only made the pain worse.

He may as well have stabbed her, and the jolt of reality nearly sent her reeling backwards. Lashing out, he'd wanted to wound her, too, and he'd done a fine job. Her eyes burned and her hands shook.

She'd promised herself she'd never beg a man the

way her mother used to beg her father. And even though her world, the new and improved version of her world since she'd come to California and met Joe, had just been ripped from her, she wouldn't beg.

A sudden surge of anger and pride made her jaw clamp shut and her shoulders straighten. Joe was damaged and wasn't open to reason. There was just no point in trying to get through to him. "I'll be out by the end of the week."

She could scarcely believe her own words, but now that she'd said them she'd have to make sure she'd carry them out. No matter what.

CHAPTER NINE

NEXT WEEK AT WORK, Carey still reeled from her final confrontation with Joe. They'd been avoiding each other like a deadly disease ever since. What a mess. She'd promised to be gone by the end of the week, and had put the word out with the nurses on her floor for any leads on small apartments to rent.

She sat in a corner, scrolling through all of her assigned patients' labs for the day, insisting on giving them her full attention. Afterwards, she'd do her morning patient assessments then pass their meds. Sometimes putting her life on hold for her day job was a relief.

"Carey?" Dr. Di Williams stood behind her.

"Yes? Anything you need, Dr. Williams?"

The middle-aged doctor offered a kind smile. "I hear there's something *you* need."

Carey quirked her brow. "Sorry?"

"An apartment?"

"Oh. Yes, well, something will pan out, I'm sure." She prayed it would because it was Wednesday and she'd promised Joe she'd be out by the weekend at the latest.

"I've got an in-law suite at my house. No one ever

uses it. It's got a private entrance and even a small kitchen. It's yours if you'd like it."

A few people were beginning to realize she was pregnant. Unfortunately, Stephanie had seen her go to the Parentcraft class, so probably the whole clinic knew by now. Obviously, Dr. Williams knew from when Carey had been her patient. "That's very kind of you, but—"

"It's a nice place. My partner and I have a house right here in the Hollywood Hills. Lisa made sure the place was comfortable and inviting, but her parents won't come to visit, and I've given up on mine coming around for years now. So what I'm saying is you're welcome to live there. I know you've had a rough time and I'd like to help you out."

Touched to her core, Carey jumped up and hugged Dr. Williams, who looked both surprised and uncomfortable. "You're a godsend. Thank you."

It was the first time Carey had ever seen the doctor grin. "We thought about adopting once, but our jobs are so demanding we decided it wouldn't be fair to the baby. Plus we're both, well, you know, getting older." She gave a self-deprecating smile. "So we'll enjoy meeting your bambino when the time comes."

She patted Carey's stomach, and Carey fully realized the reality that, yes, her baby would be born, and that after tomorrow, when she'd had another sonogram, maybe she'd even know the sex. Which made ner think how Joe had always called her baby little Spencer. It hit her then. She *really* needed a place to live. She was ready to "nest," as she'd learned the word in her parenting class. She wanted this, and the good doctor had just solved her problem.

"But I have to insist on paying rent."

Dr. Williams tossed her a gaze that perfectly expressed her thoughts—*Please, I'm a rich doctor and do we really have to negotiate money when we're having such a good moment?* "Whatever you want to pay is fine. Money isn't an issue for us. In case you didn't know, Lisa's a doctor, too."

"I'll be in great company." Carey beamed while she talked, never having felt more grateful in her life. Well, after her unending indebtedness to Joe, of course. She gave an amount she felt she could afford, nothing close to what the place would be worth, she was pretty much sure of that. But she was being honest, though, not wanting to insult the doctor by going too low, since she'd have to live on a tight budget. Especially as she'd have to return the rental car soon and would need to find a used car for transportation. *One step at a time, Carey.* Thank goodness she'd banked some unused vacation time at her hospital back in Chicago and they'd sent the final check to Joe's address last week.

"That works for me," Di said. "I'll bring the key tomorrow and you can start moving in right away."

The doctor turned to walk away, but Carey grabbed her hand and shook it, well, over-shook it, because she wanted to make her point. "You and Lisa are lifesavers. Thank you, thank you, thank you."

"Like I said, it'll be fun." Before right this moment fun would never have been a word she would have associated with Dr. Di Williams. Who knew?

Along with the warmth Carey felt for the incredible kindness of others, especially from Joe, and now from a woman Carey hardly knew, she felt new hope for her and her baby. She just might be able to pull this off, start a new life in California and move on from her past once and for all. One sad and nagging point kept her from full elation.

Joe.

She loved the guy. And she'd never get to tell him. But she'd learned her lesson in life well. Just because you wanted something, it didn't mean you'd get it. It would be too much to ask of him to love her and to accept her child, too. Not after everything he'd been through. She understood that now.

She sighed, a bittersweet thought about leaving Joe's sweet little house for her new and as yet unseen place nearly making her cry. She'd gotten so used to living with him she hated thinking about not seeing him every day. Was this really happening? Maybe she was still in a coma and this was one big Alice-in-Wonderland-style dream. The thought amused her briefly.

But she had labs to look at, and one of her assigned patients had just put on their call light.

Thank heavens for the distraction of her day job.

In order to avoid Carey and every disturbing thought she dredged up in him, Joe worked several extra shifts during the last week she lived with him. On Friday he'd even stayed on for an extra night shift so he wouldn't chance seeing her move out. The thought of watching her go would only widen the gaping wound inside him.

He'd finally opened up and told her everything, and she'd seen how messed up he truly was. Even then he'd felt her need to comfort him, but he'd held her off, pushed her away, then, once she'd seen there was just no point, that he'd never let her in, she'd agreed to move out. Whatever they'd once shared had breathed its last breath, and all the CPR in the world couldn't revive it.

It had been a crazy evening on the job with nonstop calls, and truthfully, Joe was grateful for the constant distraction.

James had thought of everything when he'd set up the hospital for his private and exclusive clientele. One perk was an emergency box in every home that went directly to The Hills emergency department instead of the more general Los Angeles system.

At two a.m. another call came through, this one from an affluent area, the Los Feliz Hills, east of The Hollywood Hills Clinic. A woman reported her husband in sudden pain that was shooting down his left arm. The emergency operator sent the message to Joe and he grabbed his team and hit the road within two minutes, siren switched on.

The five-mile distance would take fifteen minutes, thanks to the winding roads in both of the hilly communities. While they drove, the emergency operator stayed on the line and gave instructions to the wife of the patient, in case she needed to begin CPR.

Once in front of the ornate house Joe's team grabbed their emergency kits and EMT Benny rolled in the stretcher. A young housekeeper waited at the front door to the huge several-storied home and directed them up an open stairwell to the master bedroom. Joe couldn't help but notice the largest chandelier he thought he'd ever seen in a home. He quickly recalled the Hills ER operator having mentioned that the patient was the head of one of the movie studios in town.

Joe found the white-haired patient on the floor, unconscious, his wife kneeling over him in near panic.

"He just passed out," she said, fear painting a frightened mask on her face.

"Does he have a history of coronary artery disease?" She nodded.

Joe rushed to the patient's side, finding him unresponsive. He checked his airway and found him to be breathing, then he checked his carotid artery for a pulse.

"Let's get him on the stretcher," Joe directed his team, taking out the portable four-lead ECG machine and hooking up the patient for an initial reading as they applied oxygen and rolled him onto the adjustable stretcher. Then, in an effort to save more precious time, he started the IV as they transported the man down that huge stairwell. Once that IV was in place, he checked the initial four-lead heart strip, which showed possible ST elevation. Once Benny and his partner got the patient in the back of the emergency van, Joe jumped in, immediately switching the man to the twelve-lead EKG for a more thorough reading. Applying the leads, Joe was grateful the old guy wore loose-fitting pajamas, making his job a little easier.

Time was of the essence with MIs and seconds after securing the stretcher in the safety lock in the back of the van Benny and the other EMT shot to the front, turned on the emergency lights but not the siren, as a courtesy not to add stress to the heart patient, and sped down the winding hills.

Now with proof the man was in the midst of a STEMI, thanks to the twelve-lead EKG but still maintaining a decent enough blood pressure—he was even coming around a little bit, giving occasional moans— Joe added a nitroglycerin IV piggyback, gave him morphine through the IV line and aspirin under his tongue. He might not be able to stop the ST elevation myocardial infarction, but he hoped to at least help decrease the patient's pain. All this was done while the ambulance tossed and rolled around the hills, heading for Los Feliz Boulevard and onward toward Hollywood and the clinic.

Without the benefit of lab reports, he couldn't treat the patient more aggressively. And since the definitive treatment for an MI was catheterization, Joe's one job was to keep the guy alive.

The man looked ashen and his breathing had become more difficult. Joe repositioned his head for better airway and increased the oxygen one liter. oxygen sats stank. Then he checked his blood pressure, which was even lower than previously, but assumed it could be due to the nitro and morphine.

The heart monitor started alarming. Damn it, the guy was crashing. At times like these Joe felt frustrated with his role as a gap-filler until the patient got to the ER and could be hit with all the fancy lifesaving drugs. If only the ambulance could get there faster.

When the monitor went to flatline, Joe immediately started CPR, and continued to do so for the last five minutes of the ride to the clinic and the ambulance entrance where the medical big guns waited.

Unfortunately for the patient, medically the future didn't look too bright. In an oddball nonmedical way, Joe could relate.

Joe parked the car in his garage, closed the door, and headed into his house from the backyard entrance on Saturday morning. He hated how the house had felt since Carey had moved out yesterday. Had it only been yesterday? It seemed more like a month or a year even since he'd last seen her. Before, there had been this incredible life force radiating from her room. Today all he felt when he walked near it was his energy getting zapped by pain and regret. Well, he planned to save himself the angst and head right to his room to sleep.

After the stress of that morning, with the Hollywood

movie tycoon who'd wound up dying despite all emergency measures, he felt dejected and needed to sleep. It seemed typical of issues of the heart, and maybe even a metaphor for his own life lately, especially where his relationship with Carey was concerned, and with all the practical training in the world he still couldn't fix his own messed-up heart. Come to think of it, he might tear a page from Carey's story—a short-term coma would be a good thing right about now.

As usual, with any downtime, Carey was foremost on his mind. The word "coma" brought unwanted thoughts about a lady he'd once sat vigil for at her bedside. What had he done? He'd lost her. Sent her away. He unloaded the contents of his cargo pockets onto his dresser top then dug out his cell phone.

Wait a second. He'd worked all night and hadn't turned on his personal phone so he'd missed a text from Carey. He was so tired he squinted to read it.

It's a girl. Latest sonogram. Yes!

The words nearly brought him to his knees. Little Spencer was a girl. Carey didn't have anyone in her life to share the news with but him. A sudden feeling of sadness punched his gut. He'd been so selfishly focused he hadn't considered what moving out had meant for her. She'd volunteered to go and, like a wuss, he'd let her.

She deserved so, so much more. Yet, with all the bad things life had dealt her, she insisted on being upbeat. Yes! she'd written. The text was short but so touching, and all he wanted to do was find her and hold her and tell her how he really felt.

It wasn't going to happen. It wasn't possible.

He should leave well enough alone.

His house had never felt so big or empty since she'd moved out. Only yesterday! Damn, it already felt like a year. How would he go on without her?

"You did the right thing," he said aloud, glancing into the mirror above his dresser. He had to believe it because otherwise he'd go crazy. He was so messed up. Carey and the baby only would have left at some point anyway, so it was better it had happened sooner rather than later, and as *his* idea, not hers. In a childish way he admitted it felt better to have forced the change because he couldn't have survived Carey leaving him. By his spin, sending her away had been the most unselfish thing he'd done in his life.

Besides, she deserved a man with more to offer, someone without baggage like his. Anger, mistrust, suspicion, yeah, he was good at those sorry emotions. She'd had all of that tossed in her face long before she'd met him, beginning with her father and ending with that scumbag Ross. It was Carey's time to catch a break. He'd given it to her by pushing her out the door. Because he knew she was the special kind of woman who would have stuck around, put up with his sorry attitude, and tried to make the best of things if he hadn't made her leave. Beyond a laundry list of the ways she'd be better off without him, the main reason still stood out. He'd come around enough to know that Carey was nothing like Angela. He could trust what she said and did. She was as stable as they came, despite her tough life before coming to L.A. The issue was still with him.

He thought about her ultrasound and the fact her baby was a girl. The crux of the matter was that he would never know what it was like to have a woman he loved carry his baby. A kid who might look like him. And he was too damn messed up to get over it.

Better to set her free now before it got even more difficult because, honestly, he hadn't been prepared for the level of pain her leaving had unleashed. Sometimes he could barely breathe.

He thought about what he'd said to her the other night and cringed. He'd been harsh, insisting he couldn't get past his wife cheating on him, and he'd held it against a completely innocent person. What sense did that make?

He flopped, back first, onto his mattress, hands behind his head, praying sleep would find him and put him out of this torture, if only for a few hours. He'd tried to make peace with his decision about letting Carey go, but deep down something still didn't feel right.

Why, even now—when she'd found a great place to live, from what he'd heard floating around at work, and when she had nothing but good things to look forward to, a solid job, the upcoming arrival of her little baby girl, a bright future—things didn't feel right to him.

Why did he still have the foreboding sense she needed his protection?

He squeezed his eyes tight. *Go to sleep. Just go to sleep. You're getting delusional from lack of rest.*

He was bound to settle down soon because his body was completely drained and his mind so weary he could barely put two coherent thoughts together. Yeah, he'd get some sleep today, he promised himself. But first he needed a glass of water. So he hopped off the bed and headed to the kitchen for a drink.

Carey wanted to scold herself for accidentally taking Lori's clothes along with her when she'd packed the few meager possessions she owned and had moved out. Joe's sister had been nice enough to loan her some jeans and tops when she'd first moved in with zero belongings left to her name. Now she'd have to face him again, as painful as that would be, to return them. Truth was it had hurt to the core when he hadn't even bothered to reply to her text about her baby being a girl. She guessed he'd already moved on. Didn't care. Hadn't he said all she did was remind him of what he'd never have?

An ache burrowed deeply into her chest, not only for herself but for him, too. She still loved the guy. Had she imagined every good thing about Joe, or was this just how it felt to lose him? She was positive she'd never get over him, and had missed him every second since she'd moved out.

Mid-morning, she parked the rental car across the street from his house on the small cul-de-sac, thinking the car was another topic she had to bring up with Joe. As soon as she found a used car she could afford, she'd make sure this one got returned to Mr. Matthews. She wanted to make sure Joe knew she didn't expect to keep this car forever. Just for a little longer. She promised.

She reached around to the backseat and grabbed the tote bag with Lori's clothes inside. Carey had gotten the bag from the clinic the day she'd been discharged and Joe had taken her in. She'd almost slipped up and thought "home" the day when Joe had taken her home. Because that was how it'd felt when she'd walked through that door with him. She glanced at the small sage-green house across the street. Yes, he'd been a stranger then, but he'd saved her life and then kept vigil beside her hospital bed, and she'd never felt more protected or safe in her life than when she'd lived with him.

With the bag in her hand, she got out of the car and battled a feeling of half hope and half fear that Joe would be home. She'd left her house key the night she'd moved out. If he wasn't home now, she'd leave the items on the porch and make a quick getaway. On second thoughts, he'd been working so much it was possible he was sleeping and the last thing she wanted to do was wake him up. Maybe she'd just leave the bag on the lounger on his deck and not even attempt to face him right now. If she snuck off without seeing him, she'd save her lovelorn heart a whole lot of grief.

She started down the driveway, getting halfway to the kitchen-window area when she caught herself. This was cowardly. She was a big girl now. She needed to face him if he was home, though there was no sign of his car so she made a one-eighty-degree turn and headed back toward the front of the house, stunned to find a man she'd never expected to see again only a few feet away.

Ross.

How had he found her? How had he known where she'd been living? A chill zipped down her spine and her stomach felt queasy.

Then it hit her. He was the one who'd sent the flowers. How had he…? Oh, wait, he knew how to manipulate people, especially women, and had probably gotten the work address out of Polly in the employee relations department back in Chicago. Carey had been in touch with her regularly since she'd arrived in Hollywood— first to let the hospital know about her situation and to take a leave of absence, then to set up receiving her backdated pay checks, and eventually to give notice on the job and to collect her unused vacation pay. What a fool she'd been to think he wouldn't find her.

She'd thought she'd been so careful, but nothing seemed to be beyond Ross's reach. The bastard. After the quick flash of fear at seeing him she went directly into anger. The creep had another thought coming if he planned to mess up her life again. She was in control now, in no small part thanks to Joe, and Ross was powerless.

He kept his distance. Even held his hands up, all the while watching her, like a prowling animal waiting to pounce. "I know what you're probably thinking," he said, trying to sound appeasing. "What am I doing here?" He gave a poor excuse for a smile that looked more like an insincere politician's than a former lover's.

"I don't want to see you. Leave. Now."

Quickly his expression changed to that of a mistreated puppy. "I'm sorry. I've come to tell you I'm sorry. I love you. We can still be happy together. Make a life together."

"Ha! That's rich. You wanted me to get rid of my baby. That's not going to happen. There's nothing further to talk about."

She looked at Ross, tall, dark, and had she really used to think he was handsome? All he looked like now was a creep she needed to get rid of. Fast. He'd abused her, both mentally and physically. Had wanted her to have an abortion, had shoved money into her hand to do it, too.

She thought about Ross's polar opposite, Joe, and all he'd tried to do for her. How hard it must have been for him to show up at the prenatal appointments, to be the first one she shared the first sonogram with, when never being able to become a father had still been eating away at him. The moment he'd slid into that chair beside her in the parenting class had nearly made her heart burst with gratitude. He'd acted the part of being a father, even when he'd believed he would lose her and the baby, as if his past was bound to repeat itself. Yet he'd shown up and stuck with it, for her, and had never let on about the pain he must have suffered because of it. Oh, God, he was her true hero—a man to be worshipped, adored and loved. With all of her heart. And she did. She loved him.

Facing Ross, right now, she knew without a doubt what her true feelings were for Joe. Yet Joe had convinced her to walk out on him. And she'd gone because he'd looked so tortured by her being there.

She stood before Ross, a shadow of a man standing by the driveway hedge, feeling completely alone. All she wanted to do was go inside Joe's house where she'd always felt safe, and close and lock the door. Forever. On Ross.

She kept her distance, not trusting him for one second, but Ross took a single step forward.

She'd never let herself be a victim again and he'd have to hear her out. "You need to know I've finally experienced a good relationship. I know for a fact there are good, loving and caring men in the world who put their partners first. I never learned that from you, but now I have faith in the world again. In myself." She touched her heart. "You wanted to control me and tear me down to keep me under your thumb. I may have let you before but I never will again." To show how serious she was, and to prove she wasn't afraid of him anymore, she took a step forward but still kept safely out of his reach, then stared him down. "You need to leave L.A. I'll never go back to you. Never."

Ross's expectant-puppy expression soon turned to one of defeat. Did he think he could just show up and everything would be fine again? Was he that out of touch with reality? Or had it proved once and for all how he truly had zero respect for her.

Something she'd said must have gotten through to him because he actually turned to leave. Carey took a breath for the first time in several seconds. But just as quickly he turned back, lunging toward her with the look of pure rage in his demon eyes.

His first mistake had been showing up uninvited in California. His second mistake was to grab her wrist and clamp down hard enough to cut off her blood supply, then raise his other hand ready to slap her.

Instead of pulling away, fighting mad, Carey growled and steamrolled into him. Catching him off guard, her knee connected full force with his groin, the V of her free hand ramming with all her might smack into his larynx. Everything Joe had taught her about self-defense came rushing back with a vengeance.

Ross doubled over in pain, unable to gasp or shout. And, of course, he'd let go of her wrist. Shocked she'd actually pulled it off, Carey stood there dazed for one second, her body covered in goose bumps, staring at him while he writhed in pain on the driveway.

Well, plan A had worked like a charm. What was she supposed to do next?

Run! Run for the car and get the hell out of there. She turned to make her getaway, but slammed into a brick wall of a man.

CHAPTER TEN

JOE CAME FLYING out of the kitchen door the instant he'd seen the man lunge for Carey. He'd watched the whole encounter between the guy who must be Ross and Carey, the woman he loved and his new superhero, from the window above the kitchen sink.

He'd known Carey needed to face down her demon once and for all, and he'd been ready to pounce if she'd needed him. So, as hard as it had been, he'd stayed on the ready just around the corner and waited. She'd stood up to the man, not wavering for a second. When twisted reasoning hadn't panned out, the guy had lunged at her. Joe had rushed through the back door and flown outside, but she'd beaten him to the punch. Like a pro, she'd taken down her attacker. It had impressed the hell out of Joe, too. Great going.

Pride for Carey mixed with pure fear that she could have been hurt by the bastard from her past made him take her in his arms and hold tight. She didn't fight it either, just leaned into him.

"You okay?"

She nodded, then pulled back to look into his eyes. "Did you see that? I decked him! Thanks to you."

He laughed, all the while watching Ross, who slowly began to get onto his hands and knees.

"Do as Carey says, just stand up and leave. Don't ever come back," he said, with Carey safely tucked under one arm, ready, if necessary to take the matter into his own hands if the guy made so much as a hint of a move in the wrong direction.

Now Ross stood, anger still plainly carved in his face.

"The police will be here shortly," Joe said. "I called when I first saw you. She's also got a restraining order out on you in case you ever get any ideas about coming around again. Consider it your 'go-straight-to-jail' card and this is your final warning."

Ross took one look at Joe, saw the don't-even-think-about-messing-with-me stare and took off, running to the street and back toward Santa Monica Boulevard.

With arms still wrapped around each other, they watched him disappear round the corner.

"I don't have a restraining order out on him," Carey said.

"He doesn't know that."

"And the police, are they coming?"

"Again, he doesn't need to know I was just about to call when I saw you kick his ass, so I hung up to help you." Joe flashed Carey a proud grin. "You were the bomb, babe."

She laughed. "You taught me everything I know."

He pulled her near and hugged her tight. God, he'd missed her. To think he'd almost let her get away sent shivers through his chest. "You're all right? Let me see your wrist, it looked like he had a firm grip." He checked out the area around her thin wrist, which was reddened and showing signs of early bruising. Like a dope, he kissed it because it was the only thing he could think to do, and he wanted more than anything for Carey to understand how precious she was to him. "You need to know something. I said things the other night that were horrible and not true. The only person you remind me of is you, and I never want to lose you. Or your daughter."

She disengaged her wrist from his hands so she could stroke his cheek. Looking into his eyes with her soft green stare, she smiled. He got the distinct message she had a few things to clear up with him, too.

"I never want to lose you either. Standing up to Ross just now made me realize he was the one who should feel ashamed, not me. That dark past I dragged out here needs to stay in Chicago with that loser. It shouldn't have any influence over me or my future. I've started over again. That ugly shadow is gone for good."

He believed her, too. She stood before him a woman of conviction, nothing like the frightened victim he'd first met two months ago.

She went up on her toes and delivered a light kiss. He matched it with a kiss of his own, and damn if it didn't feel like a little piece of heaven had just tiptoed back into his life.

"I meant what I said to him, too," she said, her arms lightly resting around his neck. "You've given me faith again in love. You helped me learn that it's not weak to open myself up to someone and to love again. Even if you didn't want me to." Her eyes dipped down for a second then swept back up. "I couldn't stop myself from loving you. I do, Joe, I love you."

Now he felt like the coward, well, until five minutes ago anyway, when he'd watched Carey confront her biggest fear and kick its ass, and Joe finally knew without a doubt that he loved her, too. No matter how hard he'd tried, he hadn't been able to stop himself from falling in love with her. He'd pulled out every old and sorry reason to keep from loving her, but she was meant to be loved, and he was the guy to do it. And for someone whose thoughts sounded suspiciously like a caveman's—*Me Joe. You Carey. We love.*—he had yet to voice the most important words he'd ever say. He just stood there, staring into her eyes, stroking her hair, loving her in silence.

"It's especially nice when you love someone." She cleared her throat to draw his attention away from her eyes and back to noticing all of her. "If that someone loves you back."

Hint, hint! There was that tiny mischievous smile she'd occasionally given when making an obvious point, and he'd missed it so much.

The ball was clearly in his court, and it was time for him to say what he felt and mean what he said. Without a doubt he loved Carey. So, still being in caveman mode, he bent down, swept her up into his arms and carried her up the steps to his front door.

Once inside he planted another kiss on her, and got the kind of reception he'd hoped for. But he knew he couldn't get away with a mere display of affection. If ever a person deserved, or a time called for, words, it was now. So he gently released her legs to the ground, snuck in one last quickie kiss, and stepped back.

"Please forgive me for pushing you away. I was hurt. And afraid. Still am. And if you don't think that's a huge thing for me to admit, you don't know me like you think you do."

"I totally understand how huge that is." She groped around his shoulders and chest. "Just like the rest of you."

He went along with her making light of things, because the topic was difficult and heavy and loaded with old habits that needed to be set free. They'd both been through so much lately, but he had one more thing to say and he needed to say it now. He cupped her face between his hands.

"I'll understand if you can't see a future with me, because I'm sterile and I can't make babies with you."

"Stop right there," she said. "You really don't get it, do you? Did you not hear me say I love you? You may not be the biological father of the little lady here, but you've acted nothing short of a true, loving, and beyond decent father. Actions really do speak louder than, well, other actions in this case, I guess." She screwed up her face in a perfectly adorable way, having briefly confused herself. Right now there wasn't a single thing she could do wrong. "I know, terrible analogy."

He laughed lightly, while understanding exactly what she'd meant, because that was part of what was so right about them, they always *got* what each other meant, spoken or not.

"But it's all the family we need," she added, and he loved her even more for her generous thought. But the truth was a small family could never be his style, that's why he'd decided to never be in the position to have a family at all. Until Carey had shown up and changed everything.

"You don't want her—what are we going to name her?—to have sisters and brothers? How about Peaches?"

"Name my daughter after a piece of fruit?" she playfully protested.

"Our daughter, you just said it, so that gives me equal naming privileges. Besides, I thought Peaches might be significant since I'm planning to make the famous Matthews ice cream just for you after dinner tonight."

"You're making me peach ice cream?"

"How else can I make sure you'll never leave me again?"

"Ah, your father's secret ingredient."

"Yes. That. Plus the fact you have no idea what a hellhole it's been here since you left, and I'll never let you go again."

"And…?" she encouraged him.

"Because I love you and can't imagine my life without you." He kissed her again, because there was no way he could say what he just had without needing to touch her, with the best expression of love he knew. Physical touch.

"Neither can I," she said. "And if we want to give, well, I'll agree to give her the nickname of Peaches, but honestly we'll have to come up with something better than that for real. Anyway, if we want to give her siblings in the future, first one step at a time and all, right? Let's see how this little one turns out. But, honestly, in this day and age, if we want more children, we can find a million ways to do it. Right?"

"Right, as usual. Sorry I've been so dense about that topic for so long. I've been too busy wallowing in my pain."

"And *that* should never come into play with us again. Okay?"

"You got it. Because I intend to spend the rest of my life showing both of you how much I love you."

She sighed her joy and nuzzled into his neck, which felt fantastic. "That works out perfectly because I intend to spend the rest of the afternoon showing you exactly how much I love you."

For a guy who'd been up all night and who earlier could hardly keep his eyes open, Joe suddenly felt full of life, love, and, right this instant, intense desire. He pressed his nose into her hair and inhaled the smell of fresh coconut shampoo, thinking how he could contentedly spend the rest of his life simply doing this. He smiled widely, knowing she had a far better idea. "I like your plan."

She gave him a long and leisurely kiss in case there was any mistaking what her intentions were. He loved how well they communicated.

"For the record," she whispered into the shell of his ear, "you had me at homemade peach ice cream."

* * * * *

MILLS & BOON

THE HEART OF ROMANCE

A ROMANCE FOR EVERY READER

MODERN

Prepare to be swept off your feet by sophisticated, sexy and seductive heroes, in some of the world's most glamourous and romantic locations, where power and passion collide.

HISTORICAL

Escape with historical heroes from time gone by. Whether your passion is for wicked Regency Rakes, muscled Vikings or rugged Highlanders, awaken the romance of the past.

MEDICAL

Set your pulse racing with dedicated, delectable doctors in the high-pressure world of medicine, where emotions run high and passion, comfort and love are the best medicine.

True Love

Celebrate true love with tender stories of heartfelt romance, from the rush of falling in love to the joy a new baby can bring, and a focus on the emotional heart of a relationship.

Desire

Indulge in secrets and scandal, intense drama and sizzling hot action with heroes who have it all: wealth, status, good looks...everything but the right woman.

HEROES

The excitement of a gripping thriller, with intense romance at its heart. Resourceful, true-to-life women and strong, fearless men face danger and desire - a killer combination!

To see which titles are coming soon, please visit

millsandboon.co.uk/nextmonth

It might just be true love...

MILLS & BOON

MEDICAL

Pulse-Racing Passion

Set your pulse racing with dedicated, delectable doctors in the high-pressure world of medicine, where emotions run high and passion, comfort and love are the best medicine.